Maxine McArthur was born in Brisbane in 1962. As a child she also lived in New Guinea, Darwin and Mittagong. In 1980 she went to study in Japan, where she lived for sixteen years. She now lives in Canberra with her family and works at the Australian National University. *Time Future* is her first novel.

Time Future

Maxine McArthur

BANTAM BOOKS
SYDNEY · AUCKLAND · TORONTO · NEW YORK · LONDON

TIME FUTURE
A BANTAM BOOK

First published in Australia and New Zealand in 1999 by Bantam

Copyright © Maxine McArthur, 1999

National Library of Australia
Cataloguing-in-Publication entry

McArthur, Maxine, 1962–.
Time Future.

ISBN 1 86325 194 4

I. Title.

A823.3

Transworld Publishers,
a division of Random House Australia Pty Ltd
20 Alfred Street, Milsons Point, NSW 2061

Random House New Zealand Limited
18 Poland Road, Glenfield, Auckland

Transworld Publishers (UK) Limited
61–63 Uxbridge Road, Ealing, London W5 5SA

Random House Inc.
1540 Broadway, New York, New York 10036

Cover illustration by Greg Bridges
Typeset in 10.5/13 pt Sabon by Midland Typesetters
Printed and bound by Griffin Press, Netley, South Australia

10 9 8 7 6 5 4 3 2 1

In memory of my father

Acknowledgments

A totally inadequate thank you to my editors: Viki Wright, whose patience and encouragement over two years kept me going through every draft; and Louise Thurtell, whose skill and perceptivity turned the final draft into a publishable manuscript.

Time past and time future
What might have been and what has been
Point to one end, which is always present.
> 'Burnt Norton', T.S. Eliot, 1944

Dream the centre far for me
When it burns then we may see
Paths outflung in fixity
Deceive us

Cry the centre close to me
Let the burning rivers flee
Tears we shed together will
Redeem us

Sing the centre into me
Fill the light and set me free
Now and then forever be
Within us
> 'Invidi chant', from *A Child's Book of Alien Verses*, 2098

Before

When I was a little girl my great-grandmother would tell me stories of the days before the Invidi came to Earth.

She would sit in her room under the frangipani and I'd bring tobacco for her to smoke in secret in return for the stories. She'd suck and puff until the thin pipe drew properly, then lean back in the creaky cane chair. I can't remember her face – only the long arms and heavy voice, both of which are now my own. That and the flowery-smoky-musty smell of her room.

Always the same beginning to the stories.

'Listen now, child. This was a town of women. When Marlena Alvarez became mayor, she asked me to be chief of police because she knew I could do the job.

'The old mayor and judges were dead. They'd been murdered by the very thugs who put them in office. The old police chief and his deputies had disappeared, either dead or in hiding. Or they'd joined one of the gangs.

'The able-bodied men? Mostly dead, drafted by the militia or arrested by them – it came to the same thing in the long run. Everyone who could afford to go to the cities did so. Many of them couldn't afford transport but they went anyway. Better to brave the dangers of disease, famine, guns than stay. The only ones left were the old, the sick, the very young, and the women who looked after them.

'God, those politicians hated her. They tried to scare us out of town, they tried to force us to do what they wanted. They tried ridicule and starvation ... death threats all the time. Tried everything to wear us down.

'Marlena never said anything, but I watched her grow old before my eyes.'

Her tone would become softer, reminiscent. The pipe would go out.

'We did a good job though. Rebuilt the town. She never turned away refugees. They needed shelter, we needed the labour. Marlena pestered the state and central governments for funds. We got media contacts, too, and told everyone what was happening. After years of bargaining and compromise she finally placed the town off-limits to all armed groups.' Demora would roll her eyes. 'Mad, we all said she was mad.'

Sometimes I would sneak away at this point, before she reached the end of the story. It didn't matter whether anyone was listening or not. She had to say it, had to relive it and forgive herself again.

'Marlena died on January 3rd, 2017. I should have watched the roof. We never caught the sniper. I remember it was about dusk because I couldn't see the colour of her eyes when I held her.'

The town of Las Mujeres had no public money and no resources beyond its people, and their lives changed little during the twelve years Alvarez was in office. But by the time she was assassinated in 2017 the groundswell she had created was unstoppable. I grew up hearing the name Marlena Alvarez as though she were an eccentric and beloved aunt. It was years later that I realised her actions in the town of Las Mujeres sparked the original

EarthSouth movement, and that she was a legend to freedom fighters everywhere.

The EarthSouth movement demanded social justice and economic reform and provided the precedent that persuaded the aliens to sign the Mars–Invidi Agreement on Species Rights in 2080, and to admit Earth as a member of the Confederacy of Allied Worlds in 2085. Marlena Alvarez played her part in bringing us out here and history says that her death was not in vain. But my great-grandmother knew better.

I am not blind to the parallels between Las Mujeres and ourselves. We are isolated, surrounded by enemies and indifferent friends. We have no resources and cannot decide our own fate, which is what they used to say about women in those times. We are divided among ourselves and cannot conquer our own weaknesses, which is how the galaxy sees humans now. The big difference, though, is that we have no Marlena Alvarez – only me.

PART ONE

THE SPINNING WORLD

You'd think on a space station this size there'd be an all-night food dispenser open.

I thumped the ringlift controls in a useless attempt to make the door close faster. If I hadn't had to search vainly for a meal after the Engineering briefing I would have had more time to catch up on the backlog of urgent administrative tasks. And now I was going to be late for the comet presentation. Not a good example from the head of station.

The doors wheezed shut with maddening slowness, and a faint, transitory lightness in my feet told me the ringlift had begun its descent from Alpha to Gamma levels. The throughways had been deserted earlier. Perhaps the stall owners who usually wander the lower level at night were preparing for the coming festival. There certainly wasn't much business any more from shift workers – the Seouras blockade has destroyed most of our production capability and there is no longer any need for a 24-hour workforce. The majority of residents now follow the same diurnal schedule. Earth's, for convenience, although our orbit around the planet below is completed in about half that time.

I'm hungry, having forgotten to eat anything since lunch yesterday. I'm overdrawn in space rations, too, or I might have resorted to ingesting my quota of those.

The ringlift jarred to a halt. I left it and threaded my way through the morning crowd, fastening my jacket as

I walked and trying vainly to tidy my hair. I hope my face doesn't look as tired as I feel.

Fifteen pairs of eyes turned to watch me as the meeting room door opened. I get this sort of intense regard much more as head of station than I ever did as head of Engineering, and it still stops me momentarily in my tracks.

'Commander Halley.' Lieutenant Gamet, a trim woman with hair pulled back tightly from her face, nodded to me from the far side of a round table. I took my place next to Bill Murdoch, the burly head of Security, and smiled a greeting to the others. Of the department heads only Murdoch, my friend Eleanor Jago, the head of Medicine, and Veatch, the station manager, had accepted the invitation to the briefing. Eleanor, cool and tidy in her hospital whites, half-smiled back at me but her glance was more professional than personal. Veatch stared back impassively through alien eyes. The other participants were a mixture of EarthFleet, scientific research, and Engineering staff.

Murdoch caught my eye as I looked around the table. 'You should have made it an order to come,' he rumbled, leaning sideways so no one else could hear. 'You need to give people more incentive.'

I frowned. Surely a rare interstellar phenomenon was incentive enough? And I'd hinted at the prospects it offered us to break the siege. Either the other department heads hadn't understood, or they were becoming jaded by our frequent failures.

The room darkened and in place of the panel lighting a starfield blossomed brightly above the centre of the table as Gamet activated a holomap.

We could see an asteroid belt, one planet close enough to be warm and hospitable, and two more far-off frozen ones orbited an unassuming orange star. The Abelar system seemed to grow as the holomap's magnification increased. A tiny disk representing Jocasta orbited the inner planet. Nobody commented on the lack of correct scale – it felt good to confirm our presence, and it was a while since most of the officers here had seen such a good show. Engineering is the only place on the station that still has functioning holovids.

'Comets were regarded as omens of evil in many ancient Earth cultures. For us here on Jocasta, it may be the opposite.' Gamet pushed a slim forefinger into the map on top of the space station and swirled it around the planet in simulated orbit.

The officers seated around the holomap table in the dark room leaned forward to see better.

'The comet has passed its perihelion and is now on the second day of its four-day trip out of the system.' She added the last element to the holomap with a flourish, and there was a murmur of appreciation as the comet winked into existence and its bright tail streamed away from the star.

Gamet was always a stimulating presenter, which was why I'd chosen her for this one.

'Have you given it a name?' an EarthFleet ensign asked slyly.

Murdoch jabbed me in the ribs with his elbow. I started out of my half-doze. The double-nighter was starting to tell.

'A number will be sufficient,' I said coldly. The ancestors on my maternal grandfather's side may well have been distant relatives of the astronomer who bequeathed his name to Earth's most famous comet. Then again, it might be mere coincidence. In any case, one Comet Halley in the astronomy database is plenty.

'The orbit of Comet 002,' continued Gamet, with a regretful glance in my direction, 'passes between our planet and the sun on its way out of the system. Which means that particles from the tail will saturate this area of space.' She activated a simulation and we all watched as the comet sped outward again and the dust, gases and ions released by the star's warmth sprayed the darkness in a glittering stream.

'We believe this comet is releasing a type of particle particularly disruptive to communications.' She paused to give them time to consider the implications.

'Which means?' Jago's impatient voice added an uneasy note to the general atmosphere of interest, and Gamet hastened to explain.

'I beg your pardon, ma'am. It means that our sensors will be unable to function adequately,' – someone laughed shortly but she ignored them – 'and there will be some interference with communications outside the station.'

The same person muttered, 'What's new?'

'By the same token,' Gamet said loudly, 'the Seouras ships' sensors will not work either.'

There was complete silence. The Seouras ships surround our station and block communication with the outside galaxy. One remains in a close companion orbit with the station and at least three more cover the approaches to the system with efficient menace.

'The only window of opportunity for this exercise will be . . .' Gamet waited until the comet was just past the pale planet in the map, 'here'. She halted the simulation to give everyone a view of the tail streaming past Jocasta. 'If we set a probe to "follow" the tail out of the system, it might be able to avoid interception by the Seouras ships before the tail itself dissipates. The probe will then send a message to the Confederacy as it continues along a course set to intercept a major trade route.'

Assuming, of course, the Confederacy of Allied Worlds is still there to listen to us. The invasion might have happened there, too.

She touched the last known positions of the grey Seouras ships, which appeared as tiny triangles, greatly out of scale on the map, but much too small for the weight they occupied in our minds.

'Any questions?' She moved quickly to this last segment because we'd agreed that people wouldn't absorb information unless it was directly related to their own jobs.

'Why not send a crewed ship?' the EarthFleet ensign asked.

Our main defences, two squadrons of EarthFleet fighters, had been decimated in the initial Seouras attack. The remaining personnel now worked in other areas, but many, like this ensign, itched to do something more.

'We're not *that* certain it'll work,' I said, and a couple of people chuckled half-heartedly. It wasn't a laughing matter. Six months ago when the Seouras attacked, most of the residents with the means to do so had attempted to leave. All of them died when the grey ships fired on them. Since then we've tried to sneak a couple of small ships out at various intervals, but so far we've lost them all.

'Do you require any particular cooperation from my department?' asked Veatch, the station manager, in his aggrieved drawl. His department was Administrative Affairs.

Gamet returned normal lighting to the room as she answered. 'Only the requisition details for the shuttle, sir.'

'Then I fail to see why I was encouraged to attend this meeting.' He probably didn't mean to sound quite so petulant.

'We thought you might be interested, seeing that the plan involves the entire station.' Gamet's normally placid face was taut. 'Like everyone else.'

'Perhaps I am not like everyone else.'

'You can say that again,' the EarthFleet ensign commented under his breath.

'It was only twenty minutes. Surely you can spare that,' said Eleanor Jago. 'We're all busy.'

'Twenty-two minutes.' Veatch couldn't resist the pedantic correction. It was one of the reasons the Melot were such brilliant bureaucrats.

Murdoch nudged me again and I stood up.

'Engineering will contact each department if they require any assistance,' I said. 'If you have any suggestions or other input, I'm sure they'd be delighted to receive it.'

Jocasta is Earth's first outspace station, established five

8

years ago in 2116. Three rings like a corrugated discus spin around a central core, where the modified alien engines nudge us back into correct orbit every twenty-two days and provide backup for essential systems in case the solar reflectors fail in an emergency. Such as a blockade.

The station had only been in Confederacy hands for two standard years when it was handed over to Earth. It had been under construction when the Tor abandoned the system after losing their decades-long war with the Invidi and the Confederacy. Abelar was a former Tor colony system, but after the Tor withdrew, the Confederacy of Allied Worlds, of which Earth is a minor member, was busy with economic problems in the inner sectors. The Confederacy was slow to begin taking an active part in the administration and protection of this obscure system on the edge of a barren outer sector. ConFleet patrolled only occasionally. Opportunists moved in quickly and by the time the Confederacy finally asserted its rights over the system, the area had become a haunt of pirates and unaligned, unregistered traders.

Then someone had the bright idea of finishing the space station that the Tor had begun. Not only was this cheaper in the long term than maintaining a mobile force in the area, but it was also less of a threat to the balance of power here. That balance consisted of a tentative stand-off between two or three huge trading conglomerates that maintained mercenary fleets and acted in the interests of different factions on the Confederacy Council, and the Danadan, a spacefaring race who have traditionally pirated this area of space after their homeworld was destroyed by the Tor centuries ago. As well as these major players, there were a number of small, unaligned trading companies, and pirate gangs, all of whom jealously guarded their right to plunder what they could of this isolated and resource-poor cluster.

Then the Confederacy decided to 'give' the station to Earth. It was a generous gesture for the Council to approve administration of a sector facility by one of its minor members, and none of the eight other non-jump species had ever been accorded a similar honour. A gesture it remained, however. The four founding member species – the Invidi, the K'Cher, Melot and the Bendarl, the 'Four Worlds' – have always refused to allow the lesser members independent use of faster-than-light spacedrive, so Earth was forced to bow to the schedules of Sector vessels or rent private shipping to transport its personnel and sublight ships to the station. Without this cooperation we are completely isolated.

I arrived here as one of the engineering crew in the second year of the reconstruction and the year before Jocasta officially became an Earthstation. It wasn't my first job as overseer but the others had never been as chaotic as this. Work was constantly disrupted by the non-arrival of supplies and personnel, booby traps left by the Tor, and occasionally by attacks on the station itself. We only ever finished because the Danadan became embroiled in territorial squabbles with the Seouras and the other two largest pirate fleets engaged in a bloody feud for nearly a year. Even then, the outermost ring was still incomplete at the inauguration ceremony.

Relations with Sector Central were further soured by

difficulties in getting the station running smoothly. There were four station heads in that first year: one quit, two committed suicide and one was poisoned. By the time I found myself the unwilling and ostensibly temporary holder of that office, as head of Engineering and the most senior ConFleet officer, most of the construction crews and ConFleet forces had pulled out. No respectable trader would come anywhere near the station – many didn't know we existed – and to cap it all, it seemed that Jocasta's charter stated that the head of station was also obliged to act as governor of the Abelar system. This meant I had to worry about two battered and almost completely useless planets with tiny mining colonies and the usual one light-year territorial boundary as well as the station itself.

It took nearly three years of hard work to achieve a precarious stability both in the running of the station and between the species who visited and lived here. The Danadan threatened to upset it all when they declared this had always been their space and demanded special trading privileges. At about the same time the Seouras presence along the Confederacy border grew stronger and the two species clashed frequently.

The Seouras were an unknown factor. It was rumoured that they had returned to claim the area for their own, but in fact their ships made no aggressive moves against the system or Confederacy traffic. There was no indication that the Seouras had aggressive intentions or that they possessed the level of technology necessary to effect a seizure. Their ships then weren't half as big as the ones watching the station now, and the design was different.

The Danadan and mercenary fleets ruined trade and filled the station with refugees, which we could ill afford; because of the lack of support from either Sector Central or Earth, the only way for us to become self-sufficient was by trade. Even then, we were always low on essential stocks – medical supplies, delicate equipment replacements. To provide a counterweight, I suggested a treaty between Jocasta, the Danadan, and the Seouras as we then knew them. The captain of the Danadan ship that was disturbing trade around the system at the time agreed to consider a compromise. Murdoch was appalled by the idea and said so.

It took several weeks of intensive diplomatic effort to hammer out an agreement basically satisfactory to all. Both the Seouras and Danadan were to suspend hostilities in the Abelar system and a surrounding twenty-light-year radius. No force was to be used against Confederacy ships or installations in said area. Both species were allowed full access to and trade privileges on Jocasta. If one party broke the treaty, the others were to come to the aid of the injured party.

The Danadan were not happy at the prospect of losing a profitable area of pillage, but perhaps they considered the benefits of having a powerful ally such as the Confederacy worth conceding a demilitarised buffer zone in and around the Abelar system. The Seouras seemed pleased to be rid of the Danadan and expressed an interest in both trading and communicating with other species in the Confederacy.

Unfortunately the trading conglomerates and their employees at all levels of Confederacy government were not pleased, and neither were the K'Cher trade barons who manipulated them. Nor were Earth administration (because Sector was upset), crooked traders and agents on the station (because station Security now found time to deal with them), or elements within the Danadan hierarchy who thought the loss of their piracy income too high a price to pay for a peace they'd never wanted. As they say, you can't please everyone all the time.

The Abelar Treaty seemed a good idea at the time, and it worked for a while. It kept our space free from large-scale fighting between Seouras and Danadan and let us concentrate on removing smugglers and pirates, and on attracting genuine traders. We had nearly a year of peace and prosperity afterwards. The Seouras kept their distance, the Danadan visited only to trade.

A few refugees took advantage of the peace to seek safety with the Confederacy, it is true, but one hundred years ago Marlena Alvarez never turned refugees away and I was damned if I would now. Some trade from the main jump routes began to spill over to us and representatives of the sector's largest mercantile financier and the K'Cher trading fleet opened offices on the station. Sector Central even sent a team from the Audit Ministry to complain about our management structure.

All that changed in a few hours when the grey ships came.

'You really think it'll work?' Bill Murdoch leaned his elbows on the table between us and kept his voice low. He is a big man, broad and heavy-muscled, and his uniform always seems a little tight over the shoulders.

'It's the best chance we've had for a while to send a message.' I stifled another yawn. I'd been working all night with the engineering team to prepare the probe. The trouble was, I'd also been kept up the night before that when the Seouras called. They send a certain signal to the station when they want me over on the ship. As soon as the signal comes, I go. The last session had been a long one, almost twelve hours, leaving me feeling completely ragged.

Murdoch pushed his chair back and looked at me with an expression that could have been either exasperation or concern. 'Hard night?'

'Two of them. I'm going back to my quarters.' I stretched stiffly. Joint pain is one of the side effects of the Seouras interaction. Murdoch watched without comment as I flinched and rubbed. The intensity of his round, dark gaze made me stop, embarrassed to be revealing a weakness here.

The other officers got to their feet also, murmuring to each other. They filled the room, which looked smaller in the light – the sky blue of EarthFleet, the navy of ConFleet, Murdoch's olive-green Security jacket, the brown suit of a civilian researcher in Astro, and Veatch's slim, grey form. Jago's white-jacketed figure disappeared quickly – she was on call at the hospital.

The other colours left space around Veatch's grey. It was a deliberate snub. Veatch was a Melot, a 'humanoid' species – how they hated that phrase. They had essentially the same form as humans: bipedal, forward-facing eyes, a respiratory system etc, but they were one of the four founding species of the Confederacy. There were nine other member worlds/systems/species in the Confederacy, making a total of thirteen, as well as dozens of affiliated worlds that were not formal members but had economic or cultural ties with Confederacy worlds. The Four Worlds made it quite clear who the senior members of the partnership were, and the Nine Worlds, as the rest of us were called, put up with it because . . . it was true. If it had not been for the technology and knowledge of the Four, most of the Nine would have still been clawing our way out of our respective atomic ages. Or have destroyed ourselves first, as the case may be. But it was not pleasant to be reminded of one's own inferiority, and Veatch's insensitivity fanned the embers of resentment onstation against the Four, and against the Confederacy in general. The Confederacy that had not saved us from the Seouras.

In their first attack the grey ships approached the station, ignored greetings and then warnings, and blocked our communications with anyone beyond the system. At the time, I hadn't wanted to make any aggressive moves – they were obviously better armed than we were – but they got closer and closer. They sent no communications and we had no idea who we were facing.

The EarthFleet officers, whose fighter squadrons formed our first and only line of defence, wanted to give a warning followed by some aggressive posturing by the squadrons. I resisted this, because the ships had made no attack on us, although the squadron leaders pointed out that to isolate us from the Confederacy could be interpreted as a hostile act. This initial tension continued for hours, while we tried desperately to find some method of communication, and ended tragically when a couple of the traders docked at Jocasta tried to make a run for it and were swiftly, effortlessly shot down by the nearest grey ship.

So began the blockade. I gave in to recommendations from EarthFleet and ConFleet officers to retaliate. The fighter squadrons were destroyed – shot away as they attacked, picked off as they retreated. The station's residents panicked. Many of the traders and those residents with access to transport tried to leave, against our direct orders. The grey ships destroyed them too. The station was in an uproar. Already overtaxed environmental systems started to fail and damage to reflectors plunged whole sections into darkness.

We kept sending a message of surrender but there was no sign the ships received it, until they sent us a message that bore the signature we'd used for the Seouras in the treaty negotiations. We couldn't understand why they were doing this when they already had access to the station. We still don't understand.

They called me over to the ship in the same way we'd negotiated for the treaty. Like those other Seouras they did not seem able to communicate either verbally or electronically in a way we could recognise, and they used the implant their predecessors gave me, by which their 'thoughts' or 'moods' – neither, really, but there is no word in our vocabulary to describe it – are directly communicated to my mind. I couldn't do it back, but they seemed to understand me when I spoke.

All they said this time, though, was 'Wait'.

So we waited.

They returned force with force and their defences were far more sophisticated than any weapon we possessed, as we found to our cost. It might have been easier if we had known what they wanted. Why they were cutting us off from the rest of the galaxy and then leaving us to our own devices on the station. Why they would not talk except to one representative. Why they attack shuttles or small ships. Why they take nothing from the station, but hold it hostage for my good behaviour and vice versa, send for me arbitrarily on an average of once a fortnight, wring me sometimes to the point of insensibility for whatever they get from our 'conversations' . . . and then let me return. Why, if they needed nothing, they were here. And so on and so on. It nearly drove me mad at first. Then I finally realised that it was a waste of time trying to understand why they were doing this to us. Now I think about what we do know – six months' worth of sensor readings on their ships – and leave motive to the gods. There has to be an answer somewhere in the data.

All we can do is wait, while the station falls apart around us.

The wall comm link beeped through the low hum of conversation.

'Commander Halley?'

I reached past Murdoch and tapped open the screen. 'Halley here. What is it, Baudin?'

Lieutenant Baudin, EarthFleet and proud of it, calling from the Bubble. He didn't have to lean into the visual pickup so far. The tip of his considerable nose was quite blurred.

'We've detected a jump mine explosion. On the edge of the asteroid field.'

All conversation in the room ceased. Every head turned to listen.

It took a second for his words to penetrate and the adrenalin to kick in.

'Have you picked up any sign of a ship?' I said. Jump mines can only be set off by ships.

'We can't tell at this distance. Backburn from the mine is disrupting sensors.'

'The Seouras? Are they doing anything?' Perhaps they knew that any ship caught in a jump mine would no longer be a threat. Perhaps their sensors had been disrupted by the comet sooner than we'd expected.

'There's nothing from them.'

'Keep monitoring it. I'll be right up.' The screen darkened.

There was a short moment of frozen disbelief, then the others scrambled for the door.

I glared my way through first – rank has its privileges – and walked quickly to the nearest ringlift, Murdoch close behind me. The throughway outside the building was crowded and his bulk came in handy.

Veatch, who had left before Baudin's message, was waiting in front of the ringlift and he looked around with a surprised tilt of his antennae as we rushed up. The door opened.

'Going up?' Murdoch reached past Veatch and tapped in the code for the command centre.

'Yes.' Veatch was unsure of the protocol for rhetorical questions, although he often gave what I felt were rhetorical answers to my sensible questions.

The doors wheezed shut and the floor pressed briefly against our feet as the ringlift rose to Alpha level.

'How could it possibly have been set off?' said Murdoch.

I shook my head. 'I've never heard of one blowing by itself. Has to be a ship.'

Jump mines, weapons left over from the war between the Confederacy and the Tor, were seeded indiscriminately across the sector by the Tor and activate when a ship leaves a jump to return to normal space. Most of the mines have been collected or destroyed, but the number of places possible for a jump in or out of hyperspace were limited and occasionally these points drifted into a forgotten mine. Big traders and ConFleet ships had all developed defence grids, so the main casualties were small or obsolete craft.

'Commander?' Veatch conveyed censure without frowning.

'We detected a jump mine that activated within the system,' I explained, fidgeting against the slowness of the lift. 'On the edge of the asteroids.'

'I see.'

'Aren't you excited? This could be our first contact with the outside galaxy in six months. It could be a ship from the Confederacy.'

'Most ConFleet vessels are equipped with mine detection devices. And I do not see how contact with a radioactive wreck will prove of any use to us.'

'Cheerful, aren't you?' Murdoch grunted. 'Does the word "morale" mean anything to you?'

I tapped the status screen on the lift wall that showed the position of the closest Seouras ship. I like to know where it is, to be able to 'see' them, even if only on our inefficient sensors. The ship was in the same place as it had been for weeks, on the far side of the station, facing the Confederacy and the bright swathe of the inner galaxy.

'It might not be of any immediate use,' I turned back to Veatch. 'But if we can analyse the wreckage we may find out why the ship jumped into this system, whether it's from the Confederacy or not.'

The jump in itself was unusual. Normally the drive was not activated inside a populated system even if a jump point were available, a matter of both safety and courtesy. Nobody wants even a controlled singularity – at least, that's what we thought it was – opening on their doorstep. We didn't know much more about the jump drive. The Invidi often pointed out that our greatest mathematical minds have failed to understand it, but I think they should let an engineer have a go.

'I would've thought you'd be glad of a chance to get news from home,' said Murdoch to Veatch. 'Must be hard for you, stuck here with all these lesser species.'

I looked more carefully at Murdoch. Sarcasm was not his usual style. His blunt, brown features looked tired.

'I do not regard anyone on the station as a lesser species.' Veatch was making his opinion clear. Another first.

'Maybe, but you gotta admit the whole administrative

process is designed to humiliate whoever tries to use it.'

My heart sank. If Murdoch came out on the side of the anti-Four lobby, things could get tougher for me, caught in the middle between them. Until now, he has been admirably neutral.

'The administrative process is designed for efficiency,' Veatch's normal whine grew sharper in defence of his territory.

'It wasn't efficient the other day when I tried to file a complaint about recycling.'

'Perhaps you did not utilise the process correctly.'

'Nope, I put the stuff in the chute, but it didn't . . .'

'I refer to the administrative process.'

I tried to ignore them and think about the ship but their voices were like the fizz of loose circuitry, impossible to ignore. They were a strange pair – Veatch must have been born knowing every Confederacy regulation; Murdoch was quite capable of ignoring the rules when it suited him. Murdoch had been assigned here because in his former post he refused to take the usual bribes and tried to arrest his CO. Veatch must have trodden on someone's toes at Central, because there was no other reason a career bureaucrat would be sent here. And I'm sure I was given the Jocasta reconstruction project because someone hoped I'd get blown up by a Tor booby trap.

The door wheezed open at the lower entrance to the main complex.

'See you later,' said Murdoch curtly, and pushed his way out ahead of Veatch, who inclined his antennae and followed. The lift rose another half-level and the door opened on the Bubble.

The murmur of voices faltered only momentarily as I stepped onto the upper platform. I hadn't felt this much excitement on the top level for months. Instead of the usual three or four staff monitoring main systems there must have been at least twenty people there, and the narrow, circular space was hot and cramped. Baudin bent over the person on duty at the main sensor console and a ConFleet ensign, Lee, was seated at Ops.

'Where is it?' I squeezed past Baudin's salute – he was too excited to remember I hated that – and looked over Lee's dark blue shoulder. Her eyes slanted back at me briefly and her trim fingers tapped the information onto the screen.

'Drifting past the last asteroids now. And Commander – there's a ship.'

A ship. We haven't had a ship dock here since the Seouras blockade began. Our last contact with an outside source, and that by sensors only, was when a tiny prospector blundered through the asteroid belt three or four months ago. The prospector must have evaded Seouras sensors somehow to get that far, but as soon as it left the belt they destroyed it while we watched. Stupid, sad, waste. Something that small could be no threat to the huge, grey ships.

It gave us ideas, though. Of sending a ship to sneak out of the system via the asteroids. So we sent two volunteers and never heard from them again. We tried again a little while afterwards, using the tail of a comet similar to the present one. That ship was damaged and we had to watch it drift away from us, the pilot condemned to wait until his air ran out. We wished the Seouras had fired.

The Seouras might not let us intervene. The trouble is, we won't know until we try, and it means risking one of our two shuttles and several lives for a radioactive wreck.

I didn't like the idea. We'd lost the EarthFleet squadrons in five minutes when the Seouras first attacked and I didn't want to lose anyone else.

No movement from the grey ship. So far, so good. I peered at the readings. 'Have we got an ID?'

Lee frowned at the console as though it had insulted her personally. 'No, ma'am. Radiation from the mine's interfering. And the ship itself is hot.'

We had to know where the ship came from. It could carry a message from the Confederacy, from Earth. It could mean the end of our isolation. It could also, I rubbed the implant in my neck, just be another lost prospector.

'It'll take a bit longer, but we'll send the probe,' I decided. The probe is a battered robot with basic sensor arrays and limited propulsion, designed to investigate the geological composition of asteroids and the only one left out of our original complement of five. After the Seouras came we modified the robot's sensors so they could be used to repair the reflectors. The fewer live targets we provided, the better.

Lee nodded and sent a message to Engineering, but Baudin's face fell in disappointment.

'The probe can't bring the ship in,' he ventured. 'What if there are survivors?'

'We'll retrieve it then. After we make sure.' I could see

why he chafed at the enforced patience of our dealings with the Seouras – our only way of resistance is to do nothing. But the likelihood of survivors is small, and there's no way he'll persuade me to risk more lives without good reason.

The question was, why had the Seouras let the ship past? Perhaps it surprised them, and when the mine blew, they felt it wasn't worth finishing the job.

Unless ... I tried to think back to my most recent session with them. Were they any different this time? If they were letting down their guard, becoming careless, we might try slipping a shuttle 'out the back door' again as well as the comet probe. We don't have any jump-capable ships here, but we still do have a couple of shuttles, two old fighters and an assortment of motley freighters like the *Queen*.

Perhaps there had been a change in the Seouras lately, the way they felt inside my head. But not a slackening. Rather, an intensification of purpose, a sharpening of will, of voice. As though more and more of the voices had decided to agree.

I needed to think. 'I'll be in my office. Call me as soon as you have anything.'

Even now, weeks since the blast, the mess in my office still comes as a surprise. Murdoch's investigation still hasn't found the culprit, but the bomb itself was a small, homemade device. Designed, Security thought, to frighten rather than kill. It certainly succeeded. I was sick with apprehension for days afterwards, even though I was not in the office at the time of the explosion. Lately, though, my habitual fog of fatigue has cushioned fear, and the mess has become merely an inconvenience.

A chaos of filepads, data crystals, and console components littered the desk, and the lower half of the office door and the bank of interface consoles beside the desk were covered in blackened dents and cracks. The main interface bank was dead, and its dark monitor gave the small room an air of abandonment. The single live interface stood on the desk, swamped in clutter. On the wall next to the door a two-dimensional print hung askew, although the blast had not been able to damage its clear container. That print has survived two global wars, three major depressions and an Amazonian flood. An ancestor of mine who assisted the Meiji government in building its first iron and steel mill brought it to Germany from Japan. Engineering runs in the family.

The print shows a village marketplace in Japan with a curving bridge in the foreground and figures bustling around it. Behind the town towers an immense, cone-shaped mountain with a far-off traveller scurrying for shelter from a squall. Looking at it now, I sympathise with that traveller. I had the feeling we were in for a storm too.

Before I'd even sat down Veatch entered through the connecting door from his office. As station manager, officially Veatch oversees all the major departments of the station and then brings any problems that involve stationwide decision-making to me. In practice, however, the department heads have more autonomy. Bill Murdoch runs Security, the chief magistrate, Lorna deVries, never consults anyone about Judiciary, Mac has his own little dictatorship in Engineering, and Eleanor Jago takes care of the medical staff and systems. The rest of the station comes under Administration and its many divisions, except for EarthFleet and Customs, which are nearly irrelevant now.

Veatch always seems happy to immerse himself in the convoluted world of Confederacy bureaucracy that regulates the official minutiae of station life. This is not surprising, for the Melot clerical caste dominate the huge, unwieldy bureaucracy of the Confederacy for a reason. Veatch runs our administration with comparable efficiency, unfazed by military defeat and alien occupation. I find it difficult, though, to decipher how he feels about being sent to a post so obscure and isolated, let alone his feelings about the blockade. Does he see his posting as punishment? Perhaps it is merely another job to be performed as best he can in spite of the amateurish assistance of human administrators, many of whom resent his presence as proof of Confederacy interference.

A slight shabbiness is the only sign he shows of the past six months' turmoil. The collar and cuffs of his suits droop and recently he has taken to wearing the same pair of shoes two shifts in a row. But his coppery skin of tiny overlapping scales is as iridescent as ever and the great gold eyes stare at me with the same deceptive innocence.

'What is it?' I thudded into my desk chair.

'Commander.' Veatch inclined his head. 'Is there to be no rescue operation?' Presumably he'd called the upper level for an update.

'Not unless we confirm the presence of survivors. Do you think everyone's heard about it?'

'The Station Times broadcast the story on the 0900 news.' His finely scaled face was expressionless, but I caught a distinct impression of distaste. 'They scooped, I believe the word is, the official announcement.'

I groaned inwardly. Dan Florida, one of the station's more enterprising civilian residents, recently decided we needed an independent news service to supplement what he called the 'paucity of official information systems'. He pays to use part of the station comm net and then charges his viewers a small fee. Granted, the service broadcasts in a variety of minority languages, which the official net does not, and therefore employs more refugees, but it seems strange to make people pay for information that should be public.

Veatch seemed a little brisker than usual, perhaps the Melot equivalent of being excited. 'You did not meet Mr Florida?'

'No, thank goodness.'

'He contacted me to arrange an interview with you. I told him he would have to make an appointment and he said he would check the time with you.'

'Well, he hasn't,' I snapped.

He tapped his comfile with a steady, soporific rhythm. 'You have not forgotten the Smoke residents meeting at 1800 hours?'

I shook my head and choked back a yawn. Staying awake was proving impossible.

Veatch's voice is a leaden whine. Both irritating and mesmerising, it engenders a desire on the part of the listener to disagree' with whatever he's saying. At the same time his manner is lofty and disdainful. At first I thought he was just like that with me, regarding me as a sort of mechanic, incapable of understanding administrative issues. But as the months have passed, I notice that he's the same with everyone.

'The efficiency reports from last week are cause for concern. Three departments are down more than two points. It would be appropriate to bring the matter up at the senior staff meeting tomorrow,' he droned on.

'I'll look at the data first.'

Eventually Veatch folded his three-jointed fingers in a complex pattern, a movement that indicated a desire to change the subject. Before I could suggest we talk later the door chimed and opened to admit Ellis Walsh, our EarthFleet liaison-cum-personnel officer.

She walked quickly, a little behind the momentum of her own pace, a stack of filepads nestled in the crook of one arm.

'Commander . . . Oh, Mr Veatch. I didn't know you were here.' She flicked a long, blonde fringe away from her eyes.

Veatch inclined his antennae diffidently.

Walsh pulled over the other chair and sat. She had the air of someone settling in for a siege and I rattled a data crystal irritably on the desk. All I wanted was a quick nap.

'I've been trying to reach you for days, Commander.'

Veatch took his own filepad off the desk. 'Interview requests are considered according to station priorities.'

'I've been with the Seouras,' I interjected hastily. 'What is it you wanted to see me about?'

She glanced at Veatch, who showed no sign of moving. 'It concerns him directly.'

I felt a little more alert. Dissension in the ranks. Walsh is a member of the EarthFleet administration that is supposed to run Jocasta. To keep staff numbers up, though, over half the positions are filled by ConFleet people, like myself, and those seconded from Sector Central administration, like Veatch. Politically it's no accident that even though we are an Earth base, the head of station, station manager, and head of security all come from the mixed Confederacy forces.

Not that it matters any more. We're all stuck here together.

'He keeps blocking me on the development plan.' Walsh tapped her filepad.

'Development?'

'The Alpha redistribution project.' She frowned at my slowness. 'The RRC – Residential Reform Committee – met and discussed the matter last month.'

I took the proffered datachip and called up the information on my own interface. It's a wonder the thing still works. I've removed visual cueing, retina scans, voice cues, and direct cranial enhancement, which I don't use any more, and any other modifications in the hope of increasing efficiency in its main functions, but the bomb blast left problems.

'It was agreed to negotiate with the owners of dwellings in sections three through twenty-four regarding the conversion of that space into either agricultural extension or high-density residencies,' Walsh continued.

'Ye-es.' As far as I could remember 'agree' has never been something the committee has done very well, but this wasn't the time to mention it. 'I'm familiar with the proposal. How is it being blocked?' I was interested to hear what she had to say about Veatch. Ordinarily, he kept a claustrophobically well-controlled department, and for one of his staff to approach me directly argued great frustration boiling away below the surface.

Veatch recrossed his legs, unworried.

'Commander, I must protest the expression "block",' he said. 'It implies a hidden agenda and/or deliberate malice. I have merely . . .'

'Oh no. This is my complaint.' Walsh leaned forward and stared across at Veatch then back at me. 'Let me tell it my way.'

'Fine.' I glanced at Veatch. He shrugged without moving his body and settled back in his chair.

'Things aren't moving ahead at all,' she continued. 'I try to process drafts of, say, preference surveys for current residents or environmental impact assessments, but they just disappear after they leave my terminal.'

'Disappear?'

'Yes. When I chase things up, they're stuck at the

bottom of someone's In file. Or in the wrong directory. Or the hardcopy's been mislaid. It's more than inefficiency – this is deliberate obfuscation.'

I couldn't stop the yawn escaping. 'Any comments, Mr Veatch?'

'It needs to be investigated according to protocol,' he said. 'Without undue haste.'

Walsh snorted. 'Haste? Have you noticed our situation lately? We're not exactly on the main supply routes any more. We need to use space as efficiently as possible, as soon as possible, and Alpha has too many Class Four areas.'

Class Four areas were set aside as recreation or 'open cultural' space in the station's original plan. Places like parks, stages, concert venues. In practice, the well-off Alpha ring residents kept and expanded these areas while people in the crowded lower rings have had to use the space mainly for accommodation. It feeds the anti–Four Worlds sentiment on the station because the majority of Alpha residents are either K'Cher or those who've prof-ited by their association with the K'Cher. The K'Cher aristocracy controlled the economy of the Confederacy in the same way the Melot controlled its administration and the Bendarl its defence. Not overtly, but with great efficiency. Except, perhaps, for the Bendarl, who wouldn't recognise subtlety if they died of it.

Despite Veatch's unpopularity as a member of one of the four 'major' species, it was unlike him to oppose anything that improved the efficiency of station admin-istration, provided it did not mean a flow of power out of his hands. Which this project did not. There would be

31

plenty of opportunities for him to assert control.

Veatch inclined his head a little too much. 'All properly formatted material is processed through due channels.'

'Are you suggesting my drafts were not formatted correctly?' Walsh snapped.

'Perhaps we should continue at a more appropriate time.' Veatch added insult to injury by looking at me. He was definitely protesting too much. Surely he must realise, first, that Walsh was right and, second, that we couldn't afford to exacerbate the dissatisfaction on the station.

'Now is appropriate,' she said. 'We'd like to present an interim report to the committee next week.'

'That is hardly enough time to make sure all departments . . .'

'Ahem.' I didn't like interrupting Veatch, but he can spout excuses for hours on end. Walsh should know that confronting a Melot brought no solutions – they just retreat into ambiguities until you feel as though you are wrestling smoke on a high-gravity planet.

'Veatch, we really have no choice about this. The crowding in Delta and even Gamma is putting unacceptable strains on environmental systems, particularly waste recycling and water supply. You've read the reports.'

Walsh nodded. Veatch listened impassively.

'We can reallocate Alpha areas arbitrarily or we can do it with consideration of the residents' wishes. But it's going to get done, and soon.'

He snuffled, the Melot noise equivalent to clearing his throat. 'And the matter of compensation?'

So that was it. The K'Cher and their affiliates must be

pressuring Veatch to make the best deal for them.

Walsh laughed. 'You're kidding. We lease them the property, remember? Jocasta is an Earth station.'

'The administration must honour the terms of the lease or offer due compensation for not doing so.'

'They don't decide what is due compensation.'

'I do not need to remind you that Jocasta is in fact leased to Earth.'

'Yes, and we haven't got any compensation for the invasion, have we? Occupation by hostile aliens isn't in the terms of our lease, either.'

I winced. This is the real issue. None of us understand why the Confederacy did not retaliate when the Seouras took Jocasta. The grey ships are powerful, true, but the warships of ConFleet are crewed largely by the Bendarl, one of the most warlike and ruthless species in the known galaxy, and Invidi technology had been able to defeat an enemy as strong as the Tor. None of us doubted Con-Fleet's ability to defeat the Seouras ships. But we had begun to doubt the sincerity of Confederacy intentions.

Unable to voice their protest directly to the Confederacy, people expressed their feelings of betrayal and the uncertainty and fear of the future in resentment against the administration's cooperation with the Seouras – against me. They also resented the station's one Invidi resident whom they felt could have stopped the invasion or called for help, or something. An Barik, the Invidi 'observer' from the Confederacy Council, was never sociable, but these days he stayed in his quarters all the time.

I sighed. I'd had enough of the Nine versus Four

conflict when I worked in the inner worlds. It had been the catalyst that destroyed my marriage. Now it was dividing Jocasta.

Veatch and Walsh were still waiting for my response.

'You can work out some kind of compensation package,' I said.

Veatch flicked his antennae in a satisfied way.

'But they must understand that it will have to go through a judicial screening process before being approved. And whatever is eventually agreed upon, we can't actually give any sort of compensation until the blockade is ended and we have sufficient resources. And,' I added, 'they'll have to agree to something within the week.'

Walsh smiled and was about to make a comment when the comm link beeped and Baudin mercifully interrupted.

'The telemetry's coming through now, ma'am.'

'I'll be right out.' I turned to the two administrative officials. 'If you'll excuse me?'

They both opened their mouths to have the last word, caught my eye, and decided against it.

There was a living face in the coffin. A human face. Young, female, asleep.

Whatever I'd expected to see through the probe's telemetry, this wasn't it. The visual pickups moved down to show the owner of the face floating peacefully in her narrow world of aquamarine gel, oblivious to the chaos outside.

Harsh white light streamed in through a jagged rip in the spacecraft hull, so bright that vision filters flashed a warning when the probe turned that way. It chequered the mess of floating, twisted metal and left the far corners of the cabin impenetrable. Tendrils of coolant sifted across the floor, dispersed like smoke on wind by the touch of the probe's passage. A curlicue of shining metal danced end over end.

The initial blast fused ceiling and entry at the nose end in a tangle of metal. Coffin-like berths were overturned or pulled loose from their supports. Some of the containment locks had failed, the pods had opened, and bodies floated within an untidy cloud of stasis fluid. The pods would have been arranged in even rows along opposing walls. The other wall carried the remains of a magnetic tread – that must have been their 'floor'. At right angles to this were banks of controls and monitoring devices, some apparently unscathed, others blackened and melted.

The coffin shuddered as a floor panel shifted. The ship itself was creaking apart. Outside it trailed a cloud of debris and water vapour as momentum from the explosion pushed it closer to the station.

'Can we remove the coff—. . . the pod without disconnecting the cryosystem?' My voice fell flat into the scene inside my eyes, echoing in a way that should have been impossible in vacuum. There was a curious sense of dislocation to this conversation with someone who my senses told me wasn't really there. I pulled my head out of the virtual hood with a grimace of distaste and returned to the physical present – an engineering console in the Bubble. The probe continued sending information.

'There are humans in there. In cryostasis. Where did

they come from? Someone froze them and sent them here?' Lee bent over the screen as though it would yield more information that way.

A present? I dismissed the ridiculous image with regret. It would be nice to think that someone out there liked us.

'It's an old ship, so possibly they're from a human colony we don't know much about. It would have to be from close by, given how slow that ship is.'

'Three of the pods are still functioning, and that's a miracle.' MacGuire, the chief engineer, had grumbled at the necessity to come up to the Bubble from his office in the lower ring, but the excitement of the occasion seemed to have affected even him now. He tapped a monitor screen and both Lee and I peered over his shoulder to see three highlighted rectangles overlaid on thin blue lines showing the ship's layout, all put together from the probe's information. Figures continued to appear as more information from the robot's telemetry was processed.

'We can assume the pods have backup circuits, or they wouldn't still be alive now,' he said. 'But whether the backups will keep working long enough to get them back here alive . . .'

'We'll have to hope their backups have backup. And that the pods have good radiation shields.' I thought of the gel and the lid of the coffin and the waiting dark. You would have to be very sure the opsys knew how to maintain and then reverse the cryogenic process before willingly being frozen in there.

'We could nudge it over to one of the docks,' Lee ventured.

Mac snorted wetly in my ear. 'Not on your life! I'm not having that Christmas tree disrupting every sensitive comm facility on the station. And it'll contaminate the entire dock area.' He tapped me pointedly on the shoulder. 'You do know some of the rad shields in the docking bays aren't working?'

Lee mouthed 'Christmas tree?' to herself.

'I know.' I drew away from his thick, freckled finger.

He waved a hand in a circle to indicate the whole station. 'We risk disrupting the main field, too. After all that trouble getting it online again.' Mac straightened with an air of finality. 'Pop it out in close orbit for a couple of days. Then at least the really nasty stuff from the mine will have dissipated.'

'You can't leave them out there for *days*!' Lee's round face glowed with indignation. 'Their cryosystems might fail. We could find corpses if we wait too long.'

'We won't leave them.' I wanted to look at the ship sooner than that. 'You sent the probe's information to Medical?' I asked Mac.

'They're looking it over now.' Mac glowered. Our relationship of mutual professional trust and personal distaste had not changed since he arrived from Titan to take over my post of chief engineer three years ago.

We were going to have to send out a crewed ship to remove the survivors and manoeuvre the wreck into place. Most of our large-scale dock equipment had been damaged in Seouras attacks, otherwise it might have done the job for us. If we used the little tug-shuttle we'd have to be quick, because its shields weren't designed to cope with the kind of radiation it would encounter from the mine.

'We haven't got anything that will grapple the wreck properly. And you'll want a medic.' Mac read my mind easily – he'd been doing this work for about forty years longer than the rest of us, after all.

'Yes. To keep an eye on the cryosystems.'

Baudin was speaking into a monitor on the other side of the Bubble. He caught my eye, spoke again, and came over.

'Commander, the K'Cher trader Keveth is offering to assist in towing the wreck. In return for the usual consideration of second option on salvage rights.'

'Keveth?' Why should Keveth volunteer to risk its life for some unknown humans? Normally the K'Cher was particularly careful of its own safety. When the Seouras attacked Keveth had not even attempted to flee. Then again, Keveth was the black sheep of the remaining K'Cher traders on Jocasta and fraternised with lesser species, such as humans, even when not doing business, something the others never do. It was probably also desperate to get work, especially something that would give it an edge over the other K'Cher.

I noted Baudin's carefully neutral expression. One of the other EarthFleet staff was frowning in our direction and another was flipping open a section of her console with unnecessary strength. There was considerable resentment on their part that while EarthFleet pilots had sacrificed their lives to defend the station, aliens from the Four Worlds such as the K'Cher had kept themselves safe and were now enjoying the rewards of cowardice, however meagre those rewards might be at the moment.

'Has the *Rillian Queen* got the equipment?' I asked Mac. Keveth's old ship hasn't even got a K'Cher name.

'Aye. If Keveth hasn't sold too many important bits.'

The *Queen* could grapple the wreck and place it in a safe orbit. We could then send a doctor and a couple of the engineering staff in a shuttle and the *Queen* could bring the survivors back in her cargo bay. The Seouras had never attacked anything so close to the station, not since that first day.

'All right.' No reason we shouldn't use what few resources we have. 'Inform Keveth that we appreciate its help. But it'll have to apply for salvage using the proper protocols.'

Last time the *Rillian Queen* picked up some refugees, in pre-occupation days, not only had all the victims signed five-year contracts with its captain to work for a pittance, but we had had to buy pieces of wreckage for analysis from the conniving alien under some little-invoked rule of salvage.

'We won't be able to see what it's doing,' ventured Baudin, referring to Keveth. 'Not with the radiation as well as the Seouras jamming. It doesn't let humans on the ship.'

I didn't trust Keveth either, but there was little choice. 'The probe will show us a bit. We'll need someone to pilot the shuttle,' I added. That should make EarthFleet feel wanted.

'Aye, ma'am.' Baudin wasn't happy but he said no more.

It was almost comical how fast the rumours had

spread. Keveth had known about the shipwreck less than an hour after we'd sent the probe.

Mac spoke to his people on another link, sorting out a strategy for removing the pods. I'd have dearly liked to go in the shuttle too, but Security would have a fit.

'Here's the breakdown.' Lee tapped a neighbouring monitor then moved aside for me to sit before it. The probe's information was regimented into neat ranks of pale blue figures on deeper blue.

'Why should the mine blow?' she pondered over my shoulder. 'This ship doesn't have a jump drive to set it off.'

A glance at the figures confirmed it. This was an ancient ship, nearly a century old. More to the point, how could it have travelled this far without a jump drive? Jocasta is way out on the back fence of Confederacy space, more than five jumps from the closest inhabited system. It takes from three days to three weeks of real-time travel to reach here and close to a week of our time for a high-priority message to reach Sector Central.

The wreck itself looked like one of the old runabouts used around the inner worlds of the Confederacy. Outdated enough to be used independently by the Nine Worlds because the ships don't have a jump drive, but still functional. I scrolled down the columns. This one had a lot of unusual modifications, but only normal spacedrive.

'I wonder where it started from,' said Baudin.

'I wonder how it got out here,' I echoed him unconsciously.

'Could something else have activated the mine?' asked Lee.

'We haven't picked up any other ship signals. Those mines are pretty unstable things. Might have activated by accident,' Mac replied from the engineering console. He didn't sound convinced.

'Never heard of that happening before.' I stood up, joints jabbing with pain. Now that the initial excitement was wearing off, tiredness had crept up on me again.

'I guess we'll just have to ask them.' Lee's face was calm but her voice danced on the words.

'Let's hope they survive that long.' I yawned. Much as I wanted to stay and watch the rescue operation, unless I took a nap I wouldn't be lucid enough to ask the survivors anything.

The illumination failed to come on as I entered my quarters. I tripped over something soft on the floor, cursed half-heartedly, and tapped on the lights manually. Sensor relay's malfunctioning again.

A pile of dirty clothes lay on the floor near the doorway where I'd put them to remind myself they needed recycling. I stepped over the now-scattered pile and past the table occupied by two interface monitors and a mess of disks, data crystals, plastic hardcopy and dirty cups.

Originally the unit was designed as reasonably spacious quarters for one, possibly two people. After the Seouras ships arrived the living space allowance for everyone in the administration was reduced. Personnel had offered to let me have my own quarters, but I thought that smacked of preferential treatment. Later I regretted agreeing we should all make sacrifices when it transpired that those sacrifices included sharing a bathroom with three other partnerless females. The four sleeping rooms cluster around a central kitchen and the communal bathroom/head designed for one. We all miss our privacy.

My room had the resentful air of a place unloved. I only returned here to sleep, and not every night. It was a single room with a bunk along one wall and a square regulation wardrobe at its foot. The decor was plain, its saving grace an absence of the pale blue that coated the rest of the station's interior walls – it boasted varying shades of recycled grey and non-regulation cream. My grandmother's quilt was the only splash of real colour, a glorious blaze of kaleidoscopic gaiety folded untidily against the wall. A thermasheet trailed from the narrow bed where I'd dragged it as I got up, midnight the night before last.

As I bent and tossed the sheet back on the bed, its corner swept a photograph off its stand. I picked up the flat frame and wiped it carefully. Five familiar faces looked back at me from the monotone 2-D picture. A real photograph, it is the only thing my great-grandmother left me when she died. She must have known I would have no use for land or fortune. Inside the clear casing it is faded and tattered, the features of the women difficult to discern. The more I stared, the more the lines shifted and blurred. An eye socket became a leaf shadow, a strand of hair a gust of wind. But then the light and dark lock into place and the group look out at me as they stand casually on dusty ground beside a great tree.

In the background children's shadows play against a rough concrete wall.

The tall figure of my great-grandmother looks both embarrassed and defiant, her long arms folded as if to ward off enemies. Demora Haase was pig-headed and hot-tempered even in the last years of her life, but I loved her with that passion that young children sometimes have for elderly relatives, and she encouraged all my bad habits, according to my grandmother. Next to her is the short woman who headed the district court, her expression calm and efficient but her hands twisted together in a nervous ball. Then Marlena Alvarez, a little self-conscious: a plump, motherly figure in a cheap cotton dress, her tired eyes look straight through the camera into the distance beyond. Slightly behind Alvarez, in a white coat, stands the Indian representative in the provincial government, Dr Nerise Kauni. She is the only one smiling, although whether at a joke or for the camera it was hard to say. She became minister of health the year my great-grandmother retired. Standing apart and side-on to the others, as if to express the difference between them, is the last of the area's great landowners, stony-faced and elegant. After all the other *rancheros* were driven away or fell in with the drug barons, she donated her land to the town and remained to oversee the revival of its economy in the hands of guilds and collectives.

The town was named Los Lagos Gemelos on maps, named for the twin lakes that lurked in the lower reaches of the valley and flooded every rainy season, but everyone knew it as Las Mujeres. In a curious coincidence, the constellation closest to Abelar and visible from

Earth with the naked eye is Gemini, the Twins.

Their faces fascinate and console me. I look at the flat black and grey image and wonder where they found their strength, how these ordinary-looking figures managed to accomplish so much.

I put the photoimage down with a sigh, thudded onto the bed and started to ease one boot off by treading on its heel with the other, plagued by a nagging feeling that I'd forgotten something.

Food, that's it. I promised Eleanor I'd try and eat regular meals. With all the excitement about the sleeper ship, I'd forgotten again. No wonder I felt a bit woozy and lightheaded.

We receive two days' worth of stored 'space rations' per week, which I always finished in the first few days, and after that we were supposed to utilise other sources. I sighed and dragged myself into the communal kitchen to rummage through the rations cache. I hate cooking, but it was that or trek over to a cafe on the other side of Gamma.

The light sensor belatedly picked up my movements and brightened the small room to reveal rows of gleaming metal drawers topped with a narrow, waist-high bench. Ensign Lee, who was one of my unit-mates, always complained about lack of space in which to work. She stacked her esoteric culinary accessories – choppers, mixers, zappers – on the floor and under the round table. We were forever tripping over these machines.

A container on the bench held some tuber-like vege-tables. I took one and hesitated over the choice of setting on the cooker. Should it be 'firm', 'soft', 'puree' or 'pulp'?

I selected 'soft' and added the 'spice' option, not bothering with settings because we only ever get one flavour from the blasted thing. The cooker purred reassuringly when activated, and I decided it was safe to leave it while I undressed.

God, I'm tired.

Going over to the Seouras ship always leaves me with irresistible, leaden fatigue. Eleanor Jago says it's something to do with neurotransmitters. During a consultation once she'd described it to me as backlash, a reaction to the unnatural form of communication with the Seouras.

I prised off the boots and my jacket joined the pile of clothes on the floor. The uniform belongs to the now-defunct Engineering Corps. Murdoch says I wear it from affectation and Eleanor says from sentiment, but the truth of the matter is that the glorified maroon overall with roomy pockets and utilitarian belt is comfortable. I've worn it for nearly twenty-five years now and would hate to have to change it for the stiff navy suit that ConFleet officers wear now.

The trousers slid off easily. I haven't regained the weight I lost during those first negotiations with the Seouras last year. The odour of their nutrient slime would take away anyone's appetite. Greenish, stinking, opaque gel, it fills their ship from wall to wall and sticks to every surface, even seeping through the joins of our environmental suits. The stench of it clings to my hair and on my skin, and I can't smell anything else any more.

The cooker still purred as I padded barefoot across the

kitchen to the bathroom. It had steamed up completely inside and I couldn't see what it was doing to the vegetable. Probably a good thing.

It wasn't worth trying to take a shower here – we hadn't had any decent water for weeks. I would stop off at the senior staff locker room on my way back to the Bubble, but for now I needed to wake myself up enough to eat dinner. Or breakfast, for those who preferred circadian rhythms. The airwash still works, so I stuck my face into its lukewarm gush without enthusiasm, avoiding looking in the mirror at the new grey hairs.

The grey bothers me. I can ignore other problems like the uniform becoming looser, shaky hands, and the dark circles around my eyes. It's the grey hair that I notice on the rare occasions I do look in the mirror. It leaches the contrast between skin and hair so that a pale, ageing stranger stares back at me. This is not how I like to see myself.

I have always looked like my grandmother Elvira, especially the expression – the same slightly self-conscious defiance, the stubborn set of the jaw, the quizzical lift of dark brows. The face that stares from the photoimage in her sitting room at home, the one that leans carelessly against a row of sun-faded leather spines, its metal frame clouded with a lifetime of tiny scratches. Elvira in a black dress at eighteen, the year she defied Demora and ran away to join the EarthSouth movement. She met Jack Halley there and returned to the town nearly twenty years later with him and the child that was my mother. Elvira – quick to anger and heavy on discipline, with none of Demora's measured silences. My mother's reaction to her was to fade out of reach, but mine was to resist, and we had some hellish fights before I ran away to join the engineering corps.

Elvira is the last person in the family I want to resemble, but she is better than this pale stranger in the glass.

The mirror was more fogged than usual. I rubbed at it with Lee's flowered handwipe without visible improvement. Maybe it was my eyes. I really need at least eight hours' sleep after talking with the Seouras.

When I let myself think about it I am shocked at the ease with which new routines have been established since the blockade began. In the face of death, pain, and oppression I find myself insisting on cobbling together some kind of schedule, as if I can hold everything together by doing so. Not that I really believe in the schedules any more, or in the value of order. I submit to the forms of procedure because their fragile shell of normalcy is better than no protection at all against the vacuum.

It was very like grief, I suppose, those first few months. At first a numbness, an inability to fully comprehend what was happening. Periods of furious activity aided by insomnia, interspersed with black depression. We accomplished a lot in the time – engines fixed and orbit stabilised, minimum necessary reflector arrays replaced and online, expansion of primary production facilities . . . But I remembered few of the day-to-day details. It remained a distorted image filtered through the window of guilt and fatigue.

A muted clang and a curse from the kitchen indicated that someone had stubbed their toe on Lee's cooking tools. I came back to the present with a start – I'd been almost dozing over the airwash – and poked my head cautiously around the door. It was foggy in the kitchen too.

'. . . not all of us are on early shift,' muttered Flight Officer Tana Burrows, late of EarthFleet and at present attached to station administration. She caught sight of me and pulled her gown tighter with an irritable twist. She is a petite woman, even smaller than me, but her smouldering scowl makes her appear taller.

'What were you trying to do?' she demanded.

I realised that the fog in the kitchen was centred on the cooker. Tendrils drifted from its joins and there was a faint odour.

'I was hungry. You didn't need to get up.' We'd agreed that there was no place for rank in the unit, but sometimes I thought Burrows took unfair advantage of this. She saw all her fellow pilots die in the Seouras attack and quite clearly holds me to blame. She hates the Four Worlds with equal passion.

'Not get up?' she said. 'Can't you smell it? It's a wonder the alarms didn't activate . . .'

'What's going on?' Shuab Goro, plump and imperturbable, appeared in the far doorway. She was an assistant in engineering, and I must have woken her up because she'd been at the meeting last night, too. She rubbed her eyes and sniffed. 'Somebody forgot to set the burner again.'

'Halley.' Burrows put as much venom as she could into my name and stomped away. 'Who do you think?'

'Give her a break, Tana,' Shuab said to her retreating back.

'Don't worry.' I inspected the cooker with a sinking stomach. A thin dribble of yellowish sludge had escaped under the door. Maybe this was the 'pulp' option.

'She's pissed off because the K'Cher keep returning their surveys about the planning changes.' Shuab passed a cleanwipe along the bench below the cooker and tried to key open the door. 'Tana gets the fun job of calling them and asking why.'

'Why do they return the surveys?'

'They're not interested, I guess.' She finally opened the door and a cloud of steam rose and dissipated through the kitchen. From the look on her face, it can't have smelt good. 'Do you want this?'

I shook my head. I spend too much time in the Seouras ship to enjoy eating something sloppy scraped off cooker walls. I felt guilty for recycling the food directly rather than through my digestive system, but we were both too tired to care.

'I'll get something on the way over later.'

'Sure. G'night.' She yawned all the way back to her room and I did the same.

Baudin's voice woke me from a strange dream in which the K'Cher Keveth pursued me through the corridors of the station, clutching a filepad and flicking back its long, blond hair with its front feeler.

'Halley here.' I sat up stiffly, heart pounding, and tried to focus. I'd fallen asleep seated on the bed. My hand reached out automatically to touch open the screen that I keep set to show the Seouras ship positions. They were unchanged and I relaxed a little.

'We've got them,' said Baudin.

'Good work. What's their ETA?'

'About twenty minutes. The medics want to get the pods off the *Queen* and onstation as quickly as they can.'

'The prognosis?'

He paused. 'Pretty good, they think.'

'That's great. I'll come up.' I was pulling on my trousers as I spoke.

If the survivors managed to get through the transition from cryostasis to normal time, we'd have a lot of questions for them. The only human settlement this far out is Jocasta itself. They couldn't have travelled from further inside the Confederacy to here at sublight speeds – it would have taken centuries. The ship had no jump drive to get it here, but the evidence of the jump mine proved hyperspace had been disturbed in some way. If we could work out how they got in, maybe we could get out.

A lot of questions.

It hadn't taken as long as we'd feared – within a couple of hours the survivors had been brought back to the station, thanks to Keveth's help. Hopefully its intercession will improve K'Cher relations with the other species here, or at least stop them from deteriorating further.

Baudin's report noted there were three survivors, two men and a woman, and at least ten bodies in the wreckage. The former were in the hospital, the latter could be brought out when we had the wreck secure. Eleanor would tell me when I could talk to the survivors. Meanwhile we needed to access the wreck's opsys and any data that was readable. Navigational data particularly. We had to know how it got here.

I stared at the neat 3D representation of the shattered vessel, now tethered to one of the maintenance platforms around the station. Unfortunately the interior was too dangerous yet to allow a hands-on investigation and we were still dependent upon virtual information. It would be several hours, perhaps a day, before the dangerous debris was cleared away, the bodies removed, and the radiation dampened to an acceptable level.

The explosion had been quite close to the asteroid belt – possibly the mine's sensors had allowed it to drift right into the inner system. The old ship was unlucky – eventually we'd have picked up the mine on our sensors and disarmed it when it got close enough, for one thing Jocasta did possess was an elderly minesweeper.

'We're going to take what's loose and recognisable

from the main cabin, so we need somewhere to put it.'

I tapped up a section of the central cargo facility. We scrolled through bay after bay, all full.

'You'd think that with no trade for six months the place'd be empty.' Lee shook her head. Over at the centre console Baudin frowned at her familiarity.

The station's population had exceeded our designed maximum of twenty thousand sentient humanoid-equivalent lifeforms a year after I took over this job. By the time the Seouras ships arrived we were half that again, not counting the refugees, stowaways, and unannounced passengers who'd slipped through gaps in the Customs net. Murdoch thinks we have about five thousand illegals. I estimate twice that number. It places a terrible strain on all the environmental systems, hence Walsh's concern about unused space.

The Seouras attack destroyed some of the solar reflectors and processing platforms, which made certain areas of Jocasta temporarily uninhabitable. We also had to increase our food production to compensate for the loss of trade. Large quantities of unwanted building materials had been popped out into orbit to make more room, while potentially useful materials and personal belongings had been packed away in the micro-g holding areas in the centre. We never had enough space in the storage bays.

'Here!' said Baudin, leaning over and tapping the screen so enthusiastically that it changed programs.

Lee retrieved the image with a long-suffering sigh.

'That'll do,' I agreed. 'It's near an airlock where the

Queen can dock, and far enough from the nearest spoke that nobody's going to float in by accident.'

'What do you want to salvage first?' Lee's fingers paused on the touchpad.

'The main log, if we can get it,' I said. 'We need to check their route, see if they had some peculiarity that got them past the Seouras sensors. And any personal stuff that's more or less in one piece.'

'And the bodies,' she prompted softly.

I cursed my thoughtlessness. 'Those too. You'd better contact Dr Jago about stasis. I'll be down at the hospital. Give me a call when we bring the logs in.'

The ringlifts that form the station's vertical transport system are relatively well-repaired, as nobody likes clambering down the narrow access chutes between the three rings. The karrikars that travel along within each ring, however, are less of a priority, and we all do a lot more walking within the rings than we used to. The uplift system in the spokes are a problem – no contact with the outside galaxy means the majority of residents have little need to travel to and from docks in the centre. Nor does anyone now work on the processing platforms, in case the Seouras decide to use the facilities for target practice again. We now use only two or three working cars out of twenty in each uplift. The others came in handy for spare parts. People worry about evacuation, but as Murdoch says, unless all thirty thousand of us take turns to jump out the empty docking hatches, it's hard to see how the uplifts would help. Besides, we need storage in the spokes and centre because there are five or ten thousand more bodies to house in the rings than the station's planners first envisaged, and the capacity of the living quarters is stretched beyond its limits.

When the ringlift doors opened outside the hospital, I thought for a moment it was the wrong level. The sudden commotion of raised voices and press of bodies was like the Hill. The level indicator in the lift was right though, and as I stepped out the clear lighting and wide throughway confirmed it was Gamma, the middle ring.

The crowd, perhaps fifty or more people, was gathered around the main hospital entry. It was a curious mixture of human and alien, most of them refugees or unemployed dockers in shabby clothes, although with a sprinkling of EarthFleet and ConFleet uniforms. I pushed my way past a group of wildly gesticulating Garokians and was pushed aside in turn by two children chasing a third, yelling a tattoo of simulated weapons fire. This was not the usual Gamma crowd. People must have come from all over the station.

There was even musical accompaniment, in the person of a thin, dishevelled man playing a string instrument in the corner. It gave the whole scene a holiday atmosphere. The man strummed the slim oval box with grimy fingers and tapped his foot in time, seemingly oblivious to the bustle or to whether any tokens had been tossed into the upturned helmet at his feet.

The words 'ship', 'jump mine', and 'survivors' were repeated in Earth Standard and half a dozen other tongues. It looked like the rumour mill had been busy while I napped.

'Commander!'

I turned with a sinking feeling towards the hearty voice. Dan Florida, self-appointed information crusader and minority advocate, was nearly upon me. His dark head reached above most of the crowd and his broad shoulders cut an easy path through them.

'Commander Halley.' His voice penetrated the babble and three flamboyant Dir merchants turned to observe us. Two of the EarthFleet heads turned too.

'Good morning, Mr Florida. Do you mind? I have business at the hospital.' I cursed my lack of foresight – I should have taken the other ringlift then the karrikar that goes past the hospital's back entrance.

'So we hear,' he said, and stood casually in my path. 'When's the administration going to tell us what's going on?'

'When there's something to tell.'

He is about fifteen years younger and fifty kilos heavier than me, and he should have known better than to try force. I gave him my best 'who d'you think you are?' stare and hoped Murdoch had sent someone along from Security.

'I know nothing at all right now, and unless you get out of my way we won't learn anything more.'

He didn't shift. The merchants and assorted other onlookers moved closer. A couple of comments along the lines of 'What's going on?' and 'Where's the ship?' flew back and forth.

'I have it on good authority that a Confederacy ship tried to set off a jump mine on top of the Seouras,' said Florida. 'Have you got survivors in there?'

'No comment.' I elbowed past him, feeling the hard muscle of his chest. At least he had the grace to yield ground. Then a harder grip on my wrist jerked me to a halt.

'Do you intend keeping this secret too?' The Dir trader thrust his face into mine. Not that he meant to be threatening – that's how they talk. But in humans it creates a nasty adrenalin surge and flight-or-fight reaction. I pulled back without thinking, Florida stepped forward to put a huge restraining hand on the Dir, the other traders objected, and two ConFleet ensigns with engineering badges appeared beside me to face off the Dir. Florida was asking me something, the traders and ensigns were arguing, everyone was talking at once. Several EarthFleet personnel joined in, slanging off ConFleet. This was ridiculous. I wrenched away from the trader and slid back between the ensigns, treading on toes. The crowd closed up again in a noisy knot.

'What about the rumour that they're sleepers?' Florida called after me, his head above the edge of the crowd. A couple of excited children picked up the word and danced around his feet, chanting 'sleepers, sleepers'.

'What?'

'You know, cryostasis. Deep-freeze sleep. Sleepers.'

I mouthed 'no comment' and entered the hospital.

Eleanor Jago was waiting for me in one of the labs. She was going over the cryostasis pods we had taken from the mysterious wreck. The pods were inside one of the quarantine operation theatres. Eleanor and two medtechs were directing the robot sensors to investigate its mechanism. It looked like a coffin with trailing wires and a coating of glistening fluid, strangely at home in the blue light of the theatre. Of course, for most of the passengers in the old ship the pods *had* been coffins.

I was still a little shaky after the incident outside. The crowd had not been hostile exactly but in that excitable mood that can swing either way. I hadn't realised there was so much tension among the 'ordinary' residents. They rightly wanted to know what was going on. But it was more than that. I couldn't help feeling that Jocasta's isolation had touched off a deeper problem, a problem that stemmed from the very fact of our existence out here. Nobody likes being at the bottom of a hierarchy, but that is where Earth and the other Nine Worlds had been for the entire sixty years of the Confederacy's existence. Unless the Invidi started sharing their technology and the K'Cher their wealth, something was going to give. It looked like being my station.

I leaned against the glass wall and stared at the coffin while Eleanor, who had seen me come in, finished whatever she was doing on the interface. We haven't talked as friends since her partner died. Leo was one of fifteen people in a repair team who got stuck out on an unstable platform, about two months into the Seouras occupation. An explosion trapped them inside the platform where they were unable to access the emergency controls, and they drifted out of our 'safe' zone into the path of the nearest grey ship. From the station we took over the controls, as well as sending a shuttle to get them. I did have brief access to the platform's thrusters, but not long enough. I really had them. When the Seouras weapon touched the platform with tendrils of green energy and it broke up, my first emotion was disbelief. I thought, this can't be true. We were about to bring them in, dammit. I wanted to go back again, do it quicker, do it better. Do something.

After Leo's death Eleanor retreated completely from me – she accepted condolences politely, was composed at the memorial service, and returned immediately to work. Which was good, to tell the truth, because at the time we couldn't spare any of our medical officers even for a couple of days. But when she did finally meet my eyes, it was with a distant, measuring stare that made it impossible for me to reach past my own guilt.

We should have talked it over, but I was scared of what Eleanor might say, and she seemed always to be angry at me about something. She looked all right, but then it was difficult to tell what she felt at the best of times. And these are certainly not the best of times.

'How are they?' I nodded at the pods.

'I've been able to keep them off life support equipment,' said Eleanor. She is tall and big-boned, her movements considered but not slow, and she never raises her voice. Her accent, earthy and unpretentious, softens the initial impression of coldness.

'The cryostatic medium protected them from the worst of the rays. It's interesting stuff. We're running an analysis now. Their pod systems functioned perfectly and woke them with minimal physical trauma.'

'Why didn't the other ten function as well?' I peered

into the coffin. There was padding under the sticky coating of cryogenic fluid.

'Mostly physical damage to the pods from the explosion.' She nodded in the direction of the corridor. 'Let's go. I've told the three survivors what year it is and that they're among friends.'

'They're able to talk?'

'I'd prefer they didn't.' She nodded to one of the medtechs as she left. 'But one of them is a bit upset. Considering the circumstances, I thought it better to answer his questions before he upsets the other two.'

She led the way out into a wide, sunny hallway. Reflector repairs over the hospital had been a priority after the Seouras attacks, and in spite of being in the middle ring, it was one of the lightest areas on the station. Every time I drag myself down here to see Jago I feel my skin bask in the warm, safe radiation.

She placed her palm on a security pad beside the next door, which opened to let us pass. Voice and visual interaction is down in this area too.

'When can they leave the hospital?' We walked past more doors, some open, some shut. Several patients watched us curiously and one waved to Eleanor.

Eleanor nodded to the security guard who had straightened to attention beside the next door, and paused with one hand over the control pad. Her big frame was angled away from me. 'A couple of days probably. But I think they should be given quarters here, maybe over in Rehab. We'll keep their surroundings as consistent as possible while they cope with everything else.'

The survivors – the 'Sleepers', as Florida had called

them – were in a room together. The three beds were in a row against a wall, a wall that was in fact an opaque light-curtain concealing medical equipment. The ceiling was high. The walls stop and the space soars up to meet banks of reflectors that look like a louvred sky. Filters keep the light gentle and golden. If only we could do this for the rest of the station.

'I want to talk to the captain!' Peremptory tones could not conceal the voice's weakness.

Eleanor remained at the door, her attention on readouts from one of several monitors, and I walked over to the bed from which the man had spoken. Next to him a young woman with tangled dark hair followed my movements with her eyes. The face in the coffin. The numerical recognition code above the bed had been changed to a name – Rachel Dourif. The third patient, a young man, was asleep.

The older man's head turned restlessly on the pillow as he demanded to see Authority. His voice was hoarse and the accent unfamiliar. The skin on his face and hands was flaking and sore-looking around the chin and mouth. One of the faces in the pods had had a long white beard.

He saw me and focused immediately. 'I want to talk to the captain.' His voice was clear and words were comprehensible despite the accent. One of the base languages for Earth Standard.

'Go on, then. Talk.'

His voice cracked in disbelief. 'You're the captain?'

I caught a glimpse of myself in the wall mirror beside their beds. Small woman in rumpled uniform overalls with no rank badge, untidy hair, shoulders bent, and face tight with fatigue. No wonder he had doubts.

I pulled my shoulders straighter. 'What's your name?'

'Griffis. Professor Hannibal Griffis,' he said reluctantly.

'Welcome to Jocasta, Professor. This is not a ship, it's a space station. My name is Halley. I'm the head of station. Your ship was involved in an accident. We brought the survivors here and treated you.'

'What year is this?'

'It's 2121, Earth time.' Perhaps he hadn't believed Jago.

'Where is this station?' Griffis's sharp, nasal accent was confusing. I had to concentrate to distinguish the words.

The woman kept her gaze on us without comment.

'We orbit a K-class star several thousand light years from Earth along the galactic arm.'

His pale blue eyes widened further. 'How did we get here?'

'We were hoping you could tell us that. Where did you come from?'

His eyes searched my face, puzzled. 'Earth, of course.'

'No, I mean, where did you board your ship?'

He sniffed. 'I'm telling you. We left Earth for Alpha Centauri in May, 2026.'

Three years after the Invidi arrived. Nearly a century ago. I was confused. Did we simply not understand what each other was saying? 'That's impossible. Was your ship able to travel through hyperspace?'

'No.' It was the young woman next to us. Wine-dark eyes and skin like honey. 'I was the assistant engineer. *Calypso*'s engines were a kind of hydrogen fusion type I'd never seen before. It took all our attention just to follow running procedure.' Her voice would be deep and pleasant when it grew stronger. 'As far as I know, there was nothing that could have been used to enter hyperspace. I'm assuming you'd need vast amounts of energy.'

'Yes.' Probably. We don't know how the jump drive works, because we don't have access to one. The Four Worlds maintain their secret very well.

'Your ship – *Calypso*, was it? – couldn't possibly have travelled between here and Earth at sublight speeds in ninety-five years.'

Griffis and Dourif looked at each other.

'Well, excuse me, but I think we know where we started from,' said the young woman.

Either I'm mad or they are. I glanced at Eleanor but she half shrugged and turned her eye to a monitor. I tried a different tack. 'You said you came from Earth nearly a hundred years ago. How did you develop the cryostasis technology?'

'They helped us.'

'Who?'

'The aliens.'

'The Invidi?'

'That's what they called themselves. Do you know them?'

'I . . . we have worked together.'

'So we finally got along okay?' Dourif said.

I glanced over at Eleanor again. 'I'm not sure what you mean by "got along". Earth is part of the United Confederacy of Allied Worlds, which was founded by the Invidi and three other alien species in 2061.'

'Confederacy . . .' He repeated the word slowly.

Jago caught my eye and made a cutoff motion with one hand. 'They can talk again later.'

There was so much we needed to know. 'But you said the Invidi helped you. I thought they didn't give humans anything but medical technology in those first decades?'

'Cryostasis is medical technology,' said Griffis. He frowned. 'Did you say your name was Halley?'

'Yes.'

'I knew a man called Halley. In the Movement. He . . .'

'You should rest now.' Jago stepped between us. I chafed at the interruption but didn't dare object.

'Wait.' Dourif tried to prop herself on one elbow. 'What happened to the others?'

I glanced at Eleanor. Surely she'd told them. She looked back at me but her face was closed.

'I'm sorry.' My voice wavered on the words. 'None of them made it.'

Griffis turned to Dourif, face bleak. 'Rachel . . .'

'Oh god.' She turned away from us all, hunching into the bed. Griffis put out a hand helplessly then let it fall between them.

Eleanor and I walked back along the bright hallway to one of the labs.

'Sit down.' Eleanor pointed the scanner at a padded bench and turned to the monitor.

'Why?' I wanted to get back to investigation of the sensor data on the wreck. There was no way that ship could have left Earth nearly one hundred years ago and ended up here, now. Either Griffis and Dourif were lying or they had been deceived, or something had happened while they were in cold sleep that had brought them here.

'Because you're supposed to come straight here after you go to the Seouras ship. That means after your shuttle docks.' She tapped open the screen and then ran the scanner over my back. It tickled and I sat on the bench to get further away from it. 'Why didn't you?'

'We had to bring this ship in.' I didn't know what to make of Griffis. 'Eleanor, it's incredible. How could a century-old ship without jump drive get this far? Why should it end up here?'

It must have been in a jump or the mine would not have activated. Could their ship have somehow been caught in another ship's jump field? No matter that this was theoretically impossible – I'd consider anything. But if so, why didn't we pick up that ship on our sensors?

'Hmph.' She ran the next scanner around my head. It tickled too. 'When did you last sleep?'

I scratched my hair where the scanner touched a hard-ened streak of slime. 'I got in a couple of hours this morning. Eleanor, is there any medical evidence to suggest they mightn't be from the past after all?'

She put the scanner back and made a note with the stylus.

'No. Their EMGs show classic cryogenic distortions and there are substances in their blood that humans haven't had for decades. Charming carcinogenic compounds, hydrocarbons, things like that.'

She sighed and sat next to me. The bench sagged under our combined weight and I tensed against slipping against her. Yet on a different level I wanted that comforting contact.

'Halley, forget them for a minute,' she said. 'Let's talk about you. You're underweight, anaemic, and exhausted. I don't have a clue what this implant,' she touched my neck lightly, 'is doing to you. You've got to eat and sleep more.'

The problem is, I can't keep food down. It's not like the slight queasiness everyone feels in lower gravity – some days I throw up continually. It's probably stress related, although I've been under stress before and never experienced anything like this. Even thinking about it makes my stomach churn.

'What do you want me to do?' Even as the words snapped out I regretted them. 'Tell the Seouras I'm too tired to make it over there today, but that's okay, you can take potshots at the station until I feel better?'

Eleanor stood abruptly. 'I didn't say that. But you can't make objective decisions in this state. You might be able to fool everyone else, but not me.'

I didn't understand why she was trying to undermine my remaining control.

'Why are you saying this?'

'Don't be so goddamn paranoid.'

That was all right for her to say, she hadn't seen the crowd outside. I swallowed my retort.

'All right. I'll be more careful. And in the meantime can you take a good look at those cryosystems for me? I want to know why they kept functioning for nearly a century when it takes less than fifty years to reach Alpha Centauri. Did they wake up and then go back to sleep?'

We looked at each other and I could see she was beginning to see how very strange it was.

Four technicians were gathered around the maintenance access panel in the last of the hospital corridors. I had to pass them on the way to the karrikar and couldn't help stopping to see what was the matter.

'Recycling,' said the one in charge, a round-faced human whose rainbow-stained overalls indicated long maintenance experience. 'Got a big problem with waste disposal.' He ran his eyes up and down my uniform then evidently decided I might understand more than the bare facts. 'Looks like there's been a break in the flow in the under-level, but we can't do anything about the amounts we're sending down. Something's gone wrong with the whole program, don't know what.'

I peered at the figures on the small screen. It looked more like a faulty connection than anything else.

'Have you got someone down there?'

'Yup.' We all looked at the deck beneath which laboured the machines that enabled life to continue on the station. If we couldn't recycle waste products, we'd run out of raw materials within a month.

'I'll take a look on my way out.' I might as well find out how serious a problem it was now rather than later. It might mean that we would have to reinitialise this particular part of the system or even isolate it if the problem turned out to be a virus, which was doubtful. The station's systems were built for resistance rather than speed of operation. It's not so bad now because there is no input from outside, but before the Seouras came vast amounts of 'dirty' data were entering and circulating, not to mention illegal hardware modifications and additions. The systems had to be able to cope with this sort of corruptive influence.

Maintenance hatches open on to each ring from the recycling level below the deck, and allow access to the maintenance tunnels that run behind the main walls. This one opened onto a narrow, dark space dropping straight down for two or three metres before changing direction in a short diagonal at an intersection and dropping a further one or two metres. Two humans might fit at a pinch. A ladder was set in one side and the other three were covered with check points for the security network and the rough side of conduits.

I clambered down, treading on each rung carefully to keep away from live circuits and 'hot' plasma relays. My body blocked out most of the light from above, but small emitters in the tunnel itself gave off a weak glow. The bend was more difficult to negotiate, but after that the ladder ended quickly in a narrow space that opened via another hatch into the maintenance level beneath the ring. By the time I got through the hatch I was breathing heavily. I'm out of condition, need to start running again.

Recycling is a long, low room that stretches away into gloom and the upward swing of station distance. The lights are set as single units, unlike the ubiquitous glare of the upper levels. Shadows gather under conduits or beside stacks of containers and pool in the mess of catwalks, cables, and control boxes in the ceiling. It is a separate world of waste disposal pipes and processors, power cables and conduits, cleaning 'bots and work-rooms, vats of solvent and great, roaring oxidisation chambers. The huge vats run above the floor along opposite walls and beside them containers block all but the main path along the middle of the room. The noise is constant: vats rumble, pipes gurgle, pumps hiss and make sudden explosive swooshes. Droids whirr and AGVs clatter as they go about their business.

It was not difficult to see the problem. A trickle of dark sludge ran down the side of one of the first-stage vats. There was a dingy pool around the base, too, and stains splashed as far as the walkway. Several inactive cleaning droids were positioned around it, and two of the main-tenance crew were observing the mess in a depressed way. One of them wore a standard atmospheric protec-tion mask, the other had a piece of material tied over her nose and mouth. I sniffed but could only detect a faint pungency behind the stink of Seouras slime in my nose.

'What happened?'

The masked man turned with a start at my shouted question. 'What ... Oh, Commander Halley.' He gestured at the vat. 'We had a pressure problem here. It didn't come up in either the regular report or the diag-nostic this morning. By the time we realised what was wrong the thing had actually blown.'

The woman pushed down her homemade mask to speak. 'They think the problem might be in the centre, in the main connections.' Her skin had a sickly tinge in the erratic light.

Meanwhile somebody had to clean up.

A heavy hand descended on my shoulder and it was

my turn to jump. Murdoch stood there, nose wrinkling and face screwed up. The shadows gave his olive green Security uniform a brownish tinge and he seemed to loom over me more than usual.

He looked over my head at the tank and gave one of his rare, subversive grins.

'Yup, it's really hit the fan, all right.'

I let out a deep breath in the hope of calming my jumping pulse. 'Did you want to see me?'

He nodded and jerked his thumb upwards. 'It's about that lot in the entry.'

I didn't know why he wanted to see me. 'I can't do much about it. A ship arrived, people are excited.'

'You can say that ag— . . . Phew.' He pinched his wide nose as if it would keep out the odour. 'Let's get out of here. You might not be able to smell any of this but I can.'

The maintenance technician looked up sourly from where she was programming the cleaning droid but Murdoch's burly shoulders had already turned away.

'Make sure I get a full report,' I said to her and followed him.

His words took me back three years to his first days on the station and my own disbelief that anyone who worked within the ConFleet hierarchy could be so rude. He was assigned here nearly a year after my appointment, and arrived at a time when the station itself and the political situation were particularly chaotic. He'd made the mistake in his previous post of being too diligent in pursuing officials accused of taking bribes, not realising until too late that one of them was his commanding officer. I didn't care what his record was – I was just glad to have a chief of security to take some weight off my shoulders.

Which he does well. He divides his time between the two main Security offices, one in Gamma and one in the Hill. Before him, there was no Security cell in the lower ring and no permanent reminder of their presence – it was a dangerous place then, and if Security showed at all, the officers patrolled in fours and fives. When Murdoch arrived he made efforts to bring the area under control, but it was the Abelar Treaty that really made the Hill cleanup possible, mainly because it freed personnel from fighting an external force – the Danadan and other pirates – to mount an intensive campaign against the crime networks on the station. I like to remind him of this when he grumbles about what a hare-brained scheme the treaty was.

Our relationship changed after the Seouras blockade. Until recently we disagreed about most issues in a relatively civilised manner. He thought the Abelar Treaty was a terrible idea, had always been opposed to taking in refugees, and was overly concerned about personal security issues. Maybe the tension is getting to him, but lately he seems to often become argumentative for no reason at all before, the next moment, being overtaken by a mood of quixotic humour.

We climbed back up to the Gamma throughway, this time via one of the larger tunnels, passing a technician on his way down steadying a fully laden maglev platform. I twisted awkwardly to avoid him and Murdoch put out a hand to steady me without comment.

'I've got enough on my plate as it is with the festival preparations,' he said as we emerged from a side alley onto the main throughway. 'We're going to need some help. What about using some of the EarthFleet reserves?'

At this time of the station year a Garokian festival coincides with the end of Ramadan, an important observance for a good proportion of the human residents, and every year the station plunges into celebration with uncharacteristic gusto. For the Garokians it is the Renewal of Souls – an annual preparation for death, which they see as the ultimate renewal into a wider consciousness. The anniversary of Earth's entry into the Confederacy falls on the next day, which means our official ceremonies are always brief and sparsely attended as we all cope with hangovers. It is one of the busiest times of the year for Security.

'Don't see why not.'

He looked surprised at not being offered any argument. 'Can't you issue an official statement about this ship and tell everyone to go home?'

'I don't know enough yet to say anything.' I stopped in front of the nearest karrikar. 'I'll try and think of a way to put it that's not too . . . provocative.'

Murdoch fidgeted. 'So what'll you say?'

Then it hit me. He wanted to know too. 'You saw the status report earlier?'

He nodded. 'Yeah, a ship that couldn't have got here.'

'The survivors say they don't know what happened.'

'They wouldn't, not if they were in deep freeze.'

'It's incredible to have people from a century ago here, now.'

'You mean, to have a ship here.' Sometimes Murdoch's flat, dark stare is too perceptive. 'You're thinking, if one got in, one could get out.'

He's right, of course. The Seouras situation is always my main priority. 'That too,' I said quietly, and keyed my code for the karrikar.

He hooked his thumbs into his wide utility belt and drummed his fingers on it, a particularly annoying habit. 'Don't get your hopes up. They probably stumbled onto an old jump site or some natural anomaly, that's all. We can't use their ship for anything, that's for sure.'

'I know,' I snapped, and called up a review of the grey ships' positions on the wall screen while we waited.

'I just meant, don't get obsessive about it, that's all.' Murdoch let his own irritation show.

I glared. 'I'm not obsessive about anything.'

He looked pointedly at the screen where the Seouras ship data was displayed. 'So why do you keep checking up on them?'

'That's different. For goodness' sake, Bill, all I meant was it's exciting to have a ship from the past here.'

'Yeah, right. Where are you off to now?'

'I want to talk to Quartermaine.' As the lift doors opened I quickly confirmed the Seouras ships were where they should be and closed the screen. 'The . . . Sleepers' – what the hell, it was a handy name – 'said an Invidi helped them. Brin can tell me more about that.'

Murdoch grimaced. 'Sleepers, huh? Guess it's a label. While you're there, get Quartermaine to ask the Invidi if he's remembered how to get us out of this mess.'

'I will not,' I began, but the doors had already wheezed

shut. If anyone else had said that I would have been forced to discipline them for inciting unrest. Only the other day, though, I'd heard Murdoch tell an ensign that she should remember who paid her wages before she complained about the Four Worlds and the Confederacy. I don't know where he stands on the whole complex issue of the Four Worlds and the Nine, technology such as the jump drive, and autonomy. He will keep order on the station impartially, that I do know.

Brin Quartermaine is our liaison officer with the Invidi representative of the Confederacy Council. The Invidi, An Barik, was supposed to 'observe' our progress, or lack of it, in administering the station. Quartermaine forms a buffer between him and us and, by extension, between the Four Worlds and the Nine. It is surely the most uncomfortable job on the station.

The first time I spoke to Quartermaine with anything other than official politeness was shortly after the Seouras took the system. I had half expected to find that An Barik had fled in his little ship, undetected in the chaos. Most of Delta was in total darkness but when I reached the non-oxygen breathers' section called the Smoke, his quarters were still dimly lit and Quartermaine was there too, waiting.

'We thought you'd come soon.' Quartermaine's light voice was steady in the mask's ear-pieces, eyes calm through the visor.

I was strung tight with tension. 'They destroyed all the fighters. Then every ship that tried to leave. I've closed all docking ports. Nobody is to try to leave until we work out why they're here.'

Quartermaine's mask nodded. 'Including him?' An Barik didn't move.

'We were wondering . . . Invidi ships have special capabilities. Is it possible he could get through and warn the Confederacy?'

Quartermaine turned his back on me and faced the Invidi. He spoke, but must have filtered the channel in my mask because I couldn't hear him. The Invidi's reply was inaudible too.

I paced in the thick, red light until Quartermaine turned around.

'I'm sorry. He can't do that.'

'Can't, or won't?'

Quartermaine's very calmness was a rebuke. 'Both, actually. We don't know if his ship can withstand the Seouras weapons, and he won't try. He is not allowed to interfere, you understand.'

'No, I don't understand!' I pushed past Quartermaine, right up to An Barik. He was so tall that the edge of my mask made it impossible to see the top of his form. 'Surely you have technology that might help us, if not beat them, then at least contact the Confederacy? Help us prevent more deaths.'

Quartermaine stood close behind me. 'And you're willing to risk his death? That's very noble of you, Commander.'

'I . . . no, I didn't mean that.'

'Nobody else can pilot an Invidi vessel. Do you have any proof it would be resistant to these alien weapons?'

74

'No, of course we don't. We're not allowed to touch his ship, let alone analyse its capabilities.' I could feel the hope slipping away, as all other hopes had. 'Dammit, he'll be stuck here with the rest of us, for however long we can hold out. Doesn't that worry him?'

Quartermaine hesitated. 'Apparently not.'

I clamped my mouth shut over the flow of anger. If we really are to be stuck here, we'll have to work together from now on.

'Hope he enjoys it.' I turned and left, conscious that I'd never behaved this way in an Invidi's presence before.

Quartermaine caught up with me as I left the Smoke. One blue emergency light shone beyond the end of the corridor, and a faint murmur of frightened voices waxed and waned. The mechanical sounds of the station were different too – the background noises that we don't notice until they're gone. Some systems were silent, some rattled or hummed louder than they should. My engineer's ear, attuned to the smooth harmony of integrated functions, found this more unsettling than the visual evidence of failure – darkness, flickering conduits, ceramic shards scrunching underfoot, people crying in fear and confusion.

'He can't help you. The sooner you learn to live with it, the better.' Quartermaine's face was barely discernible in the glow from the airlock window.

'If he doesn't help us we may not live much longer,' I snarled, and kept walking.

'What did you expect?' Persistent man.

The truth was, I didn't know what to expect from An Barik. There was just the feeling that we had some right

75

to their help, the hope that they would care enough . . .
It was not until much later that I felt any shame at
making my mistakes their responsibility.

'Is he upset?' I hoped he was.

'I don't think so.'

Then the Seouras summoned me and it was weeks
before I thought of the Invidi again.

Quartermaine has never demanded much from our
friendship – I am the one who needs the support of our
occasional conversations, although it took me a while to
acknowledge it. After Eleanor retreated into silence he
was the only person willing to talk to me outside work
time. Not that we ever touched upon personal matters,
for he kept his life carefully locked away and I had none
to discuss. His reminiscences and advice about aliens
were enough, though, to maintain my contact with a
world outside the spiral of guilt and depression.

A quiet, self-effacing man, he is very different from the
cynical, capable Murdoch or the overconfident Florida.
His shyness is genuine, and not helped by his position
between the Confederacy representative and a large
group of people who believe the Confederacy has
betrayed them. I don't think he has suffered any personal
attacks other than verbal abuse or electronic graffiti, two
unpleasant aspects of my own life also, but he has
become almost as much a recluse as the Invidi, moving
between his office in Linguistics and his quarters, with
an occasional visit to An Barik.

He always acknowledged the Invidi's extraordinary
faculties but refused to be awed by them. I thought now

of the analogy he'd given to try to describe Invidi powers.

'In our understanding of the universe,' he'd said, 'humans stand on the page of a book and can only turn forward one page at a time, never knowing what is ahead or how to go back except in memory. But the Invidi have the index – all the page numbers to turn to at will, all the cross-references, the network of meaning that most of the time we forget or can only guess at.'

'You're talking about gods.'

'Heavens no, love. When did you ever use a perfect index? There's always something missing. Or half of the entries are irrelevant.'

I met him in the senior officers' messhall in the Bubble complex. He needed an outing, and Alpha ring was safe enough. I was also starving – I still hadn't eaten anything since yesterday. I sat down to wait for Brin at one of the low tables arranged in rough circles in front of serving and recycle hatches. No restful wall holos here, thank goodness. The only sound was a murmur of conversation from three of Veatch's staff sitting at a centre table.

I turned my face to the feeble warmth from the window. Some wit once dubbed the product of our reflector system 'second-hand sunlight', but it was better than the artificial light in the lower rings.

'You'll get freckles.'

I opened my eyes with a start as Quartermaine placed a tray containing two cups and a full plate on the table and sat down himself. He wore drab civilian clothes and might have been a caricature of a genteel academic.

'How's the Bubble?' he said, taking the plate and cups off the tray.

'Fine. How's An Barik?'

'Still here.' The old joke was starting to sound a little sour. Even Quartermaine didn't know why the alien was still here, given the likelihood that Invidi technology would allow him to leave the station whenever he felt like it, Seouras or no Seouras.

The plate held two sticky-looking Garokian pastries from the Hill bakery. 'What's this?' I asked hopefully.

'You haven't eaten.' It wasn't a question. 'Those are fresh.'

'How do you know?'

'That they're fresh?'

'That I haven't eaten.' I started one of the pastries.

'You look terrible. Washed out.'

'Thanks a lot,' I said with my mouth full. 'You look a bit tired yourself.'

'It's been noisy the past few nights. I haven't been able to get a decent sleep.'

'Festival?'

'Mmm.'

The pastries tasted much better than they looked. The bakery was deservedly popular. Garokians were refugees – among those both Sector Central and many voices on the station had cautioned me against admitting.

'Now tell me about this mystery ship.' He leaned forward. 'Is it true it came from Alpha Centauri?'

I groaned through a mouthful of tart, chewy flakes. 'We're going to have to do something about Florida.'

'What?'

'We found the wreck of a ship with its crew in cryostasis. Looks like it hit a jump mine. The strange thing,
though ...' I leaned forward too, glanced around and
dropped my voice to a whisper, knowing he enjoyed
melodrama '... is that they're human.'

His reaction was gratifying. He pushed his cup aside
and sat on the edge of his seat. 'From where?'

I made a little heap of purple crumbs with one finger.
'You're not going to believe this.'

'Try me or I'll make you drink another cup of this
disgusting coffee.'

'They're from Earth.'

He shook his head, puzzled. 'But you said ...'

I told him about Griffis, Dourif, and the other man
whose name I couldn't recall. About the wreck that
seemed to have hit a jump mine, but without jump capability so it couldn't have set off the mine – yet without
using hyperspace it could never have reached here so
quickly.

'Brin, Griffis said that the Invidi helped them to modify
the cryostasis technology.'

He seemed shocked. 'That's not possible. Invidi don't
interfere directly. And there's no record of any such
expedition.'

'How do you know?' His certainty had sparked my
curiosity.

'It's my business to know about Invidi–human relations. I'm liaison officer, remember?'

'Why should Griffis lie?'

'I don't know. It makes more sense, though, than

supposing the Invidi did something so totally uncharacteristic as helping a specific group within an alien society. Then concealing that fact for a hundred years.'

'But they gave us medical technology, didn't they?' I wished I was better versed in First Contact history. I'd have to read through the database tonight. 'What's so different about helping with cryostasis?'

Brin shook his head. 'They didn't help us to get into space. We had to develop spaceflight technology ourselves, once we'd cleared up the mess on Earth. Which they did help us to do.'

He had a point but ... 'Griffis didn't strike me as untruthful. Can you see if An Barik knows anything about it? It might be common knowledge to them, but they've never realised we wanted to share it.'

'All right.' He wasn't enthusiastic.

'What's wrong?'

'I don't know if we should bother An Barik with this.'

It was my turn to be shocked. I held his soft brown gaze. 'This is important. If they did blunder into an unknown jump point or something similar, we might be able to use that knowledge to get a message to the Confederacy. Or even get a ship away to ask for help against the Seouras.'

He dropped his eyes. 'Why do you think that would make any difference?'

I actually felt the blood drain from my face when he'd said the words. It left a fuzzy white noise in my ears and a sensation of floating. He was saying that what we had sometimes suspected was true – the Confederacy had abandoned us to the Seouras.

'Do you believe it?' I whispered the words.

He smiled without humour. 'In all honesty, I don't know.'

'But you think it's possible?'

'I think anything is possible, because we can't possibly comprehend their motives.' He looked at me worriedly. 'Halley, what does it matter? We put ourselves in their hands a century ago. They saved us from destroying the planet and ourselves. What do you think would have happened if they hadn't come?'

There it is – the question that haunts us all, always. I don't know what would have happened. We might have muddled along in the same way, decimating other species and our own at an ever-increasing rate until eventually we realised what was happening. Or we might never have realised, and blundered our way to extinction. Or a trillion other possibilities. Whatever the outcome, if the Invidi hadn't visited Earth we wouldn't be here on Jocasta now.

'All we can do,' he continued, as passionate as I'd ever seen him, 'is put ourselves in their hands again. Have some faith. They haven't hurt us yet.'

No, but I was shaken. If we can't count on the Confederacy eventually saving us from the Seouras, how else can I get rid of them?

'Just ask him, will you?' I said stubbornly. There was something about the Sleepers' arrival that tugged at my intuition.

Brin smiled, this time with affection. 'For you, I will ask. And I must admit, for myself as well. I still think these people are lying.' When I didn't reply he leaned forward and patted my knee. 'Remember *desada*. This could be yours.'

I sighed. Invidi concepts were too slippery for me. 'I still don't understand what you mean by that. Is it a pivotal event?'

He seemed dissatisfied with the words. 'Only in simplistic physical terms. It's more like "soul". It's the defining quality of sentience, of people-ness. A time – but they use a word that means place also – a time to which we return again and again in the course of our lives.'

'What, like being born?'

'For some people, yes. For others, an event in childhood. For yet others, an event on the eve of their death, or somewhere in between.'

'Do you mean some trauma that leaves scars?'

'Not necessarily unpleasant. Or major in the sense of changing the physical course of a life. But pivotal, yes.'

'How do we know what our *desada* is?'

'They say,' and he sounded less sure, 'you know, if not during your life, then at the moment of death.'

... *the moment of her death*. My great-grandmother's raspy voice rose clear and unbidden in my memory.

I was with Marlena at the moment of her death. We'd gone to the capital to negotiate with the new government for district autonomy. They were all shaking hands on the steps of the high court. It was raining and the place was crammed with reporters. A security nightmare. Marlena shook hands and turned away from the president. She looked up, some of the idiots said afterwards to heaven, but I think she got a glimpse of the gunman – he must have been on top of one of the surrounding

buildings. I think she got a glimpse because she turned
back to the president and took his arm. She wanted to
get him inside in case there really was a sniper up there.
Well, there was. And to this day nobody knows whether
the target was Marlena or the president himself.

I went to my office and buried myself in the telemetry records from the wreck. Until Eleanor let me talk to the Sleepers again, this was the only source of information on how and why they had arrived here. I'd tried to contact Keveth to ask whether it had noticed anything about the wreck during the rescue, but the K'Cher trader was either out of comm range or ignored my calls on the public system.

When I finally pulled away from the hood, hours later, I knew nothing more about the Earth humans, but I knew their ship well enough to navigate around it in the dark without gravity. It was an old Nukeni freighter – built solely to haul unambitious loads for short distances. It looked like a planet-hopper, with a basically conical, streamlined shape to facilitate atmospheric entry, and was at least six times the mass of our little shuttle. Half of that mass was engines.

Top acceleration on boosters about one-third light, cruises about sublight ten. The original cramped ops room and crew quarters had been merged with the main cargo bay to form the cryochamber-cum-control room. It was now littered with twisted metal and debris, but the plan was clear enough.

The front half was torn open in a dozen places and black with blast residue. A faint miasma of water vapour, probably from the last dregs of atmosphere leaking out when the rescue team withdrew contact with the hole they'd cut to reach survivors, gave the wreck a soft halo.

The jump mine had blasted the rear of the ship almost completely away, leaving shreds of metal trailing behind like streamers after a wild party. Emergency containment shields had activated inside the cryochamber, but they were compromised, and the damage inside the chamber seemed to indicate that some of the inner systems had exploded as well. It was unusual to see the engine section at all in a mine accident – a typical mine sets off a reaction within the engines themselves, usually followed by emergency jettison of the engines. This seemed to indicate either that the mine was unusual, part of the Tor smorgasbord of destruction that we hadn't sampled yet, or that *Calypso* was unusual in some way. I spent another half-hour sifting through records of previous jump mine accidents. None of them involved, or mentioned, a mine detonating by itself.

Who did all the work, I wondered, while the rest of the crew were snoozing peacefully in their sub-zero beds? Engineering maintenance, environment monitoring, defence. The ship's opsys would do most of it, but even in our most advanced carrier ships there's always an organic caretaker. It reflects less on the state of technology than on the reluctance of organic species to entirely trust that technology. Surely a century ago they would have been even less willing to allow an opsys to determine their fate? Would someone volunteer to stay awake the whole time? They'd be elderly, to say the least, when the ship finally arrived at its destination, and a prime candidate for space-sickness well before then. Maybe the opsys woke them in turn and then they put themselves back down when each 'shift' ended? That still

85

seemed to leave a lot of loose ends, but I suppose people on a venture like this must take chances.

I leaned back in the chair and tried to rub some focus back into my eyes. Bent down and poured the last cupful of tea from a large jar beside the desk. Think.

If the *Calypso* had no jump drive, it couldn't have set off the mine. Therefore, unless the mine had activated itself by chance at the very time *Calypso* appeared, something else must have set off the mine. Our sensors had not detected any other ship. But then, our sensors had not been state of the art when they were installed three years ago. Since then they had been damaged in Seouras attacks, jammed by Seouras interference, and repeatedly reconfigured to try to reach beyond the grey ships. It would not surprise me if we hadn't picked up a tell-tale sign of . . . what? Why should anyone visit us?

I tried Keveth again, with no result. Keveth was the most likely to have seen something out there. If it felt like divulging the information to us.

It wasn't merely details about their voyage. I had so many questions to ask the Sleepers. Griffis had mentioned a man called Halley in the EarthSouth movement. It could have been my great-grandfather, John Halley, who seemed to have been active in a number of areas at that time. I knew only his son Jack, my grandfather, who inherited John's passion for justice and who eventually settled in Las Mujeres with my grandmother Elvira. Griffis was old enough to have seen the end of the twentieth century, the beginning of the twenty-first, and most of the great struggles of that era. No wonder every historian on the station was clamouring for an interview with him and his companions. I'd left the task of organising a roster to Veatch.

There were so many questions about that period left unanswered. Too many records had disappeared in the great Net Crash of 2055, and many of the witnesses to the period died in the political unrest that followed the technological reforms set in motion by the Invidi in the 2030s and 2040s. We don't know what happened in isolated places when the Invidi came, don't know the reaction of ordinary people in different Earth cultures. Because Marlena Alvarez and that era were so important to my family, the pre-Contact period seems close to me, but to the average Jocasta resident it was ancient history, pre–anything interesting. We should be more interested, for there are many parallels with our own situation.

The connecting door chirped.

'Good afternoon, Commander.' Veatch, as fresh and calm as if it were morning. He stood with hands clasped behind him, indicating it was a short visit. 'How do you wish the new residents to be registered?'

'New residents?'

'The Earth humans from the cryogenics ship. They are not Confederacy citizens – neither are they refugees, strictly speaking.'

I dragged my mind back from the past. 'Earth's a member of the Confederacy.'

'At the time they left there was no Confederacy.'

'Does it matter?' I didn't know why we bothered to argue. However they were classified, they would be medically treated, clothed, and fed. Six months ago it would have been a question of which IDs to give them and who to send them on to, but the Seouras weren't sending anyone anywhere.

'Matter?' Veatch's antennae were stiff with shock. 'How can I file a report if they are not registered correctly?'

'Oh. Of course, forgive me. The report.' For posterity, no doubt, since nobody at Sector Central would read it. 'Isn't there a time dilation clause somewhere in the Immigration regulations?'

'But that ship does not have jump capability.'

'No, but . . .' It must have used hyperspace somehow to get here. Either that or magic. 'Tourists.'

'I beg your pardon?'

'Until we work out the classification problem they can be tourists. Give them temporary holding visas, like we used to do with the Garokian refugees until their asylum was processed.'

Veatch's antennae twitched as he considered the idea. It's been a while since we had any tourists here. Even before the Seouras Jocasta was not exactly on the scenic route – a resourceless, burnt-out system does not pull in crowds.

'That is a possible solution,' he conceded. 'I will organise the applications.' He started to leave, then turned back. 'Commander, you have not forgotten the Smoke residents' meeting at 1800 hours?'

I've had too much practice to start guiltily but I probably twitched.

'Of course not.' I wasn't looking forward to that one. Last time it had taken fifteen hours to accomplish any sort of understanding about what the residents wanted, let alone come up with solutions. It made our petty humanoid disputes seem positively pre-Atomic in their simplicity.

'I don't suppose they have any sort of agenda?' I asked, not very hopefully.

'The Nerossi wish to discuss the right of sentient beings to be consumed as sustenance. By the Nerossi, of course. The !Ghplpp! want three more rooms and another methane pond. The Tell say nothing. The Invidi wishes to discuss the philosophical implications of the hatch on Level Fifty that was broken last year – or it might be next year, he wasn't specific. And . . .'

'Right. I get the picture,' I interrupted. 'Maybe it's better if I come at it cold.'

'I have flagged the report in your In file,' he reminded me, and left.

Then Eleanor called to say the Sleepers were able to talk and I forgot about the residents' meeting.

They were sitting up in their beds now. Dourif had kicked off her thermasheet and stretched sturdy, tanned legs on top of it. Ariel Kloos was awake. He leaned his close-cropped dark head against the wall between the other two beds. He had a wary young face, not open like Dourif's, and a lilting accent.

We went through the preliminaries again – who they were, who we were. I had spoken to the doctors and the magistrate earlier about what information the new-comers should be given. Legally, they had the same access rights to public information as any Confederacy member and Earth citizen.

Their story was that their project, to send a manned vessel to Alpha Centauri, had been planned for fifteen years by an ex-government astrophysicist named Tan Nguyen, a grassroots activist and geochemist, Hannibal Griffis, and a Russian aerospace scientist, Gregori Ilyanovich. They gathered a variety of sponsors for this clandestine experiment, which was presented to the public, when news leaked out, as being for the purpose of scientific observation and experiments on zero-g manufacturing techniques at the abandoned skylab platforms. The platforms were leased to them by a government discouraged by a series of dramatic cost overruns in aerospace research and a construction industry unwilling to invest in building a ship. The Invidi explained, said Griffis, that they could not share their jump technology. But they did offer to assist in assembling a cryogenic system that would preserve the passengers for the fifty-odd years necessary to approach the nearest star system at sublight speed. The humans accepted the offer, at the cost of keeping the trip a secret from all but those involved.

Rachel explained that the ship wasn't made on Earth and it was possible to modify it at one of the space platforms. More or less abandoned in 2020, the platforms weren't even monitored. Nations had given up space programs as too expensive.

The head of the project chose the people, and he was careful. They came from different backgrounds and while most of them knew him, they knew none of the other workers before they joined the project. Even after that they only talked with members of their particular group.

Many of the support personnel thought they were working on a top-secret government mission and were sworn to silence.

'I suppose that's why we haven't been able to find any record of your expedition in either Confederacy or Earth databases,' I said, not really convinced. It was hard to believe Earth's first interstellar flight could have been kept a complete secret. According to the files, the people lying here did not exist and neither did their ship – the one that couldn't have got here.

'Perhaps your data is incomplete.' Kloos's suggestion was made diffidently, but he could be right. We've suffered any number of general and specific systems failures over recent months and that particular data could have been lost. Except that neighbouring files are untouched and the historical databases are relatively undamaged.

At the time the Invidi came to Earth the project had not progressed much beyond plans for the ship. They'd considered modifying an old WorldSpace ship, but the public profile was too high and the potential for success – considering the quality of the ships – was too low. The Invidi, whose name was An Serat, approached Nguyen first. Griffis and Ilyanovich were not keen on accepting help, for the Invidi were still largely an unknown force then.

Everybody now knows how Earth's very first contact with aliens happened. It is something we learn at our parents' knee, in school, at play. No human child grows up without knowing that the Invidi came in quietly. One day they weren't there, the next, twenty little ships were grouped in a neat pattern to cover every centimetre of Earth's airspace. Way above, the satellites transmitted a belated image of the mother ship. By the time the heads of government of the most powerful nations had conferred, the Invidi greeting had arrived on every broadcast system, every networked screen, every public telecast: Greetings. We are the Invidi. We come in peace.

Anyway, Nguyen and An Serat must have agreed on terms, but Griffis said he didn't know the details. They gained access to a ship with near-lightspeed capable engines and cryostasis technology. Dourif added that the ship's doctor had done most of the work adapting cryostasis units for use with human physiology. None of them knew what the Invidi gained from helping them – nothing, as far as they could see. Still, An Serat sounded far more communicative than any Invidi I'd ever known.

'Are you sure they offered to help you?'

Griffis nodded. 'The head of our project was the only one who ever dealt directly with them. I coordinated the scientific operations side. As far as I knew, only An Serat had contact with Tan Nguyen.'

The other problem was how.

'Did you do any work on the engines? You didn't notice anything strange about them?' I asked Dourif.

She grimaced. 'Everything was strange. This was an alien ship, remember? I could barely carry out a diagnostic properly.' More soberly. 'It was one of the most humiliating experiences of my life.'

'Commander, what went wrong?' Kloos hadn't spoken for so long that I jumped when he leaned across to look at me. 'What happened while we were asleep?'

'I don't know. We think your ship hit a gravitational anomaly that brought you here. There was nothing you could have done,' I added, trying to be reassuring.

'Why didn't someone find us?' asked Griffis, and I could see the suspicion in his eyes. Perhaps he thought we'd left them asleep all this time as part of some experiment.

'I don't know that either.' He was right to be suspicious. For the first half of their journey there was no spaceflight from Earth – humanity was busy cleaning up its own backyard – and the Invidi kept the whole sector relatively clear of interstellar trade. But the second half of the twenty-first century saw a blossoming of space travel both within the solar system and within a short jump of it. It seemed impossible that nobody had noticed the old freighter limping along its programmed path. I made a mental note to have another look at the historical database for that period and area.

'What's to become of us?' said Dourif in the kind of voice that is harsh because the owner doesn't want to be tearful.

What could I say? It must have been a terrible shock to wake up to their companions' deaths, and then to learn that they had arrived fifty years later than planned, and countless light years from where they wanted to be.

'For the moment –' I glanced at Eleanor, but she merely lifted one shoulder – 'I'm afraid you're stuck here, like the rest of us. When you feel up to it you can choose an area that interests you on the station and train to work there, if you like. When we've resolved this Seouras problem, then I'm sure you can go back to Earth if you wish to do so.'

There was a short silence. Griffis and Kloos looked down at their sheets, while Dourif pushed herself up with a little grunt and walked unsteadily to the side of the room where she turned as if at bay.

'What's Earth like now?'

I started with the Confederacy of Allied Worlds and Earth's role. This point seemed to worry Griffis in particular. I told them how Earth is one of the Nine Worlds that have a kind of junior partnership with the four founding members, the Invidi, K'Cher, Melot, and Bendarl. That the Nine have no jump technology but that they do have a vote in the Confederacy General Council on a representative basis – a certain number of councillors per head of population, with minimum and maximum representation. He didn't like the idea that the larger worlds have more power.

'Not ethically sound,' he said.

'But they do anyway, don't they? Have more power? You know, Hannibal, bigger is stronger.' Dourif didn't sound bitter, merely pragmatic. Almost amused at Griffis's frustrations.

I felt sorry for Griffis, but he would have problems if he tried to fit the Confederacy into twenty-first-century Earth categories. 'I understand what you're saying, Professor, and Earth's assemblies are still a one-member one-vote system. But the Confederacy is a union of alien species. You think the old United Nations had problems? Some of these species don't even agree on what is sentient life, let alone basic concepts such as law or rights.

Everyone made compromises to get the present representative system up and running. We should be glad it's one familiar to us.'

The political situation on Earth was easier for them. They could accept that there were two great representative units of government but had trouble at first understanding that the names EarthNorth and EarthSouth had no geographic significance and were no more than labels held over from their own time, when the planet was divided between rich and poor.

'Let me get this straight.' Griffis smoothed his pale blue thermasheet and drew map lines on it with his finger as he spoke. 'What you call EarthNorth is the Pacific?'

I nodded. 'The Pacific Union. That's former Australasia and the Pacific states. And all of Eurasia including the Indian subcontinent and northern Europe. The capital is Sydney.' Which was, I recalled, Bill Murdoch's home town.

'And EarthSouth is the rest?' He enlarged one side of his diagram.

'Yes. The Americas, Africa, and the Atlantic Alliance. Oh, and Antarctica.'

'How do people feel about the aliens?' Kloos asked. He seemed less at ease than the other two.

Eleanor Jago smiled at Kloos from where she was slotting some filepads into the beds' interfaces. 'That's a good question. Humans like Commander Halley here have lived with aliens all their adult lives. They are quite comfortable with the idea, but they tend to forget how some of the people back home feel.'

'Plenty of people live away from Earth,' I said, annoyed

by her presumption. 'The big colonies, Io and Triton, have two or three million inhabitants each. Mars is semi-independent.'

'That doesn't mean everyone loves the aliens,' she said. She was calm, as always, and I had to control the urge to break that control with sharp words. 'Not everybody thinks Earth should have joined the Confederacy.'

Griffis nodded. 'Not everyone thought so in our time either. When we left there were a lot of people who still didn't even believe aliens were real. What convinced them?'

'Time. And the fact that the Bendarl came a generation later. It's difficult to ignore two alien species and concrete proof of the existence of more,' said Eleanor.

'The knowledge that we are not alone in the universe,' she continued, 'was the greatest single scientific revolution our world ever experienced. Greater than heliocentricity, greater than the theory of evolution, greater than the computer. Our whole identity is still reeling from the shock of finding that we aren't the centre of creation. We're only among the bit players.'

Even so, after three generations it is difficult for me to imagine a worldview without that underpinning.

'But the Invidi came in 2023,' protested Dourif. 'What did they do all those years, nurse us along?'

'They brought in medical and agricultural technology. They . . .' I looked helplessly at Eleanor. Hard to describe the last ninety-plus years in a few sentences. 'They made it quite clear that we now had the means to change the world. There was no longer any excuse for not doing so.'

'Some of us tried,' said Griffis. 'Even before they came.'

I had been waiting to ask him about this. 'Professor, you said you knew someone in the "movement" with the same name as me. Was that the EarthSouth movement?'

'It was a precursor. We were an organised group but we didn't have the grassroots support that the later movement gained.' He looked at me as though trying to see someone else's face in my own. 'I didn't know him personally, but the man's name was John Halley. He worked with our agriculture branch. Last I heard, he was settled in East Africa.'

Jack Halley, my grandfather, had grown up in the grasslands of Serengeti.

'I think that was my great-grandfather. My grandfather was part of the EarthSouth movement. He met my grand-mother that way.'

Griffis leant forwards, entranced.

'You come from a revolutionary family. You know something of the Movement, then?'

Dourif groaned. 'Don't get him started on that. He can go on for hours.'

'I grew up with stories of that time,' I said, with an apologetic smile at her. 'I'd be very interested in hearing about it first-hand.' And not merely because of what light it could shed on the mystery of their arrival. Lately I couldn't get Marlena Alvarez out of my head.

'One of my great-grandmothers on the other side of the family worked with a woman called Marlena Alvarez in the pre-Movement days. Have you heard of her?'

'We all have,' Rachel recovered quickest. Even Kloos had looked up at the name.

Eleanor leaned on the interface at the foot of Dourif's bed. 'I've heard the name, but . . .'

I could see she was trying to get them to talk so didn't point out that she'd probably heard it from me. Alvarez is my first name, then Maria, after my mother.

'I heard her speak once, the only time they let her leave the country.' Griffis half closed his eyes, squinting back what was less than ten years for him, ten times that for us. 'It was at a meeting organised by World Free and Amnesty. At one of those huge outdoor concert venues that we used before holovid became affordable.'

Kloos and Rachel nodded. I exchanged a glance of bewilderment with Eleanor but said nothing.

'Alvarez climbed onstage, dragged the microphone off its stand, and came right to the edge. It was daylight but the vid people were waving at her to get back into position for their lights. She ignored them. She wanted to be as close to the audience as she could.'

'Was she standing with the audience?' I didn't want to interrupt him, but I couldn't get a clear picture of the scene in my head.

'No, on a raised platform, a stage. I'll never forget it – 130 000 people waiting to hear this dumpy little woman speak.'

'Well? What did she say?' Rachel moved away from the wall and sat on the foot of Griffis's bed.

He paused and shut his half-closed eyes completely. Then opened them and looked at me.

'She was so angry. That's what I remember most. She had a sharp voice, the sort of voice that acts like a burr under your seat. She said . . .' He thought for a moment.

'She said, "Who gave them" – meaning the official international bodies – "who gave them the right to decide if we live or die and how? When they sanction or punish governments that we did not choose, when our governments that we did not choose punish others under our name, who suffers? Not you."'

'She meant,' Griffis added, 'citizens of the wealthy democratic states. She said that it was the people like her who lost, whom the governments rule by force.'

Eleanor frowned. 'When was this?'

'The middle of the second decade in the twenty-first century,' said Griffis. 'But plenty of people before Alvarez had made these points over the years. That's why there was an increasing international tendency to bully wayward governments back into line, which never worked. Just left economies in a shambles and minorities as scapegoats.

'Alvarez,' he continued, 'spoke in a mixture of Spanish and English, mixing it almost like poetry. She told us we had a choice. We could go on just as we were now. I remember the words that became one of the Movement's catchphrases – "conscience is not enough". Or we could act in support of people who were not as free to act. She didn't urge us to pressure our governments – she said *we* were our governments. She told us that her people had discovered they were not powerless, and that it was about time we did the same. She was quite specific – said there were networks in place to convey food and goods, enough groups willing to donate arms and use them, enough laws to invoke if the will could be found to speak the words. Frankly, I was surprised they let her speak.'

'She couldn't have said it in her own country.' I remembered Demora's stories.

'I heard she was so vocal that her own government first thought she was a harmless idiot,' said Kloos.

I remembered another thing Demora had said: For years we walked a tightrope between the government's regulations, its police, the revenge of the opposition, and the scrutiny of foreign eyes.

Griffis cleared his throat. 'What would you say is the greatest benefit the aliens brought to Earth?'

I gave him the stock answer, no less true for that. 'Their presence united us, faster than anyone thought possible. You saw the very early days. It must have been obvious by the time you left that the Invidi hadn't come to invade or conquer.'

'Nobody knew what they wanted,' said Griffis slowly.

I didn't say that we were still unsure.

'We should think of their coming as a reprieve,' he said.

Rachel snorted. 'From what?'

'From the need to balance everything. Ever since mankind discovered nuclear fission our history has been one big balancing act.'

'You think they "saved us from ourselves"?' Eleanor leaned forward. It is a question that divides humanity still.

'We wouldn't have made it otherwise.'

'They took away from us the chance to decide for ourselves,' said Rachel loudly.

I thought of Alvarez. She started a snowball of far-reaching social change, true, but how long would it have lasted without the Invidi? Would the damage to the planet have been too great? Yet I couldn't see the Invidi as good samaritans. They must have had their reasons for contacting Earth.

'Are there any Invidi on this station?' asked Dourif.

I thought of An Barik with a mixture of fondness, incomprehension, and exasperation. 'At the moment there's only one. He's the Confederacy Council observer.'

The comm link beeped and we all jumped. Eleanor was closest. 'Jago.'

She listened for a moment then looked at me. 'She's here. Hang on.'

It was the EarthFleet lieutenant on duty in the Bubble. The Seouras had sent the signal that meant they wanted me to go over to the grey ship.

I turned to the Sleepers. 'I have to go.'

Rachel leaned against the wall, arms folded in a defensive way. Kloos looked puzzled and Griffis frowned from his bed.

'Are these the aliens that are blocking your communications?' he asked.

I nodded. 'I'm sorry we have to cut this short. Let's continue tomorrow.' I left without leaving them time to reply.

I was halfway down the corridor when Eleanor called out. She had a tight, almost hostile expression.

'Can it wait?' I fidgeted to get away. 'I've got to get to the shuttle and do the pre-launch.'

She caught up. 'Halley, don't go.'

'What?'

'You just got back from twelve hours over there. As

your physician I don't know if you can take it again so soon.'

I groaned with impatience. 'Eleanor, we've been through this before. I'm fine. And I don't have a choice.'

'Have you ever asked them to wait?'

'I can't "ask" them anything. And yes, remember what happened after the fire?' Two months ago, a fire had broken out in the Hill. It had taken three days to get it under control and another week before the state of emergency was lifted. Murdoch had been incautious enough to inhale too many noxious fumes on the second day and I'd directed the whole affair pretty much alone. When the Seouras called after the fire I was so exhausted I couldn't get into a shuttle. Three of the grey ships closed in, weapons primed. The state of emergency onstation resumed for another twelve hours until Eleanor managed to stabilise me enough to go. We'd been lucky that time – the Seouras didn't fire – but I didn't want to try our luck again.

She was right, though, in that it was unusual for them to call again so soon. Could it have something to do with the change in the tone of their voices that I'd felt recently? I was getting worse dreams too, if that indicated anything other than my own worries.

'I don't think it'll be very long this time.' I tried to sound reassuring. 'They probably forgot something.'

She gave me the look of scorn this inanity deserved. 'What about these dreams? You said it happens sometimes when you're awake.'

'I haven't had any for a week or so.' I shrugged uncomfortably. 'Maybe the other times were coincidence.' Then

I remembered what I'd asked her that morning.

'Did you look at the cryosystems for me?'

She blinked at the change of subject then recovered. 'They were fine.'

'Fine?'

'They were exactly what they should be. Basically Invidi medical expertise was used to build a system using materials from that time and place – forensics confirms this, by the way. As far as we can tell, the settings were for fifty-one years, which would have taken them to within a couple of months of deceleration for Centauri.'

'What did the timer say?'

'If you mean how long had they been in stasis, it was nearly the whole time.'

'Fifty years?' Which left a gap of forty-five years.

She nodded. 'I know it doesn't make sense. But our readings could be mistaken. The pods could have reset everything for another fifty years.'

I clenched my fists in frustration. Another dead end. I had a premonition of what would happen with the Sleepers: we would pursue every clue as to how they got here, every possible opening, without success. Meanwhile station life would go on as usual and the Sleepers themselves would begin to be a part of it. Soon we would forget they had offered any mystery, any hope for change, and settle back into routine. And I'd still be going over to that goddamn ship.

The shuttle swung away from Jocasta. The view is impressive. A bright dusting of faraway stars and the closer jewels of Abelar's two outer planets. Swathes of translucent colour show the remains of two more planets vaporised by the Tor before leaving for wherever they had gone. The same view from Jocasta used to be enlivened by ships passing, some close enough to make out registration details, others like miniature comets too small to ascertain any feature but movement. There's no movement now. Our planet is a pale ghost left radioactive and useless by the Tor.

I used an airlock to enter the grey ship. Even if the space beyond was not as oxygenated as Earth's, even if it was knee-deep in slippery, slimy stuff, an airlock was an airlock. The ship had gravity. Within the Confederacy, only the Invidi have invented a gravity field for stationary vehicles that doesn't rely on momentum or spin. Either the Seouras had acquired Invidi technology or they had a similar level of technology themselves. Which didn't seem right. If they had that kind of ability, they shouldn't have been interested in Jocasta, with our pitiful technological situation.

The dreamlike gloom was lit by luminescence from the slime that dripped from the low ceiling and sucked at my feet. It wasn't a large room. Tunnel-like passages ran off it at various angles but it was hard to see where because distance was flattened and distorted in the light, as if we were underwater. Once I had pushed my arm into slime up to the shoulder and felt a hard surface underneath.

Here they were. Two of them today.

If they have a shape it is impossible to tell exactly what it is, because their whole form is constantly shifting in tiny movements. From a short distance they seem to shimmer. As you look it is like bringing a microscope to bear on a colony of minute living things that seems a solid lump but resolves into countless short, slim, squirming shapes. These, too, dissolve and shift under scrutiny, as though it is all held together by some field that can form and reform. I imagine it forming into shapes that we know or maybe a giant nightmare shape, but so far they have remained roughly cylindrical blobs, about our height and three times as wide. Coloured slime-green. Or so coated with it that I couldn't tell what was underneath. I was slime-green by the time I got out of there too.

The walls and ceiling seemed to squeeze me in. Like being inside a digestive tract . . . I had the same thought every time, that I was to be broken down and absorbed, used to provide energy for . . . Calm down. Don't breathe too fast, sometimes that messes up the implant in your neck, calm down.

Come go stay help attack

I shook my head against the insistence of the call. It hurt when they got 'loud'. A sharp pain drilled behind my eyes, and more spread in short bursts from a point above the breastbone through shoulders and neck. I wished I knew what they wanted. Lately it was as though they were arguing among themselves. I rarely got a clear message.

This way.

No, here.

A cacophony of urgent needs. I used words to order the impressions in my mind, but they didn't actually speak.

Go now.

Stay.

Open.

I wasn't sure if they meant my mind or the station. Neither, I stated firmly, was available.

Their disappointment hurt.

Rush along a long, dark tunnel faster and faster, nothing but the noise of passage until at the end there's a point of solidity. Not visual but I'd describe it visually if there were anyone to describe it to – a small, half-naked human slumped barely upright on a slippery surface, an image only until the downward swoop gets closer and closer and *whump*, I'm in me, with the sour-sick stench of slime all around and the ocean-green light that has no depth. The voices have retreated.

It hadn't been too long this time. I stretched out an arm and the muscles responded immediately but stiffly. I clenched and unclenched my fingers, felt the stickiness. It was possible to swallow – throat dry and tight but not hopelessly closed. I gagged on the taste of slime, but didn't have quite enough saliva for spit, then rolled over on hands and knees and tried to stand. Shards of pain scattered from stomach and joints to gather in my head. Surely it hadn't been this painful the first time I 'talked' to them? It was getting worse each session.

The shuttle was still there. It was always a surprise and a relief to glimpse it through the murky windows in the Seouras airlock.

I slipped on unsteady legs and crashed into the airlock entry. It opened obligingly and I slid the rest of the way into the shuttle. My knee cracked on the side but I didn't feel anything. They let me leave because they must have known I'd never survive in the heat and slime. Since the slime seeped through the joins of our environmental suits, I gave up on the suit after the first few trips and wore only boots and trousers. I'd left those off a couple of times too, but while I could struggle into a jacket on the way back in the shuttle, on bad days pulling on trousers in zero-g was beyond me and I thought it probably not good for morale if the head of station were caught with her pants down, so to speak, when the shuttle docked at Jocasta.

I keyed in my code on the controls, letting each blip be a signal to open my eyes. I needed to stay awake until the shuttle was clear or the whole autopilot sequence became terribly complicated and I might not get back for days. Blip, blink, blip. I checked the time – it was nearly midnight. It was scary, the way time drained away when I was in there. Nearly five hours gone. At least I had missed the Smoke residents' meeting.

Trouble is . . . I gulped a half-litre of water, rubbed off the worst of the slime with a drywrap left here for this purpose and hauled on my jacket, strapped myself in the zero-g net and tripped the departure switch before the thought could make its way through my pounding head. The trouble is, each time I hoped it would be the last.

Every time I made it back alive with the station unharmed, it was a spur to try harder to find a way to get free.

I couldn't think of a way to do it. So far, all our efforts had been directed towards getting a message to the Confederacy, always presuming the Confederacy is still out there and not also under Seouras control. If what Quartermaine suggested today was true, though, maybe we have been wasting our time. What if the Confederacy thought the treaty with the Danadan and Seouras meant we'd allowed them into the Abelar system's space, or even that we'd formed an alliance with the grey ships? Surely they'd have contacted us to confirm or deny such a conjecture.

It wasn't the first time I'd had these thoughts, but Quartermaine's words earlier had been such a shock that I found it difficult to control the panic. Panic that rose up in my throat like vomit whenever I contemplated the alternatives before us. Without the prospect of Confederacy help, what could we do? Wait, as the Seouras had said, as An Barik seemed to be doing? But the station was falling apart, and I wasn't far behind.

The sudden tug of the strap on my bruised knee woke me. The shuttle had changed direction. Background buzzing gradually resolved itself into a voice.

'Jocasta to *Eliot*. Commander Halley, we have put the shuttle on auto for landing.'

How long had they been calling? The grey ships put out a jamming signal that prevents long-range communications, but short-range is possible in a narrow radius around the station. I might have slept through five minutes of voices.

Open your eyes, idiot. I could have taken a pilot with me every time the Seouras summoned, as Murdoch has urged me, but I prefer not to put another life at risk when the shuttle can be easily handled by one.

The station loomed close in the forward viewer. Lovely. I said it again, aloud. A great, untidy white top spinning against the black. I stared at a point on the outer ring and began to count as it moved around, one, two, three . . . hoping to see the same point come round again in sixty-two seconds, but I must have dropped off again briefly then opened my eyes as the shuttle hugged the long, pale curves of the habitat rings and snicked between two angular reflectors. It flew along one of the connecting struts towards the centre. An uplift moved inside the strut almost in time with the shuttle and I waved stupidly at the tiny window. As if anyone could see me from there.

Above the centre and further away from the station, was the wreck of *Calypso*, a white shape blurred by debris and vapour. It was tethered to the flat, open slab of a maintenance platform, and I could just make out two spidery probes on its pale surface. They were de-radiating the wreck so we could access it directly, and the sooner they finished, the better.

I undid the net straps, gave myself a quick push over to the flight panel and pulled down into the pilot's seat, hooked my feet under the console and belted in.

'*Eliot* to Jocasta. It's all right, I've got her. Switching over.' I wished my voice didn't sound as thick as my head felt.

'Jocasta to *Eliot*. Confirmed. Nice to see you back so soon, Commander.' Whoever owned that slightly sarcastic voice on traffic control knew my habit of bringing the shuttle in unaided. Not flying manually, because nobody in their right mind flies a high-performance space vehicle manually, but I needed to keep control of the shuttle's systems. Be able to act if anything went wrong. Eleanor calls it compensatory behaviour. Murdoch calls it being pig-headed. It keeps me awake.

Swish, thud. It took a second before I registered that the karrikar door was open. A long, long day – days. Seouras, Sleeper ship, unsolved mysteries.

The sticky heat of the Hill rolled into the lift. Sweat prickled immediately in the slime under my jacket and on my upper lip. This is the outer ring, the lowest circle, and the slightly higher gravity causes a fullness of hands and feet and momentary shortness of breath. I walked slowly along the rows of covered stalls and booths that lined the marketplace. It was simply from habit, because my old quarters had been down here before the Seouras came. I liked living here. It was good to know how the other half of the station lived – the stowaways, refugees, contract workers. Many of them stayed because they couldn't afford passage off and then were caught here when the Seouras came.

Blue night lights, not as many as there should be. Down here, people often put extra demands on the system or diverted the power to illicit uses. The grime and cheapness was hidden by the kindly darkness. A few people still staggered to and from bars and gathered in little knots around portable lighting units, their yellow glow comforting against the blue of the main illumination. There were smells, although my slime-deadened nose couldn't catch many – like hearing only the loudest notes of a symphony but knowing that the rest of it is playing. One of those notes was a fishy, charcoal smell. Someone had been using a true flame grill again, in defiance of all safety regulations.

This place is full of such anachronisms. It has an infrastructure of high technology – from the Tor engines, of which we understand little, and the Invidi gravity wells, which we do not understand at all. Side by side with this we have shoemakers and corner shrines, tiny foodbearing plants raised in a spot of sunlight on a bed of shredded spaceship cushions, and endless modifications to official building codes that have made a dark maze of the lower level.

Basic technologies exist in pockets – Garokian refugees who live by selling sandals made from scraps left over after glass filament recycling, for our stocks of footwear from Earth are nearly exhausted and recycling has its limits. Their shoe repair business does well too. I've had my old running shoes resoled twice now.

The K'Cher regard ability to improvise as the defining quality of sentience. Jocasta seems to prove them right.

Tiny alien food stalls spring up every night down here, as suddenly as rust appears on iron in space station humidity. The owners use unwanted material from the black market to produce meals far more appetising than official rations. The Office of Public Health raids the Hill regularly but the stalls never disappear. I'd been unlucky last night but hoped one would still be open tonight, because after this morning's fiasco in the kitchen I had no intention of trying to cook something for myself.

The only booth with a dim, orange light still showing was obviously finished for the night. Three folded stools leaned against the cooking box, and a cloth sign-curtain was furled beside them. I poked my head over the box, which formed a low, U-shaped counter and tapped it twice.

'Nothing left for an old customer?'

A broad face turned upwards and the light glinted gold on scales as the Garokian owner of the stall stood up, a blackened pan in each webbed hand. I repeated the question in case she hadn't caught my lips and she shook her head, well versed in human body language. She shifted from one foot to the other, clacked the gills on her neck and upper shoulders, and turned her head to look at me with a sideways, bird-like glance. A head that was more like a chinless continuation of the thick neck, which in turn flowed smoothly into shoulders.

Her eyes were large, silvery clouded irises filling the whole eye, which was surrounded by a fine filigree of triangular scales. Her clothes, designed for a human, hung loosely on her hips and stretched tight across her back and shoulders. She was about my height but solid. Garokians acquire a weight problem when they live here. Their stocky, cylindrical bodies pout sideways in protest at a lack of exercise and a diet that Confederacy nutritionists insist is adequate. It obviously isn't satisfactory, because the Garokians gather together at close of day in clan or neighbourhood groups, clumps of silent, gesticulating trolls hunched over pots of bubbling delicacies. They make pastries out of the residue that Achelian restaurants scorn and boil up unlikely brews with plants bartered for homemade sandals from creatures in the Smoke who have many feet.

This Garokian was wider than most. Like all large

'people' she had a presence that demanded to be noticed. Her body created a wash ahead of itself, a cushion of loaded air, and she occupied even more space in my mind than in reality. So solid, so grounded, soft heavy flesh and triangular scales with an oily sheen. My own body felt insubstantial as a drift of gas in comparison. I hitched up my trousers, suddenly self-conscious. The belt has no more notches left to tighten.

She slapped the pan down behind the counter with a bang, then held up one digit for me to wait and rummaged around below. The reward for my patience was a small, wilted dumpling, which I knew would contain a curry-like puree. It must have been her own supper. Perhaps she would be up all night preparing for the imminent Renewal of Souls.

She pushed the dumpling into my protesting hands, the whole conversation (this is yours – no, take it – it's all right, I'll try somewhere else – forget it, I said take it) conducted in silence. In the end I took the dumpling and chewed it gratefully on my way to the ringlift, leaving the careless, unheard clatter behind.

The Garokians and the mess in the Hill are part of the other world of the station – the rich, suspicious chaos that Veatch and Walsh would like to dilute to their own image. A whole world that I couldn't begin to describe to the Sleepers because I'm too far removed from it. But it was a world I would like them to see.

'Commander Halley?' A vaguely familiar voice.

I turned quickly and peered at the owner in the gloom. It was Rachel Dourif.

'What are you doing here?' I swallowed the last

mouthful of dumpling hurriedly and stepped closer to
her. She was wearing a generic grey overall and, from
what I could see in the half-light, an expression of
determination.

'I'm going for a walk,' she said, as if it were the most
natural thing in the world. 'What are you doing?'

'I'm getting supper.' I wasn't sure if I should stay with
her or not. The Hill may be dirty and overcrowded, but
it is seldom dangerous. On the other hand, she had few
survival skills for this century. I didn't think she'd
wander out an airlock but . . .

'Dr Dourif, maybe you should go back to the hospital
and come again in the morning.'

'Call me Rachel, please.' She glanced around and sat
on an upturned container beside one of the silent,
shrouded stalls. After an awkward moment, I sat beside
her. The throughway was quiet except for a hum of
voices further along and the occasional clatter from one
of the open stalls. I leaned back against the corrugated
side of the stall and felt the incredible busy-ness of the
day begin to recede, draining away into the stained deck
through the soles of my battered boots. Rachel's voice
startled me back to wakefulness.

'When I was a student I used to walk a lot at night.
We'd spend all day in labs, sitting in front of a computer.
By evening I was stir-crazy. I'd get outside into the street
and walk and walk for hours. I'd finish up at the other
end of town, the harbour end. The place was full of street
people then. Do you know about the "clean-ups" of the
early 21st century?'

'Not much.'

She smiled ruefully. 'It was such a big thing when I was a teenager. The government was going to find homes for everyone, but we ended up with more ghettos.'

'Very little really changed until after the Invidi came,' I said. 'Socially, I mean. That's why a lot of people say that if the Invidi hadn't come, we would have eventually destroyed ourselves.'

'What do you think?'

'I don't know. There were people like Alvarez and Hannibal Griffis, too. Maybe they would have done it.'

Rachel made an unconvinced noise and we sat in silence.

She turned and peered at me. Her eyes picked up a reflection from the night lights and seemed to flash with strong emotion. 'Do you know what it's like to go from a small town to the big city? Sort of like going from Earth to space, it's such an upheaval.'

'I know what you mean,' I said, 'I ran away from a small town to join the Engineering Corps when I was fifteen.' As I said the words I thought again how I had more in common with my grandmother Elvira than bone structure. We had both run away, she from her mother and I from her. At least she'd returned to the town.

Rachel snorted. 'People still run away from home? Guess children haven't changed much.' She thought for a moment. 'But I thought you were from some famous family. Griffis said . . .'

'Not my family. Alvarez was famous.'

On the wall of the dwelling opposite someone had scrawled a rude cartoon of a K'Cher manipulating several stick forms representing humanoids. Even the graffiti was becoming more primitive. Feeling was running high against the Four Worlds down here. I glanced at Rachel and thought how much simpler it must have been in her day.

'Why did you do it?' I blurted out. 'What was it like?'

'It was . . .' Her whole face glowed with remembered joy. 'It was wonderful. I have to say that first. When *Calypso* left the orbital platform on its run out of the solar system I thought, that's it, we're the first to leave. This is history. It doesn't matter what happens after this. This is enough. And it was.' She looked around and shook her head. 'But now . . . Probably on some level I never expected to wake up at all, and this is confusing me.'

'What did it feel like to wake up?' I imagined the second of panic as consciousness faded away, the relief when it returned. No wonder they were glad to be here. I would have been glad to wake up anywhere.

She stared past me as she searched for the words. 'I heard a voice. I don't know whose – it might even have been yours. I couldn't understand the words at first, but the sound was like an anchor that stopped me drifting any further. Then everything slowly came into focus – sensation, thoughts, a sense of identity.

'Like a landscape emerging slowly with the dawn. You know, there's no single moment of clarity, but then by the time you realise what's happening, everything is clear.' She glanced at me to see if I understood.

'When I was studying I'd spend a couple of days at home every month or so. I used to catch an early bus to get from our village back to the coast where the city shuttle left, and from the bus I'd watch the hills turn from black to grey to colours. I was the first girl from our village to finish a graduate degree. My grandfather boasts about it . . . used to boast about it. I guess he's . . .' she hesitated over the word, then sighed, 'dead now. Commander, when can we get things off our ship?'

'In a couple of days, when the worst radiation has dissipated. Why?'

'I have some photos – you know what photos are?'

I nodded.

She dug at the deck with her sandal. 'Of my family. I'd really like to see if they were okay. The photos, I mean.'

'What about the things we brought over from the wreck?' I waved my hand upward to indicate the storage bay in the centre. 'There were some personal belongings in there.'

'Can I see them?' Her tone was so hopeful that I felt guilty immediately, not wanting to be responsible if she were disappointed.

'Soon.'

She shook her head. 'You're all so damned unselfish.'

I looked at her, puzzled. She stared back, flushed, then looked away again. 'Chief Murdoch's the same. And the doctor. They work their butts off, and for what?'

'We're a bit . . . fixated on our work here, but that's unavoidable given the circumstances.' I wondered why it bothered her. 'Your project was visionary. You must have worked hard on it too.'

'You don't get it,' she said. 'You're different, you all are. Hannibal can't see it. Ariel can sort of grasp what I mean, but I think he likes it more than not.'

'Likes what?'

'Feeling like a lesser form of life.'

I stared at her, dismayed. 'Is that how you feel here? I didn't know . . .'

'A less evolved lifeform,' she conceded. 'It's how I felt when the Invidi came. One of the reasons I joined the project. I knew that they meant us well, but I couldn't forgive them for taking over our future.' She said the 'our' possessively, hungrily.

'So you wanted to get away?'

She nodded.

'What were the other reasons?

She took a long time to answer. 'I couldn't stand it.'

'Couldn't stand what?'

'Everything.' She pulled savagely at her overall hem. 'The . . . the world as it was. Feeling like I felt all the time.'

'How did you feel?' I said softly.

'Like watching a glass fall off a table on the other side of the room.' She shook her head as though the words were wrong but continued anyway. 'You can see it start to fall. You know it's about to shatter. And you can't do a damn thing to stop it.'

I shivered and pulled my sodden jacket closer. I knew exactly how she felt.

I left Rachel at the hospital entry in Gamma and continued on in the uplift. Her words had rekindled my curiosity about their arrival and what might be different about their ship.

The loose items we'd collected might contain a clue.

Exhausted though I was, I knew I wouldn't sleep properly until I'd checked them personally. I could have taken Rachel with me – there was no reason she shouldn't see the objects – but it would have been inappropriate, somehow. To me, the salvage was a collection of curiosities that might or might not yield treasure. I might equally dismiss it as junk. To her, they were objects hallowed by familiarity and their connection with the dead.

There is close to zero gravity in the centre. We do have the option of using the Invidi gravity field, but no engineer likes using something they don't understand, even when it works so well. The field came with the engines, so to speak, and I think it had something to do with the way the Confederacy defeated the Tor, but they don't tell we junior members such details. It allows us to use the micro-g areas to best advantage and keep partial gravity for the people who supervise the work done in the centre. But I still don't like it.

In the uplift the gravity diminished gradually and with it my stomach's reliability. I hooked my arms over one rail and toes under another and stared out of the window.

'Below', the curve of the habitat rings fell away in a gleaming arc, the shine of the reflector panels marred in dull patches where repairs were incomplete. I stared at the blazing stars in an uneasy reverie until the lift jolted to a halt. If I shut my eyes I end up not knowing which direction is which.

I headed across the centre to the storage bay, kicking

off first then steadying myself on the handrail. The corridors are narrower here, with low, padded ceilings. No attempt has been made to create an environment that would shelter the occupant from claustrophobia or solipsism – the corridor is no more than a simple channel from A to B, or in this case from the small freight elevators to the storage bays. The walls are unpanelled, unlike those of the habitat corridors. Different-coloured cables and heavy plasma conduits like ridged hoses snake naked along the walls beside me, interrupted by irregularly spaced breakers and control panels. When motion sensors flick on the light it is bright and harsh on the eyes – no discreet backlights or second-hand sunshine here.

Something touched the very edge of my vision. I twirled myself around with a hand on the wall to look behind me. Nothing there. Stop imagining things. You're too tired to be up here if you're seeing things. Security had cleared the area when the rescue operation docked this afternoon. The section was more or less deserted anyway. Before the Seouras came there would have been a work shift moving around even at this hour, but not any more.

I pulled myself along a bit further then drifted without touching the rail. Someone was here. This time it was a sound on the edge of hearing. I somersaulted gently ninety degrees and looked behind again – nothing. Teppits, maybe. Teppits used to be found only in the lower levels, but lately they were everywhere. They probably didn't mind even micro-gravity. There are several theories to explain why these small creatures are found throughout the inhabited galaxy. Like most humans, I tend to keep quiet about their resemblance to Terran cockroaches. Some contributions to galactic culture are best left unsung.

I cleared my throat. 'Hello?'

My senses might have been scrambled by fatigue and tension, but the sensation of being watched was unmistakable. There was something else in this corridor and it wasn't human. I thought uneasily of smugglers and substance dealers and bombs in my office. Better keep going. I shouldn't have assumed Murdoch would have someone up here. The Sleepers' ship was out at the platform, Keveth's ship and the shuttle back in their docks. Why bother to leave a guard on a storage bay full of radioactive junk?

It's impossible to walk backwards in micro-g, so I proceeded in a series of slow and clumsy somersaults from floor to ceiling and back again, and by the time I reached the next corner, I was giggling. Good thing Baudin didn't see that.

The light activated obediently as I kicked around the corner. Storage bay Sigma 41 should be the one in the middle. The one with the door open a crack.

The one with the door open?

I grabbed the railing to stop myself and tapped open my comm link.

'Halley to Security.'

'Sasaki here.'

'Are you monitoring the Sigma storage bay where we stored the Sleeper ship equipment?'

'We're having a bit of trouble with that, ma'am. Sergeant Kwon's on his way up now.' Sasaki is

Murdoch's second-in-command. She is too well trained to ask a superior officer what the hell she was doing, but the query was in her voice.

'Thanks. I'll wait for him, then.' I closed the link and stared at the narrow, dark space where the door should have been sealed. Security personnel could open it, as well as anyone else with a level five or above clearance, but if the lock had been touched Security should have been alerted.

Kwon's taking his time.

I drifted cautiously closer to the door. Paranoid. Maybe Eleanor was right. It was probably simply a malfunction, hardly surprising on this station.

There was no movement inside. I did feel stupid, hanging there staring at a door. I spun right side up and checked the control panel visually. The problem was immediately obvious. The lock command had not been input properly. It was a wonder the last person out hadn't noticed.

I waved my arm next to the door's movement sensors and it opened with a swish.

A shock of freezing air. I kicked off the floor to go in. Might as well look. There didn't seem to be a problem other than someone's carelessness. The light activated and I was looking at rain.

Tiny blue drops, some formed into globules, scattered all over the small room. Liquid does that, left to itself without gravity. But there's no rain on a space station. Something else floated, mainly in the middle, what looked like broken pieces of thin shell trailing glutinous lumps and long strings of . . .

I flailed backwards as my brain finally processed what it was seeing. A body, not human, and very dead.

Something touched me and I bit off a scream.

'Oh my god,' said Sergeant Kwon.

Murdoch hung onto the wall-rail, talking to a medtech. Two other white-suited and helmeted figures stood normally in the middle of the bay, which meant they wore magnetic boots. The air still had a bluish tinge, although they'd collected all the droplets.

I kept shivering in the cold, and wished Murdoch would hurry up and give his report so I could go and be sick again. Tiers of containers bobbed against the far wall, kept in place by softmetal gridlines like greasy, malleable rope. Normally gridlines wouldn't be necessary in a null-gravity area, but in our case there was always a risk of the Invidi gravity field engaging at an inopportune moment and the lines were there as a safety precaution. Against the near wall another container bobbed, this one marked with a radioactivity warning seal. The salvage from *Calypso*.

Murdoch finally swung around and pushed himself over to where I hung by the door.

'K'Cher. We're checking who it was. Must have been in the last hour or so.' He was furious – the blaze of emotion exposed his usual off-handedness for the thin veneer it was.

'They say,' he jerked his chin at the medtechs, 'that it was decapitated and cut open with a large, sharp weapon. A thin, curved blade, not laser. There's no sign of cauterisation. They're running a metals residue analysis now.'

There were species in the known galaxy who wore their knives in their sleeves, so to speak, on the ends of limbs or in toothed tentacles or even in the lash of telekinetic ability. As far as I knew, though, none of these species were on Jocasta, and none of the other inhabitants of the station seemed likely candidates for such a flamboyant xenocide.

Apart from the containers the bay was empty. Conduit and junction boxes jutting from the walls offered little concealment and there was no room between the stacked containers. It wasn't a large room – none of our rooms are large. Surely the victim could have seen an attack coming? Unless . . . I looked up into the untidy maze of conduits, hookways, control boxes and mag lines that covered the ceiling of the bay nearly a metre deep beyond the long illumination rails that hung just above our heads. There was a kind of catwalk up there too, useful to cling to when the lower spaces were busy with loading machinery.

Murdoch followed my gaze. 'Yeah, that was my guess too.'

Blood had stuck to the light. That implied considerable momentum – it must have sprayed wildly. I looked away, half gagging again. A broken cable waved from one of the catwalks and small pieces of unidentified metal and plastic, the debris of heavy work, littered the bay. A broken lunchbox hung forlornly against the back wall.

Why do this? There weren't more than half a dozen K'Cher traders remaining on Jocasta. Two of them are members of the main 'family' of the K'Cher aristocracy and have remained cloistered in their spacious quarters since the Seouras arrived. Two more are middlemen for station administration's purchase of nearly everything and are probably the only traders on the station who still make a profit. There was Keveth, the lone wolf, and the remaining one was the unfortunate captive of a debilitating addiction to certain illegal substances. 'Which one of them do you think it was?'

'I dunno. We'll know in a tic.'

I shivered again.

'D'you want to wait outside?' Murdoch's gaze returned from wherever his thoughts had taken him.

'No.'

'And there's that.' Murdoch pointed at the container that held the *Calypso* salvage.

'What about it?'

'Someone's tried to force the opening. Not very well either.'

That made no sense. 'There's nothing valuable in there.'

'Souvenir hunter?'

'Or the murderer.'

There was a short silence. Voices crackled from the open comm link. Murdoch's eyes kept moving over the bay. Security would have scanned it for lifesigns before entering and he wouldn't have let me in if there were any danger, so it must have been an automatic reaction, a policeman's reflex to keep observing while the scene was relatively undisturbed. His hand weapon was charged and the holster cover open.

'One more thing.'

I looked at him warily. I hate the way he always leaves the worst news until last.

He detached a flat security scanner from his belt and activated the little screen. The scanner can record electronic and visual data and perform basic chemical analyses. All Security personnel carry them. 'When we examined the door lock . . .'

'It wasn't shut properly, I know. Why wasn't that picked up by your surveillance systems?'

'Normally it would be. But we found this.' He held the scanner out to me. On the screen was an electronic map of the door's circuitry and something else, a small loop device by the look of it, that sent the alarm signal back on itself rather than to the security network.

'What is it?'

'Hard to say.' Murdoch took the scanner out of my hand without asking. I resisted the temptation to tug it back. 'It's gone now.'

'Gone? Someone took it?'

'Nope. There's been a guard on the door the whole time.'

'So what do you mean, "gone"?' I could hear my voice rise in frustration on the last question. What does he expect? It's two o'clock in the morning, we're floating in a zero-g midden, and I haven't had a proper sleep in three days. I should just have gone to my quarters. Behind us, scrape, snip, squelch. One of the medics laughed.

Murdoch hooked his boot under the lower railing and used both hands to tap out his information again. Either he hadn't noticed my bad humour or didn't think it worth acknowledgment. 'It sort of melted away. I think we're looking at some very advanced shit here. And I ask myself, who on this station has access to stuff like this?'

'Nobody. Unless ... someone found a way to bypass the blockade.'

Murdoch looked at me with a strange expression, his eyes hooded. 'Yeah. But look at the energy signature.' He passed me the scanner again.

I stared at the screen, frowning as the image blurred in time with my shivering. 'Invidi?'

'Looks like it.'

This was totally unexpected. Nobody except the Invidi themselves has Invidi technology. They don't share more than a fraction of it with the rest of the Confederacy. Humans don't understand it, and everything they've given us over the years has turned out to be actually from other species and civilisations closer to our own. While I stared, dazed, Murdoch's comm link chirped. He listened, then turned to me.

'Looks like it's Keveth. All the others are in their quarters.'

'Oh, hell.' Unlikable as Keveth had been, it had provided a link between the K'Cher and the rest of us 'minor' species. And it had lived on my station, under my protection.

'We'll look into Keveth's movements after it got back from the salvage operation.' Murdoch reached for his scanner, but I was still looking at it. 'There's only a couple of hours to fill in, shouldn't take long.'

'Keveth volunteered to help with the rescue. Perhaps it saw something then and offered to show someone.'

'I thought the *Queen* going out was suspicious.'

'Maybe Keveth tried to open the salvage. Were there any K'Cher traces on the container?'

'Haven't found any so far. Keveth had a lot of dicey contacts and some of them might be prepared to pay for old Earth curios. We'll interview 'em all if necessary.' He sighed and stretched. 'I get the feeling we're going to be doing a lot of footwork on this one.'

'Murdoch, why wasn't the bay monitored by Security?' The whole station is supposed to be accessible to surveillance, with limits on its use in the residential quarters.

Murdoch's face darkened at the implied criticism, justified though we both knew it was. 'I don't know. We have a record up to about midnight.'

'That's over an hour before I got here.'

'I know, but we're bloody shorthanded at the moment, what with the festival and all. Sasaki sent Kwon up to have a look – that's why he got there just after you did.' When I said nothing, 'Well, I didn't think anyone would be interested in a load of radioactive parts a century out of date.'

I sighed. 'Neither did I.' There was another possibility to consider. 'Do you think it's got something to do with the latest anti–Four Worlds feeling? There's been a lot of unrest the past few weeks.'

His wandering attention fixed on me with almost embarrassing intensity. 'Have you had any more trouble?'

'What, like my other office being blown up?'

He glared, and I regretted the sarcasm. 'Sorry. Could a human have done it?'

Murdoch accepted the apology. 'Nah. The angle of swing is too high and wide. They'd have to be three metres tall with arms to match.'

'Maybe the murderer wanted the body found like this, which is why they didn't use an energy weapon.'

'Or they didn't care. And where does this Invidi lock-breaker fit in?'

He reached for his scanner but I shook my head.

'Uh-uh. I'll need this when I talk to An Barik.'

'Sooner you than me,' said Murdoch, satisfied. He can't cope with Invidi. 'Want to watch while we turn the gravity on?'

'No, thank you.' I managed to wait until I got outside before being sick again.

Second day, 3 am

The ringlift took me close to the entrance to the Smoke, the section of Delta ring set aside for non-oxygen breathers, its unofficial title from a K'Cher epithet for the Invidi.

I'd decided not to call Quartermaine. It was too late, and the only thing I wanted from An Barik was for him to confirm that the lockbreaker Murdoch had found was Invidi technology, and whether it was his or not. I knew the Invidi did not keep the same diurnal rhythm as we did and could therefore be approached at any hour. Besides, I was a little sick of always having Brin as a buffer between the Invidi and myself. Sometimes it even seemed as if the alien was hiding behind Quartermaine.

I walked along the darkened passages of the Hill with increasing unease. Only a couple to go before the Smoke entrance. The lights were off almost completely. Someone must have bled too much off the mains. It was quiet now. I could hear only the occasional rumble of conversation from doorways, and a few dark figures passed silently. A loud curse nearby was accompanied by a clatter of falling metal. I was sweating. Images of Keveth's scattered body parts rose unbidden and unwanted in my mind. The darkness that had concealed the grime earlier now held more sinister possibilities.

I finally reached the main airlock. The buzzer sounded and two warning lights went off. There is another light that humans cannot distinguish. We have seven different species on the station who do not breathe the same atmospheric mix as humans, so supplying their needs makes environmental control extremely complicated. In an emergency we have to be able to shut off this section separately, for their protection and our own.

I wore a mask, as regulations demand, though I can pass through without one, thanks to the breathing device the Seouras implanted in my neck at our first meeting. It was not a long operation and involved no pain, but Jago thinks the organic technology they used allows the device to 'grow' into the recipient's body. It didn't hurt when the original Seouras used it to communicate, unlike our present invaders, who may be creating the pain deliberately, or perhaps they're just not as proficient at communicating. Our doctors say they can't remove the implant while it's active, so it stays in the hollow above my collarbone, a raised starfish shape under the skin.

It was a strange and frightening sensation to stand in the Smoke surrounded by poisonous gases and yet remain untouched. The first human divers to use portable gills in Earth's oceans must have felt this way.

The main corridors of the Smoke keep an atmospheric mix that four out of the seven species find bearable. There is a thriving subculture in here, with bazaars, entertainment, and eateries, although most of the humans find it all too alien to visit regularly.

The corridors beyond the airlock seemed shrouded in fog until I put on the mask, which filtered out some of the shadows. Most of the doors were shut, some of them with double and triple airlocks to contain particular atmospheres. As I walked to An Barik's door a Tell rolled around the corner from the opposite direction. It stopped immediately and I felt somewhere, somehow, the feather-light touch of its mind as it confirmed my identity. I smiled and walked on past. I can't help smiling at Tell. I like them immensely. They are perambulatory balls of blueish fuzz, with no apparent features or other distinguishing characteristics. They do nothing to or for anyone and never, ever complain about anything. What station commander wouldn't like such residents?

I paused outside An Barik's room. I hadn't encountered him (they say it's the correct pronoun – the only pronoun) in a while. Invidi are always willing to talk, but they rarely answer a question in the way you expect. They also seem terribly interested in the unsaid.

I often get the feeling with the Invidi that they are filing their observations away into a great pool of information about humans. Despite their being the first aliens we encountered, they know a lot more about us than we do of them. Perhaps it is due to environmental barriers – we usually only see them when they wear breathing apparatus for our atmosphere. That is one of the reasons I try to meet with An Barik in his own surroundings. Certainly it puts me at a physiological disadvantage, but it does let me do some observing of my own.

The door opened. The room was large, to match its owner, and the air seemed clearer than outside. It was gloomy to human eyes, and I switched on the infrared filter in the mask. The tall, hooded figure of An Barik stood in the centre of the room, silhouetted against weak lime-green light from a brazier against the far wall. A line of poetry rose unbidden from childhood readings:

O sages standing in God's holy fire /As in the gold mosaic of a wall . . .

'Good peace.' I didn't worry about greeting gestures, as I didn't have enough arms to do it properly. 'I trust you are in health, Master?'

An Barik stood quite still too. 'Governor Halley. The one is honoured by your concern. And of the title "Master" unworthy.' His voice echoed from the translation device concealed somewhere on his person.

I'm never sure how far to extend the greeting stage. When he switches to more colloquial language it's usually the sign that we might discuss specifics, but it can take hours to reach this point, depending on his mood.

'It is I who am unworthy of speaking to the Master. But I would be grateful for the opportunity to do so.'

An Barik made a remarkably expressive snorting sound and turned slowly.

'Humans make problems with time. You should let it use you more gently. Remember, "time is the bone of the soul".' He glided backwards as he spoke. Invidi have a caterpillar-like method of propulsion on the underside of their tall, knobbly bodies. It is ironic that the first sentient alien species to visit Earth and the most benign of our visitors should have looked like all our fears and nightmares of invaders rolled into one. They have no distinct head or face and long, prehensile tentacles, glistening greenish skin, wrinkled and bubbly in places like a toad. They must have seemed terrifying at first, even wearing their body suits, which had snaking cable-like protuberances and metallic drapes.

I followed An Barik to the lighted area around the cere-monial brazier. There were a couple of stool-like fittings that he kept in concession to weaker races' need to sit.

'How may the one be of service?'

Well. He was coming quickly to the point today.

'Thank you.' I did not sit, disliking the physical and psychological discomfort of looking up. 'Early this morning there was a murder in the centre storage bays.'

An Barik's smaller tentacles twitched rapidly in consternation, and even the larger ones swayed restlessly. 'Condolences.'

He used this expression to honour our customs. We don't know how the Invidi feel about death and/or an afterlife. They are a secretive people and we know nothing of their customs regarding the dead – how they treat the body: burial, cremation, abandonment, con-sumption, assimilation ... possibilities as many as there are species. For that matter, what were we to do with Keveth's remains? The K'Cher have elaborate rituals for those which die before Changing, but I had no idea what the process involved. And Murdoch wouldn't want to release the body until his investigation was complete.

'Accepted with thanks. It was one of the K'Cher traders – Keveth. Did you know the individual?'

'Not known.'

'The body was found in a bay that should have been locked. We don't know what Keveth was doing there but security scans of the bay revealed a small device that could have disrupted the door signal. That device had an Invidi energy signature.'

'May the one observe?'

'I'm afraid not. It disappeared.'

'Unfortunate.'

'Very. But that is a characteristic of certain Invidi technologies, is it not?'

Two of his smaller tentacles twisted around each other in a gesture irresistibly reminiscent of hand-wringing, and rows of spots down the side of his body seemed darker. I knew enough of Invidi physiognomy to realise An Barik was upset, but not whether it was distress at the news or something else.

'Was it yours?' No human ego to bruise here, although I could have used more formal language.

'The one cannot answer that question.'

'Why not?'

'Does not see device in question and therefore the answer is unknown.'

I pulled out the security scanner and isolated the energy signature readings for him. 'You may be able to tell from this. Was it yours?'

As I held out the scanner one of his smaller, thinner tentacles snaked over and caressed it. Close up, the tentacle was a soft green, the underside covered with a fuzz of tiny hair-like projections. I watched, fascinated. How does he 'see'? Does he absorb energy directly into his body and distinguish the tiny electromagnetic fluctuations? What if he touches me?

I didn't think An Barik was involved. He has been on the station for over two years now. Unlike the previous 'observer', a K'Cher which used to take every possible opportunity to retreat to the civilisation of the inner sector, An Barik has not been off Jocasta since he arrived.

He appears dutifully at official functions but otherwise keeps quietly to his quarters. It was possible that someone had stolen something from here – I'd have to speak to Quartermaine about security. Strictly speaking, Quartermaine should have been here with me to talk to An Barik.

The tentacle retreated and the voicebox made a sound like an embarrassed cough. 'The one knows not.' He swayed back slightly from me.

He was lying. I knew it as surely as I stood on the hard deck.

I'd asked Quartermaine once how he understood so much non-verbalised language, both with the Invidi and his fellow humans, and he'd laughed at me. 'You do it yourself, m'dear.' Then, at my puzzlement. 'Gut, just gut. Disengage that analytic brain for a bit and you'll be surprised what the universe shows you.'

That an Invidi could lie to me was inconceivable. I trust them more than I trust most humans. Maybe my gut was wrong, but I could hear the sound of a paradigm shattering. We don't know how they think. We can't know how they feel. All we have is a set of case studies, a collection of examples. With each addition, the paradigm shifts. Without a shared perception of the world we cannot say Invidi will act in such-and-such a way. All we can do is admit that, up until now, we have seen most Invidi do so-and-so. But if An Barik was capable of lying, what else might he be capable of?

The silence lengthened as I stood there like an idiot. What could I say? Sorry, but I think you're a liar? Maybe they don't have the concept of lying. An insidious little voice whispered, what does it matter? He's given you the perfect way out. Murdoch will worry about it for a while but then the whole thing will be put aside. It was only some maverick trader anyway, you've got more important business to worry about . . .

'Are you sure? Have you perhaps had anything stolen recently?' Sometimes I listen to the little voice, sometimes not.

'Not stolen.'

'Do you have any explanation then?' I persisted.

He swayed again. 'We stand at a . . . node of extreme flexibility.'

'A "node"?' The interpretation chip had, unusually, hesitated over the word. The effect was like a static blip, immediately distinguishable from a hiatus in normal conversation.

The tentacles shivered. 'The expression is unclear?' he said at last. 'Concept is familiar to your species.' The simulated voice managed to convey a touch of reproach.

'I understand the word to mean the point at or from which an unspecified number of paths diverge . . . Master, please remember that my temporal perception is linear and limited.'

'Yes. The one attempts to restrict explanation.'

The Invidi, as far as we can tell, have the ability to see in time much as we see in space. They can walk freely on the road that we call the future, although their view is limited by the horizons of possibility and blocked by the obstacles of choice. How they see what we call the past and whether it is differentiated from the rest of time, nobody knows. Nor is it clear how they relate space and time. They regard us as we might regard someone who proceeds through the universe able to see only the ground one step ahead of her on a single plane – with pity, concern, and a certain amount of irritation.

'There are a great many possible continuings in this area,' he explained patiently. 'The one cannot quickly discern the brightest one.'

I rubbed at the implant in my neck, fingers unconsciously tracing the familiar shape. 'Are you saying we're heading for a crisis soon?'

'Soon?'

He didn't need a semantic explanation – he wanted to know the specific content of the word. I cursed myself for using a temporal expression, and a vague one at that.

'I refer to a period extending from this particular moment to and including an unspecified one along our entropic line that corresponds to approximately fifty-five planetary rotations.'

'That is acceptable. Not soon.'

So we were all right for a month or so. He didn't deny the 'crisis' bit. Not for the first time I wondered why An Barik hadn't warned us about the Seouras, or at least got himself out of the way before they came. He had asked us to shelter him, to keep his existence a secret from them, in case they proved to have an appetite for Invidi technology. I'd suffered for that secret, and others might yet.

'Is this "node" connected to Keveth's death?' I tried to bring him back to our present.

He didn't answer, but ran one of his smaller tentacles up and down the same spot on his torso, like me rubbing my neck. He'd lied about the device, true, but there might be other questions involved here – security, cultural taboos, lack of preparation. I got the impression that he genuinely could not understand the urgency of my questions. I needed to talk to the liaison officer about this. Brin always said, 'First blame the translation program. Then check your hardware, clarify your own interpretation, and be positive you both have the same information. Then, and only then, dare you begin to suspect irreconcilable cultural differences.'

'I'll talk to you again later, perhaps', I said to An Barik. 'If you have no objection?'

'Later?'

'Unspecified,' I amended hastily. 'Period extending from this moment into unspecified future, probability of within one diurnal unit.'

'Acceptable.'

There was one more thing. We could tell this from the sensor logs but Murdoch would ask and I might as well spare him the trouble. 'Master Barik, were you in your quarters the past twelve cycles station time?' Did he realise what I was implying?

'The one remains in same space. Movement limited.' Yes, I was the one who had cautioned him to stay within the most heavily shielded parts of the station to prevent the Seouras picking up his lifesigns if they scanned us.

'Thank you. Your leave.'

The tall, irregular silhouette watched me go without further comment.

I hadn't handled that conversation very well. My head felt as though it was stuffed with slime. And dammit, I forgot to ask An Barik about the Sleepers getting help from the Invidi all those years ago. I'll just wait for Brin to tell me tomorrow.

By the time I reached my quarters I was asleep on my feet. The lights failed to come on and I knocked something off the table but didn't care. Blue light made the bed look deep and inviting. Marlena Alvarez's face accused me from the photoimage – what are you going to do?

I grumbled to myself and tipped the frame over so she couldn't see me. I will get us out of this. But not tonight.

The quilt smelled of slime as I sank into it and oblivion.

There's a metallic taste on my tongue. Blood. My face is ground down with brutal force as they hold my arms. I can't move, a hard weight on my back. Oh god, help me ... One of them grabs a handful of hair and shoves my head forward into the slime. The stuff is in my eyes, nose, mouth, I can't breathe. It's going into my lungs, I'm drowning ... impossibly sobbing at the same time, screaming, enough enough enough ... I try and twist around to see who it is. I can almost see his face but it begins to disintegrate, eaten from within by a twisting, writhing movement that breaks into countless tiny wriggling shapes. Shapes that grow larger into long feelers, tentacles that snake along my bare legs with a cold smooth touch of horror.

No, this is wrong – they don't touch me, they never touch me. Leave me alone ...

Help us. Stay away. Come. The voices conflict, clash inside my head until I can't hear anything else.

'Oh shit.' I curled up on my stomach and cried into the sheets that were already wet with sweat. 'Only a dream, only a dream.' Too many dreams lately. What if Eleanor's right and I am going mad? Maybe it is the implant. But they've never 'talked' at this distance before.

I scratched uselessly at my neck. Wish I could get rid of this thing.

I loathe it when they're in me, even though I remind myself this is the only way they can communicate and it's better than having them blow up the station out of frustration or pique. They told me I must come when called and I do. It isn't telepathy – there's no emotional link at all. I don't feel an actual presence but I know they are there, more than one of them. It's like walking through a familiar room in the dark and putting your hand on something you know shouldn't be there. The worst of it is not the pain, it's the fact that they don't communicate anything. Are they learning about us? If so, they're certainly taking their time.

I slipped into an exhausted doze back to the flat plain under a sky low enough to touch. I reach up and familiar viscosity licks at my fingers. Slime underfoot gives off a greenish luminescence that rises to fill the world with a sweet, sour, acrid smell. It is so familiar now, I wear the odour like a second skin. What do they want from us?

'Halley.'

What am I going to do about them?

'Murdoch to Halley.'

How could Murdoch be calling me in the Seouras section? Communications are jammed. Unless he's here too. I moved my arm through viscous air and hit something with a sharp crack. Station wall. Wake up.

'Halley here. What is it?' My heart was pounding so loud and fast that I thought he'd hear it through the link.

To my horror, the visual component of the wall comm unit flickered into life. It hasn't worked properly, to my knowledge, since I moved up here. Murdoch's face blinked at me.

'We need to . . .' He raised his eyebrows.

'Visual off,' I snarled at the interface and pushed the

manual cutoff too. Blast the man, it's not as if I'm naked or anything. Merely a thin singlet and a face full of sleep.

'We need to talk about last night.' His voice was amused. 'Can you come now?'

'Now?' The events of the previous day and night came crashing down into the forefront of my memory in a tangled cacophony. The jump mine, cryostasis travellers from Earth in a ship that couldn't have got here, Seouras, Keveth's blood like rain . . .

'Yeah, I got a couple of minutes before we start the day down here. How about you?'

I rolled out of bed, stumbling over the thermasheet. Coffee. I have to get a coffee subroutine in my kitchen.

'Where?'

'How about breakfast? Main messhall.'

'Right.'

I rummaged through the mess on the floor to find the uniform I'd tossed away before crawling into bed, pulled at my hair ineffectually with a comb, fastened the same shirt, closed the jacket and cinched the belt tighter. Jago is right – I can't afford to lose any more weight.

I squeezed into the shower alcove, held my face in the airwash for a long minute, and groaned at the puffy eyes in the mirror. Sometimes I feel I inhabit a strange, stretched state in which each day runs into the next, in which there is no break between the end of yesterday's work and the beginning of today's. My real self is shut up in a tight little box somewhere near the top of my head and I've gradually learnt to leave her alone. In the end I forget about her. But somewhere, a feeling that there's a gap – a breach where something ought to exist but doesn't.

It was going to be a long day.

The main Alpha messhall below the Bubble was three-quarters empty, which suited me. The command crew has four shifts and the other departments three, both sets staggered to begin at 0900. At this hour the mess should have been full of first- and third-shift diners, but it seems that more and more people are eating elsewhere. The few here were all human, mostly in EarthFleet uniform, some reading tabletop screens, others chatting or chewing into space as they endured whatever was on special.

One wall was taken up by serving hatches and the others boasted holo-pictures designed to give the illusion of space – calming seascapes, wind-blown meadows, tree-lined streets, that sort of thing. The pictures were stuck as usual, and one was down completely. Personally, I thought the grey wall studded with tiny emitter relays was far more restful.

I weaved between the lines of long tables and stood at one of the serving hatches. Three Customs officers seated at a nearby table whispered obviously and one of them laughed. I receive more open hostility from crew members, surprisingly, than from residents. Many residents came to Jocasta from such appalling situations that the Seouras blockade must seem like a minor inconvenience. The crew, on the other hand, are divided clearly on the question of surrender. I'd like to think the majority agree that it was the only way to preserve the station, but at times like these it seems doubtful. I used to sit with whoever was in the mess, but lately it's been too much like a gamble with the odds stacked against me.

I fished my ration card out of an inner pocket and pushed it into the machine. Not many choices lit up. The mess menu was an orthodox blend of representative human dishes and a basic selection of alien fare, all clearly labelled and colour-coded for taste, digestibility and so on. If you ordered a dish unsuitable for human physiology – nothing on the menu was poisonous, but some selections could make you quite sick – an audio warning clicked on automatically, accompanied by flashing lights. This annoyed Veatch and a couple of other aliens on the staff, but most of the officers were human so the warning stayed.

I pushed the numbers for fruit salad, coffee, and churros. We'd tried voice commands but the hubbub of conversation from the queue – mostly conversation about food – had been too confusing for the interface. I mentally timed the food being brought out of its storage containers, placed on a tray, and shunted back to the hatch, but the tray lurched out of the serving hatch sooner than I expected. I grabbed it as the movement of the conveyor slopped coffee onto thin slices of batter and a small, round fruit. Obviously the morning's supply of fruit salad was finished.

Further away in the room a voice rose with an edge to it, '. . . coming in here! What a hide, huh?' Shushing noises followed.

I turned around, tray in hand, and the noise level

dropped suddenly. One of the Customs officers deliberately shifted her chair as I walked past. I sat at a far table and took a sip of lukewarm coffee, though it might have been tea.

I put aside the question of An Barik's possible lie until I could talk with Brin Quartermaine. He would enlighten me about Invidi concepts. I hoped he had asked An Barik about the Sleepers and Invidi activities around the time of the First Contact. I washed down a tasteless, doughy mouthful with tasteless liquid and hoped my stomach could take the punishment. I doubt any of the human staff have reservations about alien food now – not if this is the alternative. Officially the fresh food supplies we produce onstation go to the hospital and shelters, but a small, significant percentage ends up in the restaurants and markets in the Hill and lower Gamma. The messhall makes do with recycled concoctions and the ever-dwindling stocks left over from before the blockade.

Another tray slid onto the table with a crash that made me jump.

'That's all you're having? No wonder you're so skinny.' Murdoch squeezed his bulk into the chair. His tray held a plate of greyish, greasy mess that smelled so strongly of curry that even my slime-sodden sinuses could tell. Also an enormous pile of batter slices and a jug of reconstituted juice.

I looked away from the tray quickly and let the personal comment pass. 'After last night's little episode I'm doing well to stomach anything.'

'Ach,' he waved a hand in dismissal of such frailties.

'It gets to you at the time, but you put it out of your mind afterwards.'

'It's not my mind that's the problem.' I tried to peel the fruit. The tough, purplish skin refused to come away in one neat piece and had to be scraped off with what I call my fingernails.

Murdoch drank a deep draught of the juice and shuddered slightly. It was probably made from this same underripe fruit that had been in stasis for months.

'So,' he said, mouth full of dough, 'what do you think?'

'Either Keveth opened the door or someone else did. The idea of Keveth getting its feelers on Invidi lockpicks is so far-fetched I'm assuming the latter. An Barik says it wasn't his, by the way.'

He made a short exclamation of interest through the mouthful, drew a filepad from his jacket and laid it on the table. He made an entry on it with one hand and poured the rest of his juice with the other.

I popped a pale green segment of fruit into my mouth. It was sour and bitter at the same time. 'Well?'

'We got two distinct DNA traces, both confirmed. At least, one ID'd as Keveth. The other – it's human, by the way – we haven't got a match for yet.'

'Why?'

'Medical says no record.'

Which meant someone who entered the station without going through immigration procedures and who has had no medical treatment, and no employment or criminal record. Murdoch would have made sure it wasn't one of the records we'd lost in the Seouras attack either.

He demolished the last batter slices. 'Nothing from

Keveth's contacts so far, but we did find someone who saw Keveth coming out of Trillith's place in Alpha yesterday afternoon at about two o'clock.'

A couple of hours after the rescue operation concluded.

'Could it have been working for Trillith?'

Murdoch tapped the table in disgust. 'If it was, we'll have a hell of a time tracing anything.'

He read the information on the screen then pushed it over to me while he finished the curry. 'Keveth's been here on and off for more than three years now. That's longer than the K'Cher usually stay anywhere.'

I skimmed through the information. Keveth had been charged several times with minor offences, all Customs in-fringements. Two illegal substances, four non-declaration of taxable goods, and one late docking fee. It had paid all fines up front even though the attached financial records showed its business to be in debt. A couple of times it had been up before the bankruptcy court. Someone had bailed it out each time, although the record didn't mention who.

'It doesn't seem likely that Keveth would deal with the other K'Cher.' It had quarrelled publicly with them and made its opinion of any sort of authority quite obvious.

Murdoch grunted. 'The K'Cher have their black sheep too, eh?' Even aliens send their misfits to Jocasta. 'All we can do is wait and see if we get a positive ID from the lab on that human DNA. And the weapon. Then it won't matter who Keveth's connections are.' Murdoch had recovered his poise, and with good cause. He could arrest the K'Cher onstation and their powerful aristocracy couldn't do a thing about it, thanks to the Seouras blockade.

'Looks like Trillith was one of the last to see Keveth alive.'

'Yup.' Murdoch took the filepad back and frowned at the screen.

'Keveth volunteered to help with the rescue. Perhaps it saw something then and offered to show someone.'

'I thought the *Queen*'s going out was suspicious.'

'You've got nothing on the weapon?'

He sighed noisily. 'I've got my people doing a quick search while they make their inquiries. We found enough weapons to set up a bloody army. Knives . . . well, take your pick, carving knives, ceremonial knives, paring knives, sharing knives . . . I tell you, we need to go back to square one with our dangerous weapons regulations. It's not even as if they can smuggle them in. But none of them is a forensic match.'

He clicked the filepad shut, pushed his tray aside, and absently activated the tabletop screen – holographics weren't working but we got a reasonably clear flat image. An educational program on responsible waste disposal.

'So what've we got? Keveth and some human were in the storage bay with a load of old building materials . . .' In response to my unspoken query. 'We checked. Nothing of interest, unless Keveth wanted to corner the shower slab trade. And the stuff from the Sleeper ship. The door was open when we got there. It had been opened with an Invidi lockbreaker that then conveniently disintegrated or melted or whatever.' He leaned his elbows on the table and counted the points off on his fingers. He has nice hands, strong, long fingered, well kept. Unlike my own bitten, plasma-stained digits.

'Our resident Invidi says the lockbreaker wasn't his. That's about it for the Invidi connection at the moment.'

'I did ask An Barik where he was last night.'

'And?'

'In his quarters, of course. I suppose you checked the Smoke airlock logs?'

'Yeah, but those things aren't infallible. Where was I?'

'You've got Keveth connected with *Calypso* through the rescue and connected with the K'Cher through Trillith.'

'And the K'Cher mean the Invidi and the Four Worlds.'

'Not necessarily,' I protested. 'The Invidi don't have much to do with K'Cher business.' This seemed like as good a time as any to broach the next subject. 'Bill, is it my imagination, or is the anti-Confederacy feeling growing worse?'

He looked at me warily, as if gauging how much he should say. 'There've been no major incidents. At least, not since that bomb. And the Gamma trade hall thing.'

He meant a protest that had been staged by the Small Businesses Union against the monopoly of storage space by big merchants, notably the K'Cher and their affiliates, despite the fact that no interstellar trade was currently being conducted. They'd wanted the space to establish small-scale manufacturing facilities for immediately useable consumer goods. The protest had turned into a near-riot, thanks to the arrival of a large, intoxicated group of ex–dock workers from the Hill, who began by supporting the Union and ended by attempting to trash the K'Cher warehouses. Murdoch's job had been complicated by the fact that most of the Security personnel clearly supported the dockers and small businesses.

Weeks later we'd finally forced Veatch to complete the new factory legislation to pass to the magistrate, who pushed it through immediately. It had left the few big merchants who remained on Jocasta extremely dissatisfied with the administration.

'No major incidents, no. But plenty of little ones. Graffiti, trouble with the Smoke environmentals. Recycling to Alpha residencies blocked up, that sort of thing. Administration officials being called collaborators.'

Murdoch frowned. 'Who called you that?'

'It doesn't matter who. But what's your feeling about it?'

Murdoch leant back and stared at the tabletop screen. He passed his hand over it and back again, peering at the visuals through splayed fingers. 'You can't blame people,' he said finally. 'Earth's been a member for thirty-six years. They think we deserve better than this.'

'We don't know what's happened out there. The Confederacy might be under attack too.'

He drummed his fingers irritably on the screen, which changed channels obediently. 'You don't really believe that with all that Invidi technology they couldn't get a message through to us? That ConFleet couldn't jump a fleet into the middle of those grey ships and take them out before they knew what hit them? I saw Bendarl ships on suicide runs in the border wars. They'd eat these Seouras for breakfast.'

I was shocked, not by what he'd said but by the fact

that he'd said it. 'Bill, if you feel like this, why haven't you said something to me?'

'Hey, I only mentioned it because you asked what I thought.' He gave me one of his rare wry smiles. 'Besides, what can we do about it? You've got enough on your plate without me whingeing.'

In just two days, two of the people closest to me on the station had revealed their disbelief in the Confederacy's good will. First Quartermaine, now Murdoch. It shook my own faith, and it was also propelling me into panic as I considered what I should do if they were right. And why had they, particularly Murdoch, continued to support my pro-Confederacy stance when they thought we'd been abandoned?

A familiar voice probed the edge of my hearing and Murdoch reached for volume control. At his tap the screen had automatically switched to Dan Florida's alternative channel. Florida was interviewing Rachel Dourif and Hannibal Griffis.

Dressed in hospital gowns and jackets they sat stiffly on the edges of their chairs facing Florida. He sat back with legs crossed casually, urbane in a dark suit, tidier than I'd ever seen him. It was probably about five minutes into the interview, because usually he started by standing to welcome his guests and spent a few minutes on introductions. It must have been conducted yesterday afternoon or last night, after I'd talked to them and while I was over on the grey ship.

'. . . the voyage was illegal?' Florida sounded as unconvinced as I felt.

Griffis waved a hand in dismissal. 'Illegal in the sense

that it didn't have government sanction. But there was no law to prohibit private citizens from leaving the planet if they chose.'

There wouldn't be, not if doing so was impossible. Interplanetary travel was fifty-six years away, well after the formation of the Confederacy.

'We're all interested in how you feel about this incredible experience.' The camera focused on Florida's face. 'Remember,' he spoke directly to his audience, 'these people were asleep for nearly a hundred years. This morning we spoke of the Rip Van Winkle legend in Earth's past and several similar stories in other cultures. Professor, if you could turn back the clock now, would you?'

Murdoch raised his eyebrows at me. I looked around at the other diners – most of them were watching their screens, and I didn't think it was to learn about recycling procedures.

'I don't think we have anything to regret,' said Griffis slowly. 'And I don't think we'll have a lot of trouble fitting in here. It's not as if we came from before First Contact.'

No, they had already made that conceptual leap of recognising that we weren't alone in the universe. Anything after that was a matter of degrees.

I still didn't understand why an Invidi had helped Nguyen and his band of visionaries. Why become involved in what must have seemed a pitiful attempt to reach a star so close that most of our ships use 'half-jump' mode? What profit – now I'm thinking like a

K'Cher – could the Invidi possibly make from such involvement?

Florida asked Rachel and Kloos how they felt. Both of them answered diplomatically that they felt a little at sea, but looked forward to becoming useful members of our society.

'Ah, one last question. You said that Dr Nguyen didn't come with you. Why was that? Surely he wanted to see Centauri?'

'He died,' Griffis said slowly. 'In custody.'

'But ...' The shock on Florida's face did much to reveal the falsity of his Hardened Reporter guise.

I remembered Demora's stories about Las Mujeres – the terror squads, the disappearances, the desperate resistance. It was eminently possible that Nguyen had died in the prison of a repressive government.

The program ended with thank yous to all. Murdoch tilted his chair. 'Kind of makes you want to reread the history files, doesn't it?' He scratched his close curls. 'I didn't think we'd issued a pass to Florida.' Security was still keeping away the crowds of curious residents from the hospital and the Sleepers' room. It was no wonder Rachel had sneaked out in the dark last night.

'I specifically told him he'd have to wait for a story.' I thought Florida would find a way to get to the Sleepers if forbidden to do so. 'It won't satisfy the researchers, but if we get some information on the newsnet, the thrill-seekers might be satisfied and go home.'

Murdoch chuckled. Then he let the chair fall back with a thud.

'Invidi interfered in Earth's affairs a century ago. What

makes you think it's any different now? We don't know what they're thinking, but we do know they have lots of handy gadgets – like the one that opened the storage bay. Why do you think he's being uncooperative?'

'He's always uncooperative. Or it looks that way.' I leaned forward. 'Bill, you don't seriously suspect him, do you?' The idea that an Invidi would deliberately hurt another being was as startling as it was repugnant. I had never seen them even touch anyone. 'Think of the practical problems. People are going to notice a two-metre alien in an atmospheric suit skulking around. And he knew he could be vulnerable to Seouras scanners if he left the Smoke.'

Murdoch's face settled into its customary stubborn mask. 'The only hard evidence we have is a record of Invidi technology. He's the only Invidi on the station. I have to follow up the lead.'

'I know. But consider who you're dealing with.'

'Look, I'm not going to speculate about motive. That's bad enough when it's only humans involved, let alone aliens.'

I thought of my own struggle with Seouras motives. How can we possibly know? And should we not try to know? Quartermaine says we don't need understanding to live together – just guidelines. Understanding comes later.

The problem was, if Murdoch could watch Florida's interview and suspect the Invidi, so could the rest of the station, even if they didn't have our knowledge of the connection with Keveth's murder. Maybe I shouldn't have let Florida do the interview after all. On the other hand, the murder victim was a K'Cher. If it had been a human there might have been trouble, but with any luck people would see it as a Four Worlds problem . . .

'Halley?' Murdoch was leaning over the table frowning at me. 'You with me?'

His expression was serious, which made me even more uncomfortable than the thought that I'd been caught daydreaming.

'I think you should get Dr Jago to look you over. You never used to brood like this.'

'I don't brood.'

'Whatever. You just sort of fade for a minute.'

'I was thinking.' He was starting to annoy me.

'It's been getting worse these past few weeks.' He really doesn't know when to quit. 'Maybe you need a rest.'

'Leave me alone, Murdoch.' The words emerged sharper than I'd intended. A flicker of anger lit his features and he opened his mouth to retort, then shut it again.

'All right. It's all right.' His voice was unexpectedly gentle.

The tone surprised me and I had to look down at the remains of breakfast for a moment before I could return to our immediate problem. 'What's your schedule?'

He stood and flexed his shoulders. The dull green material stretched alarmingly over them. 'We'll search for the weapon, go over the bay again, get onto Keveth's contacts. Talk to Trillith. And I'll get Quartermaine to interview the Invidi with me.'

'I'll tell him. There's something I asked him to do for me yesterday.'

'Whatever you like. Tell him I want to do it this morning. And no rubbish about it being the wrong time.'

Murdoch swaggered out. I sat and stared at the remains of breakfast, trying to recall whether Rip Van Winkle told the people of his new village how he got there.

I needed to talk to Quartermaine. First, about An Barik's reactions to my questions last night on the evidence of the lockbreaker found at Keveth's murder scene. Second, regarding the help that the Invidi had allegedly given the Sleepers so many years ago. Now I had a name to give him – An Serat. Maybe the name had cropped up in Brin's research.

Brin lives in one of the most pleasant areas of the station, the three Gamma sections directly below the agricultural sections of Alpha ring. My quarters are on the edge of the residential areas, in the less desirable corridors near the main trade halls, where offices and bazaars spread out in noisy confusion.

Brin's residency allowance was for somewhere near the Invidi, but he likes comfort and doesn't mind paying extra for it. I stood in front of his door and waited for the sensors to tell him I was there, but there was no answer. Curious. He always kept to a strict morning routine: up at five, breakfast, toilet, prayer, work. Never varies. By my calculations he should be at the peppermint tea stage. I pushed the manual buzzer but there was no response.

'Computer, activate. Bioscan these quarters.' No reaction. Voice interaction is down again. I flipped back the control panel's cover and keyed in my access code. Slow, slow. The poor opsys has a lot on its mind. I wonder which part of the grid has blown this time.

So where was Quartermaine? The interface finally told

me there was no one in his rooms. I walked back down the hall to a public comm panel, called his main office, and got a recorded message. He wasn't in the Linguistics department either – when I rang, a sleepy voice said she'd been there all night and hadn't seen him.

There was one other possibility, but I was loath to use knowledge of his personal life to intrude when it wasn't really an emergency. It could wait, particularly as I had an Engineering meeting now and had promised the Sleepers a tour at 0900.

'Today?' Griffis repeated Eleanor's words and they all stared at us.

'If possible.' The doctor was sympathetic but unrepentant. 'Tomorrow at the latest.'

Kloos stared at the floor and Rachel jiggled her foot so hard that the bed she was leaning on rattled against its monitor.

'What does it matter?' she said. 'It's only a . . .' she waved her hands in a circle. 'A formula for goodbye. Today or tomorrow, it's still goodbye.'

'Yes, but . . .' Griffis sighed and scratched his nose miserably.

Beside him Eleanor clutched her filepads.

'I'm sorry you don't have more time to prepare, but the radiation that the bodies absorbed makes it impossible to keep them in stasis for very long,' I began.

'At all,' Eleanor interrupted, as though it were my fault. 'Anyway, the stasis equipment needs repairs. We reserve it for emergency medical cases. I'm sorry.'

'So I need to ask you,' I continued, 'what arrangements

you'd like made for services and the disposal of the bodies.' The phrases came out smoothly. I've used them too many times in the past months.

Rachel gestured again helplessly. 'You tell them, Hannibal.' She rose and went to stand with Kloos, who had turned his back to us and was staring at the wall holo.

Griffis seemed to stoop more at the words. He took a large, square piece of material like a cleanchif out of his pocket and used it to blow his nose.

'We all knew how dangerous it could be,' he said finally. 'We all signed an agreement that if anything happened to any of us during the flight, the service was to be left to the discretion of any survivors. And our bodies were to be burnt either in atmospheric entry or in the engine boosters.'

'Or whatever else possible,' said Rachel without turning around.

'We generally do the same thing,' I said, relieved. We'd run out of cemetery storage space many months ago, and one of the administration's continuing headaches was the friction this caused with some of the religious groups on the station. 'The bodies of ConFleet and EarthFleet personnel are sent to burn up in the planet's atmosphere. We have a program that lets you watch from here, if you want to.'

Griffis nodded and blew his nose again. There was a dignified silence.

'You can fix up the details of the service with your counsellor.' I knew it sounded as though I was rushing

161

through this, but I couldn't help it. The memory of other funerals crowded the silences.

Rachel turned around. 'Will you come?'

'I, er. If you want me to.'

'We do,' she said firmly. Griffis nodded.

Hell. The last thing I need is another funeral. And what are we going to do with Keveth's body?

I'd thought a short tour might divert them, if not cheer them up, but I was starting to regret the offer. The Engineering meeting about the comet probe had not been encouraging, and I wanted to spend some time looking for mention of *Calypso* in our historical database. Somebody must have seen them during that whole century.

Dan Florida came scrounging for another interview as we left Rehab for the tour. Griffis glanced between Florida and me as we argued the protocol of Florida's accompanying us.

'I find it unusual for a military installation to have a public media, a free press,' he said.

'It's not a military installation, Professor,' I said wearily. 'We have an official news bulletin and ... Mr Florida's venture. Whether he provides a public service or not is a matter of opinion.'

Florida pointed the recording sensor down to cut it off. 'We provide a necessary service.'

'For your own profit,' I reminded him.

'If we didn't tell people what was going on, where would they find out? I don't think you realise how much distrust of the administration there is, Commander.'

'Why distrust?' Griffis asked.

Florida started to explain the dissatisfaction members of the Nine Worlds felt about the Four Worlds' dominance of the Confederacy.

'*Some* people on *some* of the Nine,' I reminded them.

'But you say the Four don't share their jump technology because the Nine can't understand it,' said Griffis.

I was going to agree but Florida got in ahead of me.

'We have to live in the world of the Confederacy, which means we use the technology anyway. To get as far as this station, for example. But we have no control over it,' he said.

I hated this debate, having lost it endless times with my ex-husband. I could never get around the feeling that if we can't understand the jump technology, why should they share it with us?

It was the Sleepers' first walk outside the hospital, or, in Rachel's case, her first daytime walk. Every curve in the walkway, every alien scent had to be exclaimed over and analysed. The main throughway is an open space that continues nearly halfway around the Gamma ring. Ten metres across at its widest point, it once contained most of our better-class shops and the offices of high-profile businesses. Many of the shops bear 'closed' signs now, and some enterprising stall-owners from the Hill have taken advantage of the free rent and grand position to tote their own flimsy wares. To me, its shabbiness is familiar and unremarkable, but as the three humans turned this way and that, their mouths open in amazement, I wondered what they saw.

Was the light too diffuse for them, too far away? Here in Gamma the central throughway was open to reflected light from Abelar, but it was much gentler than the bright glare of sun through atmosphere. The internal reflector panels are nearly three hundred metres away on either side. They reach from halfway up the sides of the ring to the opaque top. From here, they are simply a bright expanse. Buildings rise on both sides of the ring in steep tiers, in some places encrusted on each other and blocking or diverting the throughway. There are recognisably human designs, notably the standard round prefab colony residences like tall beehives, plus a few that could only have originated on other planets. Would Rachel find the jumble oppressive? Had Griffis perhaps expected a streamlined, gleaming vision of humanity's triumph in space?

'It reminds me of somewhere . . .' Rachel's long features pulled into a V of concentration as she glanced around.

'Shanghai,' said Kloos.

'Barcelona,' said Rachel.

'Abidjan,' pronounced Griffis, and the other two agreed.

How little we know about the cities of their time. When I first came to space, in my early years in the corps after completing training on Earth, the closeness had been oppressive. It hadn't occurred to me that the Sleepers might find the crowds and multicultural bustle of Jocasta more familiar than I would have.

'This is like the main street. We call it the Boulevard. On either side are residential areas and business offices. Further along this level are trading halls, where you can rent space to conduct business in private.'

'What about the social structure?' Griffis glanced at my

uniform, then around at the controlled bustle. 'I presume you follow military hierarchy?' he continued uncertainly.

Florida took Griffis by the arm and gestured grandly as they walked. 'It's a bit like a layer cake, Professor. Or like the rings on the station, actually.' He smiled appreciatively and repeated the metaphor to himself. 'At the top of the ring you've got the original ConFleet officers – like our gallant commander here. Then, still up the top but down a bit you've got the administrative staff from Sector Central. Not all of them are human. Like the station manager, Veatch . . . You haven't met him yet?'

Rachel had taken Kloos lightly by the arm, too, and murmured to him. He shook his head and removed his arm from her grip.

'Still in the inner ring but below the Sector Central staff are the EarthFleet staff. Then in the middle ring are us civilians from Earth and the colonies, who came out here to make a living either on the station or from the ships that stopped here. There are some Confederacy traders caught here too, so I guess they should be above us in the middle.'

'Why?' Griffis was overly sensitive to the issue of Earth's minority status.

Florida shrugged. 'That's how it goes.' He continued before either Griffis or I could interrupt. 'In the very outer, lower ring live the small-time traders and family businesses. And at the very bottom are the refugees and illegal entrants. After all,' with a calculating glance in my direction, 'out there on the bottom the reflectors are still unrepaired, it's closer to cosmic rays and most vulnerable to attack . . .'

I wasn't really listening. It had struck me that back in the Confederacy it was humans who lived in the outer ring, so to speak. In the gaps and slums of alien society.

I watched Griffis from behind as we walked. Tall and long-legged, he shambles, with a forward teeter. His stoop is not self-effacing but part of a trademark, an instantly recognisable image, a caricature of himself by himself. He seems arrogant and opinionated yet can charm as well. I like the way he's already managed to tread down the heels of his new sandals and bag the seat of his trousers. The shirt sags unevenly around his waist, weighted by three different types of handcoms he insists on carrying and uses at every opportunity. He seems determined to come to grips with this century – perhaps a little too frantic, as if scared we might throw him back if he doesn't.

Kloos's bristle of short hair and smooth skin have blue highlights in the second-hand sun. He listens to explanations, turns the datapads over in his hands, but it is impossible to tell if he has absorbed any of it.

And Rachel – my first impression of her as reserved and self-assured was changing each time we spoke. As she faced me outside the hospital bed, healthy and upright, it became obvious that she was a person always physically involved. A stocky, taut ball of nervous tension.

The sounds of the Boulevard became more insistent as we moved along. The air was filled with echoes of conversation in a multitude of tongues, overlaid with translations in Standard. Or not, as the case might be.

As this is an Earth base, the translators are officially set on Earth Standard speech, but the more complex Confederacy Standard is nevertheless popular among the big traders. I've been trying to understand Con Standard for over two decades and still can't do much more than pass the time of day.

The Sleepers didn't need to use a translator, but many of their words were only vaguely familiar, echoes of phrases from my childhood, the meaning of which I could guess at but not really understand. They were probably guessing at the meanings of many of our words too, but at least they had the things around them to refer to.

I also found their accents, especially that of Griffis, difficult to catch, and it turned out he felt the same way about mine.

'It's familiar yet unfamiliar.'

I nodded. 'I speak Standard to you and you understand because Standard is close to your old English, but my linguistic background isn't English.'

'What's your mother tongue, then?' asked Florida curiously. If he'd done his background checks properly, he'd have known.

'A mixture of Portuguese, Spanish, German, and native dialects,' I grinned. 'You wouldn't understand a word.' Besides, I do not have an accent. Everybody else does.

There was a moment that amused them for some reason, when Rachel asked me about the station's 'gay' community.

'We're not very happy at the moment, what with the blockade and everything. Still, I think generally people . . .' I began, but stopped as even Griffis snorted with laughter. Rachel couldn't choose between a grin and looking concerned. I glanced at Florida and he shrugged back.

'I'm sorry.' Rachel forced her mouth straight. 'It's an expression we use that means homosexual.'

'Oh.'

She glanced at the others in genuine concern. 'You do understand . . . ?'

'Yes. It's something that's been around for a while,' I replied wryly.

We discussed words that indicate the mores of the society in which they were used, and the fact that human sexuality became a broader issue when seen in the context of the variety of alien solutions. The facts of alien reproductive habits tend to challenge our assumptions about our own. My former husband was H'digh, humanoid but not human, which was about as far afield sexually as I wanted to go. But, I reminded them, I was fairly conservative.

'Was it an important difference in your time?' asked Florida. I was quite happy to let him run with the ball.

Rachel shrugged. 'I guess we were all a bit preoccupied with sex.'

'Sex. You mean the biological differences between human males and females?' Florida was obviously making notes in his head.

'Not necessarily. We often use it to mean the act of copulation. You don't use it in that sense?'

'Not in Standard, no.'

'You don't have a gay community then?' Rachel pressured me with the intensity of her gaze.

'No, I don't think so. Not in the way you mean.' Primitive the station might be, but at least we've left that sort of sexual apartheid behind.

Humans in EarthFleet blue, humans in other clothes. A sprinkling of ConFleet navy. Two Security guards trying to shift one of the pedlars. Most of the scruffier people were human. The rest were humanoid species like the Dir, busy cheating their latest customer, and Achelians, furred and spindly limbed. They made an interesting contrast: the Dir are angular, ascetic-looking humanoids who practise a rigid, cutthroat code. Achelians are cuddly, furred creatures like urbane koalas, equally adept at transferring the wealth of others to their own dark, long-fingered paws.

There are also a few H'digh, Lykaeat, and more Garokians. Some of them, like the H'digh, are almost indistinguishable from humans. Taller, more slender and better muscled than most humans but still similar. With others, like the Garokians, the only thing we have in common are two legs, two arms and a head.

I glanced at Kloos beside me. He stared at everything with a mesmerised gaze and his movements were a little unsteady, as if his brain had disconnected links to everything but his eyes. I hoped he wasn't in danger of some kind of sensory overload. Griffis was listening carefully to Florida's explanation and Rachel's dark hair bounced as she looked from one side of the throughway to the other.

One of the K'Cher traders, not Trillith, came through a doorway as we passed. It ducked to get under the lintel then stretched to its full height in a confusion of jointed limbs and feelers before ambling down the street away from us.

'What was that – the praying mantis-y thing?' said Rachel, startled.

'K'Cher,' said Florida, and gave her a condensed version of K'Cher history and culture.

Kloos's pace faltered and I waited for him.

'How do you do it?' he said.

'Do what?'

'Live with the aliens. The differences. Have human beings changed so much?'

'I don't think so.' I'd expected them to feel uneasy. 'We've just had a bit longer to get used to the idea, that's all.'

'It doesn't bother you?' His voice shook.

It was difficult to be honest and reassuring at the same time. 'Not the physical aspect, except in the sense that it's part of what defines our other differences.' Old memories surfaced unbidden. 'I once went for three years without seeing another human.'

'What was it like?'

'It was very . . . stressful. You have to constantly think about how you relate to others and the environment. There's no autopilot. You can't trust your common sense because you have nothing in common with anyone else.'

'You weren't afraid?'

'Constantly.' I struggled to explain the positive aspect of it. 'But there is a freedom too. You can be completely yourself – no point in pretence. And you can expand physical borders – it's as if you see with your nose or smell with your ears. Everything a couple of degrees off balance.'

He managed a feeble grin. 'Sounds like a good high.'

'A what?' It was funny to hear the word perfectly, just not know what he meant.

His grin grew wider. 'Hallucinogenic trip – don't you use recreational drugs?'

'Some people do.' I didn't add that avoiding reality in that way had backfired on me once in a big way. In fact, applying for jobs in alien space had been how I coped with it. At the moment I didn't think my body could handle even a glass of wine.

'We knew there were other aliens out there.' Rachel heard us and stepped back a pace. 'We just didn't give them much thought. I mean, we communicated with the Invidi all right, and they seemed friendly enough. We kind of assumed the others would be obliging.'

I winced, thinking of the pirates and salvagers who prowl space outside treaty zones. It seemed incredible that they had failed to detect *Calypso*. It *was* unbelievable.

'What about fun? Don't you have any hobbies?' asked Rachel.

Fun. Now there's a concept I haven't used for a while. 'I used to run quite a bit.'

They stared at me. 'Run? Where?'

Florida rolled his eyes. 'She gets in people's way.'

'Nonsense. It's a good marathon around all three rings.

I used to do it in a bit more than three hours.' I haven't been for months now.

'I have a lot of fun writing new entertainment holos,' said Florida unexpectedly. 'It's more difficult to grasp alien humour than you might think.'

'I'm sure it is,' said Kloos, his eyes on the passers-by.

'Everyone needs a hobby,' said Griffis firmly. 'It helps you keep perspective on things.'

The pale blue panels ran back smoothly. A collective gasp rose from three throats behind me. I think it's pretty impressive too.

We are supposed to preserve long lines of sight all over the station – a measure to keep space sickness at bay. Unfortunately, reality often does not measure up to specs, and much of Gamma and all of Delta rings have been built over to cope with our excess population. Here in Alpha, though, you can see the sky.

Not blue sky, to be sure. But sunlight bounces off banks of reflectors to form a vault of tinted alien gold. Only in the Alpha ring do you see light right above, for Gamma's sky is Alpha's base, and Delta sits under Gamma, as far as the spinning top's gravity is concerned.

A single long path hugged the lowest point between beds of grains, vegetables, fruits, fungi, and gillus that rose in terraces on either side to meet the edges of the vault. The lower fields have a base of artificial soil, the higher ones are hydro- or aeroponic. The air is warmer, thicker, wetter, and I wish I could smell the scents.

Griffis gestured at the coloured terraces. 'I presume you have a self-sufficient food supply?'

Florida settled his beltful of equipment comfortably over one shoulder as he answered. He looked so at home out in the open. His movements were less jerky, his big hands and feet more relaxed. His slight squint had seemed calculating inside – now it was merely the result of looking into the distance. I could imagine him as a pioneer on a colony planet, enjoying the struggle to build a new world. Why had he come to Jocasta?

'The purpose of all this is self-sufficiency,' he said. 'But they always seem to have problems. Food rationing is a fact of life.'

It certainly was. Photosynthetic productivity was never constant and we've had some difficulty with viruses. The station wasn't designed as an agricultural settlement and when we modified other systems to compensate, that threw additional stress on those areas. The population is already too large to allocate any more space to food production.

In the early days the station was a ConFleet base, and most of our supplies were imported. Then supplies dwindled and support from Earth faded. While complaining to Central we stepped up research on food production and expanded trade. When the Seouras removed the trade option altogether, we had already started producing staples. But there are so many random factors – too many illegal entrants and their associated bacteria floating around. The most we can be certain of is that any strains of foodstuffs that do survive are hardy.

'It's all right for civilians,' I reminded Florida. 'Staff still use a minimum of twenty per cent space rations.'

Rachel grimaced. 'The gunk in tubes?'

'Uh-huh.' Processed nutrients that taste fine in free fall – anything tastes okay in free fall, as long as it doesn't go up your nose – lose their appeal squeezed onto a plate as part of a normal meal. I'm not the only person who has lost weight in the past few months.

And the refugees, the illegals, what do they eat? The people who have slipped through the bureaucratic net, who haven't registered for medical checks, accommodation benefits, employment lists. Like the unknown human who was in the storage bay with Keveth last night. People who live off the records. We can calculate approximately how many extra people are here by using oxygen consumption and waste recycle figures as a base, but pinning them down physically isn't as easy.

'How about backups for the main computer systems?' Kloos asked.

I didn't know whether to laugh or cry. 'That's what we're running on now.'

'What do you mean?' He looked shocked, as any good systems engineer should.

'Not completely on backups. Some of the systems are still run on the centreline, which has its main access nodes in the centre. Some are run on backups, though, because either we couldn't fix the centreline functions, or we couldn't afford to keep them running on centreline. This is one reason we have such patchy performance in various systems. Some access for these is in the rings, some in the centre.'

'Sounds like a maintenance team's nightmare,' Rachel said.

'It's ironic in a way, isn't it? That we should come so

far, only to find ourselves back at the starting point.' Griffis spread his arms to encompass the whole station. 'I mean,' at my puzzled look, 'you have so many similar problems to Earth in our time – overpopulation, resource management, recycling, isolation. All the problems of a closed system.'

Close curve of sky bright with captured alien light. The horizon curves up ahead to meet the sky and disappears around its immense corner into a grey blur of buildings. My engineer's eye notes missing panels in the reflector grid and gives me a critical appreciation of the balance in shell thickness that can withstand the greatest stress with least mass. But lately another eye has been drawing my attention to the chequered effect of borrowed sunlight on green growth. This other eye – has it been with me always, recording and delighting but unheeded? I squatted down to see what my new eye made of damp soil and pale green borders trodden by incautious boots. Thick, brown clods stuck to the stubbed treads of my boots, leaving a half-moon indent in the earth. Earth. This is not earth, merely dirt. A mixture of waste sediment, compacted vegetable matter, and sterilised processing waste. No more than a thin skin laid over the metal bones beneath.

The warmth on my neck was intoxicating. So strong after the diffused artificial light of the inner corridors. The sunlight promised more delight if I let it flow down under my collar. A great wave of desire to see Earth broke inside me. To feel a breeze that had not been recycled and programmed. To be immersed in the constant subtle variations of shadows that only atmos-phere can provide. Leaves scattering golden light through an afternoon breeze, ozone-pungent greenish portent of an afternoon storm, great trees with roots that reach deep into time past. Rain.

I haven't been back to Earth for over twenty years.

'Wouldn't you agree, Commander?' Florida sounded smug. He must have made a telling point.

'I beg your pardon? I was thinking of something else.'

'I was telling our guests,' Florida said, weighing his vidcom in one hand as if deliberating whether to throw it at me or not, 'how we've been virtually under siege all these months. The Confederacy must really be in trouble with these aliens, but the administration gives out no infor-mation. Maybe you don't know what's going on? What's the chance they've taken over Sector Central too?'

'I don't think that's likely.' I wished he hadn't brought it up.

'Why hasn't the Confederacy contacted us, then?'

'They probably don't want to risk losing the station if the Seouras attack.' My irritation grew with each ques-tion. This was not the time or place for putting the administration on the spot.

'What do you get out of it, talking to them?'

'I resent the implications of that question.' I was about to explode with anger and frustration when I realised that while Florida's question was intrusive, his voice and eyes were not. There was misery in his expression, and a desire to be reassured.

I sighed. 'I just want to keep everyone safe.'

He seemed relieved. 'That's what I thought.'

His words had wrenched me back to the present. 'If you want to help, you can do some research for me.'

I hadn't expected him to show any interest and was surprised when he accepted the assignment with alacrity. He was to go through any records in our database that might shed light on where *Calypso* had been all those years. Ships' logs, travellers' diaries, news items – anything and everything. With two of us working on it there would be a greater chance of success.

'Thank you,' I said.

He bowed. 'At your service. If you want information, come to the professionals.'

'And thank you from us,' said Griffis. He'd been listening carefully as I described *Calypso*'s course to Florida.

'Yes,' put in Rachel. 'It'd be good to know what was happening while we were asleep.'

'How we got here,' added Kloos.

My comm link beeped. Engineering wanted me to come and look at the latest update on the comet's position. The Bubble staff wanted me over there too. They were expecting large-scale sensor interference and burnouts from the dust. Taken together with the recent opsys problems in the centre, it seemed we were in for a busy few days.

Rachel looked at the link. 'You're going?'

I nodded. 'I'll see you later. Mr Florida? They're to be back in Rehab at midday. Without fail.' It was hard to be strict with the sun warm on my neck.

Florida sketched a rough salute, a parody of Baudin's crisp movements. Must admit I like Florida's better.

I finished in Engineering sooner than I'd expected. The probe was nearly ready and there wasn't that much else we could do about the dust and debris from the comet except batten down and keep taking observations up until the last possible minute.

No one had any new theories about the arrival of *Calypso* or why the jump mine had activated. I'd gone over the data, and the best I could do was that the Sleepers were caught in an anomaly similar to a wormhole and ended up here. It wasn't as far-fetched as it sounded, because there are recorded jump points from near Centauri to a long way away, although in a different direction from Jocasta. The radiation *Calypso* dumped when coming out of this anomaly, because similar to that from a controlled jump, could have set off the mine.

We could try to get a ship back to Centauri the same way, but we had no time or resources to spend experimenting with hyperspace, and the theory would have to remain a theory.

Quartermaine still wasn't in his quarters. I hesitated before keying in the number of his sometime partner but we needed Brin's help with An Barik and . . . I was starting to worry.

'Ranit here.' The voice on the comm link was sleepy. Maybe Ranit was on second or third shift this month.

'I'm sorry to disturb you. This is Commander Halley. Have you seen Brin? I need to contact him urgently.'

A short silence. I was about to repeat the question when he answered.

'No, I haven't seen him in weeks.' The voice sounded more alert. It was a pleasant, light-brown baritone. 'Isn't he at work?'

'No. Thanks anyway.'

'Is everything all right?' A definite sharpness now.

'Fine, fine,' I lied easily. 'We just need him to do a bit of interpreting.' I cut the connection and this time used my code to open a limited call pattern. 'Commander Halley to Mr Quartermaine. Please contact the command centre or Security immediately.' The message would go to all staff offices and public places. It was one way of communicating with someone who, like Quartermaine, had turned off a personal comm device. Only the command and senior staff are actually required to carry one at all times and most of the other residents don't bother or can't afford it. The public comm system is free and ubiquitous and they use that.

I decided to give Quartermaine half an hour to check in, then tell Murdoch. It wasn't like Brin to go off somewhere, particularly without telling someone.

I ran a hand through my hair. It felt stiff and scratchy and a headache lurked behind my eyes. Brin was missing, we had a murderer loose on the station, cometary debris sleeting through the Abelar system, and a spate of mysterious opsys failures.

Oh for hot running water and twelve hours' uninterrupted sleep . . . Fat chance. I could do something about the hair, though, before I went to see Murdoch.

The karrikar stopped in the familiar heat and dinginess of the Hill. By this time of the morning the throughway was crowded with loiterers, hawkers, legitimate shopkeepers, and their customers, and there were fewer unlit corners. Today it was even more packed than usual because of the festival preparations.

Preparations involved a great deal of cooking and chatting, and also the job of clearing the main throughways of anything large enough to interfere with the procession. The array of dancing, gesticulating Garokians that formed the backbone of the celebration would wind its way through Delta, ride an uplift to Gamma and parade through there, then take another uplift to Alpha, where it would annoy the hell out of our more genteel residents. Last year, the third year they'd held the procession, they had also taken an uplift right to the centre, made a nuisance of themselves in the docks, and come down again to Delta where the participants dispersed to eat and drink in earnest.

If it were only Garokians it would be a quiet affair, but unfortunately the rest of the station treats the whole thing as an excuse to make up for the lack of other excitement, and the procession becomes a kind of interspecies conga line that meanders in an increasingly rowdy and drunken way for most of the night.

I like the idea of the Renewal of Souls. As far as we can tell, it is a yearly revision of one's actions and involves thinking through the consequences of those actions and what to do about them. This soul-searching is conducted through a kind of structured and ritualised group discussion, incorporating all members of the community regardless of age or status. Some of the discussions continue for weeks, but at the end everyone seems able to make a 'clean' start again. I find it comforting that they recognise firstly that we must act and secondly that we are responsible for those actions, but not necessarily alone.

Usually I enjoy the festive atmosphere, but this morning everything annoyed me and fed my anxiety – voices raised in once-a-year songs, the sound of sputtering oil, the fierce bustle of spring cleaning that sent scurries of dust and debris under my feet from open doorways. Doorways too close to the throughway to be legal. Rooms had been added to existing buildings until the whole edifice leaned outward to meet the opposite buildings overhead. Even if the reflectors were not offline, there wouldn't be much real light down here. I flattened myself against the wall to avoid a multi-species group carrying a long table from one dwelling to another. Didn't they know we were under siege?

At any rate, there was no sinister feel to the place this morning, and I felt ashamed of how I'd hurried on my way home last night after finding Keveth's body. The whole incident was probably a misunderstanding among the K'Cher. Nothing to do with the rest of us, certainly no reason for unrest onstation. I should leave the investigation to Murdoch and get on with our comet probe project.

'You haven't got an appointment?' The human hair-dresser, Mrs Giacommetti, was busy with another customer when I arrived.

'Sorry. I thought you might fit me in . . .'

She swung around and looked at me closely. There was something bird-like, almost reptilian in her bright gaze. 'Have a cup of tea while you're waiting.'

I filled a cup from the tray on a table by the door. Mrs Giacommetti's tea was legendary. Her salon was a long room with multidirectional mirrors down each side and chairs in front of them. There were tall stands of equipment beside each chair but the Giacommettis haven't let any of their customers use a machine in years. They specialise in a personal, hands-on approach.

'Over there.' She indicated the last seat in the row, then turned back to the customer, a human male with a shock of stiff reddish hair that fell in quick whisks to the floor as she cut. I sat in the chair and sipped my tea until it was finished. It tasted faintly of oranges. Concealed ceiling ventilation gave off a steady hum, occasionally punctuated by a swishing clatter. Voices were raised beyond the adjacent door that led to the family residence, but not in anger – they ebbed and flowed like my breath in the cool, peaceful air . . .

A warm hand tightened on my neck and squeezed the taut muscle with practised strength. 'You're going to have to stay awake while I cut it, you know.'

I inhaled sharply and met Mrs Giacommetti's amused eyes in the mirror as she picked the empty teacup out of my lap and set it on the ledge in front of me.

Water rationing meant that instead of a real shampoo

I sat with the sonic helmet on my head for two minutes, but the neck massage was the same as usual. Mrs Giacommetti worked silently, a frown of concentration pulling her round face into a square at the mouth. As the tension knots melted away I felt more alert than I had in days.

She picked up her scissors and started cutting. Another eccentricity, real scissors. Real blades. A bother to keep sharp and their use imposed up to an hour's inaction on the part of the customer – unthinkable in our automated world. Yet even before Jocasta was isolated from the rest of that world Mrs Giacommetti had not lacked customers. She and her bright scissors held comfort for many people.

Snick, snick. Soft brown tufts on the tiled floor. Voices rose in altercation outside and there was a rattling crash as a trolley collided with, I hoped, something inanimate. Alien curses. Another day in the Hill had begun. I began to relax. Then Mr Giacommetti bustled into the room, buoyed on the never-failing waves of his own self-importance.

'*Buongiorno*, Commander Maria! Wonderful to see you again! You have been avoiding us, no?' Mr Giacommetti is a born-again Italian and takes my middle name as a personal compliment. 'You need the cut, this is true.' He inserted his pudgy blue face between mine and the mirror and pretended to inspect my head. 'Shape around the neck more, my dear.' He straightened up and waved an admonishing appendage at his wife. 'A nape of such beauty should not be concealed.' Mrs Giacommetti ignored him completely.

The other customer finally heaved himself out of his chair and paid Mr Giacommetti at the door. He glanced quickly at me and muttered something about staying on the good side of the administration, which Mr Giacommetti deflected with a cheerful farewell. I met Mrs Giacommetti's eyes in the mirror. She half-smiled then went back to concentrating on the cutting. Nevertheless, her attention kept drifting towards the doorway where her husband stood looking out at the Hill.

'If it's . . . inconvenient for you when I come here,' I began in a low voice, 'please say so. I don't want to cause any trouble.'

She glanced at the doorway again, then returned to cutting. 'You're all right,' she murmured. 'That lot don't know how lucky they are. There are plenty worse places in the galaxy than here.'

Which was true, but a qualified compliment if ever I'd heard one.

Mr Giacommetti turned his back on the Hill. 'I have just heard the most amazing rumour.' Mr Giacommetti is also a gossip *extraordinaire*. I said nothing as he rearranged objects along the mirror ledge. Later one of the apprentices would move the things back.

'There has been a terrible murder,' he continued when it was clear I was not going to comment.

The scissors paused almost imperceptibly then continued on their measured course. Mrs Giacommetti's face in the mirror showed nothing but a deepened frown. I could see her husband, though, waiting eagerly for her reaction, his eyes fixed on her almost in supplication. He gave up after a minute or so and threw up his six-split fins in exasperation. 'The woman is made of stone. A murder, I said! Don't you want to know who it was?'

Mr Giacommetti is Lykaeat, a knobbly skinned humanoid race of brilliant imitators and mimics. Many is the time I've heard the story of his first visit to Earth, how the great monuments and people of a Gibraltar Bloc country called Italy had been imprinted upon his young and impressionable psyche, and of how he vowed he would become one of them. One particularly crowded day the whole salon was held hostage for an hour while he revealed intimate details of his first gelato. We never hear how he met his wife, though – a taboo subject. Genetic incompatibility has not prevented them from having a family. They've adopted five children ranging from six to sixteen, all of whom speak fluent Italian.

'Remember that rude K'Cher who used to hang around the bar?'

'Keveth.' Mrs Giacommetti didn't take her eyes from the scissors.

'How did you know?' I turned my head to look directly at her. She stilled the scissors with a sigh and her other hand turned my head back.

'Even aliens drink tea,' she said. Snip, snip. 'How did it happen?' She asked me rather than her husband.

Several of the mirror angles showed Mr Giacommetti lean forward, gills fluttering eagerly. Oh well, better he should spread an edited version of the facts than unbridled speculation.

'It was up in Sigma. We don't know yet who did it.' When I met her eyes in the mirror they were wet with unshed tears.

'Is it true there were strange religious markings on the floor?' Mr Giacommetti slid along the mirror until he was almost in my lap.

'No! Nothing religious at all.' We have enough problems on the station without creating religious tension. 'You haven't heard anyone threaten Keveth, have you? Has it upset anyone at all lately?'

The Lykaeat shrugged theatrically. 'Not that I've heard. But the creature was infuriating most of the time anyway. Taunting and ranting.'

Then he realised the potential of the situation. 'I, Giuseppe Giacommetti, will make discreet inquiries for you. You know, Maria, that everybody tells me everything eventually.' He could barely contain his glee, and I didn't have the energy to resist.

'Make sure you tell Mr Murdoch anything you might hear, *capisce*?'

He clapped his thighs in delight, not having the right mouth for smiling. '*Capisce, capisce.*' Then suddenly he was serious. 'I should mention the other K'Cher perhaps.'

'What other K'Cher?'

He looked down, fiddled with a brush then met my eyes again. 'When I opened the salon this morning, they were talking outside.'

'Who was talking?'

'A woman called Gress. She works for one of the K'Cher, one who lives in Alpha.'

If he was right, Murdoch could trace which of the other K'Cher it was. 'Who was she talking to?'

'Why, *Signore* Jones. The musician.'

Jones, Jones . . . I couldn't place anyone called Jones.

'He plays the mandolin,' said Mrs Giacommetti. 'You probably saw him standing on a corner somewhere.'

I recalled there had been someone like that in the crowd outside the hospital the day the Sleepers arrived. And this morning he had been talking to one of the many humans who worked in the Alpha residencies for one of the K'Cher. These jobs were not popular and would gain the person who did them much criticism, but they paid well. There was never a shortage of applicants for jobs in Alpha.

'Jones, he is also not the sort of man to leave unattended for a moment, if you know what I mean.' Mr Giacommetti leaned over me again confidentially.

'No, I don't think I do,' I said.

'His fingers are very active in pursuit of other people's property, to put it another way.'

So Jones was also a sneak-thief. Well, the station had a good number of them.

Mrs Giacommetti placed the scissors on her tray, removed the shoulder cover, and whisked stray hairs off my neck. 'Finished.'

My hair looked shorter, neater, and ... 'It's awfully grey.'

Mr Giacommetti tut-tutted. 'No problem, *bella mia*. What colour would you like instead? Green? Purple?'

I looked at his wife in the mirror. Her round, not-bird eyes watched me impassively. 'This is fine.'

She didn't smile, but when I left several minutes later she joined her husband in the doorway.

Quartermaine still wasn't anywhere he should be. I called Main Security.

'No, ma'am. The Chief's down in Hill Central. Do you want me to ask him to come up to your office?'

'No, I'm down here now.' I was standing at the main intersection in the Hill, with the burnt-out section in front of me and to one side, and a jumble of two-level buildings behind and to the other side. It was just before the main shift break and there was a steady stream of traffic, mostly bipedal, along the main throughway. Occasionally an AVG or freight trolley would try to wind through the jungle of legs, stilts, and tentacles, but moving around the Hill usually confused the automatic sensors so much it was quicker to rely on organic power – messengers and deliverers.

The crowds made it seem hotter and I took off my jacket. The 'street' was like a sauna. The main Security centre for the lower station is down here, past a sonics repair stand and a pawnshop. The other Security office in Alpha Four deals with problems in the centre and the more refined white-collar crimes of Alpha and Gamma levels. The Hill office gets landed with petty thieving, sordid domestic and interspecies quarrels, and the tracking down of refugees. In the months following the Seouras attack much of the petty crime died away when it became obvious we were not going to let people starve, although in those horrible weeks after the fire everyone came close.

The Security building was our ops centre during the Hill fire. Its blackened side was evidence of the heat of the blaze. There was an open space beyond the building, gloomy without lights, where the flames had eaten through into the maintenance levels beneath and it was too dangerous yet to rebuild there. It was strange to see so far on the station – almost to the horizon that curved protectively until blocked by buildings. That tight curve was a reminder of how easily we forget where we are – inside a narrow torus of life that spins around a still centre.

The main doors swished open and I almost ran into the tall figure of Helen Sasaki.

'Oof! Sorry ... Commander Halley. I beg your pardon.' She grabbed my arm to prevent me from staggering back into a passer-by. Sasaki was promoted to Murdoch's deputy weeks before the Seouras came. She is shy, brusque, tenacious, and inventive, and we have relied on her strength in the past months.

'Good morning, Lieutenant. In a hurry?'

'We might have a couple more witnesses for Keveth's movements yesterday afternoon.' She pitched her voice low and her face was impassive as usual, but her eyes shone. 'I'm going to see them now.'

'Good luck. Is the Chief inside?'

'Yes. In his office.'

'Thanks.' I watched her smooth dark head and wide shoulders disappear into the crowd. She looks well. The strain shows in her face but serves only to etch lines of character into its smoothness.

The station inside was a microcosm of the passage

outside, the crowds compressed into a smaller area and heated further, in a sort of Brownian frustration. The desk sergeant argued in sign language with three Garokians, oblivious to the verbal assaults of several humans. Benches lined the wall, their occupants representative of the mixed population down here: humans, Garokian refugees, Dir shopkeepers, a couple of furry Achelians, and one mound of sticks and fluff that would unfold itself into a Hoffa. The light was brassy and artificial compared to the 'day' outside. It looked to me as if the whole lighting system in the building could do with a refit.

Murdoch's office was little better, although he does have a panel positioned to direct light at his desk. The desk was nearly as untidy as my own. Banks of monitors lined the walls behind it, many of them running visual links to security points all over the station. I could make out the main Customs gate in Alpha Three, now the coordination centre for agricultural research. Also one of the entries to the Hill, and a stretch of corridor that looked like Sigma 12. Pity they hadn't been watching Sigma last night.

'Put it on the desk,' he growled, then looked up and saw who it was. 'Ah, I was just about to call you.' He leaned back and looked at me with insolent intensity. 'Nice haircut.'

He only does it to make me nervous. I chose not to answer.

'I can't believe they're going ahead with the festival.' He slapped a filepad irritably on the desk.

'It's a religious thing.' There were two extra chairs, and

I chose the one that looked the most sympathetic to human physiology.

'Yeah, I know that. But dammit, we're being held prisoner by hostile aliens. There's a killer still loose on the station. Nobody knows what'll happen tomorrow.'

'That's probably the point.'

'What is?'

'That we don't know what the future holds.' I thought of An Barik. 'Most of us.'

'You'd think they'd hold off a bit,' he grunted. Festivals are never much fun for those who have to keep the peace.

I shrugged. 'I can issue a curfew if your investigation is going to be compromised.'

'Oh yeah, and who gets to enforce the curfew? My people have plenty to do already. We'll leave the drunks to kill each other.'

'Come on, Bill. It's not that bad. Mostly clan reunions and people stuffing their bellies.'

'Don't know what they'll stuff 'em with,' he grumbled, tilting his chair back at an acute angle.

I saw how fatigue had drawn the lines tight around his mouth and felt my own face soften in sympathy. 'I'm not staying. I just wanted to get your update and give you one from Engineering.'

'We talked to some people who knew Keveth,' he said before I could start. 'They couldn't understand why Keveth volunteered to help with the Sleeper rescue. Especially as there was no guarantee of payment.'

'Keveth might have gone to Sigma to check on what he might get in payment.'

Murdoch didn't look convinced. 'We're still looking

for someone who could open the door with forbidden technology.' He slammed his chair down. 'Did you tell Quartermaine I want to talk to the Invidi?'

'Wait a minute. I just spoke to someone in the Hill. He saw a human, a woman called Gress, who works at one of the Alpha K'Cher places. She was speaking to a man named Jones in the Hill this morning.'

Murdoch sat up a bit straighter. 'If the person works in Alpha, their medical data will be online. But Jones is a possibility.'

He'd lost me for a minute until I realised he was thinking of the unregistered DNA traces we'd found in the bay with Keveth's.

'Murdoch, about Quartermaine – that's what I wanted to tell you. I can't find him. He's not in his quarters, his office, the hospital . . . I'm worried. It's not like him not to leave a message.'

Murdoch's chin rasped as he drew his fingers over the greyish stubble. He dropped his chin and raised his eyebrows at me. 'No, it's not like him. He has access to the Invidi quarters, hasn't he?'

'Yes, but he can't help us with An Barik if he isn't here . . .' At last I caught on. 'Oh no, Murdoch, that's preposterous. Brin could no more attack and kill a K'Cher than I can breathe in vacuum. Don't even contemplate it.'

He shook his head. 'I've got to contemplate it. We found traces of his DNA in the storage bay, over by the wall in the overhead conduits. He probably hid up there.'

'What about on the door and around the container?'

'Nothing, but that doesn't mean he wasn't there. Face

it, Halley, unless it was the Invidi himself, Quartermaine is the only one who could have got that lockbreaker. And if he got that, he could have got something else to wipe personal traces.'

'Why didn't he wipe overhead too?'

Murdoch shrugged. 'Too much of a hurry. Maybe forgot.'

'Why would he go there? If it was to look at the Sleeper salvage, he had Invidi equipment, so why the clumsy attempt to open it?'

'If he's innocent, why is he hiding?' It was a predictable question but Murdoch seemed somehow preoccupied.

'Have you considered Quartermaine might be in danger? He saw what happened to Keveth and he's in fear for his own life. Maybe he knows the identity of this other human. Or of the killer.'

Murdoch drummed his knuckles on a corner of the desk. 'Until we find him we don't know. And if he was lying hurt somewhere we'd have found him by now. We've gone over the upper levels and haven't picked up anything. He's hiding down in the Hill or somewhere with background interference that makes it impossible to pick him out on sensors.'

Would Quartermaine hide from us? From me? I thought he was my friend, inasmuch as either of us had any friends, and felt hurt that he hadn't come to me.

I didn't like the idea of him being Murdoch's prime suspect, but at least they'd find him quickly. I wanted to see Quartermaine safe, wanted to hear his explanation for this business. He could never be involved with a brutal murder, that was certain. He has spent so long with the Invidi that he displays many of their characteristics – he was quiet, enigmatic, elliptic in conversation, and solitary. He spends most of his free time reading obscure historical texts and working on improving translation algorithms between Earth Standard and the Invidi languages.

'What about Engineering status?' Murdoch seemed jittery. He pushed his chair away from the desk and began to pace up and down in front of the monitors as he listened. This was strange – usually I'm the one who paces.

It was hard to drag my thoughts away from Quartermaine. 'Did you get my report about the disruptions in the centre opsys?' Engineering had sent me a message that environmental controls in the centre had shut down early this morning, and when they investigated they'd found a series of severed conduits. This was what had caused the malfunctions in the hospital recycling system yesterday. A repair team had been dispatched.

He nodded. There was something almost furtive in the way he ran his thumbs along the inner edge of his belt and back again, taking comfort in its shiny solidity.

'We've been monitoring the comet's projected course,' I continued. 'Tomorrow morning at 0800 we'll launch the probe.' Even though Brin had thought there was no point, in absence of evidence to the contrary we must assume the Confederacy is out there and waiting to help us.

'The Seouras have been a little more ... confused lately. If they've got to the stage of letting something like *Calypso* through, we might have a chance.'

Murdoch didn't respond to the enthusiasm in my voice. 'Great.' He paused, silhouetted against the screens. 'Halley, we got some more forensic evidence from the storage bay.'

'Yes?' I wished he'd let me finish one topic first.

'The good news is, we won't have to search for a weapon. The bad news is we know who killed Keveth.'

'Why is it . . . ?'

'We just got the lab results back. There's K'Cher all over the room. And DNA from the unknown human. Trouble is, there's another trace we didn't notice at first because it was so close to the K'Cher.' He finally looked at me. 'It's Q'Chn.'

The old K'Cher military caste. My first reaction was relief at such an obvious mistake. 'Can't be.' I even tried some heavy-handed humour. 'There aren't any Q'Chn on the station. I'm sure we would have noticed. Must be a mistake. They're extinct.'

He didn't laugh. 'Look for yourself.' He swivelled one of the monitors to face us and called up a report. 'The lab has been told to keep this quiet, by the way.'

I glanced at the screen. The results were clear. 'The analysis program must have a bug. Either that or the scan results themselves are screwed. Did you take another reading? Run a diagnostic on the equipment?'

He nodded wearily. 'All the hardware checks out. Forensic says there are no metal residues in Keveth's wounds. But there is a biocompound that's consistent with an organic weapon. Like a Slasher.'

The colloquialism penetrated my disbelief where his rational explanation had not.

Q'Chn, also known as Slashers.

They said the Slashers were bigger than other K'Cher. They said you never saw them coming. They said the Slashers never spoke so all you could hear was the sound of your own screams ... I could see the same fear in Murdoch's eyes. We are not equipped to handle monsters on the station, and we can't call for help.

'Nobody's seen anything?' If it really was Q'Chn nobody ever saw anything, not until it was too late.

He rubbed the skin around his eyes as though it was too tight. 'We don't have enough information about the things. All we know is that they were genetically engineered and that the K'Cher agreed not to make more when the Confederacy was formed. The damn database tells you the history but not how to beat them.'

All we had was forty or so years of hearsay. The K'Cher had always taken the attitude that keeping something out of sight kept it out of mind. When they did speak of Q'Chn it was in a way that implied they had been created for the sole purpose of defending the K'Cher from a hostile galaxy, but in fact a millennium ago the K'Cher had possessed a vast empire and at one stage the Q'Chn warrior class came close to outnumbering the others. At a time humanity struggled against feudalism and plagues, the Slashers patrolled trading lanes and system borders in their big ships, giving no warning before they attacked and no quarter when they did. Their squabbles with the Bendarl and other species who preferred to remain independent and who could hold off the Q'Chn had gradually reduced K'Cher territory to its present abbreviated space.

Two centuries ago the Invidi had made a stand against that empire. I still didn't understand the reasons for the Invidi–K'Cher war or how it could have been fought – the Invidi today use only one-pilot ships and usually don't venture out of their own system. Thirty or so years after they contacted us the war was over anyway, and shortly after that the Confederacy of Allied Worlds was formed. All this is history. But nowhere can one find details of the Q'Chn appearance, their fighting methods, or, more importantly, how to stop them.

'I want to talk to the Invidi,' said Murdoch. 'Maybe he's got information about them. And we should talk to one of the K'Cher. We may need to sound a general alert once we have some idea of what it's likely to do.'

'How the hell did it get here?'

He stared at me. 'Who the hell cares? It's here and we gotta do something about it before someone else gets hurt.'

'We haven't had any ships enter the system since the Seouras came, except that prospector and *Calypso*. There's no docking records except for the shuttles. And the Q'Chn certainly hasn't been lurking around up there for the past six months. Firstly, the environmentals have been off for most of that time and secondly, we would have noticed something. So it must have arrived recently.' I felt quite queasy with fear and excitement. This station was supposed to be isolated, but since the jump mine exploded we'd had one, now two visitors from outside. Maybe the Seouras were losing their hold.

'Can we find out where it is?' I thought out loud. 'Locate it with the internal sensors?'

'You know what our sensors were like even before the Seouras jamming.' The internal sensors were designed to cope with only half the volume of living things that we have now, and not even a quarter of the variety. We keep reconfiguring the system but it never keeps up. 'I can track you if you have a comm link or a specific e.m. signature device, and I can track movements in a specific area, but as for picking out a single string of DNA from all the others . . .' He drummed his fingers irritably on the active monitor, which skimmed rapidly through several directories in response. 'Bugger. I hate this new interface.'

I leaned over and restored the previous screen, a diagram of the Sigma bays.

'I suppose we don't even know if it's still in Sigma.'

He gave me a 'thanks, I needed that' look. 'Sigma's the most likely place for it to hide.' He paused. 'If it wants to hide. There's very little chance of anyone seeing it there. Who goes up to view empty docks?'

'Can you secure the storage bays without locking out Engineering or the docking ports?'

'I already did. But now I want to do a full isolation routine. Then we can eliminate areas as we go.'

I considered the idea. A full isolation alert meant that the centre – docks, main engineering section, storage bays, processing facilities – would be completely evacuated and all access spokes sealed both at the centre and at their entry points to the rings. Murdoch could make a sweep of each spoke in turn and perhaps catch the Q'Chn there or in the centre. It could work, and there would be less danger to the rest of the station. Time enough to decide what to do with the thing when we did catch up with it.

'Did the repair team report in?' I was suddenly afraid for all the people in the centre – Engineering staff, dock maintenance workers, businesses in the spokes . . .

'Not yet. I mean,' he amended, 'we heard from them earlier but they haven't filed a proper report yet.'

We should get everyone out of there. 'I read somewhere the Q'Chn can go through forcefields.'

Murdoch grunted. 'Overrated things, forcefields. Give me a good duranium airlock any day.'

The chair was suddenly constricting. I pushed it away and paced up, down.

Murdoch scowled. 'Somebody's making Q'Chn again.' He gave the observation the moment of awed silence it deserved. 'They were bloody indestructible, y'know? Says here,' he jerked his chin at the interface, 'they could breathe pretty well any atmosphere, even exist in a vacuum for a short time, withstand different gravities. Their "skin" was perfect armour, it adapted against the harmonics of almost any energy weapon . . .'

'Murdoch, if we can talk to it . . .'

'What?'

'We must find out how it got here. Don't you see? It got past the Seouras somehow to get onto the station. Maybe we can find out how and send a ship out ourselves.'

His reaction surprised me with its vehemence. 'You're mad.' He stared at me in disbelief. 'You don't *talk* to Slashers.' He spoke each word slowly and clearly. 'They . . . kill . . . you.'

'Why is it here? To pay a visit to an isolated station and give us a bit of a scare? Someone sent it.'

Murdoch folded his arms stubbornly. 'I'm not sending my people in after it. Too great a risk. I don't give a fuck how it got here. We've got to find a way to get rid of it quickly. Think of the casualties if it ran wild in the residential levels.'

'I'm not suggesting you put your people in danger. I'm asking you to think of the larger issue here. We have to pursue every chance to get out of this stalemate. How do you know it won't talk to us?'

'You're asking me not to try and kill it?'

'If necessary, yes.'

Both hands banged flat on the table as Murdoch pushed himself to his feet. 'You ask me to think of the larger issue, but you know what? I think you're so obsessed with this larger issue that you can't see straight any more. Listen to yourself! You're saying, let's put the station in danger for the sake of a possible chance of getting it out of danger.'

I flinched.

'What if we have massive casualties in the short term and then the Q'Chn can't or won't talk to us?' He leaned over the table. 'One Q'Chn could practically take this station if it wanted to, you know? That's what they were bred for. To go in and destroy K'Cher enemies. Not capture or ask them to surrender. Not talk to them. Just kill and go on killing until ordered to stop. Do you want to be responsible for that?'

'You say you can't possibly defeat it. So what choice do we have but to talk to it?'

'Jesus. *They don't talk!*'

'Murdoch, we need to know how it got on the station.'

We glared at each other across the chaos on his desk, then at the same moment we both stepped back. This was no time for competitive pig-headedness.

I still found it difficult to believe we were arguing about a Q'Chn. The stuff of legend, of horror stories come to life. As if Murdoch had come to me and said, By the way, we've got a little vampire problem.

'There shouldn't be any Q'Chn still alive. The K'Cher said they'd stop making them when the Confederacy was formed. The Change comes in about fifty Earth years, so they should all have Changed.'

'Looks like they didn't keep their word, doesn't it?' Murdoch growled. 'We need more information.' His expression became sly. 'One of the other K'Cher.'

I saw where this was leading. 'Oh no, Murdoch. Trillith and I do not get along.'

'It won't talk to me,' he protested, and this was too plausible for me to question. The most senior K'Cher trader, Trillith regards natives of the Nine Worlds as barely necessary irritants in a galaxy arranged for its own convenience and well-being. It considers we are well below the K'Cher on any scale, evolutionary or otherwise. 'It insists on talking only to the highest authority. Which is you,' he added with relief.

'Trillith detests me. The treaty got rid of half its revenue from this sector. And it blames me for our getting stuck here.' I searched for another excuse. 'Anyway, this station operates under Earth law. Trillith has to comply with your request.'

Murdoch looked as if he'd swallowed something prickly. 'I'm telling you – Trillith quotes Confederacy law at me. It insists that members of the Four Worlds don't have to conform to our system.' He sighed and drank his now-cold tea in one gulp. 'I know I've got the right to go up there and drag Trillith down to Security for questioning. But it looks bad, you know? And someone could get hurt.'

'So you want me to persuade it to come down?'

'Yeah.' He rubbed his nose and added with studied casualness. 'Or get the information while you're there. And don't forget to ask about Keveth being there yesterday afternoon. I'll follow up this lead of yours in the Hill.'

'All right, all right.' I tried not to sigh. 'You take care of the isolation procedure, I'll see if Trillith will talk.'

He had the easier job and his expression said he knew it.

Veatch caught up with me at the Alpha ring karrikar. He wore a dull cerulean suit that I had never seen before. New clothes? We don't have resources to spend on fashion.

'That colour suits you,' I ventured.

'Good morning, Commander. Thank you.' He paused, then added almost reluctantly, 'I had a grey suit redyed. I'm gratified that the effect is satisfactory.'

'Oh, very.'

Veatch watched me expectantly. 'You require my presence here?'

I started walking along the Alpha south throughway. 'Not here exactly. We're going to see Trillith.'

'The K'Cher trader?' He didn't move.

I glanced behind and caught his expression – body stiff and antennae curled over in tension. He roused himself and stepped after me, but the reaction was unexpected.

Does he know Trillith? The trouble with reading too much into unexpected alien reactions is that sometimes your expectations are unreasonable, not the reaction. Why shouldn't Veatch know Trillith, either professionally or socially? They are both members of the Four Worlds, two of the few left on Jocasta, and Trillith is notorious for its contempt of 'lesser' species. It might well want to spend time with Veatch.

'Yes. Mr Murdoch wants us to ask if it knew Keveth. There's evidence that links them.'

'That is hardly likely, given the differences in their

social status. Does Chief Murdoch believe Trillith is involved?' His tone was as indifferent as ever. As station manager he'd have received a report from Murdoch.

I probed his facade. 'I don't think he had any particular suspicions. You heard about the Q'Chn?'

'I received a report from Security only minutes before you called.'

'It seems logical to assume one of the K'Cher would know about the Q'Chn first. It is a K'Cher construct. Part of their culture, their genome.'

Veatch said nothing. Even his antennae were expressionless.

Trillith lives in the station's so-called luxury quarter. The greatest luxury is access to unlimited sunlight on the same cycle as the agricultural section, and the lesser gravity of the innermost ring. Not that much less in absolute terms, but enough that in the levels below there was always, by contrast, a drag on body and spirit.

The section lies between the main administrative blocks that house the Bubble and part of the hospital and research labs on one side, and the agricultural section that has expanded to cover over one-third of the ring surface on the other. It retains some of that idealistic quality you can see in early representations of 'Cities in Space' – a central throughway open to the 'sky' and leafy shrubs scattered around aesthetically arranged terrace housing. Open, light, and clean. And totally unaffordable by most of the station's residents, including myself. But it was an unpleasant fact of life that to maintain our stocks of essential goods without assistance from Central, we had had to levy as much duty and taxes as possible.

The Alpha residencies were part of the 'package' to attract those who could afford it. Like Trillith. I don't like such inequity, which is why I was supporting the Residential Reform Committee's drive to redistribute some of the space.

'Can I ask you something?'

Veatch started slightly. 'Yes?'

'Why are you opposed to the RRC proposals?'

He was silent for a moment, huge eyes fixed on the pinkish ceramics of the walkway, antennae bobbing gently with each step.

'I am simply opposed to precipitating action that may be irreversible. A redistribution of the population on this scale involves an immense amount of preparation. We must be sure we do not waste time and resources.'

'We're considering it to save resources,' I pointed out. Could Veatch be receiving some kind of payback from the present residents to preserve the status quo? Surely not.

'Are the results of the DNA scan beyond question?' he asked suddenly. 'I find it incredible that a ——' – Veatch used a non-Standard word, presumably meaning the Q'Chn – 'should be alive today. There is no record of thefts, experiments, or disaster that could be connected with such an abomination.' He made a curling movement with one hand on the last word, like a gesture to ward off evil.

'As far as we can tell, yes. The forensic evidence supports the theory. But the pattern of behaviour is not as clear.'

'That is my point. Surely if it were a Q'Chn we . . .'

'We should be dead,' I supplied glumly.

'Yes.'

'I don't know, Veatch. All we can do is build on the evidence we have now. Which tells us there's a Q'Chn on the station, lying low. We're going over the observation records from the centre in the hope that one of them might have picked up something last night before the surveillance system crashed.' The security pickups work on a simple time lapse circuit and the records are sent to Main Security, where they are retained for twenty days. A long shot, but you never knew.

'If you have any suggestions, don't wait to let us know,' I added.

'I would not presume to tell you or Mr Murdoch how to do your job.' Melot society is arranged around castes, or sub-species, each of which has a distinct role. Evidently Murdoch and I fit into a different caste from Veatch himself.

There was no sign of upheaval caused by the Q'Chn in Alpha, that much was certain. People walked or rode – bicycles mainly – along the walkways and between the residential blocks. An Achelian flitter glided silently overhead, the only form of artificial flight permitted in the rings. The few humans that could be seen were rushing on work errands. Security kept the less desirable elements away from the neat gardens here. But there were few voices, no children calling or shopkeepers hawking their wares, and I never wondered what drama lies behind the tightly shut doors and upward-facing windows. It is the most alien place on the station, in spite of all the Terran vegetation and human-designed architecture.

Trillith's block rose straight from the throughway, plain, staggered grey tiers that managed to be opulent. We walked through a high arch into a courtyard then into a carrier, also high-ceilinged. The sensation of feeling small was familiar from when I'd worked on alien ships. Voice commands in the carrier were working normally here and it took us to the appropriate floor in smooth silence. None of the karrikars in the Bubble work this well, and I made a mental note to discuss priorities with Maintenance.

We stepped into an immense room filled with glowing pale light and silence. You could almost reach up and touch the curve of the sky. Closed doors faced us on the other three walls.

I put my hands in my pockets and casually surveyed the room, for the benefit of whoever was watching. 'Very nice, mm? Colour scheme's a bit dull but we can't have everything.'

Veatch was silent, outwardly calm but he started visibly at the sound of one of the doors opening. The one we hadn't noticed, behind us and next to the carrier.

'Can I help you?' Human, male. A polished neutral voice to go with the polished bald head, wearing a streamlined beige bodysuit. Expressionless brown eyes moved from me to Veatch and back again.

'Er, I don't know. We're looking for the *kuvai* Trillith.' I used the same term of respect that emerges from every K'Cher voicebox.

The man ignored the attempt to curry favour and

bowed slightly from the waist. 'Who shall I say is calling?'

'The head of station and the station manager.'

Not a flicker of recognition or interest. 'This way please.'

We followed him back through the door. A holo-projector was turned on in what was probably a small room, giving the impression of a starfield, stretching above and around us. Only the floor beneath our feet still felt normal. It was an extraordinary feeling, as though we'd stepped into space without an environmental suit. For a millisecond I actually held my breath against vacuum.

'I will present your request to the *kuvai*. Please wait.' The man disappeared.

I let out the breath and looked at the stars. 'Whew.'

Veatch fixed the blazing multitude with a critical eye. 'This would seem to be night above the K'Cher home planet.'

'It's glorious.' I tried to calculate how much power this sophisticated projection would use. Unfortunately my field is engine modification, not holotechnology, and I couldn't begin to guess. 'Has Trillith declared use of an independent power source of any kind?'

Veatch considered. I could almost hear the files on Trillith opening in order. 'Some solar batteries, nothing exceptional.'

'Hmm.' Wonder if we could beg a loan of those batteries – for the Hill clinic, say.

The man in the beige suit appeared again, scattering

stars before him, an unlikely messenger god walking the heavens.

'The *kuvai* will see you now.'

How generous.

I'm always vaguely uncomfortable around K'Cher. There's no sense of physical threat, only an unacknow- ledged tension. They don't hide their scorn of anything non-K'Cher, although in the case of Invidi, Bendarl or Melot the scorn is tempered with tolerance. Melot are humanoid, but perhaps their sheer numbers – they are by far the most numerous species in this part of the galaxy – have convinced the K'Cher to accept them. Among the non-humanoid ships I worked on before coming to Jocasta were K'Cher freighters. At the time it suited me to be left to myself, but with hindsight those engine rooms were not pleasant places. A couple of times I got caught in conduits or plasma-burned and they offered no help. Even a ConFleet officer was more expendable to them than the salvage equipment or maintenance robots.

The trader was in another large, light room. I didn't waste time looking around, pretending to be impressed – K'Cher don't notice things like that. They notice what you say and every possible nuance to be wrung out of the words. Trillith raised a front feeler in less than enthu- siastic greeting. It reclined – sat – leaned against a complicated arrangement of softmetal strands.

'Commander Halley. How may I help you?' Unlike Keveth's creaky and unreliable voicebox, Trillith's was smooth, vibrant, and programmed with truly obnoxious personality markers. The words rustled from the tiny areas on either side of Trillith's upper thorax where a vibratory organ produced sound by friction, at the same time as it issued from the voicebox below its head.

'Good morning. This is Mr Veatch, the station manager.'

'So it is.' Trillith dismissed Veatch with a sway of one leg, at least until it wanted something out of him. 'What do you want? I am extremely busy.'

'I'm sure you are, what with all the trade around here lately.' I coughed down the rest of the sarcasm as Veatch's antennae dipped disapprovingly. 'We are here on a security matter. Last night a K'Cher named Keveth was killed. Did you know it?'

'Yes, yes. I am familiar with the issue. Your Security chief called and I told him I have nothing to say about the matter.'

'We need to fill in a few details, that's all. I would appreciate your cooperation.'

'There are no more details. I supplied all the information at my disposal. You have wasted your time.' Trillith snapped down all its legs decisively.

'There have been new developments since Mr Murdoch spoke with you yesterday. A couple of answers is all we require.' I couldn't tell if this was the usual K'Cher obstructionism or if Trillith really had something to hide, but I was getting thoroughly annoyed.

'Under section five, sub-section 32, fourth clause of the Sovereignty and Immigration Appendix, natives of the Four Worlds are not obliged to follow laws of the minor worlds if doing so would clash with the laws of their own.' Trillith sounded bored.

I glared at Veatch. He was studying the ceiling and

made an elaborate show of finally noticing me in surprise. What was wrong with him?

'Veatch?'

'Commander?'

'Are you familiar with the regulation in question?'

'No . . . yes. Not in detail, however.'

'And it reads as Trillith says?'

He hesitated yet again before continuing. 'As a matter of fact, *kuvai*, precedent supports the use of this particular clause strictly in cases of religious significance. It would be difficult to get an exemption from testifying in a court unless you could prove that doing so violated a religious precept or taboo. This proof would have to include witnesses not related to the complainant.'

That seemed to dispose of the legal angle.

The K'Cher stalked across the room to where the human stood beside the door. It said something to him in a whisper, then stalked back. The man left. Trillith stopped, much closer this time. I could see the ridged exoskeleton down its thorax quite clearly – greenish grey, faintly shiny and brittle looking. A smooth, even colour, unlike Keveth's mottled and knotted body. I had to crick my neck backwards to see its face.

'Surely, *kuvai*, it would not inconvenience you simply to answer a few questions?' I'd given up the idea of getting Trillith to come with us. Whatever we asked had to be asked here.

Trillith tilted its face down deliberately close to mine. It was an effort not to step back. 'Commander Halley, I am still not without influence, both here and in that larger world which you seem to think has conveniently disappeared. I assure you it has not. Don't do anything that you may regret later.'

Veatch intervened mildly as I tried to find words to retort. 'Threatening an official in the course of their duties is considered illegal influence.'

The K'Cher swivelled its head 180 degrees to regard Veatch. Did some unseen message pass between them? At any rate, Trillith became more civil.

'Keveth was here from early yesterday afternoon until evening. My servants will confirm this.'

'Did nobody else see it? Not that we doubt your employees' veracity, but . . .' I hoped the pause sounded as insolent as I'd intended.

'No. Nobody came.'

'Did Keveth often visit?'

'That, Commander,' Trillith rocked backwards a little, 'is none of your business.'

The door opened and a different human, young, female and wearing the same beige uniform, carried in a large tray containing plates of fat green and white dumplings. A silvery urn dribbled steam from its spout. The maid walked past us as though we weren't there and lowered the tray to a small bench that ran along one wall of the room at waist height. She kept her eyes lowered on her way out too. I wondered if she was the woman Mr Giacommetti had seen talking to Jones.

'Refreshments, Commander?'

I shook my head without regret. My stomach hadn't coped well with breakfast.

'This is not a social call. Someone has been murdered. Under Earth law, if you are found to be involved you can be tried as an accessory after the fact. Is that clear?'

'Tell me, Commander, what do you suspect me of?'

'Nothing, *kuvai*. We would merely like to know if Keveth told you anything about his plans for the evening.' I hesitated over the next step, but it seemed necessary. 'Do you remember anything about that night – did Keveth return at any time? Did any of your staff notice anything unusual? We may be able to negotiate some kind of agreement about responsibility.'

'Negotiate?' Trillith's real voice crackled audibly for the first time. A dangerous rustle, like a snake through dry grass.

I cleared a suddenly dry throat. Veatch was looking at me with the kind of expression he reserved for files out of order. You never use words like 'deal' or 'bargain' or 'negotiate' around K'Cher. Not if you wanted to preserve property and livelihood.

'I mean that people who assist us to uncover the truth usually, um, have less trouble refuting ... are given consideration . . .'

Trillith turned away from me and resumed its position. I was sweating despite the cool, dry air. Dammit, Veatch, give me some backup. I wish Quartermaine was here. Not that he would have said much more than, perhaps, 'Don't give them a challenge. They love a challenge. Pretend you're a pushover.' That shouldn't be too difficult.

Trillith straightened its forelegs. 'I regret, Commander, that we are not in a position to conduct business about this matter. At this time.' The last words were not a promise for next time.

Murdoch hadn't said anything about the Jones angle, so I would leave that one. But, 'There is still the matter of the Q'Chn.'

Trillith became perfectly still. It might have been an insectoid statue. I held my breath too, and beside me Veatch's antennae were flat sideways.

'Q'Chn?' Trillith finally said the word, and the sound that underlay it was like a wave sifting onto sand. 'What Q'Chn?'

'We think there is one here, on the station. That it killed Keveth.'

Trillith swung upright. Two metres plus on four multi-jointed legs – legend said the Q'Chn were bigger. Trillith had two thick manipulating feelers as well as the slim joints on its forward pair of legs. The Q'Chn were called Slashers for a reason, and I had an unpleasant feeling that it involved that pair of legs.

'There are no Q'Chn,' said Trillith.

'The evidence,' I began, but it was suddenly close to us, nearly physically pushing us out the door.

'There are no Q'Chn,' its artificial voice was a shout. 'Leave. Leave now.'

All I managed in return was, 'We'll get back to you.'

I ran my finger under the spotless lip of the control box set into the wall beside the courtyard entrance. Every cleaning 'bot ever invented left a film of dust under there, especially in these units. It was impossible to program out of them. Trillith must employ living cleaners, and I could guess what species.

We walked away.

'Why would Trillith keep something from us?'

Veatch looked ahead, eyes narrowed in concentration. 'The foremost reason would be that it can use the information for its own benefit.'

I waited until we were out of audio pickup range of Trillith's block.

'What's going on, Veatch?'

'What do you mean?'

'You're supposed to back me up, not side with the K'Cher.'

'I do not "side" with anyone. I merely administrate for the benefit of all.'

I could have slapped him. 'Don't give me that neutrality crap. I'm the part of the administration that you're supposed to report to, remember?'

He met my eyes with an impassive, limpid stare.

'Is Trillith pushing you somehow? Feeding you the Four Worlds Unity line?'

'I have received no information from Trillith on issues concerning the Four Worlds.'

'That's not what I mean.'

We walked on in silence. Politics. It follows us thousands of light years from home and influences what we do even in the middle of a hostile alien blockade.

Veatch's antennae were flat, and he did look miserable – perhaps I'd been too harsh. Although there was definitely something going on between the two of them.

'Look,' I tried as we reached the karrikar. 'If Trillith's pressuring you – if there's something you don't want me to know – we can work it out. Somehow. Don't feel you have no alternatives.'

He inclined his head solemnly. 'I shall bear it in mind.'

'Veatch, would you do something for me?'

'If I can.'

'Would you check our latest records to see if there's any mention of the Q'Chn – see if anyone has seen any recently or heard of any revival rumours? You're so familiar with Confederacy records.'

He didn't respond to the flattery but agreed. 'If you will excuse me.'

'You're not coming back to the Bubble?'

Still the same limpid stare. 'I have an appointment.' He walked away.

Appointment with whom? Maybe I am paranoid, but it's unpleasant always to feel so isolated. Not merely geographically – the feeling that K'Cher and Melot and Invidi are making all the moves and we're stuck here in the middle, powerless. Feeling small. As governor under Confederacy colony laws, theoretically I can veto any administrative decision Veatch might make. Trouble is, either I find out he's made the decisions well after they come into force or somehow they end up being my decisions.

As I stood there, vaguely watching Veatch's figure disappear up the curve of the horizon, another small figure caught my eye. A human in sloppy civilian clothes. She dawdled along, staring up at the reflectors and buildings.

Rachel waved as I stepped out of the karrikar alcove.

'You're supposed to be back at the hospital,' I said.

She shrugged and pulled back the dark waves of her hair. 'Not when it's such a nice day.'

'It's always a nice day.' I squinted up at the reflectors too. Always. For once I'd like it to drizzle.

There was something I'd been meaning to ask her. 'Tell me what you find strangest here.'

She shoved her jaw forward in concentration and thought for a moment.

'Tea,' she said at last.

'Tea?'

Her sombre face crinkled into a smile at my expression. 'I'm sorry. That doesn't explain much, does it? What I meant was that I didn't expect tea. Some kind of high-nutrition, dietary supplement drink, manufactured to suit individual needs, that sort of thing. But people here drink tea. All the time. They come to talk to us – I don't mind,' she added hastily – 'and what do we drink?'

I'd never thought about tea. It was just there. Relatively efficient to grow, easy to synthesise. Provides trace elements and comfort. Everyone likes it.

'Humans have been drinking tea for thousands of years. Why should we stop now?' was all I could think of.

Rachel nodded. 'Exactly. And that, to me, is the most amazing thing here. That so much is familiar. After sleeping for nearly one hundred years, we didn't expect the familiar.' She glanced up at the plain boxes again. 'Not as familiar here, I must admit. Why is it so different from down there?' This time she looked at our feet.

'The lower rings?' I kept my eyes up, deliberately

obtuse. Hoping she'd take the hint and talk about something else.

'Uh-huh.' She shot me a speculative glance that suggested she would not easily change topics for anybody. 'This is more like I imagined a space station would be. A planned, controlled environment. Light.'

'This is how they'd like it to be.' I started walking and after a second she followed. For a moment the only sound was the dull tap of my boots and slap of her sandals on the neat, planned tiles.

'And you?'

'We can't keep it like this for everyone.' The angry words spilled out before I had a chance to stop them. 'We're so limited in resources. It was all right before the Seouras came. We could get out to the asteroids and mine the ore. We processed some of it on the platforms, then we at least had something to trade. Do you know, Sector hardly sent us anything? Then we ended up with all these refugees. What was I supposed to do? Turn the ships away to die out there? For the pirates to plunder? At least if they're here they're alive . . .'

I broke off. Rachel was looking at me, more shocked than anything. We'd reached a dead end – the throughway was blocked by the uplift entrance that marked the end of the section.

'I'm sorry.' I tried a careless laugh that didn't come off. 'Was I ranting?'

Rachel's gaze didn't slacken. 'You were, a little. So you're one of the people against humans being part of this Confederacy?'

'No, don't get me wrong. I think we were right to let

the Invidi in and right to join the Confederacy. But . . .' I sighed. I'm not good at detailing emotions on my best days, and this was not one of those.

'I used to think,' I tried again, 'that the alliance was not only ideal – living in peace with alien races, how immense and incredible – but also practical, because it provided protection in a hostile galaxy. But now I'm not so sure. It hasn't provided us with protection here.'

How my ex-husband would laugh if he heard me. He swore that some day I would come round to his way of thinking. He'd be wrong though. I'm not in favour of secession, or changing the Confederacy. I just wondered about the way it was set up, if there wasn't an alternative.

'The Invidi have been our bridge to the galaxy for so long. It's as though we're so sensitive to what the Invidi say and do that we're not looking at it straight. Maybe we should be asking what we get from the relationship.'

'Maybe we should have asked that in the first place,' she said, then examined the interface panel. 'Can I get this back to the hospital?'

'Yes. Get out at Gamma and then walk. No, on second thoughts, you'd better take the karrikar around to Gamma Four.' It would save her running into the groups being evacuated from the east spoke.

'Why isn't there a Beta ring?' She craned her head back to see the spire of the uplift that seemed to vanish flatly into the sky.

'There was, at first.' I didn't want to explain. I was tired and confused and bad-tempered. There were too many problems waiting for me in the rings below.

Rachel shrugged and looked away, obviously hurt. I sighed.

'The upper part of Gamma was called Beta when we started construction.' I drew an invisible diagram on the uplift wall with my finger. She turned back and watched me.

'But then everything went wrong. We kept running into Tor booby traps, important material got lost or mislaid, systems failed for no apparent reason – a real mess. Rumours of a saboteur started, which caused a lot of tension onsite. Some people thought the project should be scrapped completely.'

'But not you?' It was ridiculously gratifying, the way Rachel hung on my words, like a child hearing a fairytale for the first time.

'No-o. I try not to leave things half finished. But I couldn't find an explanation. Anyway, finally one of the Cronites came to me with a suggestion, adding that if we didn't implement it, they'd all leave, which would have halved our labour force.' I could still see the small, intense dark face floating to attention in the tangle of conduits and consoles that I'd called my office.

'What was the suggestion?' Rachel's impatient voice.

'It said that the name was wrong. The name of the ring,' I added, seeing her take breath to ask. 'They didn't know why, but probably we'd done something inauspicious at the beginning.'

'A jinx?'

The word was unfamiliar. 'Like a bad coincidence. You can imagine what ConFleet thought about that.'

'What did you think?' She leaned comfortably against

the wall, one foot braced on it and her knee sticking out. I leaned beside her and told my muscles to relax.

'If it meant we could continue construction, I was willing to try anything, bar live sacrifices. Of course admin refused to change the name. But someone on the site itself must have given the go-ahead, because unofficially Beta ring changed overnight to Gamma ring.'

Rachel grinned. 'I wonder who gave the go-ahead?'

'I wonder. After that we had fewer and fewer hitches until the final stages went ahead. We had no more unexplained problems with Gamma or the rest of the operation.'

She shook her head. 'Do you believe . . . ?'

'Does it matter?' Tight shoulder muscles twinged as I shrugged.

'It would make me uncomfortable. Not knowing.'

I laughed and turned to open the uplift lobby door. 'You're going to be uncomfortable in this century then.'

Like me. What a hypocrite, to pretend that not understanding Invidi science doesn't make me so angry sometimes I could explode. Or to pretend that I don't hate being forbidden the chance to learn it. I didn't tell Rachel of the years of frustration at being relegated to secondary systems, of trying to study the jump drive and gravity fields from a distance. My record is dotted with disciplinary actions for trying to circumvent security measures designed to keep members of the Nine Worlds away from such technology. Once, on a K'Cher ship, they almost spaced me. Uncomfortable, indeed.

Murdoch and I argued all the way to the Smoke. About whether he should come with me in the first place, then when I lost that one, about what we should say to An Barik.

'You can't ask him straight.'

'Why not?'

'Because it's impolite and because you won't get a straight answer anyway.' We stopped for the umpteenth time as the crowded throughway jammed. Evacuation of the spokes had not dampened everyone's enthusiasm for the festivals, merely increased the density of the revellers. Rumour of the Q'Chn skimmed over the surface of conversations in every tongue, hissing in awkward pauses before people turned back to their tasks, but it was not said in fear.

'I thought you asked him straight if that lockbreaker was his?' Murdoch pushed a little ahead of me and the waves of people broke before him.

'Ye-es, but we'd gone through a bit first.'

'There's a Q'Chn loose on the station. We haven't got time to waste on chitchat.'

He was right, but I don't think An Barik sees it as chitchat.

'If you go too fast I won't have time to think. Sometimes I need time to decipher his answers.'

Murdoch drew his brows together and a Garokian child scuttled out of his way. 'Never a bloody liaison officer around when you need one.'

On that, at least, we agreed. Where had Quartermaine got to?

If the Smoke made Murdoch nervous he concealed it well. His only sign of tension was a start as An Barik's door opened before we'd announced ourselves.

'He wasn't interested in seeing Security earlier.' Murdoch's voice was muffled by the mask.

'I didn't know you'd tried.'

Murdoch had the grace to look embarrassed. 'Yeah, well. Just wanted to confirm the time he was in his quarters. Nothing major.'

It didn't bother me that Murdoch had wanted to confirm what the Invidi told me, but it must have been the first time he'd called on the alien alone.

The Invidi slid backwards as we stood inside the doorway.

'Governor Halley, Chief Murdoch,' his vocoder intoned.

To my secret amusement, Murdoch bowed shortly.

'Master Barik, you are in health?' I stepped further into the room.

The way he swung his tentacles seemed to argue a leisurely mood. 'The one is satisfactory. Considering the season.'

I let that one go. 'We have a problem and were wondering if you might help us.'

'Please specify.'

'I'll explain.' I ploughed on, unwilling to let Murdoch take over. 'Evidence suggests there is a Q'Chn on the station.'

The tentacles stilled. An expanse of puckered skin shivered, but he said nothing. Murdoch and I exchanged a glance.

'Master?' I prompted. 'You know what a Q'Chn is, don't you?'

'Invidi know.' Did that mean all Invidi or just him?

'Do Invidi have any way to fight it, then?' Murdoch elbowed me out of the way verbally, his harsh tones echoing in the murky air.

'The one is an observer.'

'Yeah, well tell that to the Q'Chn if it comes looking for you.' His reaction reminded me of my own on the day the Seouras attacked, and it softened my annoyance with his abruptness.

'Murdoch ... Master Barik, if you have any information about these creatures, anything at all, I urge you to allow us access to it. We have few resources here and many lives to protect.'

For a moment I thought he would help us. Something in the way the rounded body turned slightly. But it passed, and he trundled backwards further.

'The one must retire.'

'Master, please ...'

'The one must rest.'

In other words, dismissed. Beside me Murdoch fumed, but the room had already darkened so that we could not see the Invidi. Nothing else to do but leave.

Murdoch was livid.

'You're just going to walk out of there?'

I kept going. 'Looks like it.'

He groaned and walked after me. 'He knows something.'

'Yes.'

'Is it a matter of asking the right questions or what? How do you get through to them?'

I reached the ringlift door and tapped in my code. 'I don't think he'll tell us if he doesn't want to. And what do you want me to do?' I was irritated with Murdoch for assuming it was within my power to influence the Invidi. 'Threaten to put him up in the centre with the Q'Chn?'

Murdoch sighed and, arms folded, leaned against the wall. His large presence was both oppressive and comforting. 'Nah. He's probably got a defence against it. That's what makes me spare. Why can't he share it with us?'

I shrugged. The whole debate about whether the Confederacy had abandoned us only sent me into a panic when I thought about the Seouras. The lift arrived and we got in. Fortunately it was empty.

'Where to?' He paused, hand raised over the control pad.

It took me a minute to think. There were so many things in my head clamouring for attention. The foremost were Brin's continued absence, the Q'Chn's continued presence, and the comet's dust cloud, which must already be affecting the station's sensors.

'We need to debrief and work out a strategy,' I said slowly. 'Your office?'

'Yeah, why not?' He entered the code. 'Yours is such a mess.'

I glared at him and reached past to call up the Seouras position on the comm screen. As I expected, the external sensors were nearly useless. We could 'see' in a narrow band around the station and in the direction parallel to the comet's course but otherwise, nothing. Not even the Seouras interference had done this.

I got an empty feeling at the back of my neck when it was obvious we couldn't see where they were. I closed the screen, Murdoch's uniform rough under my sleeve as I brushed his chest.

'How long will that last?' He nodded at the now-blank screen.

'It's moving quicker than we calculated. It's the weirdest orbit I've ever seen. We'll be caught in the tail as it swings around on its way out of the system. It will be worst tonight and gradually clear tomorrow.'

'How badly will it affect the system?'

'Radiation shields are fine, but it depends on the problems in the centre how badly the rest of the station is affected.'

He was silent. I felt the whole situation closing in on me with an almost physical weight. The Seouras implant seemed to itch and I tried to wriggle my neck away from it. Murdoch looked down at me in surprise but said nothing.

We waited in his office until the desk sergeant brought in a jar of tea.

'Do you want something to eat?' Murdoch suggested, but I shook my head.

'Let's get on with it.'

'Right. What do we know?' He sat behind his desk with a thud and activated the interface. 'First, we now have a link between Trillith and this bloke Jones.'

'Don't tell me – it was Trillith's maid talking to Jones.'

'You got it. We'll question Trader Trillith next. But meanwhile,' he scrolled down the figures on the screen. I wished we had more up-to-date holoviewers for our interfaces, then I could have looked from this side without craning my neck. 'If we hypothesise that Jones is the mystery human who was in the storage bay with Keveth when it was killed . . .'

If Jones was indeed the busker I'd seen outside the hospital on the day the Sleepers arrived – can it really have been only yesterday? – then it was possible he'd avoided being registered by the system in any way. He'd had the look of someone to whom authority of any sort was worse than whatever might happen to him outside its reach.

'Then we have both Keveth and Trillith involved in some way with a Q'Chn on the station.'

'The Seouras must have let it through too.' I thought aloud. 'You know, the Q'Chn's ship, wherever it is and however it sneaked in, might have set off that jump mine.'

Murdoch nodded with barely concealed impatience. 'Yeah, well, it's here now. So we have one K'Cher killed by the Q'Chn – dunno why – and the other knows a human who was probably with Keveth when it was killed.'

'We have to find Jones.'

'We're looking,' he grumbled. 'Half the lights are off,

that bloody festival starts today, and I'm trying to finish evacuating the spokes and keep a guard on them. Give us a break.'

'No sign of Quartermaine either?'

'No,' he said shortly. 'So we've got two K'Cher and a Q'Chn. Minus one K'Cher now. Keveth also left the station shortly before its death to help rescue a ship that appears inexplicably just before the Q'Chn kills Keveth. And the door to the storage bay where Keveth was killed was opened by an Invidi lockbreaker.' He reached for the tea jar and poured two cups that were perched unsteadily among the detritus on his desk. 'That's a bloody great lot of coincidences.'

'Keveth's ship was squeaky clean, wasn't it?' I said. 'That indicates there was something there it didn't want us to find.'

'Q'Chn DNA traces maybe?' Murdoch nodded. 'But where's the Q'Chn ship?'

'If it did set off that jump mine, maybe it's in small pieces in orbit by now.'

He passed me a full cup of tea. 'I reckon Keveth and Trillith got the Q'Chn onstation in the *Rillian Queen*. Jones was probably paid to run errands. Then they had a disagreement, the Q'Chn kills Keveth.'

'Why kill Keveth if they were in it together?'

'I dunno. I told you, alien motives are nothing but a headache. Let's just look for the means.'

'Why the storage bay?'

'It was handy. The Q'Chn must have been waiting inside Keveth's ship. Normally, people'd be less likely to visit radioactive wreckage than a public dock area.'

'Except me.'

He gave me a look that said I'd just proved his point. 'Why the Invidi lockbreaker?'

'The Invidi's in on it too. He gets Quartermaine to come and open the door for the others.'

'Wait a minute. Brin wouldn't be involved in any plot to hurt the station.'

'Look, he was there. I can't believe it was another coincidence.'

I rubbed my eyes. We were going around in circles. 'Why would they bring a Q'Chn onstation?'

Murdoch drained his cup and poured another. 'I said leave motive.' But then he added, 'Why do the K'Cher do anything? Because they want something. Have you had a really good look at that salvage?'

I sighed. 'I'll go over it again. And you'd better find Quartermaine.'

'We're on it. The next thing I do is interview Trillith.' Murdoch spoke with wary anticipation. 'We'll see who's untouchable under Confederacy law. Conspiracy to restore the Q'Chn or acquisition of Q'Chn DNA is a full trial offence.'

'What are we going to do about the Q'Chn?'

We looked at each other. I saw what he did – an over-tired, overstressed human, sitting in an untidy room on a rickety space station, no special powers or abilities and with old, badly maintained equipment, talking about how to overcome one of the galaxy's most feared killers.

'What are you laughing about?' Murdoch was annoyed, although I'd only smiled.

'I was just thinking how unlikely we are to succeed in getting rid of it.'

He rolled his eyes and shoved his chair back. 'Oh, that's helpful. I suppose we should "ask" it to leave?'

It was one option I hadn't considered. 'How's the evacuation going?'

He groaned and gestured at the screens. Now that he mentioned it, every screen showed people – humans and aliens – moving along the corridors, milling in front of uplift doors, and forming long lines in the hallways.

'The centre was relatively easy,' he said. 'We don't have many personnel up there anyway. I had to send Kwon with a squad to look for the repair team. They haven't reported in.'

'And the spokes?'

He gestured again at the screens. The lower spokes, especially, housed a variety of shops, low-gravity residences, and laboratories. To clear them completely would take more than a couple of hours.

'Do you suppose it would take a runabout and leave, if we gave it the chance? Have a shuttle in the docking bay, ready, and lure it up there somehow.' I was thinking aloud, then another problem hit me. If the centre was closed off, it meant we would not be ready to launch any sort of ship or even a probe to take advantage of the comet's interference of the Seouras sensors. Damn. I began to feel personal antipathy towards the Q'Chn.

'We don't know what lure it will follow.' Murdoch considered the idea.

'Still, it would be worth the loss of one shuttle to get rid of it, wouldn't you say?'

'We only have two.'

They aren't much use now anyway. One of them carries me over to the Seouras ship. 'What about some sort of disabling gas?'

'We don't know what will affect it. We could always experiment on the K'Cher, I suppose.' Murdoch sounded as if he approved. 'And who goes in to see if it's been affected?'

'Why?' I put my cup down on his desk with unnecessary force. 'Why is it here?'

The desk sergeant stuck her head around the door.

'The Lieutenant says you might want to listen to the alt channel, Chief.'

Murdoch grunted acknowledgment and changed the topmost screen behind him to show Dan Florida against a plain blue background. Murdoch swung his chair around and tilted it back to stare upwards.

'. . . asked the Confederacy Council observer on Jocasta for an interview so we could hear what his people have to say about this interesting matter, but unfortunately he felt unable to meet me. This is a great pity, I'm sure you'll all agree, especially as it involves the past of both our species. I did manage to talk to a different member of the Four Worlds, though, to get its opinion on the matter.'

I groaned as the angular form of Trillith filled the screen. Rachel had described the K'Cher as 'those praying mantis-y things', and from the front it was an apt description. Trillith looked like it was going to pounce, and I hoped Florida could handle it.

'*Kuvai* Trillith, do you have any comment on what we heard this morning from our guests?'

Trillith waved one of its upper forearms delicately. 'I should not be surprised if these tales of Invidi interference were true. The fact that they engaged the K'Cher Empire in war for over five of your centuries shows that they are capable of interference on a grand scale.'

'But I thought their non-interference was limited to the, er, so-called lesser species.' He didn't like the phrase but managed it with a lot more grace than I would have.

Trillith, of course, had no such scruples. 'The lesser species, such as your own, are more susceptible, naturally. Considered culturally or technologically – any way at all – you are so far beneath the rest of us that it is a wonder you have survived as a group at all.

'In Earth's case, the Invidi behaviour was "passive interference". The mere fact of their appearance was enough to change your planet's history. More so when you chose to accept their technology.'

'We didn't have much choice.' Florida's jaw set. He needs more practice staying objective.

'Even on this station, which is supposed to be under your government's rule, the Invidi are actively interfering.'

'What do you mean?'

'Come now, Mr . . . ?'

'Florida.'

'Florida.' Trillith's voicebox buzzed the word smoothly. 'Don't tell me you are unaware of the recent murder of a K'Cher citizen?'

'Yes, but how does that . . . ?'

'The murderer possessed Invidi technology, did it not? And I see the establishment has not allowed you to tell us that the Invidi liaison officer is also missing.'

Florida was silent. I could almost see him weighing the profit from this unexpected revelation with the official reaction if it turned out the information was classified. He apparently decided discretion was the wiser course and let the comment go, aided by his ill-concealed dislike of the K'Cher trader. The dislike made him indiscreet enough to ask the next question.

'Regarding that murder, Trader. There is also a rumour, substantiated by several official sources, that the murders were committed by a Q'Chn that has somehow entered the station. Do you have any comment?'

Trillith made a hissing, scrunching sound. The voice-box might have been briefly turned off. It also flushed an unattractive mauve colour.

'There are no Q'Chn. This is a stupid rumour. I have no further comment.'

Florida grimaced. 'Well, folks, that concludes the program for today.'

Murdoch and I looked at each other.

'Who knew about the Invidi lockbreaker besides you and me?'

He drummed his fingers on the desk at each name. 'Sasaki. Barassi in Comtec – he's been working at it on an encrypted screen, so nobody else there has had anything to do with it. I sent a coded report to Veatch. That's it. Did you tell anyone?'

'It wasn't in the senior staff memo and you know we

never mentioned it at the security briefing. Murdoch, none of them could be involved.'

'If Trillith is deeper in it than we suspected . . .'

'It'd be pretty stupid to give us such an obvious clue. No, I think Trillith is just trying to stir things up.'

'What about An Barik?'

I sighed. 'How are you going to place him in Sigma? He can't sneak around, you know. Too conspicuous.'

Murdoch threw up his hands, exasperated. 'He might have told Trillith.'

'Who uses the information to stir up anti-Invidi sentiment?'

'Trillith is the most likely person to know the Q'Chn. You don't think he protested a bit too much?'

No denying that a K'Cher was the most logical contact for the Q'Chn.

Murdoch stood up abruptly. 'What a bloody mess. Let's just try and get rid of the thing.'

'I wish we could ask it why it's here.' We walked towards the door.

Murdoch snorted. 'The only thing we know for sure about a Q'Chn is that by the time you realise it's there, you're dead.'

He stomped out into the corridor. I followed and stepped into . . .

. . . slime that shifts and slithers underfoot. Clothes and skin coated with it, hair stiff with it, mouth raw from spitting away the stench. No gradual connection today – wham, they're here. Inside my head. A slime-filled tunnel overlapped the Security corridor. I staggered.

Go on. Who said that? *Go on, further.*

Slide, slip, crawl like an animal in a maze – is that what I am? Further, further. I try to stop, out of sheer obstinacy, but the voices propel me on. The slope is downhill now and gravity allows no dissent. A speck of light in the distance. Light at the end of a close, green tunnel.

'Halley.' How do they know my name? *Go on, go on.* Less variation within the cacophony now. More like one voice. And a note of desperation. *Help us.*

The light is closer. Shapes in it. Not amorphous Seouras shapes – hard, metallic. White light so sharp it cuts the eyes. A door. I'm looking through a doorway.

'Halley.' Murdoch's voice, hoarse, with a catch in it. He's here. He's shaking me.

He's shaking me, yes. But not in a slime-filled cavern. We're in the Security corridor. Two constables glanced at us curiously as they passed. Nobody else here, fortunately. I could still faintly hear the voices and it scared me.

I stood still, hardly daring to breathe lest it all come tumbling out, the last thing I wanted to do was scream over Murdoch in the corridor. Bad for discipline ...

Murdoch's hands were painfully tight around my upper arms and he held me stiffly at arm's length as though afraid I'd explode in his face.

'What's going on Halley? You're giving me the creeps.'

I took a deep, shuddering breath.

'Sometimes I can hear them.'

'Who?'

'The Seouras.' No use pretending, even to myself, that

I didn't know whose voice it was. His grip slackened in surprise.

'How? How can you . . . ?'

'I don't know. It's something to do with this.' I touched the implant at my throat. The impulse to pull, gouge, slice it away was strong and I had to make a fist before my hand would lower.

'I thought you used that when you were over there?' He gestured outward.

I nodded, feeling as tired as if I had been over in the grey ship. 'Yes, but lately there's been a sort of . . . overflow. I can hear them sometimes here, too.' There was something like panic in Murdoch's eyes and it scared me. 'Don't look so worried. My dreams aren't going to endanger the station.'

'How do you know? They might have invasive telepathic abilities.' He frowned and drummed on his belt. 'You should have told me.'

'It's not your problem.'

'The safety of the head of station is my problem,' he growled. 'What if something happens to you and they won't deal with one of us? Have you thought what they might do?'

I hadn't. Without the implant, could the Seouras communicate with us? I'd often wondered why they didn't fit more of us with the things – it was possible I had the only one. What might they do to Murdoch, or the chief magistrate, instead?

'Tell me if it happens again,' he continued. 'I'll talk to Jago and see if she has any suggestions.'

Eleanor would have plenty, I was sure. I felt trapped

between them and the Seouras, trapped in an inescapable and ever-tightening noose.

One of Murdoch's hands was still cupped around my arm. I shrugged it off.

'All right, all right. But it won't give me any more options.'

He sighed. 'It's not only the station I'm worried about.'

I stared at him and he shifted uncomfortably.

'Let's do something about the Q'Chn,' was all I said, but the slimy echoes had been banished by his concern.

Second day, 4 pm

Outside Jocasta, solar winds pushed the comet's tail ahead of the tiny nucleus and we were caught in the drifting strands of its long 'hair'. Particles streamed past the Seouras ships and the station, playing havoc with our sensors. The particles would also affect the unprotected wreck of *Calypso* and the station's adjacent platforms. With luck, damage to the solar reflectors and radiator discs would be minimal.

Inside, more and more peripheral systems were experiencing shutdowns. There was something wrong in the centre, and I hoped it was due to the dust and not the Q'Chn. One of the reasons I didn't like the idea of evacuating and isolating the centre was that the potential for sabotage was so great there. Some of our environmental and operational systems ran on backup, as I'd told Kloos, but many of them were accessible only through the centre core, which runs down the middle of the centre for twelve levels. Engineering had sent a repair crew and there wasn't much I could do until they reported in.

Thanks to the Q'Chn we had given up the idea of sending out even a probe to contact the Confederacy. To tell the truth, it had been a pretty long shot. Recent opinion on the station seemed to be that we were wasting our time – the Confederacy wasn't coming.

I didn't believe that. We've known the Invidi for nearly a hundred years and have been part of the Confederacy for thirty-six of those years. They're not going to abandon us now. At the moment it was important to find out why the Q'Chn – if it really is a Q'Chn – is here and what to do about it. To that end, we need to know what Keveth was doing in the storage bay. We need to know whether there was anything about *Calypso* and the salvage that could have brought Keveth there.

I sat in my office and read about Marlena Alvarez.

My main interface continued to fly messages like 'Specify Search Pattern Further' or 'Results Inconclusive' before I even entered the search sets, and refused point-blank to search the historical or operational databases. Instead I had one handcom doing a search for navigational data on possible courses between Earth and Alpha Centauri while another looked for historical references to ships on those courses during the century in which *Calypso* was making its mysterious journey.

While I waited, I looked up the official history of Alvarez and Las Mujeres. It was a curious feeling, as though something I had thought private turned out to be public knowledge. Like seeing family problems aired on the infonet.

My great-grandmother had always described Alvarez in exalted terms and with little attention to political detail, but the official version had been written with an eye to both sides of the equation, and was less generous. The story that Alvarez was at a local government conference in the city and had met my great-grandmother in a bar was true, according to the database. On the other hand, it also described Demora as a 'mercenary looking for somewhere to settle away from the European justice system'. The other details were basically what I'd been told ever since I was old enough to sit and listen:

The government of the province in which Las Mujeres was located wanted to relocate the town, and several others, to make way for a dam on the lakes. They spoke vaguely of accommodation in the city, but in essence the message was 'get out'. The townspeople didn't want to go. The police, the mayor, and most of the other councillors had been bought off. Several of the major landowners in the district, the ones with political clout, had shares in the construction and electric companies.

Marlena Alvarez had no qualifications other than a correspondence diploma in small business management. The database said this deprecatingly but I remember it as one of Demora's greatest sources of pride. 'Marlena wasn't one of those educated city people, come to tell the hicks how to do things.' She had allies. The judge of the district court, Carole Benacion, was part of the old-style legal network, judges and magistrates who were often targets for extremists in and out of government. Indeed, Benacion was machine-gunned down in front of her family only weeks before Marlena died. The doctor who ran a small hospital that supported the native title movement in the area, Nerise Kauni, also had contacts within international aid and human rights organisations, and this was how news of Las Mujeres reached the outside world. The other central member of the group was Natalie Sanchez-Verlen, the landowner the government couldn't buy off. For years she sat in her mountain fortress in the middle of the land they wanted for the dam, protected by an army of thugs who scared even the secret police. When she was finally persuaded to join

Marlena and the others the government began to get worried. Sanchez-Verlen worried my great-grandmother as well. She hated having to integrate the aristocrat's militia into her own police force and never really trusted them.

Once it became obvious that the villagers were not moving, the government stepped up its campaign of intimidation. There was little on this subject in the database, but Demora had more than made up for that. I could have written files and files about the fear and violence that dogged their lives, for the opposition parties, which specialised in organised terrorism, also targeted the village when it became clear that the women were not interested in ideological paths to glory.

The database glossed over the next few years, saying merely that 'Alvarez and her group survived a number of attempts on their lives'. Demora had emphasised, though, that things got worse when no goods flowed into the town and they all nearly starved. Medical supplies, too, were a problem – the guerillas and the militias were too much for foreign and local aid workers. The foreign connection came in handy, however, when the government moved in with demolition equipment and troops to guard it. There was an international outcry and the rebels took the chance to attack government troops and press their claims, so nothing came of it in the end. The stalemate continued while Marlena's international notoriety increased – the more the government prevented her from travelling, the more interested the media became – up until her death.

※

I checked the two handcoms, but the searches were not yet complete. It was slow doing it this way, but trying to repair the main interface would have been more time-consuming still. Needless to say, in a properly equipped station with a properly functioning interface net, the search would have taken no more than five minutes. I stretched and walked around the room, inspected the print and pulled it straight. Each time I look I find a detail in it that I missed last time. To one side of the market scene a man squatted beside a basket of crabs, his face split in a grin as a customeer peered into the basket. I had always thought it was crabs but today it struck me that they might be eels.

I wondered how Alvarez had felt. In the database she seemed so controlled, so focused and inspired. That isn't quite the image I have of her though, and I sifted through my memories of Demora's ramblings to find out why. It would be ironic if the key to our situation here had lain inside my memories all this time.

According to Demora, Alvarez was a bad sleeper, and Demora had to assign two shifts of bodyguards to her to keep up with her night-time perambulations. Alvarez disliked travel and would always be worried about what was happening at Las Mujeres in her absence. She was particularly sensitive to criticism of her refusing access to the so-called freedom fighters, the extremist guerillas. All this added up, it seemed to me, to a picture of a woman who tried hard to overcome not only geographical isolation, opposition from her enemies, and the scepticism of the international community; she also fought against doubt of the rightness of her actions, guilt over their consequences, and fear both for others and for herself. But maybe I'm imposing my own experience on hers. It's hard not to identify with her situation – I only wish I could learn something useful from it.

A transcript of her speech at the venue described by Hannibal Griffis was also enclosed in the database. I was impressed at the accuracy of his memory, although he had left out the closing words. As I read them I could see Alvarez as Griffis described her; not the fearless visionary of Demora's memory but an articulate, clever politician who used the international media to further her cause for unity. Demora had been right when she said, 'Marlena knew that the meek of the Earth weren't going to inherit anything unless they took it'.

Your governments see me as nothing more than a ranting woman from a poor country with no political or economic power. They think I am no danger to them, or I would not be allowed to talk to you here today. But they are wrong. I pose a danger to them that is radical and more fundamental than money or politics, or the question of who has the more destructive toys. I pose a real danger to them because, in spite of all I have seen, I am an optimist.

I believe that all of us have the power to look inside ourselves and see what we must do. I said that conscience is not enough, but without conscience there is no beginning. You must start with yourselves, as we have. Just because you have never acted before is no reason not to act now.

One of the handcoms bleeped minutely to signal the search was done. I scrubbed fiercely at my face to bring myself back to the present, sat down and began to sift through the results. Most of it, as I expected, was useless.

I tried to vary the pace of the screen, in the hope that I'd pick up anything significant more quickly. The room seemed stuffy, and a couple of times I caught myself taking little dives into the screen as my eyelids drooped.

The only potentially useful piece of information was in the logs of a freighter that had been carrying an illegal load through the space around Earth that the Invidi had declared a kind of alien-free zone. The master had gone on to better things and eventually opened the logs to public scrutiny as part of his memoirs.

The freighter had come across the trail of a Nukeni ship. It was unusual to see Nukeni that far from Central, and also strange to see one that kept a straight course past a number of potentially useful mineral-bearing asteroids. The freighter followed the Nukeni for a while then veered off.

I considered the report. The year on Earth would have been 2073 or '74, forty-eight or so years after the Sleepers launched. That was still before Earth began interstellar flight with entry to the Confederacy in 2085. The evidence showed that the Sleepers, assuming the 'Nukeni trader' was indeed *Calypso*, were still on course up until the projected end of their voyage and well within tracking distance of Alpha Centauri. Why hadn't anyone else seen them? I would have to ask Jago to look further at the cryosystems. If they had kicked in for another fifty years, there should be some evidence of this, even in the wreckage.

More interesting, of course, was the information that

the database did not contain. That is, any record over the next fifty years of a Nukeni freighter or any other ship on that particular course. Either they'd been hiding or someone had hidden them. It was possible that the Invidi had helped them with systems other than the cryostasis. A sensor-deflecting device maybe?

If I could find this information, so could anyone else.

Rachel and I went through the salvage.

We did not go through it by hand, of course – the centre was off-limits and the salvage itself still mildly radioactive. We sat, instead, in a booth in one of the Intatec labs before a 3D screen that showed an image of every item taken off the ship. The scanners had recorded the data before the things themselves had been stored in the container up in Sigma. Rachel confirmed the identity of some of the equipment and helped us label the personal possessions.

'I'm surprised that you haven't progressed beyond this,' she said.

Perhaps the comment was provoked by the screen having frozen for the third time in as many minutes. The round-faced technician on lab duty shot me a look of apology.

'Unfortunately this is not one of our essential subsystems.' I kept my tone matter-of-fact. She was going to have to learn to live with inefficiency. 'Security is pulling in a lot of power at the moment.'

Rachel leaned back in her chair. She averted her eyes from the still image on the screen – a piece of console casing.

'I understand that the station is low on supplies and power is rationed. It seems strange, that's all. I expected . . . differences. I mean, we had avatar interfaces in the late twentieth century.'

'Yes,' I replied. 'And how many starving children did you also have?' Shocked, I realised I had used one of my grandmother's favourite phrases. Don't tell me I'm starting to resemble the revolutionary Elvira in temper as well as features.

It was one of the things I couldn't understand about our history. How could situations have existed side by side at the same time that seem to me to belong to different planets? I wanted to ask her, how could the people of your time live that way?

Rachel seemed to search for words, but then just shook her head without replying and turned back to the monitor. The screen flickered back to life again and the uneven, fire-beaten fragment turned slowly for our perusal.

'That's fine.' Rachel confirmed our ID scan and we moved on to the next piece.

I sipped a cup of tea and tapped a filepad on the desk next to the larger screen. The filepad showed navigational data from the *Calypso*'s arrival in the system. There was an outside chance it might tie in with something in the salvaged equipment. Or we might find what it was that brought Quartermaine to the storage bay in time to witness Keveth's death. Or what brought the Q'Chn and Keveth there. And, by extension, a clue to where the Q'Chn was now.

Rachel hummed a couple of bars. Slow, monotonous

beat with a lilt at the end. When I realised what the tune was I almost dropped the cup.

'What's the matter?' Rachel stopped humming and stared as I blotted tea stains with my sleeve.

'Sorry. You startled me. With the song.'

'You know it?'

'It was family history.'

'Was your family involved in the EarthSouth movement after Alvarez died?'

I thought of Demora Haase in her ancient, creaky house. 'My great-grandmother stayed in the town. She was never very concerned with politics or globalisation. Never talked about anything but the town's affairs.'

Rachel turned her chair to face me, but there was still something wary in her expression. I shouldn't have made that insensitive crack about the children.

'Did she teach you the song?'

'No, I think Demora believed people should mind their own business.' Like me, stuck out here. We simply want to keep our own house in order. 'It was my grandmother Elvira. She caught me singing that song one day while I was playing and scolded me.' Although 'scold' was too mild for the tongue-lashing Elvira dished out. 'Said it was not a song for play, that people had died with it on their lips and if she ever caught me again she'd thrash me.'

Rachel blinked. 'Bit of a fireball.'

I thought of Elvira without fondness. She used to make all our lives hell. 'She was a . . . committed activist.' Her own words.

Rachel turned back to the screen. 'From what you say,

I wouldn't have thought there'd be much to overcome by then. All the children fed, right?'

Touché.

'So do I have your permission to hum?'

'Be my guest. Rachel?'

She stopped humming.

'Why all the secrecy about *Calypso*? Surely if you had Invidi help, nobody would have tried to stop you.'

'I told you, we only ever dealt with one of the Invidi. He suggested the secrecy.'

'An Serat?'

'Yes.' She fiddled with the corners of the monitor for a moment or so before continuing. 'We weren't privy to the details of Invidi politics, but I got the impression that he wasn't sure of himself. As far as the other Invidi went, I mean.'

'Wasn't sure, how?' It hadn't occurred to me that all Invidi might not think alike. I suppose they must allow differences of opinion.

'I don't know. I don't think any of the other Invidi knew about our trip, either.' She tried to concentrate once more on the screen, then looked away with a sigh.

'Look, I realise you need to know everything about us. But if we don't know, we don't know. I want to start getting on with my life here, not keep thinking about the past.' She paused. 'It hurts, okay?'

Before I had a chance to apologise, the comm link beeped.

Murdoch sounded satisfied. 'Come on over to Hill Security. I'm talking to Trillith now.'

'I'll be a few minutes.'

'You'll miss the fun.' He cut the connection.

I turned to Rachel. 'Will you be all right here alone? Or shall we continue another time?'

She stared at the relics. 'I'll finish it. Ariel isn't up to it and Griffis is busy.'

I left her staring at pieces of the past.

Murdoch met me outside the interview room. There were fewer people sitting on the benches in the Security corridor. Perhaps everyone was too busy with the festival.

'We've got a bit of information, but not much,' he grumbled. 'It admits Keveth came to it that afternoon and said that Jones had given Keveth a job bringing back a passenger.'

'How could Jones afford to give anyone a job?'

Murdoch shrugged. 'Dunno. He must've given Keveth some pretty big incentives. Trillith says Keveth didn't say anything about a Q'Chn, and Trillith doesn't know who Jones was working for. It isn't working with the Invidi and doesn't know anything about a lockbreaker.' He paused for breath.

'Does it say why its servant was talking to Jones?'

'Only that it has no control over who its staff talk to in their off hours.'

'It hasn't given us much,' I said. 'What about the salvage? Does it know why Keveth and Jones were up there?'

Murdoch glowered. '"There must be something there,"' he mimicked. 'Anyway, I'm about to ask it for some background info on the Q'Chn. If it wants protection it'll have to earn it.'

'But we can't protect it from the Q'Chn,' I protested as we turned to the interview room. 'We can't even protect ourselves.'

'Shh.' Murdoch put a finger to his lips. 'Trillith doesn't know that.'

Trillith filled most of the room. The chairs and table across which Murdoch would have glared at a human interviewee had been removed and his stocky form looked curiously vulnerable before the big alien.

'What can you tell us about the Q'Chn?' he asked, then added quickly, 'In general.'

Trillith hesitated before speaking. 'It is not a thing we are proud of. But at the time it was a necessary evil. Without the Q'Chn our people would no longer exist. For centuries they kept our world safe from the Bendarl and other species you do not even know.'

A necessary evil? The K'Cher empire had not been acquired by defensive action.

'Were they always under control?' I asked. 'They never got out of hand?'

Trillith shook a feeler at me as it replied. 'They were genetically programmed to obey. How could they not? In times of peace we let them Change without maintaining their numbers, and that was that. In other times we produced more of them from our first-stage young.'

'The Change comes in about fifty Earth years, right?' Murdoch said slowly. Trillith's head bobbed in acknowledgment as its legs jiggled impatiently.

'Yes, yes.'

'Then how come there are still Slash— . . . Q'Chn alive

now? It's sixty years since the Confederacy was formed. Most of 'em should have gone already.'

'Exactly.'

'So you're saying what we have here is one of the last remaining specimens?'

'*Ifff . . .*' the word hissed out like steam under pressure. 'If, human, you are not mistaken, then it may be one of the last great warriors. It's not some zoo specimen!'

I shot Murdoch a warning glance.

'Sorry,' he muttered.

The K'Cher raised itself on four jointed legs. They dislike talking about the Change – they feel we could never understand, which is probably correct. Our nature is so founded on the concept of two biological sexes that it is hard to imagine being born in batches, having one active life followed by another entirely sedentary one in which they do . . . what? We see it as a static state of preparation, the way they exude a new being – the first stage of their young. Yet, according to the K'Cher, this is where all their great philosophy and poetry is produced, and it provides the metaphysical underpinning of their society.

'When our people agreed to end the Q'Chn there was naturally some opposition. The more conservative elements felt that we had made ourselves vulnerable for a doubtful return. In the first decade of the Confederacy there were still some Q'Chn born. We admit this.'

'So some of them have twenty years or so to go?' said Murdoch.

'At the most, twenty of your years. But as the years passed we realised that union with other worlds brought us much that we could not have achieved otherwise. We would not now endanger that union by reviving old problems.' It delivered this speech with satisfaction.

'But there is a stockpile of engineered DNA?' Murdoch pressed.

'There is such a thing, yes.'

'It's maintained by a multi-species task force,' I said gloomily. 'Impossible to tamper with.'

'You never heard rumours of anyone making more?' said Murdoch.

'No.' A greenish flush crept up Trillith's ridged thorax and moved along its smooth lower body.

Murdoch paced in front of the K'Cher once, twice. 'We found Q'Chn DNA here.'

'Will it talk? What if we offered it passage off the station, providing it harmed no one else?' I stepped forward.

Trillith swivelled one eye to Murdoch first as if gauging his reaction. 'It might agree. But there is no guarantee it would keep its word. It will merely seek the path of greatest benefit at the time. If it came here for a specific purpose then it will not leave until that purpose is achieved, no matter what anyone says.'

Oh, wonderful. So it could get partway off the station and suddenly decide on slaughter. We couldn't take that risk. 'So it can talk. Would it listen to you?'

Trillith snapped its limbs again and made a noise that the translator ignored.

'Why do you think I came down here?' Its voice snapped too. 'Keveth was killed, and it is obvious that the Q'Chn is responsible.'

'I thought you said there couldn't be a Q'Chn on station,' said Murdoch smugly. 'Anyway you didn't see Keveth after yesterday afternoon. It's not as if you were involved with anything. Is it?'

'I want protection,' said Trillith. 'I have a reasonable fear that my life is in danger. You must give me protection.'

Murdoch was enjoying this. 'I don't have that many personnel. You said yourself that the Q'Chn won't leave until it's finished. Of course,' he spread his hands generously, 'if you helped us to stop it . . .'

Trillith hissed something that the translator left unprocessed. Murdoch shrugged.

'You said you saw Keveth on the afternoon of the day it died. We also know one of your employees spoke to Jones the next morning. Do you still maintain you don't know what Keveth's connection was with Jones?'

'This is harassment.' Its voice grated. 'I think Jones and Keveth have together made it look as though I am at fault. There are terrible things said against the Four Worlds on this station, Commander, which might surprise you.'

'But Keveth was a K'Cher,' I said, confused. 'Why would it frame you?'

'Keveth was not a true K'Cher. It associated with lesser beings and paid the penalty.'

Murdoch snorted. 'A Q'Chn isn't exactly what you'd call a lesser being.'

'I meant humans!' Trillith's abdomen flushed a deep, dirty brown.

'Would it surprise you,' Murdoch turned away, paced

to the nearest wall, then turned around, 'if traces of Q'Chn DNA were to be found in Keveth's ship?'

I noticed the way he framed the question and hoped that Sasaki or somebody was not monitoring the conversation. Murdoch's line of questioning was legally dubious.

'I do not know what foolish things Keveth might have done,' said Trillith. 'Merely because we are both K'Cher does not make us partners.'

'*Kuvai* Trillith.' I stepped forward until I was closer to the K'Cher than Murdoch. 'If there is a Q'Chn on this station, none of us is safe. Can you give us any idea how we might defeat it?'

Trillith bobbed its head slowly. 'The Q'Chn were undefeated. Except for the smoke-eaters.'

'How did the Invidi defeat you?' asked Murdoch bluntly. Now it was Trillith's turn to twitch.

'Read the history files,' it crackled sullenly. 'You will never defeat it with what you have on this station.'

Trillith suddenly swung its head down in front of me and I jumped back a little. Murdoch put a hand on his holster.

'Commander,' it said, and the voice was as earnest as I've ever heard from a K'Cher. 'The Q'Chn are terrible. Glorious and terrible. Do not hesitate to kill it if you get the chance. It will not hesitate to kill you.'

PART TWO

THE STILL CENTRE

We stood in the corridor outside the brig cell. Murdoch ran his hand over his face and drew the skin down as though it were too tight.

'I can't keep it here.'

'That's good,' I said. In answer to his raised eyebrow, 'It doesn't want to go back – it's scared of the Q'Chn. Let it stew a while.'

He grinned without humour. 'You're in a nice mood.'

'I'm worried about the Q'Chn, Bill.'

We had to assume it would be ready for our first, second, and probably third moves. I thought of the maintenance tunnels that connected the entire station, of the ways in which even a mediocre hacker could get into our opsys, of all the defensive weapons we did not have.

I felt Murdoch's eyes on me and straightened up. 'I don't like it in the centre. The engines are there – what if it damages them? We'd be looking at spin reduction and orbit decay.' Although the engines were still the most secure system on Jocasta.

He started to say something then gestured helplessly. 'I dunno. I never . . . who would've imagined it? We've got no protocols for this. I don't know what the thing can do. For all we know, it's finding a way through the containment doors right now.'

Murdoch panicking scared me almost as much as the thought of the Slashers.

He drummed his fingers on his belt. 'So you don't want to leave the centre and spokes isolated?'

'No. But I don't see we have any choice. We can't chance it getting into the habitat rings.'

He shot me a look. 'Glad to know you've got your priorities straight now.' He jerked his chin at the door at the end of the corridor. 'Let's get out of here.'

We found ourselves in the building's lobby. The benches had filled up since I came in. Looked like the evening rush hour. I thought we would go into Murdoch's office to talk but instead he headed for the main doorway.

'Where are you going?' I caught up outside.

He half turned in surprise. 'Dinner. You haven't eaten.' It wasn't a question.

'I am not hungry.'

'I am.' He ploughed off through the crowd, and after briefly wondering if the satisfaction of slipping away and leaving him to it would be worth having to come back again later, I followed.

The night lights down here formed a crazy kaleidoscope of colours that spilled and floated from different sources. The lights dyed the thronging figures and concealed the sticky grime and cheap building materials. Music trickled or blared from every doorway, music that was recognisable as such and some that was not. Voices provided a counterpoint in different languages and tones. The air was probably thick with exotic scents too. The entertainment industry seems to be the only sector that prospers under the Seouras occupation – I don't know how people can still have credits to spend or how the proprietors have stockpiled enough supplies to see them through, and perhaps it is best not to ask.

The main entertainment area is in the least damaged section of the Hill. After the fire the mess of bars, gambling houses, holo-parlours, and stim-joints crept over from their previous location and brought sleaze to a previously quiet district. Respectable residents migrated to Gamma.

The Q'Chn rumour certainly hadn't affected business. If anything, the evacuation had probably increased the numbers of customers here. The coming festival added an air of expectation.

The clamour and bustle made my head throb. The throughway in most of the Hill is narrow, just wide enough for two or three humanoids or one larger alien. Most of the 'establishments' jut out into it in defiance of building regulations and fall back into more extensions. Some squeeze two storeys into space meant for one and the space above is built right over. Very few places in Delta get reflected light anyway because of damage to the reflector grids. Warrens of new corridors and un-licensed entries have opened up all over the level. Security hates the place. Many of the buildings were rebuilt after the fire, cobbled together with old metal sheets and un-usable ship parts.

I looked up and saw strips of red cloth tossed through a window as banners lying limply against the grey walls in gashes of ominous colour. It was said that the only colour the Q'Chn could see was red, or at least the colour that humans perceive as red. Legend has it that when the Dir world was taken over, the inhabitants deflected the wrath of the Slashers by covering their cities in scarlet to honour the invaders. These pieces of cloth seemed to have become confused with the festive atmosphere. Were they propitiating the Q'Chn, warning off curses, or welcoming the soul's rebirth?

As we walked, I told Murdoch about Veatch's report on the Q'Chn background, which essentially supported what Trillith had said. He had added that the Q'Chn were only defeated once in recorded history, and that was in what the K'Cher called the War To End Wars. The K'Cher were the aggressors and pushed the Invidi back further and further until they were trapped in their home system. The K'Cher thought they had won, but the Invidi turned at bay and within a few days the K'Cher forces, including the Q'Chn, were defeated. Legend has it that the Invidi used a virus, a disease engineered specifically to fit the Q'Chn's engineered genes.

'Is that still possible?' Murdoch sounded doubtful.

'I doubt it. But we can talk to An Barik and see if he'll help us.'

Murdoch groaned. 'He hasn't helped us so far. If he could sit and watch us go through the Seouras invasion, why should this be different?'

'At least we can ask,' I said.

During the festival, the throughways at this end of the Hill were not wide enough for the processions to pass, but that did not deter the mobile stall holders or the roaming vendors, both those who were lucky enough to possess an antigrav unit and those who pushed their carts the hard way.

We sat on benches in front of one of the carts. While Murdoch ordered, I thought about the Q'Chn.

One of the worst aspects of the situation was not knowing where the damn thing was. Like the Seouras ships behind the comet's dust tail. They could be doing anything and we wouldn't know.

I suggested to Murdoch that if the confusion resulted from a proximity device that the Q'Chn was carrying, we might get a rough idea of its whereabouts by monitoring which sections were out of use. He wasn't impressed, and said it might have two devices or the area affected might be too large. I retorted by asking where he intended to start and he just glared. The options seemed to be either major physical restructuring of every sensor relay on the station or fine-tuning the sensors in a particular area, and neither remedy was possible at the moment because we couldn't send anyone into that area. The reason we couldn't send anyone, of course, was because the sensors weren't showing us the Q'Chn's whereabouts.

I hated the idea of it loose in the centre. What if it tried to hold the station to ransom by threatening the engines? It seemed now certain that the earlier disruptions had been the Q'Chn's work, and I had an unpleasant feeling that more would follow.

'It's all very well to keep it in the centre but what are we going to do with it?' I said, more accusingly than I'd intended, when he returned with two bowls of something noodle-like and savoury.

'We can't just sit and wait for it to do something. We need to go on the offensive,' he said firmly.

'Why?' I drummed the tabletop in frustration. 'Why is it here?'

'The good thing about keeping it in the centre is that we have space to move without worrying about civilian casualties. And no danger of breaching the habitat shells.'

A faint alarm bell rang in my mind. 'What are you planning, Murdoch?'

'A projectile weapon.'

I stared at him. 'This is the most sophisticated killing machine – biomachine – ever bred. And it's going to let you blow a hole in it?'

He set his jaw. 'It's about the only thing that might work. So long as it isn't carrying physical shields. Its natural defences work against energy weapons, not cannonballs, and there's no reason it would be expecting anything so primitive.'

'Don't they have extremely fast regenerative processes? A backup nervous system? How can you be sure of hitting something vital?'

He smiled in a predatory way. 'We're talking about a very big hole.'

I pushed the bowl to one side and rubbed my head. 'I don't want a very big hole in my station.'

'It's all I can come up with.'

'Stop looking for ways to kill it then.'

'Well, what are we going to do? Ask the slime-eaters to get rid of it for us?' He looked at me anxiously. 'That was a joke, Halley. A joke, for chrissakes. Don't even think about it.'

It wasn't a funny joke. 'Do you think it would take a shuttle and go?'

'What's to stop it doing that now? It's got free run of the docks.'

I recalled his previous comment. 'How long can they survive vacuum?'

'Dunno. An hour or so, I think. Why?'

'All we need to do is lure it into an airlock, blow the door, and wait for a couple of hours.'

He looked at me then put his utensils down deliberately. 'I don't suppose you've given much thought to who lures it in and how?'

'I'm working on it.' It all depended on what it wanted here on the station in the first place.

Murdoch's comm link beeped. He turned away from the street noise and pushed it right up against his ear. When he turned around I could see something was wrong. His face was dusty pale.

I put my cup down in alarm. 'What is it?'

'They found the repair team near the core.' His expression said the rest.

'Oh god. Were they all . . . ?'

'Three. The other three were injured. Managed to stay inside one of the smaller tunnels.' He thudded his clenched fist down on the table and everything crashed together. 'Shit, shit, shit!'

I stared at the slowly widening pool of tea on the tabletop. I knew he was right, we had to do something. What had Trillith said? The Q'Chn would only 'seek the path of greatest benefit at the time'. And that it would not leave until it had finished whatever it had come to do. We had no idea what that was, but perhaps we could manufacture a 'path of greatest benefit' that would outweigh the demands of that imperative.

'It'll go after human beings,' he said.

'What are you thinking?'

'I'll take a team up. We'll lure it into an airlock with live bait.'

'It's not an animal, you know. It will know what you're doing.'

'I know, I know. All we can bet on is that it doesn't know the station as well as we do.'

'How will you blow the airlock without taking yourselves too?'

'We need an escape route for the bait,' he said slowly. One finger traced a pattern in the spilt tea. 'The best way'll be the recycle tubes. They're everywhere.'

'You'll be recycled,' I pointed out.

'Not if we turn them off and make sure the outlets into the vats are stopped up.'

I considered it. The tubes all feed into the centre's single large recycling area under Level Six. Waste was sorted there and all inorganic material sent to the lower centre or the platforms for processing, the organic waste treated there then sent to the rings. The centre was virtually unused these days so the recycling tubes should be empty. Murdoch's idea was possible but . . .

'You won't fall in zero-g.'

'We'll have to keep the suction going but at a reduced strength.'

It sounded revolting. 'Either hold your breath or take air tanks.'

He shook his head. 'Even gills get in the way. We shouldn't be in the tube long enough for it to be a problem. We'll be practising our decompression routine,'

'There's another thing.' I didn't want to give up on a

feasible plan, but I didn't want to see Murdoch kill himself trying one that was not. 'You said they can survive in vacuum. What if it can survive long enough to crawl around and cut its way into one of the spokes, say?'

'Not if we're right up top in Level One.' The docking sections were heavily protected, designed to resist accidental collision during docking.

He stood up, face sombre. 'See if you can come up with a way to trace it.'

Up in Gamma, Eleanor was not in a hospitable mood.

'Go away.'

Her office had not changed since I was last here, around the time the Seouras invaded. A Native American weaving mounted as a wall-hanging, holo-pics arranged on the desk, impressively healthy plants looming in big pots. If you looked closely, though, it was all a bit dilapidated, the holo-pics slightly askew, a film of dust on the leaves.

Eleanor sat at the desk in an unofficial pose – feet up and glass in hand. A bottle of real whiskey beside the interface screen.

'Go away,' she repeated. 'I'm not in the mood for a lecture.'

I opened my mouth, shut it again. I'd come to ask her if she was ready to go to the funeral, but it seemed like waste of breath.

'Unless you'd like one too?' She raised the glass expectantly in my direction, shrugged when I shook my head. Took an appreciative sip. 'Then just go.'

'No.' I sat down with a thud in a chair beside the desk. She looked as if she needed someone to talk to, or at least to abuse.

'Please yourself.'

We looked at each other for a moment. Two tired, middle-aged women in an untenable situation.

'Sure you don't want a nip? Leo left me a caseful. I've been working my way through it.'

'No, thanks.' I swallowed my thirst. I don't drink – it is too easy to take the path Eleanor is following. But tonight I was tempted.

'I was thinking,' she continued, tracing her fingernails up and down the bottle's label as she spoke. 'You think I blame you for Leo's death.'

I cringed inside. 'Well?'

She frowned at me. 'People aren't as simple as your machines. Sometimes we blame the obvious person. Sometimes we even blame ourselves because something happens to us.'

'What do you mean?'

'I mean that really there's nobody to blame at all. And that's pretty hard to live with.'

She looked at me then poured herself another glass.

'So don't assume I blame you, okay? Sure, I couldn't stand the sight of you for a while, but all I wanted was some time alone. It's presumptuous to assume that's blame.' She pushed herself clumsily upright and walked over to the wall-hanging, stroked the patterns with one finger before turning. Her voice was steadier.

'It's a control thing, you realise?'

'Control?' My voice wasn't too steady either.

'Yes. Taking blame, feeling responsible – it's one way of trying to control an uncontrollable situation. Refusing to be a victim, if you want to look at it that way.'

'Spare me the console psychology.'

She startled me by taking two unwavering strides to my chair, swivelled it around and grasped both its arms, penning me in. 'I'm not sitting at a console, in case you didn't notice. And you need the psychology just as much as I do. You need something. I'm not having any patient or friend of mine come apart before my eyes.'

'I'm not coming apart,' I snapped.

She took her hands off the chair and straightened up. 'The longer you deny it, the harder it is to treat it.' She stayed there looking down at me for a moment then returned to her desk and drained the glass in one swift movement.

'I think it's that thing in your neck. It must be having an effect we can't measure.'

'I don't think so.' It would explain the occasional voices though, the strange dreams.

'Must be some effect,' said Eleanor stubbornly.

I rubbed my eyes tiredly. 'Eleanor, I just came to ask if you're going to the Sleepers' funeral.'

'No. I'm not going.' She sat again.

'Well, at least go home and get some rest.' I grabbed the bottle and tossed it into a side drawer. The drawer clinked.

'Halley, I don't want to go home.' She was crying now, tears trickling down both cheeks. 'It's too . . . full. Of old things.'

I hugged her awkwardly, her white coat cool and smooth beneath my cheek.

We've had our share of funerals here.

The first lonely requiems for those who died during the station's construction, cold stars around and alien pipes echoing in my helmet. Accidents, assassinations, pirate attacks and refugee ships that ran out of fuel too soon. Tense, hurried services performed in moments between one crisis and the next after the Seouras attacked – dark, confused scenes of emotional exhaustion. After the fire, the mixed smell of smoke and slime in my nose and the names of the dead ringing in my ears.

I haven't attended them all, especially the alien ceremonies, but the authorisations all pass through my hands. The bodies of EarthFleet and ConFleet personnel have always, unless leaving instructions to the contrary, been cremated in the atmosphere of the planet below. Lately I've sent too many little pods to eternity in a brief flare of turgid gases or, perhaps worse, read eulogies for those whose bodies we did not recover. Like the EarthFleet squadrons destroyed by the Seouras. Or after the platform accident when we lost the fifteen dock workers, including Eleanor's lover.

And tomorrow there would be three more. I hadn't had time to organise services for the three Engineering staff who died in the centre earlier today. Security was retrieving the bodies now. The fact of their deaths had only just begun to hit home, and fear of the Q'Chn and what it could do to us was growing in my stomach like an icy hole. I tried to push that fear away for the time being. My voice needed to be steady tonight.

We were in one of the few remaining observation halls on Alpha. A small room, the roof and one wall of which were shielded from reflected light and angled to give an uninterrupted view of the stars outside. Griffis, Rachel, and Kloos made an untidy half-circle with me on one end. Behind us stood a few of the people who'd met the Sleepers after they arrived. It seemed much longer ago than yesterday. Two nurses from the hospital and one of the counsellors, a history scholar, Lieutenant Sasaki representing Security, and Dan Florida. Florida had caught me visually checking his suit for signs of recording equipment and gave me an injured look. I wondered if he had discovered anything in his research on *Calypso* and made a mental note to ask him after the service.

The dark-clothed human at the door compared his filepad list with our faces and nodded to me that we were ready to begin. I took a deep breath and stepped in front of the small group, hands clasped behind my back, hating every second of it.

'Good evening. We are gathered here to pay our last respects to the recently departed shipmates of our friends.' I'd had to make some hasty amendments to the official service, and if I didn't concentrate, my tongue was likely to follow the other well-remembered words automatically.

'At Professor Griffis's request, the bodies will be cremated together, with the same honours as EarthFleet officers.' One tiny flare instead of ten. 'Owing to unforeseen circumstances we cannot use the centre ports, and the coffin will be launched by remote control from an emergency evacuation port in the Delta ring. We will be able to watch from here.' If the holo-emitters still worked. I hoped so, because Griffis, Rachel, and Kloos deserve to farewell their comrades with dignity. 'Professor Griffis has agreed to say a few words.'

I met Griffis's eyes and he stepped forward, composed, while I moved back to stand next to Rachel. She smiled briefly at me, twisting one of Eleanor's thin scarves around her fingers.

'Ladies and gentlemen . . .' Griffis paused. Perhaps he was remembering that some of our residents are neither. 'I shall not speak for very long. For the three of us this is an occasion both for sorrow and rejoicing.

'Sorrow, because so many of those who left Earth with us are not here today. Rejoicing, because we three can tell their story – they will not be forgotten. Because we did make it. Our great endeavour did not fail.'

Beyond the other side of the station *Calypso* floated, a mute witness. I wish we knew how they got here.

'We left Earth during a difficult period. Humanity had just set foot upon a road never travelled. We, too, with help from alien friends, were a part of that period. Even though it might seem we were leaving it for the future.'

Kloos shifted slightly and Rachel leaned over to murmur something to him. He shook his head. Griffis continued slowly, emphasising the words.

'That future is now our present, and we must try to be a part of it, too. We all believed in what we were doing, and we all knew the risks involved.' He stopped, his pointy throat bobbed as he swallowed. 'So we will mourn them as they would have mourned us, had our situations been reversed. They went to sleep in hope, never knew they died. Never knew the second chance we have been given. We will remember them with pride and keep their memory alive in the way we use that chance.'

Rachel pressed her trembling lips together and stared down.

I thought he had finished but then Griffis looked directly at me. 'I would like to thank the staff of this station for rescuing our ship and ourselves, at great risk to themselves.'

I thought with shame of the selfishness of my own motives. Both Rachel and Kloos, and probably Florida, were looking at me too, which made it worse.

'I hope that in the future,' Griffis continued, 'we will be able to repay the debt we owe through our contribution to the life of this station.' He inclined his head towards us and as he stepped back the lights dimmed. I crossed my fingers for the holo-emitters.

The star field jumped closer, a more even spattering than Earth's River of Heaven, but not as bright. How strange the patterns must seem to the Sleepers. An image flickered into life overlaid on the stars – a small, bright ovoid gradually diminishing in size. The coffin had launched safely. I uncrossed one set of fingers.

The music began.

They'd chosen the old Earth Anthem. Nearly every year somebody would suggest it was outdated but any change was always voted down. The Afro-Caribbean beat and epic symphonic sweeps of melody, the delicate Asian wind instruments that rose impossibly into quiet ecstasies of emotion. To these people it would be fresh and new. To us it is hallowed by nearly a century of usage.

The pod became another piece of bright dust and disappeared over our heads. Then a ghostly pale half-circle appeared across the lower half of the window. Our little planet, which the Tor had laid waste and left to tempt us with images of what might have been. Its thin halo of unbreathable atmosphere distorted the stars beyond.

The holo-emitters did work. I uncrossed the other set of fingers. We have not had an active satellite relay from the planet since the Seouras came, but sensors monitor the coffin's actual position and align it with recorded images to make a good representation of what is really happening.

The bright ovoid travelled slowly over our heads and began its dive into oblivion. The Earth Anthem chorus ripped away the shields of non-feeling and we faced the reality of loss.

I was taken back to a similar rhythm, to the smells of childhood when alien slime was not even a dream. Demora's funeral – a crush of people all over the house, unknown cousins playing under the verandah and sticky, sweet, spilled wine in the hot afternoon sun. And the empty memory of my father's funeral. Elvira said my mother should have taken me, that I deserved a last goodbye. My mother said she didn't want to upset me but now, looking back, I think it was her way of defying

Elvira. So she buried him alone and I wasn't there.

The planet's misty veil embraced the coffin. The tiny spot grew larger and brighter for a second before fading completely, leaving only the planet and the stars blurred by tears.

The melody of the Earth Anthem stayed in my mind through the rest of the evening. Through awkward condolences when the service ended. Through a flood of protest calls from owners of businesses in the spokes who had been evacuated and staff who could not get to research labs because of the isolation procedures. The calls that reached me were only a small fraction of the whole – the complaints department was working over-time, as were Security and Personnel. The evacuees had been told it was an emergency drill. Nobody believed it. I just hoped the Q'Chn was still in the centre. The evac-uation should be over by now and Murdoch could move on to planning his airlock operation.

And Quartermaine? Security had been looking for him all day and still no sign. As countless illegal residents have proved, on a station this size there are plenty of hiding places if you truly do not want to be found. Myself, I would go down into the under-levels if it were necessary to avoid detection. The labyrinth of conduits and crawlways beneath each ring's throughways and buildings carry recycling pipes, heat waste conductors, clumps of cables and maintenance cells. I hadn't even asked Murdoch if he'd got his staff squirming around down there. It would take months to cover it all and anyone in there would have to emerge eventually. If the trace radiation didn't get to them, starvation and pests would. But Quartermaine was unlikely to take that route. So where was he? And why hadn't he contacted us?

I cursed the malfunctioning shower in our quarters, pushed aside a meal of space rations, and sat drumming my fingers on the side of my desk, the only clear space on which to do so. He'd been in the storage bay at or around the time Keveth was killed. Unlike Murdoch, I still did not believe he was involved in something illegal with the K'Cher, much less the Q'Chn, so his hiding was all the more difficult to understand. Who was he afraid of? It hurt to think that Quartermaine did not trust me enough to come forward.

I stood, squeezed past the foot of the bed, and tried to see up through the window that provided reflected light during the day. But there were no stars, only a blank panel.

I felt unreasonably deprived. Here I was, stuck out in space in the middle of nowhere and I couldn't even look out at the stars as I went to sleep. The stars that had seemed so familiar from the observation room earlier. They were as familiar to me as the constellations of Earth. Until the Sleepers came I hadn't thought of Earth for months. They were so close to Earth, practically smelled of it, if I'd been able to smell anything. They carried with them a whole society, a whole age, which, while not my own, was still familiar enough to tug at the heart.

My own images of Earth are from childhood, since I have spent most of my adult life away from the planet. The memories are disconnected and localised but vivid, unchanging. Like short poems . . .

I spent a futile ten minutes searching the room for a book of poems called *Sitting in the River*. My father must have written most of them when I was quite small, for he died when I was ten and the 'scrap of child with cloudy-sky eyes' who appears in some of the poems is probably me. Simple, narrative monologues or brief word plays, the poems were a dependable doorway back to the landscapes and personalities of a planet past. They gave me fine red dust of the dry season, voluptuously soft to bare feet; village aunts in ancient acrylic dresses, attention unevenly divided between the net racing screen, burning dinner, and squabbling children. Warnings – 'Don't go near the river', and inevitable shivering moonlight forays to the creek with friends whose voices are now no more than faint flavours on the tongue of memory.

My father was a congenial but shadowy figure. Eugene – he was a novelist – used to leave at regular intervals on extended trips to 'clear things up', as he put it. When he was at home he would read to me extensively from whatever author had seized his fancy at the time, and I enjoyed the attention, if not always the works themselves. One day he simply did not return. I learned later that it was a traffic accident, witnessed by the group of gypsies with whom he had been travelling. I was mainly angry at him for leaving my mother, who seemed to find the loss tragic. Which is why I said nothing when she went to bury him without me. Five years later I left to join the Engineering Corps.

I couldn't find the poems. It was a thin, battered paper hardcopy and I hated to think it might be lost. It would probably be available on the literature database, but there are some comforts only a real book can provide. I did find another of his books, though, behind the clothes locker next to my neglected running shoes, but I didn't want to read *Moths*.

It is the story, presented in diary form, of a minor official in one of the corrupt and violent regimes of the late twentieth century. Interspersed with actual newspaper clippings and interviews of the period, it tells how this ordinary man was involved in the abduction, incarceration, and torture of thousands of innocent people. He is not evil, and not particularly weak or corrupt. One cannot even say that he is twisted in some way or rendered numb to suffering, because he does reflect on and repent his actions – he is a practising Christian. Yet he is a party to these terrible things.

There are parallels in *Moths* to our own situation that chill me more than the story itself. I put the book back into the closet with a shudder.

Where the hell was Quartermaine?

I was overdue at the Bubble. Murdoch must be nearly ready to begin the operation to get the Q'Chn to the docks.

I shouldn't have let Murdoch go ahead with his plan. They didn't have enough firepower, not even after he'd taken most of his best people off other work. It was too dangerous for the squad that would attempt to lure the Q'Chn up and into an airlock. I knew Murdoch would lead that squad himself, though he hadn't said so. I remembered the warmth of his big hand as he steadied me in corridors, in a lift, going up a maintenance shaft. I remembered his eventual unfailing support in anything I had ever done on the station, and the wave of panic that followed made me retch. What would I do if he were killed or badly injured?

I found I was crouched beside the bed biting my nails.

This is ridiculous. I have to get to the Bubble and at least monitor what is happening.

The corridor outside my room was dark and deserted. It looked like our lighting had fallen victim to the system failures.

It happened as I turned to check that the lock wasn't also malfunctioning. A feeling like a surge of physical energy that dissolved fear and depression in a wash of well-being. My face was suddenly flushed, hands and feet suddenly warm.

There was nobody visible in the blue shadows. But the feeling was familiar – it was the effect of H'digh pheromones.

'Come out, whoever you are. I know you're there.'

A H'digh warrior stepped out from behind the next corner. Even ten paces away, his pheromones had worked their usual magic. When I worked on Rhuarl, we'd taken inhibitors daily.

I peered at the stranger's face, indeterminate in the gloom. They all look much alike.

'What do you want?' I knew we had only a few H'digh left on the station. 'You can make an appointment . . .'

He padded one, two paces closer and I gasped.

It was Henoit.

His voice was light as a breath, with nothing of a human's timbre. 'Must I make an appointment to see my own wife?'

For a moment I couldn't move, couldn't speak. It was

like one of those dreams where you freeze, unable to do anything to save yourself.

'How . . . what are you doing here?' My voice rose on the words.

'Greetings, Halley,' he said calmly. He hadn't changed, not at all.

I needed to sit down.

'Come in here.' I reopened the door to my quarters and backed in ahead of him. I flicked on the inside lock to stop anyone intruding and continued until we were inside the common hallway. Then I stopped to try to get my breath. It kept catching in my throat.

Henoit watched me carefully. He stood quite still, long arms slack but ready at his sides. His short, skirted garment was in the bright colours only a prince may wear, and the tattoos that curled down his neck and along his back moved faintly with his pulse.

He was tall. I didn't remember him being so tall. He reached out – I knew that knotted red hand, every sharp joint, every line. He looked exactly as he had the first day we met, at a marathon on Mars. The H'digh are a superlatively beautiful species; tall, slim, iron-muscled hunters with smooth, red-brown skin. Henoit showed no signs of the ageing that comes on them suddenly after about fifty years of vigorous youth.

I ignored the hand and folded my arms defensively. 'I'm not your wife. Either by Earth or by Confederacy law. Three complete solar rotations with no interaction. Finished.'

They do not show much facial expression, but he seemed disconcerted. 'H'digh law does not recognise annulment of a marriage contract, even with the death of one party.' He stepped closer. I could feel the warmth of him and sense the pheromones that take humans unaware. I felt heat flushing through my cheeks.

'Too bad.' My heart thudded in an irregular rhythm. 'We're not on Rhuarl now. This is my station and you are an intruder.'

'I had hoped to be admitted as a guest.' He took one step closer and I held up a shaking hand.

'How did you get here?' I should call Security but I still couldn't believe this was happening.

He said nothing, just watched me with that calculating stare. 'How did you get here, Henoit?' I couldn't take my eyes off his face. Seven years ago those high, flat cheekbones and long eyes had been important enough to marry. A long time ago. I hadn't said his name aloud for seven years.

'I approached this station using the dust tail of the comet as cover, an old stalking trick.'

I didn't know whether to laugh or cry at the irony. We had been so preoccupied with exploiting the dust tail to sneak out of the system we hadn't even considered that someone might use it to sneak in. At least his arrival confirmed that the Seouras sensors as well as our own were blocked by the phenomenon. We could either wait for another comet or try to duplicate its effects ourselves.

'Where's your ship now? You just parked it in the docks?'

'It is concealed under a vessel already docked. You will only detect the signature of the larger ship.' He knew all the tricks – most H'digh warriors do. But there are few of them in ConFleet.

Despite their reputation as warriors, the H'digh maintain no formal military institutions. The major clans are held together by loyalty to the clan lords, and the clans gave up fighting among themselves nearly a millennium ago when they discovered how much more interesting it was to battle a variety of aliens. The H'digh are not simply warriors – they are canny traders and astounding artists as well – but their culture does refute the old human adage that any species advanced enough to achieve space flight must also be intelligent enough to give up aggression.

'Halley . . .' How strange to hear my name in his voice and how familiar it sounded. 'I bring you a proposal.'

I got the impression they were not the words he had first intended to say.

God, he's really here. My ex-spouse, one-time ambassadorial assistant to Earth, successor to one of the H'digh ruling clans.

'What's your proposal?'

He stepped closer and I stepped back, nose and ears tingling. Those pheromones can be tricky. 'You have a problem with these Seouras.'

'Did the Confederacy send you? Why didn't you tell us you were here until now? What's happening in the Confederacy?'

He watched me with topaz eyes, vertical pupils like a cat. He never quite looked at me straight; to do so was an aggressive act for the H'digh.

'The Confederacy was unprepared when this station was taken. They did not, I am told, intend to uphold

your treaty but used the breathing space to gather information about the Seouras. The Seouras, we presume, did
the same.'

'The treaty seemed the right thing to do at the time.'
It's going to haunt me for the rest of my life.

'Perhaps if there had been more time to get used to the
idea more people would agree with you. Many think you
engineered the whole thing.'

'What! Why should I . . . ?'

'It is unlikely, considering that you are trapped here
also. Besides, none of those people know you personally.
The point is that the treaty muddies the issue.'

'What do you mean?' I felt a slow anger begin to burn.
While we have been desperately trying to survive out
here, they have had time to play with rumours at Central.

'Normally, if you can call this state of affairs normal, the
invasion of Confederacy space and blockade of one of its
facilities by an alien power would demand instant reprisals.
But because you granted them access to the system . . .'

'Peaceful access. They broke the terms of the treaty as
soon as they initiated hostilities.'

'It took a while for the news to reach ConCentral. Much
of it was garbled, rumours only. Until an official investigation was sent and repulsed by Seouras ships nobody
knew what had really happened. Only that they were here.'
He made an elegant gesture encompassing the station.

'Because we couldn't communicate with Central it was
assumed we'd set up the whole thing?' I didn't know
whether to be more hurt or angry. 'Didn't anyone trust us?'

'As I said, there were some. On Earth, voices are raised
to demand ConFleet do something to get the station back.'

'So what happens to us?' I had the sick, sinking feeling that the pawn gets before being sacrificed to make a good game. Henoit has confirmed everyone's worst nightmare – we are expendable

There was silence, his breathing disciplined and inaudible, mine harsh and uneven as though I'd just finished our marathon again. I could recall every detail of that run as if it were yesterday. He had been a superb runner, intelligent and tireless. The red dust on Mars had settled on his smooth red skin like the fuzz on a peach.

He drew his hand across his chest in an elegant negative. 'You misunderstand. I did not come from the Confederacy.'

'Where . . . ?'

'I am a member of the New Council of Free Worlds.'

I'd heard of this group, in pre-Seouras days. It was large, well organised, and not above using violence to achieve its ends.

'So you finally found a group who agree with your aims.'

'We want equality for each member of the Confederacy. Otherwise it is a confederacy in name only. Surely you agree the present system is unjust?'

'How is it unjust?' I needed time to think.

'The Four Worlds control the flow of resources and the diffusion of technology – such things as the hyperspace jump technology – so important to us all. The Inner Council has members only from the Four Worlds and they have the right to veto any decision by the Outer Council. Yet the Outer Council has members from all thirteen worlds.' He made a graceful gesture of persuasion. 'You don't find this strange?'

'Jump technology and most of its spinoffs came from the Four Worlds in the first place,' I said slowly. 'Didn't your planet ask to be admitted to the Confederacy?'

'Yes. And I do not regret that, neither do I wish to take us back to the old days.' He sounded as sincere as he ever did.

'What do you want to do?'

'We want the Inner Council to realise that they cannot continue to do this to us. We have the right to be treated as equals.'

That sounded good, and in principle I agreed. But if in practice it meant allowing free use of jump technology to aggressors like the H'digh and the Ohedrhim, to offer the far reaches of space to the Dir to bargain for, to give my own quarrelsome species further territory on other planets before we had evolved a method of ensuring unity on our own planet ... I'd never been able to muster enthusiasm for the idea.

'Did you come all this way to continue our old debates?' I said sourly.

He inclined his head slightly downwards, a sign of annoyance.

'Join us.'

I stared at him.

'In return we will drive away the Seouras.'

The enormity of what he was saying overwhelmed me. 'What do you want with Jocasta?'

'We want it as a base. It is far enough from Sector Central to keep our movements secret, and large enough

284

to be useful. Once the Seouras are pushed back, we have a trade network already in place.'

'We're not a military base. We don't have the defence capabilities.'

'We don't need them.'

'But with your people here it would be a ConFleet target.' I was arguing on autopilot, unable to register his replies properly.

He had that puzzled look again. 'There are always sacrifices.'

'How do I know you can do what you claim?'

'I will show you strategic proofs as soon as you agree.'

'I can't even consider it without some proof.' I stalled.

He tapped the counter slowly. Not impatient – hunters are never impatient. 'What do you have to lose? Halley, the Confederacy left you to make whatever defence you could against these aliens. They're waiting to see what happens. You don't owe them anything.'

'I don't owe you anything either.'

'You don't have to do it for me. Do it for the station.'

Dammit, he could always argue rings around me. Always knew which buttons to push.

'Think about it.' With unerring tactical instinct, he withdrew, and was at the door before I surfaced.

'Hey!' I couldn't get between him and the door without getting a lot closer than I wanted to. 'You can't go now.'

'I will not leave the station until you give me your reply.'

'You bet you won't. You'll have to stay in custody.'

If he had been a human, he would have smiled condescendingly. 'That might prove difficult.' The door opened obediently. 'I will talk to you again soon.'

'I can't let you walk around here.'

'Why not?'

'You're an illegal entrant, for a start.'

'Spoken like a Melot.'

I jiggled one foot in frustration. 'I need to be able to contact you.'

'I'll contact you.'

'Listen.' I rounded on him, angry and frustrated. 'If you want me to trust your stories, you've got to give me some trust too.'

'I trust you, Halley.' His cat's eyes flicked to mine and away again. 'Or I wouldn't be here. But not the Confederacy.'

'What are you worried about? The Confederacy is thousands of light years away.'

'It's here too. It's everything this station is – the K'Cher with its slaves, the Invidi who never do their own dirty work, the Melot who run your life ... ConFleet as a threat of violence, the poverty and helplessness of the other species. It's all here. And you still believe in it, don't you?'

I nodded. Yes, I do. I'd always believed in the ideal.

'Well, I've lost my faith, wife. So wait for me to contact you.' The door shut. I reached out to the comm link to call Security, but it would be a waste of time. By the time they got here, Henoit would have disappeared into the mass of biosignals in the lower station. Besides, the best of the Security personnel were in Sigma right now trying to trap the Q'Chn. They didn't need distractions.

I had to get up to the Bubble, find out how Murdoch and his team were going. Henoit would have to wait. He said he would wait.

I wasted time at the ringlift, which was slower than usual. I hoped this system wouldn't go down too. It shouldn't – the access nodes were in Delta and it was well maintained.

What did Henoit really want? He wouldn't come all this way without a good reason, and gaining a base in the sector might qualify as one. I needed to know how strong this New Council had become, whether Jocasta was isolated enough to protect us from ConFleet reprisals if we did join them, how Earth would react and, most importantly, whether Henoit could deliver on his promise to drive away the Seouras. The grey ships had easily overcome our feeble defences when they first attacked.

Once here, he was unlikely to return without results. Which meant that if I refused to join them, he would get the same result the hard way – by taking the station by some other means. I had no illusions about Henoit's ruthlessness, although if I were perfectly honest with myself I might have hoped he'd volunteered for the mission so he could see me.

Seven years ago I fell for him completely, and no wonder – a sexy alien prince telling me I was his soul mate. I'd had a couple of unsuccessful human relationships and wanted to put them behind me. Henoit had trouble gaining the acceptance of the first official human–H'digh union from his family, but it didn't really matter as his political views estranged him from them anyway. During the first year we only met once every month or two because of my ConFleet job. Then I was appointed overseer on a big project in the H'digh home system and we started to live together.

Memories came rolling back – he was tidy and particular, I was messy and clumsy. He was dependent on routine, I would blitz on a problem until it was solved then laze for days. God knows how we'd ever lived together. I once asked him what happened when H'digh couples had habits that drove each other mad. Absolute monogamy would appear to be a constricting philosophy. But Henoit had answered that often such couples lived apart. It made no difference to the fact of being a mate.

For ever and always. I never really understood it. How can there be only one person who is the other half of your soul? It works for the H'digh but goes against human practices and inclinations. Nobody, it seems, makes a mistake in choosing their mate. An entire planet full of hopeless romantics. Ridiculous.

After a few months living together, though, Henoit's politics began to get him into trouble. He was leader of the most radical, anti-Confederacy faction on Rhuarl, one that was associated with the revival of the old armed resistance movement that had opposed the K'Cher when they arrived in the H'digh system a century ago. I came under pressure from my superiors and ConFleet Security began watching me. We disagreed in private too. He assumed I was as discontented as he, and I could never really see the point of what he was doing.

Our differences came to a head with an incident in which a K'Cher trader was murdered by the armed resistance group and Henoit's party didn't disown the connection between them and the group. Henoit privately admitted to me that he was part of the conspiracy. He seemed to think I'd leave ConFleet and join them. It didn't help either that I knew the murdered trader, who was the owner of a fleet, and I'd worked for it in the inner systems when I was on contract. I began to live on the project site rather than return to Rhuarl and when the job finished, I left.

The ringlift reached the Bubble at last. The late-night faces on the upper level were not as familiar as those from Alpha shift. A ConFleet lieutenant on the centre console nodded formally to me as I came in.

I asked her how the Security operation was going and she checked a screen before replying that it was running smoothly so far. I was so distracted by thoughts of Henoit and worry about Murdoch's team that I sat down at the console and called up data before realising she needed the screen. I apologised and went into my office to settle down.

Veatch was sitting at my desk, the 2D screen of my desk interface active in front of him.

I was so shocked that my first emotion was simply embarrassment – at walking in on him and also embarrassment for him. How undignified to be caught spying on your boss's interface.

'What are you doing?' I tried to keep my voice calm. There was probably a perfectly reasonable explanation.

'Commander Halley.' He had already begun to turn at the sound of the door and was standing now, smoothing his trousers automatically, seemingly more distracted than anything.

I took three steps into the room, which brought me nearly to the desk. 'Well?' He'd been looking at an access file – the password module's distinctive string was still flashing.

'I . . . I wished to access a document in your files.'

'Why can't you do it from your office?'

'The damage to your interface has caused difficulties in connections . . .' His eyes were so carefully averted from the screen that I looked more closely.

'This isn't an administrative file. It's personal mail.'

Short silence while I waited for a better excuse. Then he shook his head slightly, as if waking from a moment-ary nap, antennae bobbing.

'I wish to speak to you about this issue.' He looked at the chair. 'It may take some time.'

'Speak away.' I was still unable to believe he was doing anything wrong. Although Walsh, for one, had obviously had suspicions. I should have listened to her.

He regained a little of his usual poise and placed a hand on the chair. 'May I?'

I circled behind the desk, keeping an eye on the screen, but he made no move towards it. We both sat.

'In a way, I am relieved that you are here,' he began.
'Why?'

'May I tell you the whole story?' When I nodded, he

290

continued. 'It started when Sector Central was not pleased with the establishment of Jocasta as an Earth base. This was seen as a purely political move, liable to prove costly in terms of personnel, maintenance, and protection.'

'They were right. Except that they never spent more than a fraction of what they promised here . . .'

'No,' he interrupted. 'Which made the prophecy self-fulfilling. To continue, when the post of station manager was created, it was felt that the appointment should be filled by an official sympathetic to Central's concerns.'

'You spied on us – me – for them.'

He hesitated only a moment. 'Yes.'

I couldn't say I was surprised, but the fact left a bitter taste on the tongue. 'Did you send them everything, or did they ask you for specifics?'

'There was no information here to interest the Security division of Central. I merely provided regular reports. I presume they were passed on when necessary.'

'They were waiting for us to screw up.' Which would prove, once and for all, that the Nine Worlds were unable to operate as full members of the Confederacy.

'But you did not.'

I was glad he thought so. It all looked pretty screwed from where I stood.

'The trader Trillith somehow acquired knowledge of my semi-official reports to Central and began to demand information in return for not informing station Security.'

'It blackmailed you?'

'Essentially, yes. This did not seriously affect the quality or frequency of my reports at first, but gradually

Trillith's demands became excessive. My superiors and I had decided to end the arrangement when the Seouras invaded and cut off communications. In this new situation I would have been in an untenable position if Trillith brought evidence of our collusion to your attention.' His deadpan delivery and strange emphases made it sound like a status report rather than a confession.

I rubbed my neck in dismay. He did not sound particularly guilty. I'd heard that every senior member of the bureaucracy played politics as well. It indicated they were serious about their jobs.

'Sector, I can understand,' I said. 'Just. But dealing with Trillith might have compromised the safety of the station. You should have cut your losses and stopped.'

'With hindsight, you may be right,' he agreed, as though we'd merely decided to order an extra set of plascopy for hardfiles. His reaction was infuriating.

'This is all we need. How often have you mucked about in my interface?'

His antennae were stiff. 'Never. You would know, of course. Your ability in the AI field is at least equal to my own.'

'So what's different this time?' Had he wanted to be caught? He'd certainly been very careless.

He hesitated, hands clasped in an unfamiliar pattern, antennae twitching.

'I came here early this morning. The scan in your quarters informed me that you had risen and I assumed you were here.'

Early this morning. I'd been talking to Murdoch about Keveth's murder.

'Didn't you check the comm link indicator?'

'It was offline.' Too likely to dispute and easily provable with a glance at the techlogs.

'Go on.'

'I needed to access a file that had been sent to you most inappropriately by a junior member of the Employment Bureau.'

Unprovable, but what did it matter now? I looked at him but couldn't see any change in his face.

'And you couldn't wait?'

'I did not wait. The interface was on standby and I attempted to find the file.'

I'd come back to the office the night before to save a brief report on the Seouras meeting. It was quite possible I'd failed to log out afterwards, considering how tired I'd been. Obviously I haven't been in administration long enough to develop the right kind of paranoia.

'A particular screen came up as I searched,' Veatch continued. 'It must have been programmed to appear immediately the interface was activated.' He probably had hell's own trouble finding anything in my de-modified interface.

'It was a letter from Mr Quartermaine.'

The temperature of the room seemed to drop.

'You had obviously not seen it,' his voice continued through the buzzing in my ears.

'What letter?' I swung the monitor around and began to scan my personal files.

'You still have not seen it?' Veatch's level tones made the question a statement. 'I suspected as much from your behaviour. I did want to inform you but to do so would have put me in a disadvantageous position, so I was attempting to bring the letter to your attention when you walked in.'

Once a letter had been read, it saved itself automatically to the Pending files, not an area to which I devote a lot of attention. I barely cope with Urgent.

'Here.'

Veatch peered over my shoulder and dipped his antennae. 'That is the letter.'

I shot him a dirty look and opened it, heart thudding and stomach in throat.

Halley dearest. I'm sending this to you because, frankly, I don't have the courage to come and tell you in person. I'm not sure how safe that would be for either of us anyway.

Brin was sitting at the desk in his quarters, sideways on the edge of the chair as though he'd recorded the message as an afterthought on his way somewhere. He was dressed, strangely, in a plain black jumpsuit and his hair was mussed.

It's ten o'clock in the evening and I'm sitting here stewing. I've decided to wait until midnight – it seems an appropriate hour for possibly nefarious activities. I know you won't see this until morning so I'll send it off before I go.

Only I didn't see it this morning, being too preoccupied with Keveth's murder, the Q'Chn, and the Sleepers. I looked at Veatch. He was listening to Quartermaine intently.

The Master sent me . . . no, asked me to do something for him.

He said the next few sentences quickly, looking down.

He needs something from an area of the station he can't easily enter. It's a storage bay in Sigma. He's given me tools to get in.

Then stared straight at the screen. There was a long, deep furrow of concern between his neatly clipped brows.

I'm sorry about this, Halley. He says it's for all of us, for you in particular. He says I don't need to know the details.

I'm not certain that this is the right thing to do. The famous intuition isn't working at the moment. But he's never lied to me before and why should he now? Maybe I'll find the answer in whatever it is he wants – I don't think he's sure himself. He says it's nlitri – 'information' is the closest translation, although it covers everything from a memo to prophecy – I presume it's on a chip or other data storage device. I've got another gizmo to locate it, in any case.

His body language was stiff and uncomfortable, and there was a little pause between each sentence as though he had to force himself to continue. He didn't want to oblige An Barik, but he had.

He spread his palms in a charming gesture of contrition.

Don't be too cross with me. I have to do what he says, and as you've spent some time with Invidi you won't need to ask why. Besides, he's promised to tell me what it's all about once I get the nlitri, *and you know what a sucker I am for information.*

He half shrugged. *I thought this was the best way to let you know what was going on and to give you time to think. I won't leave any traces and otherwise you mightn't know what has happened. It's up to you whether you confront him with it or not. I don't recommend it but I know you will.*

He looked down for a long moment then smiled at the screen.

I'd rather not be present when you do because this isn't easy. I'm caught between two people of whom I'm very fond, and I hate to betray you by doing this, and him by telling you about it. Let's just get together when things have settled down and laugh about it, si? Bye for now.

I sat back with a sigh and drummed both hands on the desk. If I'd seen this earlier I could have confronted the Invidi with it. An Barik had lied to me about the lock-breaker being his. Murdoch was right – Quartermaine had opened the doors to the storage bay using an Invidi device, not stolen but received from the owner with orders to steal something from the wreck of a hundred-year-old ship. What 'information' could be so important? How could information on a hundred-year-old ship benefit the Invidi? Would Quartermaine go back to An Barik from wherever he was now? Maybe he had finished the task and was waiting to give this *nlitri* to An Barik. Maybe he'd already done so.

I turned to Veatch, who had retreated to the other side of the desk again. 'Why didn't you tell me?'

He leaned back slightly. 'One, I did not wish my past indiscretions brought to your attention. Two, I believed that we could use the information to put pressure on the Invidi.'

'We?'

'Trillith and myself.'

This sounded bad. 'You told Trillith?'

'Yes. As K'Cher representative, it is the obvious choice to confront the Invidi. As well as myself.'

'I don't suppose you considered the head of station an obvious choice?' I said, exasperated. 'Veatch, the way you've made these decisions is totally unacceptable . . .' I gritted my teeth against the anger. Now we knew who'd leaked information to Trillith. And so much for Trillith being the victim of a frame-up. He was in this as deep as anyone.

'Why did you want to put pressure on the Invidi?' I said.

He shifted back a little more. Was he afraid I'd take a swing at him? 'We felt that the Invidi might have a way to break our stalemate with the Seouras.'

That stopped me for a moment. I've often thought the same. 'Did you go to him?'

'No.' Veatch made the same evil-eye gesture I'd seen him make before. 'News of the Q'Chn precluded contact.'

'How did you intend to "pressure" the Invidi?' I couldn't help asking.

Veatch shifted in his seat almost furtively. 'I, er, believe Trillith intended to borrow any means of communication with the Confederacy.'

So they were thieves as well as traitors. What a mess. Intrigue and betrayal even before the Q'Chn arrived ... Wait a moment. We knew Trillith had seen Keveth that afternoon.

'Did Trillith say anything about Keveth?'

'Keveth?' Veatch's fingers twitched and he put his hands in his lap. 'Yes. In fact, after the scans revealed Q'Chn residue I once more suggested to Trillith that we go to the Invidi immediately.' He stopped.

'But?'

'But Trillith refused. It said there was a greater prize at stake. It said that it knew who asked Keveth to go to the storage bay.'

'Does Trillith know where the Q'Chn is?'

'I doubt it.' He sounded definite. 'But it knows who asked Keveth to get the Q'Chn.'

'That still doesn't tell us where Quartermaine is now.' I could have yelled with frustration. 'What if you've endangered him by telling Trillith?'

His antennae drooped. 'I acted in the way that was mine at the time. Quartermaine, too, acted in a less than dutiful manner. It was his way. I am not responsible for his actions, nor those of Trillith.'

I closed my eyes briefly. Sometimes it is all too difficult to even try to understand.

'You can give a statement to Chief Murdoch. I'm going to talk to An Barik. And then we're all going to talk to Trillith.'

He seemed satisfied. Protocols were being followed.

'What's Quartermaine been doing all day?' I continued. 'Why didn't he come forward?'

The interface blipped and the polite message *You have incoming mail* lit up the screen briefly. The coincidence was eerie enough to straighten my spine with a shiver.

'Open . . .' I began, then remembered the lack of oral interaction. I touched the Accept pad.

Halley, I hope to god you're there. I daren't risk the comm channels.

Quartermaine was dressed in the same dark clothes but he was dishevelled and hollow-eyed. He peered into the screen, probably a public booth, continuously glancing back over his shoulder as he spoke. *I've been hanging around all day as per orders.* Whose orders? *Meet me near the entrance to the Smoke, and come quickly. I'll wait until you come, because I'd rather you have it. I think I know why he wants the* nlitri *and I don't agree.* He touched a side pocket and glanced around. *He told me to bring it back, but I said I'd lost it. Please hurry.*

He kissed his fingers and touched them to the screen, all the while watching over his shoulders. *Bye.*

End of message.

Second day, midnight

I looked at Veatch.

'What's the time?'

He looked at his filepad – he knows the stationtimer in my interface is out.

'Eleven fifty-nine.'

I made a quick copy of Quartermaine's transmissions, saved and sent them to Murdoch's interface, slapping on the strictest security rating I could think of in the circumstances. Then I pushed away from the desk and rushed to the door in a clatter of plascopy files, crystals, and empty coffee cups.

'You too,' I yelled over my shoulder. I didn't want Veatch left in my office alone. Dammit, I should have been more conscious of security.

The Bubble staff stared at us as we ran out.

The karrikar was too slow. I fidgeted, checked the controls, glared at Veatch. Once I'd talked to Quartermaine, Veatch could explain his role in this to Murdoch. An Barik had some explaining to do too. What was this *nlitri* he wanted Quartermaine to retrieve for him? He should have asked me for access to the salvage instead of going through this whole charade.

I thought of calling Murdoch but he was up in the centre playing tag with the Slasher and could do nothing. There were bound to be some Security personnel in the Hill if we needed backup. Backup against whom? Brin hadn't sounded scared of An Barik in particular – more a generalised fear. Unless we'd all been wrong and the Invidi was behind everything after all. Perhaps someone else had found out Quartermaine had been in the storage bay that night – Trillith's interview would have told anyone – and was on his trail.

What did he have in his pocket? In his second message Brin had said, 'He told me to bring it back.' Presumably 'he' was An Barik and 'it' was either the 'other gizmo' of the first message or the *nlitri* itself. My heart pounded faster with excitement – this was what linked, for whatever reason, the Sleeper ship and An Barik and Keveth's murder by the Q'Chn. It was about time we found out what all the fuss was about.

The only recent arrival, I remembered with a small shock, who was unconnected to the contents of Brin's pocket was Henoit.

We got out near the entrance to the Smoke. The festival was in full swing. The press of people, the blare of conflicting music, and the cacophony of voices were all twice as bad as when I'd been down here earlier. The noise and movement coupled with the erratic blue night lights, flashes, and flares in other colours all served to make dark corners even murkier.

Glancing back over my shoulder occasionally to make sure Veatch followed I rushed on, panting in the heat.

Quartermaine had said 'near the entrance to the Smoke'. That could mean the main airlock, which had two corridors feeding into the lobby in front of it, or either of the two side entries, one of which was blocked off from normal use while the other was barely used.

Both of these side entries opened onto narrow corridors and alleys in the backlanes of the Hill.

On our left rose the great curved box of the spoke base, where we'd left the karrikar, and behind us spread the dark warren of the Hill. The throughways were too crowded to navigate quickly. I kept bumping into people gathered in groups to drink or talk, and they didn't appreciate it. The erratic lights hid tables and chairs until I crashed into them and children kept running in front of me. The noise was too loud for anyone to hear my muttered apologies.

'Drunk in uniform,' someone said. Other people at the table laughed hilariously.

About fifty metres from the Smoke entrance I glimpsed the olive backs of four Security guards. They were in the middle of the throughway talking to a woman. I looked around and after a moment located Veatch's antennae flat with misery about twenty metres behind me. With a wave for him to catch up, I reached the guards. Sergeant Kwon looked up in surprise.

'Commander Halley?'

I had to gulp tepid air before I could answer.

'I'm looking for Quartermaine. Have you seen him? He left me a message saying he'd wait for me near here.'

Kwon looked at the other three, two sturdy young women and a tall man, and they all shook their heads.

'Sorry, we've only just got over here. Somebody said they'd seen Jones and we came to check it out.'

An alarm rang in my mind. That sounded like another coincidence.

'I'm going over to the Smoke entrance anyway. When

you've finished, send one of your people to join me. And take Mr Veatch back to Main Security, would you? He's got something urgent to tell the Chief.' I spared a quick prayer that Murdoch would survive up in the centre to talk to Veatch, then started shoving my way through the crowd again.

Seconds later I felt a touch on my elbow.

'I'll come with you now, ma'am.' The tall guard indicated politely that I should move aside. 'I'll take point.' He moved ahead of me and began to clear a path along the throughway far more efficiently than I had. Jeers of annoyance and shouted abuse followed us but I didn't care.

It happened when we were within ten metres of the end. Where the row of dwellings fronting onto the throughway finished was a crossway and beyond, the outside wall of the Smoke and the space in front of the airlock entry. The airlock itself was invisible around the corner.

There was a flash of colour from above. I looked up to see if someone was flying illegally and the Q'Chn was there in front of us.

Almost in slow motion it reached the deck. Huge. Poised. Beautiful – a piece of reaching, flexing, living architecture. It had wings. Nobody told us it had wings.

In the same instant blood was arcing from the headless neck of a human who had been standing there. The body began to topple and the stream of blood spattered the surrounding tables and people at the same moment. The scene broke up.

Screams. Tables toppled, chairs and food went flying.

People ran towards us away from the monster, yelling and falling over each other. But the panic had not yet spread back along the throughway and the crowd became a seething mass of shrieking, yelling arms and legs as they could retreat no further.

The Security whistle blew behind us.

'Get down!'

'Look out!' They'd never get a clear shot past the crowd.

Doors grated as people forced their way into dwellings, anything to get out of the range of the spindly rainbow killer as it stalked one, two rhythmic paces this way.

'It's coming!'

'Oh god, oh god, oh god.' A woman crouched behind my knees and made herself into a ball to escape the blows of the crowd. I nearly fell over her myself, then pulled her roughly beside me as the security guard pushed me to the side of the throughway where a heavy metal flange offered the possibility of cover.

'Call Main Security!' I yelled at the guard over the screams, my eyes fixed helplessly on the Slasher.

'Kwon will. We're too close.' He shoved me against the wall and peered around the flange. I left the woman and looked too.

The Q'Chn lowered its head and the great wings – like single links of soft chain – spread once, closed again. The head tipped sideways, then it turned with unbelievable swiftness and was gone around the corner to the Smoke.

The panic had spread like a flame in oxygen and the crowds behind us were falling back into the Hill. The red alert siren rose in shrill whoops, compounding the noise.

'Commander! Are you all right?' Kwon forced his way against the faster flow of the crowd, his body sideways.

'Yes. Clear the area!' I yelled above the noise of that damned siren. I thought of Quartermaine and hoped he'd heard the screams and run the other way.

'Where are you going?' Kwon grabbed my arm as I started half running towards the corner. Quartermaine said he'd wait for me around that corner.

'I have to see . . .' I shook him off and kept going. Past the upturned tables and blood-spattered remains of meals. Past a couple of people sitting or lying groaning where the crowd had left them. Slipping in the seeping red that surrounded that first mutilated body.

Two of the guards were covering me from close behind. The young woman muttered to herself as she walked. We reached the corner and looked around.

We saw blood and bodies and the Q'Chn at the main airlock entry turning towards us.

The lights went out.

'Scatter!' yelled Kwon and I felt someone brush me as they dived away. I did the same, jumping backwards towards where I hoped the closest doorway was. Before I'd even half completed the motion, a violent gust knocked me a different way and something hit me in the small of the back with enough force to wind me completely. I slid down the wall, unable to move.

The siren whooped.

'Lights! Emergency lights!' It was the other security guard, the tall one.

'Medics over here!'

Footsteps pounded faintly below the siren. Great

timing for the lights to go. I sucked in a couple of breaths that hurt below the stomach and stood shakily with one hand on the wall, dizzy in the dark. There had been bodies on the deck in front of the airlock, human bodies.

Blue night lights fluttered on in a few places, but not enough to illuminate properly. I was facing the throughway we'd come along earlier. Wrong way, turn around. Small, bright weaving points of light suggested the right way was in the opposite direction.

Somebody turn off that bloody alarm.

The moving points of light were attached to people, crouched or standing over things on the deck.

I crouched, too, beside the nearest body. The medic shone his light briefly on my face then shook his head and mouthed something against the siren.

'What?' I yelled back, and he drew a hand briefly across his throat, then went over to a different body.

The alarm stopped.

Into the vast silence broke a woman's cry, a wail of lost hope. Back in the throughway. Someone stood beside me and shone a light on what remained of the corpse's face.

'That's Mr Quartermaine, isn't it?' said Sergeant Kwon. 'We've got Jones back there too.'

The wailing kept on. Or it might have just been inside my head.

'Halley?'

I swung around at Murdoch's call. The lights were still half functional in the Hill so it was difficult to see his expression, but his voice was shocked. 'Is this where it got in?'

I nodded. We stood in front of one of the maintenance hatches. Here, the main entry hatch for this tunnel area had been forced half off its attachment and hung at an acute angle to the deck. A team of white-suited medtechs were packing up their equipment in front of it and beside them another group, this time of engineers, waited impatiently with their own equipment.

'It can fit into the main tunnels. I don't know how.' I saw again the height of the Q'Chn – it must have been at least three metres tall. And those wings spread twice, three times that. It must be able to fold its limbs and body flat. That would make sense in a creature designed to take over enemy spaceships, the only access to which is often through tunnels like these.

'We're closing all emergency containment doors over recycling entrances,' I continued, eyes on the engineering team, which had begun to sever the damaged hatch. 'It's only a stopgap measure, and a lot of them need to be done manually because of the system failures, so we're looking at a couple of hours before it's all done.'

Murdoch was looking at me rather than the hatch. 'Let's go back to Security,' he suggested, raising his voice above the whirr of the engineering equipment. He turned and walked away. I followed, reluctantly. I'd have preferred to stay there and stare at the hatch in hope of inspiration.

Murdoch's team had pulled out of the centre as soon as they heard of the Q'Chn's appearance in Delta. By the time they got here, though, the Q'Chn had disappeared, presumably back the way it had come. Its sensor jamming continued, and we still had not been able to get the main internal sensor grid up and running to counteract this. I blamed Q'Chn sabotage for the grid malfunction, but it could have been part of our usual opsys problems.

It was still dark throughout most of the section around the Smoke. The mess of furniture and belongings in the throughway had been partially cleared, shoved aside against the walls and doorways as Engineering and Security personnel arrived. Blue night lights were on in patches, and some of them were flickering. The loiterers and vendors were nowhere to be seen. Shopfronts lining the main throughway were battened down, and a few people gathered in front of them in excited little groups that dispersed as quickly as they formed. Some rushed to and fro carrying pieces of luggage, furniture, children. Fragments of conversation flickered between them.

'. . . right below us . . .'

'They're coming in ships . . .'

'. . . only if you can get in . . .'

'Security's less than useless.' The man who made the last comment saw Murdoch at the last minute and backed away sheepishly. Murdoch scowled after him.

The number of people in the throughways grew as we left the immediate area of the Q'Chn's appearance. At least three cannoned into me and rushed away again without apology. It was unbearably stuffy and seemed hotter than usual. When I loosened my collar, my trembling fingers touched stiff, faintly sticky patches on the material. Blood, someone's blood. Brin's blood. I was glad the gloom hid my face from Murdoch. I didn't want him to see me struggle for control.

Something moved above head height and I started violently and bumped back into Murdoch before realising what it was – another piece of red material had been flung from a second-storey window to join the first long banner of supplication stuck flat against the wall.

The day lights had come on in places here and more people milled in groups.

'Where are they?' A squat woman with head covered in a patterned scarf blocked my path. She thrust her face urgently into mine. Her skin was greasy with sweat and worry carved two sharp lines between her eyes. 'When are they coming?'

I knew her. She owned one of the food stalls near the marketplace. 'Nothing's coming,' I said. 'We've got everything under control. You mustn't panic.'

'What do you expect?' she snapped back, hands on hips. 'Nobody tells us anything! People are saying you're too busy protecting the upper levels to worry about us down here.'

'That's not true. Security . . .'

'Security do something for us?' she interrupted. 'Don't make me laugh! We reckon they'll let the Sl— . . . them do the dirty work and clean up the Hill scum. Then they can all live happily ever after with their own kind.'

Several other people muttered agreement. We were suddenly the centre of a growing crowd.

'That's ridiculous.' I couldn't find the right words. 'If the situation were that bad we'd evacuate everyone in danger, no matter what level.'

The lines between the woman's eyes stayed. 'You could at least tell us what's going on.'

'We can't make an announcement because the Delta comm grid is down,' said Murdoch beside me. His deep voice and large presence calmed the crowd. 'Go back to your block reps and ask them – they'll be getting messages to pass on to you. And settle down. There's no need for alarm.'

They backed away grudgingly and we continued.

'It's a mess,' growled Murdoch. 'Panic everywhere. People are moving away from the Hill. You'd think they'd realise there's nowhere to go. All we can do is make sure nobody gets hurt in the crush. Most of the transport is down.'

We reached the Hill Security building and went inside. Past the crowds at the entrance who all tried to talk to Murdoch, past the people thronging the lobby who were all trying to talk to the desk sergeant at once, into the blessed peace of Murdoch's office.

It was such a relief to be in a familiar place away from the crowds that I had to fight a ridiculous desire to burst into tears.

Murdoch was already behind his desk, trying various surveillance and comm systems. I reached for one of the other chairs and sat, knees suddenly trembling. Murdoch looked up and muttered something, then rummaged beside the desk and lifted up a heatjar, out of which he poured a cup of what looked like tea. He shoved it across the desk, careless of spills.

'Go on, drink it.' he urged. 'Best thing for shock.'

My hands shook more tea onto the floor than went into my stomach, but it did have a calming effect. I could force myself to think straight.

'Any sign of the Q'Chn?'

He shook his head. 'Nope. No reliable reports. Looks like it's gone back to wherever it's been waiting.'

The best thing to do would have been to immediately shut off the Hill section above decks as we'd already done with the under-deck section, but by the time everyone was evacuated, the Q'Chn would have had ample time to go elsewhere. Besides, where would we put everyone?

What were we going to do? All I could think of was, wave a red flag and surrender.

'D'you want to keep the centre sealed off?' Murdoch was skimming through data. I stood unsteadily and walked around the desk so I could read it from behind him.

'The Slasher obviously isn't bothered by our confinement measures,' I said. 'On the other hand, if we've got to worry about the maintenance tunnels, the entrances from the spokes are easier to monitor.'

He nodded, then swivelled his chair so he was facing me. It was strange to look down on him from my standing position.

'I'm beginning to think you may be right about trying unorthodox methods,' he said.

'What, like talking to it?' I meant it as sarcasm – my mind was still full of darkness and blood flying and screaming. I could not consider talk right now.

He wasn't trying to be funny. 'Maybe. Think about it. This Q'Chn isn't behaving like it's supposed to. I'm not sure how far we can depend on Trillith's idea of what it might do.'

'Isn't behaving how?'

'All the records say the Slashers were programmed – they were trained as well but basically they just followed very strong instincts. They were supposed to attack, kill, and leave, all in a group. Even when the K'Cher brought them in as a threat they had to be physically confined to stop them attacking. Does that sound like our friend here?'

It did not. 'Our' Q'chn snuck in quietly on a hired ship, worked alone, efficiently killed every person associated with it, and kept hiding. 'Maybe it's learned to control some of its instincts? Been given different training . . . ?'

'Or whoever is controlling it is on the station.'

'Here?' I'd assumed the brain behind all this was parsecs away and had sent the Q'Chn to do its dirty work.

'Yeah.' He dropped his eyes and took a deep breath, one hand resting on the table and the other fiddling with the clip on his holster. 'I think we should go talk to the Invidi again.' Murdoch obviously suspected An Barik.

'We're looking for someone with the resources and backing to secretly bring a Q'Chn a quarter way across the galaxy and pay Keveth enough to risk its life,' he continued. 'That's way out of the league of your average operator here.'

'Wait.' I rubbed my head, which had started to ache. 'Before we start accusing anyone, what are we going to do about the Q'Chn?'

'At the moment I don't see what more we can do.' He said the words as though he wanted to disown them but couldn't. 'We'll finish activating all the emergency containment doors over main maintenance tunnels. Keep the spokes and centre isolated. Put extra guards, force-fields, and activation alarms on all key points.'

'There are going to be more system failures, you know,' I said. The Engineering repair team hadn't had a chance to do anything before the Q'Chn surprised them.

'Can't we keep things patched together from the rings?'

'You don't understand. We always keep things patched together from the rings. But there are certain systems that must be coordinated from the centre. If too many links are taken away, the whole chain collapses. What we're seeing now is the early stages.'

He spread his hands helplessly. 'How long before we get too far to link things together again?'

'God, I don't know.' I half closed my eyes, trying to visualise the station's opsys as a whole. All the variables – the Invidi bits, the Tor elements, the 'extra' adjustments that half the population illegally makes. What would it take to crash the lot? 'I'd have to ask Mac what he thinks, but if it goes on at this rate we have to find a way to get to the core within forty-eight hours. If there's any more sabotage, make it twenty-four.'

'Hell.'

'Did you get Brin's messages?' I was surprised that my voice was so steady.

'I got them,' he said gruffly. 'I'm sorry about Quartermaine.'

'Yes.'

'I'm going to talk to his friend Ranit, see if Quarter-maine wasn't hiding there yesterday. Yeah, I know,' he forestalled my objection. 'He told you Quartermaine wasn't there, but people can lie. Or Quartermaine might have gone there later.'

Why would the Q'Chn kill Brin? I felt sick again at the stupid waste of lives. 'Was anything found on him?'

Murdoch called up what looked like a hurried status report. 'Nothing. Not even a personal info-wafer.'

'Nothing nearby?' I felt terrible asking about objects when Brin had lost his life, but he had clearly said that he'd brought 'it' to give me. I explained that from Brin's message I didn't know whether, by 'it' he meant an Invidi device An Barik had given him to locate the *nlitri* or the *nlitri* itself.

'And we don't know what this information is about?'

'No. But An Barik is going to tell me now.' The thought of getting down to the Smoke and sustaining my anger with An Barik throughout an entire interview seemed suddenly too much. I leaned against Murdoch's desk and put my hands over my face so he wouldn't see the tears.

After a moment I heard him get up and then I felt his large, warm hand on my shoulder. Then he squeezed the tense muscles at the back of my neck before withdrawing his hand.

'Why don't you wait here?' he suggested. 'I'll go see Ranit then later we can recap and work out a plan of action.'

I lowered my hands. Everything looked fuzzy. 'Thanks. I . . . I think it's all catching up with me.'

314

'Yeah, probably.' He waited a moment without saying anything, then left.

I stared after him. It was the first time Murdoch had breached the physical distance between us in anything but a strictly professional manner. Why he'd done so was unclear – the stress of the moment, or maybe he'd always wanted to. I wondered if he was interested in exploring the new space he'd created between us and if so, how I would react. With a flush of dismay I remembered Henoit – I hadn't told Murdoch of his appearance.

I sagged into the desk chair and blinked until my eyes focused again. Goodness knows where Henoit was. At any rate, I would put off questioning An Barik until Murdoch came back. Brin might have told Ranit something about the Invidi that would affect how I talked to An Barik. In the meantime I wanted to map the pattern of environmental systems failure, in case we were missing something that might allow us to fix more of it down here in the rings, rather than going into the centre.

After a few minutes, though, I found myself staring at the screen without taking in anything but the pale blue EarthFleet background and black characters . . .

Black characters merge to form a black sky. I'm in a spaceship with Rachel. We sit, knees bent, facing each other in one of the life-pods. There aren't any tubes or goo, for which I am grateful – the stuff that the crew of *Calypso* had lain in was too much like slime. Stars stream by the window, very close. Some patter against the glass, seeds of light blown by interstellar winds.

'This is a nice dream,' I say to Rachel.

'I'm in it, that's why.' She laughs and leans forward to pat one of my knees. 'Do you know why we came?'

Change to a flat plain under a sky low enough to touch. I've been here before. Familiar viscosity licks my fingers and slime slides underfoot. It gives off a greenish luminescence that rises to fill the world with a sweet, sour, acrid smell I wear like a second skin.

Halley.

Who's calling me? The air is too thick to see, too thick to hear. The sound must be coming straight to my brain, which means it's them. Why are they calling me?

'Halley.' It was Murdoch, leaning over the desk to peer into my face. I was leaning forward on top of a stack of plascopy. 'You should go to your quarters.'

I sat up and my neck cricked painfully. 'Ow.'

'I'll get someone to walk back with you.' He turned to the office comm link.

'No.' My voice sounded weak and unconvincing. 'We have to talk. What happened with Ranit?'

Murdoch shrugged off his jacket and sat slowly in the other chair. He stretched out his legs and exhaled noisily. 'Ranit was pretty upset. He told us as much as he knew.'

Upset. Of course he was. Glad I hadn't been there for the interview.

'Did Brin go to him? Was he there when I called the morning after Keveth's murder?'

'Must have been right after that. Quartermaine met Ranit in the Hill and said he'd seen a man killed up in Sigma. He told Ranit he needed time to recover away from everybody. And yes.' There was sympathy in Murdoch's eyes. 'Yes, he was there when you called. Ranit lied for him.'

'Did Brin tell Ranit what he was doing in Sigma?'

Murdoch shook his head in disgust. 'Nope. Just said "don't ask", and Ranit didn't. Or so he says. But he does say that Quartermaine was preoccupied as well as upset, as though he had a problem on his mind as well as a shock.'

'So we're really no closer to finding out what happened in the storage bay,' I said disgustedly.

Murdoch pushed his chair back again and jumped to his feet with a sudden spurt of energy. 'Maybe there's someone who can help us.'

'As I told Commander Halley,' said Veatch, 'I desired only to be of assistance in resolving our present untenable position with regard to the Seouras ships.' He shifted uncomfortably on the hard chair. His blue suit was crumpled and dusty, his antennae curled almost double in despair. Murdoch shouldn't have kept him in a holding cell with the rest of that day's arrests. After all, he had come down voluntarily after the Q'Chn appeared in Delta. Sasaki had joked, when we saw her on the way in to interview Veatch, that the Security building had probably seemed the safest place to him with the Q'Chn on the loose. I thought that uncharitable but likely.

'Let's get this straight.' Murdoch leaned his elbows on the desk between them. 'In your eagerness to "resolve our position", you accessed a private message to Commander Halley from Brin Quartermaine, failed to inform her of the message, then passed on the contents of this message to a person outside the administration. The K'Cher trader Trillith. Am I right so far?'

'You are correct. However, I should like to point out that . . .'

'Oh, I forgot.' Murdoch interrupted. 'This was the K'Cher trader you'd been passing classified information to for months.'

'Murdoch, Trillith was blackmailing him,' I murmured.

'He says.' Murdoch wasn't giving up his Bad Cop role. 'Then you both decided you might as well find what the Invidi thought was so important. Trillith must have sent his maid down to find Jones. You knew about Jones and Keveth, didn't you? Yes, and you thought you'd get the *nlitri* thing from Quartermaine. Did you and Trillith send the Q'Chn to kill Quartermaine and Jones?'

Veatch started. 'No, don't be absurd. Neither Trillith nor I . . . we never . . . we have nothing to do with the Q'Chn, nothing at all.' He half rose in agitation. 'You, Chief Murdoch, should know better than to suggest it. Trillith went to you for protection, did it not? And you sent it away. You spend all your time and effort protecting the members of your own species, and when one of the Four Worlds actually needs your help, you refuse.' He looked at me. 'This is blatant prejudice, Commander. I wish to file a complaint with the judiciary.'

'You can't do that if you're under arrest,' said Murdoch.

'I beg your pardon,' said Veatch. 'Under subsection 33 of the Security Code modification of . . .'

'Veatch,' I interrupted gently.

He looked at me and sat down again.

'We don't know how, but Trillith is connected to the Q'Chn. Because if it's not you, then it must be Trillith.' I didn't say we suspected whoever controlled the Q'Chn was onstation. If so, it meant they might have contacted Jones far more easily than we originally thought. No need to send signals off the station.

'Do you have any idea what the *nlitri* might be and who has it now?' I asked.

His antennae perked up a bit. 'I was under the impression that Mr Quartermaine had it. After all, he was in the storage bay first. At least, the forensic evidence indicated so, did it not?'

Murdoch grunted non-committally. The area in the bay wiped 'clean' was underneath the other forensic evidence the DNA traces. It must have been done by Brin, therefore, to conceal his own traces before he hid. He'd said something like that in his message, too. We had assumed Brin arrived first and after opening the door, hid himself from the Q'Chn.

I still didn't understand why Veatch had spied on us for so long, why he'd betrayed us to Trillith with so few apparent scruples.

'Didn't it bother you that information you sent back could have been used against us?'

'I have never knowingly damaged this facility or its inhabitants.'

'Who's your real master?' asked Murdoch. 'Who do you serve in the end?'

Veatch paused. His voice when he spoke was less sure, less pedantic. 'I do not sympathise with any cause, or individual, only with order. Order is served by a balance of power. At this time, power in the Confederacy is held by the Four Worlds. Only time will tell if this is balance or not.'

'That's why you can work for both me and them at the same time,' I said, beginning to understand a little. Not that it made me any more sympathetic.

'Commander, I support you because you have always shown a preference for . . .' he paused, and seemed to be consulting a mental file, 'if not order, then at least balance. You have handled the Seouras situation admirably, although not always in a way that I appreciated at the time.'

'But you . . .' I began, then gave up.

'Tell me,' I moved my chair around the table so we at least were not on opposite sides. 'You said that you wanted to resolve our problem with the Seouras by placing pressure on the Invidi. You must also think, then, that the Invidi can get us out of this mess but hasn't.'

'You are correct.'

'Why do you think this?'

'Because it is highly unlikely to be unable to help.'

I seem to have been the only person who believed the Invidi. 'There's really no reason this station should remain part of the Confederacy, is there? What do you see as the future? If,' I added gloomily, 'we ever do shake off the Seouras.'

'It is possible to be neither Earth nor Confederacy affiliated.'

'What do you mean?'

'I refer to the status of planned neutrality. This incorporates a period after the declaration of neutrality in which the applicant's legal status is accepted as unaligned but in fact the details of whatever the final agreement will be are still being processed. In the case of a colony, for which Jocasta would qualify, although with certain modifiers, independence, neutral or otherwise, must be ratified independently by three Council members other than the member from whom the colony is ceding.'

A pretty academic problem unless we get rid of the Seouras. 'Would you recommend that for Jocasta?'

He seemed almost surprised. 'I had not considered it, but it is certainly one option. It would not, however, be practical immediately.'

Murdoch had been waiting to get a word in. 'I'm going to talk to Trillith.' He glanced down at Veatch without a shadow of trust. 'See what it says that contradicts his story. I'll see you in my office in, oh, about fifteen minutes.'

'What about Veatch?' I did feel sorry for him in that cell. Besides, the thought of my having to do the station manager's work as well as my own was too appalling to contemplate.

Murdoch stopped halfway to the door. 'Confined to quarters for the time being. All interface access privileges denied, mind you.'

While I waited for Murdoch I checked the engineering updates. No change in the opsys status – that is, no change in the way it was deteriorating. The Q'Chn had neither reappeared nor given any sign of where it might be.

Murdoch burst into the office. 'Got it,' he grinned

triumphantly. 'At least, as much as we ever get from these bastards.'

'Well?' I got out of his chair and circled the desk.

'Taking it from the top,' he reclaimed his chair and ticked the points off on his fingers as he spoke. 'Keveth visited Trillith on the afternoon of the day the Sleepers arrived, and told Trillith that Jones had asked it to pick up someone under cover of the jump mine explosion and the rescue operation, which it did.'

'Did Jones approach Keveth after the explosion or before?'

'Trillith thinks before, but without specifying a time or place. When the mine exploded, apparently Jones gave the signal for Keveth to go.'

'That means they didn't actually know the mine would explode.'

'Possibly.' Murdoch was cautious. 'Anyway, Jones apparently didn't know Keveth told Trillith about this. We can assume it was the Q'Chn that Keveth picked up because its ship was so clean. If it had been a different species' traces, our equipment would have picked up something.

'Keveth met Jones and the Q'Chn later that night in the storage bay where salvage from *Calypso* had been put. We don't know why they met there. But it was the same storage bay that Brin Quartermaine had just used an Invidi device to open and search for something for An Barik. We don't know if he found what he was looking for, but we think he hid and saw the Q'Chn kill Keveth. Jones ran off, or the Q'Chn let him leave, or he knew that it would kill Keveth, I dunno. But both the Q'Chn and Jones went to ground.'

I wished I'd had a chance to talk to Brin about what happened that night. Was it a sudden falling-out among thieves or, as Murdoch suggested, deliberate reduction of people who knew what was happening?

'By the way.' I interrupted him. 'Did we check the salvage contents after the murder against the contents when they were first put away? There was nothing missing?'

'Nothing. The next morning,' he continued, getting into stride, 'Veatch came to Trillith with news about the *nlitri* and the suggestion they conduct some genteel blackmail to get An Barik to hurry up and do something about the Seouras. Trillith, with an eye to more profitable ventures, intended to take the *nlitri* for itself. Trillith knew Jones was Keveth's contact, so Trillith contacted Jones in the hope of buying information about Jones's bosses and also about the *nlitri*, in case Jones had seen Brin take it.'

'We think Brin contacted An Barik later and was told to lie low,' I added.

'Right. Now, Jones didn't get back to Trillith, which pissed it off and it gave that interview with Florida, remember?'

'The one that virtually advertised Brin was on the run with Invidi technology, yes. So anyone might have known.'

'Anyone might have known, but it was the Q'Chn that appeared and killed them.'

'Why kill Jones, if he's part of the Q'Chn's group?' I was confused.

'Which brings us,' Murdoch sounded gloomier. 'To the things we still don't know. We don't know who gave Jones his orders and who controls the Q'Chn. It'd be handy if they were the same person. We don't know what this blasted information is that everyone's so keen about and why An Barik wants it so badly. Why did the Q'Chn kill Keveth, Quartermaine, and Jones – were they all part of its group?'

'If the Q'Chn killed Brin, surely that exonerates An Barik?'

'Unless he wanted to get rid of Quartermaine,' Murdoch said. 'Maybe, like Keveth, Brin had outlived his usefulness.'

'Usefulness for what? You're heading for a grand conspiracy theory here, Bill, but the scale just doesn't fit. This is a minor station on the outskirts of nowhere. What could possibly interest galactic-scale plotters here?'

'Yeah, well there's a link to the Invidi. That's pretty close to galactic scale.'

I sighed. 'I'll go and talk to An Barik. And don't forget,' I didn't enjoy remembering something he hadn't, 'that we still don't know how *Calypso* got here. I found some evidence that indicates their voyage was routine for nearly fifty years, but we don't know what happened after that.'

Murdoch groaned. He'd run out of fingers to tick off the things we didn't know.

He needs something from an area of the station he can't easily enter. It's a storage bay in Sigma. He's given me tools to get in.

He says I don't need to know the details.

He says it's nlitri – 'information' is the closest translation, although it covers everything from a memo to prophecy – I presume it's on a chip or other data storage device. I've got another gizmo to locate it, in any case.

He's promised to tell me what it's all about once I get the nlitri, *and you know what a sucker I am for information.*

Did Quartermaine find it? His second message seemed to indicate this. *I'll wait until you come, because I'd rather you have it. I think I know why he wants the* nlitri *and I don't agree. He told me to bring it back, but I said I'd lost it.*

Perhaps telling An Barik that he'd lost it had got him killed. Maybe the Q'Chn had taken the information and An Barik had what he wanted already. But that assumed the Q'Chn was controlled by An Barik. This did not really fit the puzzle, no matter what Murdoch said about conspiracies. If An Barik knew the Q'Chn was involved, why would he have asked Quartermaine to look for the *nlitri* in the first place? Unless he didn't trust the Q'Chn, which was a most atypical member of its species. Again, why should An Barik kill Quartermaine? He merely had to wait until the *nlitri* was brought back.

Unless, a small voice reminded me, An Barik had intercepted Brin's message saying he wanted to give it to me rather than to the Invidi. And why did Brin not agree with An Barik's reason for wanting it?

Certainly An Barik's non-interference in the station's affairs had turned out to be a joke, like Invidi non-interference in Earth's affairs. Even Veatch believed An Barik could contact the Confederacy if he wanted to. Instead of doing so, instead of merely asking for access to the *Calypso* salvage so that he could get whatever it was he wanted, he had to go and put us all through this mess.

I was terribly angry with Brin. Instead of coming to me immediately with the whole story, he had to get all mystical about loyalty to the Invidi and then float around the storage bays in his ridiculous costume, playing burglar. If I had him here, I'd . . .

I leaned my head against the wall of the access shaft and tried to control the sickening onslaught of grief. Later, you can give in to it later.

The person behind me cleared her throat meaningfully. With most of the ringlift system out, we were forced to use manual access between rings, unless it was an area handy to an uplift that was still working. Typical of this station, I thought, and started climbing down again. We cut off the centre so nobody needs to go there and the only lifts that stay working are the ones up to there. Sometimes I think the spirit of the Tor booby traps remains to confound us.

The access shafts are quite separate from the maintenance tunnels, but even so it wasn't pleasant to be in that

326

enclosed place and wonder what would happen if the Q'Chn came after me inside it.

I reached the Smoke airlock. The one on the side away from the Hill, thank goodness, so I didn't have to avert my eyes from the scene where Quartermaine, Jones, and four other people met their deaths.

The airlock door shut with a hollow thud behind me. I fitted on the mask. Faint hiss of changing air, more imagined than heard, interminable wait. Tap, tap of boot toe on floor. What could the Invidi possibly want from *Calypso* that he couldn't ask for openly? Historical data?

Would the Invidi have any use for personal data from the crew? I couldn't imagine anything important and dangerous enough to risk Quartermaine's life. But why not tell me he needed some information? Because he didn't want me to see whatever this *nlitri* was, came the answer. It had to be something Quartermaine wouldn't recognise but I would.

The 'enable' light clicked on and I ducked under the inner door as it inched open. The corridor was full of the same milky fog as always, but there was no sign of life. Nobody wanted to meet a Q'Chn and they were all battened down in their quarters.

I stopped before An Barik's door and pressed the buzzer. There was no answer. I pressed it again. I could override the privacy cover and check if he was really there, but where else would he be? We'd had no reports from Security about an Invidi outside the Smoke, so he must be here. I pressed the buzzer again, this time resting my palm there long enough to confirm the ID. The person inside knew who I was.

I leaned into the audio pickup. 'Master Barik, you know it's me. I need to speak to you. It's urgent. I shan't leave until we have talked, so you may as well let me in.' Nothing. I'll look pretty silly if he isn't in there after all.

It was quiet in the corridor, the hum of atmospherics punctuated by subdued clicks and beeps from other systems. The environmentals all seemed to be functioning here. Which is as it should be. Because of the dangers of containment failure with the Smoke's atmosphere, it had the most sophisticated backups on the station. On the other hand, if the Smoke's atmospheric containment failed, we'd know we were in big trouble.

I pressed my palm on the buzzer again and the door opened. I walked through to the inner chamber. An Barik stood motionless in the same place he'd been last time I was here. Had he moved at all? I skirted the brazier cautiously in the dim red light and approached a little closer than custom allowed.

'Quartermaine's dead.'

'The one knows.'

'Did you know he left me a message?'

'Message?' The flat baritone sounded puzzled.

'Yes, message.' Something made my voice shake. Not anger, exactly. How do you sustain anger at someone who can't return the emotion? 'You didn't think he might try to contact me? It didn't occur to you that he might feel some loyalty to his own people?' This was wishful thinking – Quartermaine's actions had shown where his loyalties lay.

The big knobbly shape rocked slightly. 'The one does not wish to speak to others at this time.'

'That's not possible. A murder has been committed and you are involved. I want to know what's going on.'

Two of his long tentacles curled up and around. I managed not to step back.

'The one . . . regrets the acts of violence.' The comment came slowly, after a long silence.

'"Regret" . . .' Yes, we all regret it. 'Master, why didn't you just ask me to give you access to the salvage?'

The Invidi swayed towards me and this time I did jump backwards. I had initiated closer contact, but not this close. The long strips of bubbly skin down his sides seemed to shiver.

'The turning is mistaken. The one attempts reappraisal.'

'What about the Q'Chn? Was it a mistake too?'

He went perfectly still. Every shift, every twitch ceased with startling completeness. He might have been a rather bizarre stone statue. I held my breath in unconscious mimicry.

'The one errs. It is necessary to reaffirm the right path. Please leave.'

'Errs how? I'm not leaving without some answers. Did you directly cause the Q'Chn to come here?'

An Barik was silent. His small tentacles wrung around each other.

'Please answer me.'

'The one is not aware of this being. Invidi knows them.'

'Yes, yes, we went through this last time. You won't help us defeat it.' I don't know what I hoped he would do – activate an all-encompassing forcefield, produce an invincible weapon from the folds of his body like a rabbit from a hat? Invidi technology is sufficiently like magic that I wouldn't have been all that surprised.

'This . . . Q'Chn is not seen clearly at the right path.'

'What does that mean? You didn't know it was coming? How far can you see into what we call the future?'

'The question has little meaning. All points have existence therefore all are visible.'

'But you said that certain nodes are important.'

'Some nodes proliferate more paths than others.'

'What about individuals? Can you see our futures?'

And do they see all our pasts, as well as who we are now – not in glimpses as we do but each entire life? Does An Barik perceive in me the jungle and Demora, Henoit, the construction of Jocasta, the slime? Could he have seen the end of Quartermaine's?

'Individuals . . .' A tremor ran through the mass beside me. 'Individuals initiate paths according to their nature.'

'So you can't predict a certain action? Is that why you didn't know the Q'Chn would come?'

'The one erred. Invidi are individuals also.'

'Why did your people come to Earth?' The question popped out to startle both of us.

Silence. Stock answers – expansion of galactic influence, benevolent conquest, to prevent one of the other races acquiring Earth's dwindling resources – are never enough.

'The one is not in that continuing. There is an issue of . . . reciprocity.' Who owes whom? 'You have the potential for *desada*.'

Ah yes, the sentience indicator. The point at everyone's centre.

'Recognising your right to be considered authenticates our relationship.' He almost sounded as if he wanted me to understand.

'You're observing us? To check if we're sentient or not?'

'"Observe" ... the connotations of this word are incorrect.'

I took a deep breath, let it out again. 'Master, listen. We've had too many casualties, including a man who worked with you for years. Unless we do something about the Q'Chn, the station is going to start falling down around our ears. If you know why the Q'Chn is here, tell me now.'

'The one does not know.' It was as clear an answer as I'd ever had from him.

'What is the *nlitri* and why did you ask Quartermaine to get it?'

'The one attempts to correct an error.'

'What sort of error?'

'Invidi learn ... not to intervene in the affairs of others. What you call the coming-to-view.'

'The future?'

'Yes. By the seeing, the thing seen changes. In the continuing to which your Sleepers belong, an Invidi intervenes.'

'You mean An Serat?'

'Correct. The one asks Mr Quartermaine to retrieve ... evidence, your Mr Murdoch would say. Evidence of this intervention.'

'The *nlitri* is this evidence?'

'Correct.'

'Why is it so important?'

He said nothing. Perhaps I should have asked to whom it was important.

'What does this have to do with the Q'Chn?'

'The one does not perceive a direct connection.'

'Then why did it kill Quartermaine? Did he bring you this "evidence" the night he died?'

'The one does not talk to him.'

He might be telling the truth. 'So you don't know if he got it or not?'

That bore out what Quartermaine had said, that An Barik 'wasn't sure himself'.

'How did you know this information was on the *Calypso*?'

A long silence.

'It is Invidi only to understand.'

And I got no more out of him.

Brin had made me his executor, damn him. In the stiff holo-testament format he calmly asked me to distribute his property in various ways. It was devastating, but finally I managed to go through his personal files. I sat in his office and recorded a message to his parents. They were frail, and lived on Earth, in a community hospice in Auckland. The message was encrypted and posted to the top of the URGENT list of missives to Earth and Confederacy that sat in the filesys and waited for the day Jocasta would be free. One of Veatch's staff regularly reviewed and weeded out the unwanted or outdated messages.

It made me think about my friend, how little I had really known him. I looked around the little office – neat, impersonal. ConFleet standard issue furniture. His real life can't have been here.

If I'd thought about it, his firm stand on the Nine versus Four problem should have given me a clue that he might side with the Invidi. He had been so convinced of their essential benevolence towards us. And who was I to disagree? He had spent most of his life trying to understand the Invidi. We have no proof to dispute their benevolence, only a great deal of circumstantial evidence that could be read many ways.

Although if you were to take the opposite position on the Nine/Four issue, the whole structure of the Confederacy was proof that the Invidi, K'Cher, Melot, and Bendarl wanted nothing more than to keep the rest of the member worlds in subservient status. In fact, I followed the unfamiliar thought reluctantly, the superiority of Invidi technology and its application in a jump drive is the keystone of that structure. If in some way you could remove it, allow the Nine Worlds to comprehend and use that technology, then the whole structure would come tumbling down. But then a century of peace might be buried in the rubble.

Brin's second thoughts were all the more shocking for his faith in the Invidi. What could possibly have caused him to disagree? He'd decided I needed to have the *nlitri*, because presumably I would use it in a different way from An Barik.

I accessed the files he'd been working on the day he died. Three of them were routine Linguistics department business, but the fourth was his research on An Serat. That name kept appearing as we got deeper into the case, and Brin's research indicated why.

An Serat had been the head or facilitator of the Invidi's first expedition to Earth. Apparently he was still alive, under a sort of house arrest on the Invidi home planet for his 'unethical' activities – including acting beyond his brief in revealing technology to humans. He was 'asked to leave' the expedition by consensus.

I suppose helping *Calypso* would qualify as acting beyond his brief, especially as Rachel's words indicated their whole expedition had been kept a secret from the other Invidi, if only for a while. An Barik must know about it now, which is why he was trying to retrieve evidence of An Serat's tampering from the wreck. The whole incident was looking more and more like an Invidi internal affair. An Barik must be gathering information to use against An Serat in some Four Worlds squabble. Brin's research also mentioned that An Serat still had support from some of the younger and more radical Invidi – obviously An Barik was neither.

But that didn't answer the question why An Serat helped the Sleepers. I didn't believe in the good samaritan theory any more. He must have seen some advantage in sending them off the planet – was it to keep something secret for nearly a hundred years?

Revealing technology to humans. That must mean technology that should not have been revealed to humans – the Invidi brought us plenty of technological advances, but only in the areas they chose. We took what we could and were grateful for it. What else could An Serat have given humans?

The first thing that sprung to mind was the cryotechnology – Griffis had indicated the Invidi offered it to Nguyen. I should ask Eleanor what else she'd found out about that technology. She'd have had time to go over the probe's records by now. I tried the comm link but it was blocked. Great, all we need is internal communications to go down.

I left Brin's office. Fortunately the hospital was on the same level, so I wouldn't have to clamber up or down access shafts.

Eleanor came from her quarters but she wasn't happy about it.

'Halley, it's half-past five in the morning.'

'I know, but we're running against time. We have to do something about the Q'Chn so we can get up to the centre.'

Eleanor moved past me into her office and activated the interface. She sighed, slid a storage drawer out from the wall, and poured herself a cup of liquid from the heatjar inside.

'Coffee?'

I shook my head. Even the idea made me feel sick.

'I know about the Q'Chn attack,' she said. 'We finished the autopsies about an hour ago.'

'Oh. Sorry to wake you.'

She leaned back in her chair, hair mussed, face pale and tight, eyes swollen from lack of sleep. She wore an ancient woven fabric cardigan over the hospital whites and it made her calmness seem more human.

'Why *did* you wake me? And sit down, will you?' She pointed at the guest chair.

'No, thanks. Think I'd better not.' I had the feeling that if I sat down, I wouldn't have the energy to get up again. 'It's about the cryosystems on *Calypso*. Can you give me a more complete report on them?'

'I already gave you a report.'

'You said they were what you'd have expected. Did you mean they use the kind of technology that the Invidi gave us in that period?'

She frowned and put the cup down. 'I'm no historian but ... no, I wouldn't have said so. The *Calypso*'s systems used nanotechnology and integrated functionality that we didn't achieve until the beginning of space flight. We didn't need it before then, of course, whereas the Sleepers did. I assume that's why the Invidi supplied it.'

That might have been what An Serat was being criticised for. The trouble was, if he wanted to get rid of evidence of his tampering, why send the Sleepers into space and why in such a haphazard way? If he wanted to conceal something, sending it to wander through a highly travelled area of space while its guardians slept was hardly the ideal method. No, I think we're off track here.

'Are you sure the wakeup mechanism was set for fifty years?'

Eleanor grimaced and drummed her fingers on the desk. 'I wish you wouldn't call it a mechanism, as though it's an alarm clock. The cryosystems are partly organic themselves. It's an incredibly sophisticated method of controlling the autonomic nervous system.'

'Fine. But when were they supposed to wake up?'

'They said they were going to Alpha Centauri. That's about fifty years.'

'That's what they said. Only we're left with the problem of forty-five years unaccounted for. What about the systems?'

She looked at me for a long moment then blinked up files on the interface, presumably of the cryosystems. I found I was starting to sway a bit and shifted my feet. Maybe I should sit down.

'You could be right. There's evidence . . . of a sort,' she said finally.

'What do you mean?' I walked around beside her and peered at the screen, which let me lean on the desk. She pointed at some figures that meant nothing to me other than that they recorded some kind of neural degradation.

'It could mean the cryosystems reinitialised and continued after that fifty years. Which is logical, considering, as you say, we're a hundred years after they left. Which means the systems were programmed from the beginning for ninety-five years. On the other hand . . .' she blinked through more data, using the retinal interface connection. I've never had enough ocular control to use one efficiently.

'On the other hand, I could be wrong. This attrition could be a function of the nanotechnology, which tends to destroy itself after a program is complete.'

'So it might have been only fifty years after all? I think

that qualifies as an impossible probable.' Fifty years is fifty years and ninety-five is a lot longer than that. I'm starting to sound like the Invidi. Profound and totally meaningless.

'Some advice from your doctor.' Eleanor had stood up and was looking at me nose to nose. Chin to nose rather, as she's nearly a head taller. 'Go back to your quarters, take a shower.' She fingered the stains on my uniform with distaste. 'Get changed. Have something to eat and a couple of hours' sleep. You'll be surprised how easy things get after that.'

The wonders of contemporary medicine. Prescription – hot water, clean clothes, food, and sleep. Amazing.

'You should probably have a good cry too,' she added. 'For Brin's sake.'

I swallowed. 'Eleanor, did he suffer?'

'No. It was very quick. He probably didn't even notice.'

She shouldn't have patted me on the shoulder. The gesture released all the tension and grief of the past twenty-four hours into a flood of tears onto her faded cardigan.

'Shh,' said Eleanor, and this time it was she who rocked me gently.

Third day, 6:30 am

I got about three minutes' worth of hot water out of the shower in our quarters, but it was enough to make a difference. I actually felt my body belonged to me again, not some stranger who wasn't listening to it saying, I'm tired, I hurt, and I'm hungry. The final spurt of cold water woke me up enough to buzz my teeth clean and wonder what to have for breakfast.

I stopped off in the kitchen on the way to my room from the shower, a drywrap tied gingerly under one armpit in case the visual interface activated unexpectedly. I was developing scattered bruises where the Q'Chn had knocked me against the wall in the Hill, and the drywrap knot caught painfully. The rooms were all quiet. Lee was pulling a double shift helping Engineering and the other two weren't up yet.

There didn't seem to be anything immediately edible. Maybe I'd sleep first, then get something at the messhall.

The door chimed. I looked in the visual scan and saw Henoit standing outside.

'You can't come in here!' I hissed.

He cocked his head at the drywrap, which had slipped with the ferocity of my reaction. I grabbed it and hesitated. If I sent him away, goodness knows when we'd get a chance to talk again. And I had to know more about his offer. The night's events had kept me preoccupied with the immediate danger of the Q'Chn, but Henoit was a danger too. Of a different kind.

'All right then. But come into this room.' I led the way back to my private portion of the unit.

'ConFleet's not doing much for its officers these days,' he commented as the door whooshed shut behind him. In a human it would have been a joke, but Henoit was quite serious.

'We're conserving space,' I said, and wished I'd got him to wait while I changed first. One flimsy layer of material between us wasn't enough. I could feel my body responding to the pheromones as we spoke. It wasn't an unpleasant sensation, just unnerving to be aroused without having thought about anything in that context at all.

I sat behind the desk and motioned Henoit to sit in the other chair, a safe distance away. He removed a stack of crystals and some underwear from the chair and sat. He said nothing, but every fastidious gesture was a criticism of my sloppiness. I drummed fingertips on the desk and vowed not to get annoyed.

'First of all, where have you been? What if I'd wanted to contact you to say I agreed with your offer?'

'Do you?' he asked quickly.

'I didn't say that. But where were you?'

'In an abandoned dwelling. In a section that seems to have been burnt recently,' he said grudgingly.

The damaged sector in the Hill. 'You shouldn't stay there. It's not safe.'

'That is irrelevant. Have you considered my offer?'

'I think you'd better tell me more about this alliance.'

He dipped his chin in assent. 'We are not a simple conspiracy. You must understand that we represent, directly or indirectly, billions of beings on the Nine Worlds who are dissatisfied with the present system. We offer an alternative.'

'If you want change, why can't you work within the Confederacy? We have a representative system.'

His mouth twisted in distaste. 'You know how it works. We have to work through duly elected representatives of the government or whatever system the planet works with. The H'digh government is controlled by senior officials who have everything to lose if the status quo is upset.'

Henoit's family is one of the pillars of the status quo on his world. He had chosen a road that defied his own traditions.

'So what does this movement intend to do?'

He raised his eyebrows in a negative. 'I can't tell you too much.'

'How can I decide without knowing?' I almost laughed at the absurdity of it. 'I don't need your strategic secrets but at least tell me your long-term objectives.'

He was silent for a moment, his cat's-eyes, never still, stroked over me, the desk, the bed visible at the back of the room. I hoped it was my imagination that his gaze lingered on the bed.

'We want them to combine the Outer and Inner Councils and give us a seat on the new one. As representatives of a significant number of Confederacy members.'

'So you don't actually want to dissolve the existing alliances?'

'No. There is too much for us to gain by keeping them. But we want to be included. Your joining us would be a tremendous example in itself. This is the only space station administered by one of the Nine Worlds. It is Earth's single extra-system base. Think how many it would persuade to join our movement if you did so.'

'Not so fast. You want Jocasta as a base. Will you bring your fleet in here?'

'I told you I can't tell you too much until we know where you stand.'

'What means do you intend using to achieve your goals, if not the official ones?'

'I can't tell you.'

'I will not be a party to terrorism. Too many innocent lives are lost.'

We glared at each other and he did not withdraw his eyes this time. Stare only at mortal enemies and mate – was I both or neither?

'Don't you want to get rid of those ships?' He sounded frustrated.

'Of course I do!' So much that I can taste it. 'But I have to think ahead too.'

'It's hard to see that it could get any worse for you here.' Maybe not, but at least the Seouras leave us more or less alone. ConFleet might not be so laissez-faire if they found we'd betrayed them.

'Besides, it isn't only me you have to convince. I don't run the place single-handed. I need something concrete to take to my senior officers and the administration.'

'You underestimate yourself. Our sources think your staff is almost undividedly loyal.'

I had a sinking feeling and wondered who else besides

Veatch had betrayed us. 'Sources? What sources? Have you been spying on us?'

'No spies,' he said hurriedly. 'I give you my word we have no spies here now.'

'But you did have?'

He sniffed and didn't answer. I wondered why he'd said 'almost' undividedly loyal. I pushed aside the paranoid thought, pulled my drywrap tighter around me and shivered.

We were getting nowhere with this conversation. Nowhere with the whole situation. He couldn't give me information until I committed and I couldn't commit without more information. The Confederacy has abandoned us and the New Council only wants to use us for their own ends.

He cleared his throat. 'Why did you leave?' he said, half turned away, his voice tense.

'Why?'

'Yes, I want to know. I have wanted to know for many years. How could you disappear without a word?'

'I left you a holovid explaining why . . .'

'You left less than nothing!' His vehemence was startling. He got out of the chair and prowled up and down the room as he spoke, his long strides covering the space quickly.

'You insulted me by not talking to my face, then further by not answering my calls.'

The accusation stung, because it was true.

'I was . . . afraid.'

'Afraid?' He said it in the way of one to whom it had never and would never happen.

'Yes, dammit. Afraid of what you'd become. A terrorist.' And afraid, too, that if I spoke to him face to face I would not be able to resist the lure to physical union. As I found it difficult to resist now.

'You are my wife. You should tell me what is in your mind.'

'You really believe this? That there's only one person for you in the whole universe?'

'Usually one person on our whole world.'

I wanted him to show me a foolproof way to understand. I couldn't accept that there could be harmony without understanding. At least, there might have been, in the days when we had harmony.

'Aren't you confusing physical attraction with . . . with some sort of mystical union?'

He looked at me and then away in total incomprehension that I took as prevarication, until I remembered that the H'digh do not admit a dichotomy between mind and body. Their philosophies contain little celebration of the dualities beloved by human thought – spirit and flesh, form and content, heaven and earth. Life and death.

He leaned over the desk close enough for me to feel the soft, warm touch of his breath on my face. ' "By time not asundered, nor by distance rendered, World cannot defeat us, nor death shall us part".'

For a second I almost gave in and touched him, gave in to the desire for his breath to be mine again.

'Let me guess – from the *Khual'anath*?' The extraordinarily long and complex epic poem that seems to provide half the sayings and precedents in H'digh society. 'I didn't know it contained love poetry.' I leaned back and

344

swivelled the chair away from him, deliberately breaking the spell.

'It is from the Marriage Ode of Queen Ser,' he admonished. 'Why do you think we mate for life? Neither of us will ever achieve such a bond with anyone else. I don't know what you mean by "mystical". This is a fact.'

I could feel the 'fact' as I prickled and throbbed under the drywrap in response to his presence. But I was older now, if not wiser, and there were a lot of things hanging over me to balance the pheromones. The Q'Chn, *Calypso*, An Barik, the Seouras. Maybe we were bonded forever. That didn't mean I had to live with him, or agree with his politics.

'Why did you come here?' I asked straight. 'Why you, and not some other persuasive bastard?' Were he and his group so foolish as to think I'd be more susceptible to his suggestions? I would have thought the fact that I'd left him would have alerted them to the likelihood of the opposite being true.

'I . . .' For an extraordinary moment he seemed to be lost for words. Normally he would never leave a gap in conversation, any more than he would leave a gap for an opponent in a duel. 'I wished to ask you the question that you have not yet answered. Why did you leave?'

'Because I couldn't live with a murderer.'

He considered the words. Moved his long, powerful hands in a rolling gesture as if to turn the words over and look underneath.

'Yet you would have lived with a warrior.'

'Don't insult me by saying you don't know the difference. Even your father didn't condone those killings.' The older H'digh lived by a rigid code. Which was one of the reasons they were losing their young to other creeds.

'I do not understand your thoughts. But however far you run, you will always be my wife.'

I shrugged. Legally we were divorced, and as far as I was concerned that was it. He could think what he liked.

'But I still offer you a chance to be together in our political activities. Join us in our fight against the hegemony of the Four Worlds.'

Say yes and we ally ourselves against our own world and its protectors. Say no and they take the station anyway. Do nothing and if the Q'Chn doesn't destroy us the Seouras probably will. What would Marlena Alvarez have done?

I shook away the thought. It was absurd to be looking for guidance to a world so much simpler than our own.

'Give me some time,' I began.

He turned in annoyance and strode to the door.

'No, really,' I said, standing to call him back. 'I have to do something about the Q'Chn, or you won't have a functioning station even if you do manage to beat the Seouras. Give me twenty-four hours.'

'Make it twelve,' he said, and left. I stood there wondering what Murdoch was going to say.

Murdoch said a lot, most of it unworthy of an officer.

I caught up with him in Gamma where he was arguing with property owners who didn't want to lend us space for residents evacuated from the Hill, even at interest. I suppose they were aware of our solvency status. Murdoch asked them to wait while we adjourned to a nearby overhang and I told him about Henoit.

I think it was the Seouras that annoyed him most. 'We've been sitting here like we're in quarantine for a communicable disease for six months. They couldn't let supply ships through, could they? Oh no. Just some ancient junk heap with frozen passengers, a bloody alien killing machine, and now a terrorist.'

Certainly the Seouras behaviour was inexplicable. But it was not our greatest worry at the moment.

Murdoch knew Henoit's name instantly. 'Your ex, isn't he?' He looked at me slyly. 'Bit of a coincidence, that.'

'It's no coincidence,' I said wearily. 'They must think it'll be easier for him to work through me.'

When I was on Rhuarl an officious Security sergeant once explained to me that Henoit had a record for political activity. There was no evidence that he had ever put a foot wrong but unspoken acknowledgment that he was one of the leaders of the anti-Central movement. The sergeant pointed out that if I had any information to add to the record, it was my duty to come forward with it. That was the sort of position Henoit had continually put me in.

'Work through you to do what?'

I concealed a yawn and rubbed tension knots in my shoulders. 'He says he's a member of the New Council of Free Worlds.'

Murdoch started, but said nothing.

'And that if I agree to join them and put the station at their disposal, they'll get rid of the Seouras for us.'

Murdoch looked up, around, then passed one hand across his head. He opened his mouth, shut it, then finally ended up saying merely, 'Shit. You said he came onstation before Quartermaine was killed?'

'That's what he says. Using the comet tail as cover.'

Murdoch snorted, amused. He saw the irony in that too. 'I wish you'd told me earlier.'

'I'm sorry. It really wasn't at the front of my mind last night.'

Murdoch folded his arms and made an exasperated 'phew' sound. He was angry, but not at me. 'Is he telling the truth? You know him better than anyone else here.'

'I haven't seen him for seven years.'

'No kidding?' Studiously indifferent. 'That's a long time.' He muttered something to the uncaring Boulevard.

'What?'

'Nothing.'

'It was not nothing.' I stepped back a pace so I could eyeball him properly. 'Say it again, if it's worth saying.'

'Jeez, what a fuss.' His eyes were everywhere but on mine. 'I said that it must have been some reunion, that's all. You'll have to adjust the record. You're down as divorced.'

I could have kicked him. 'That's no business of yours.'

He must have been ogling the Security files. Everything is on those files once you get a high-level clearance.

'This bloke enters the station in secret, doesn't let anyone except you know he's here ... everything about him is Security business. His past especially. Because it might give us a handle on his present motives.' Murdoch met my eyes at last. His own showed anger, and something else. I wasn't the only person to feel betrayed. 'So get off your high horse and tell me what's going on.'

I do hate it when he's right. 'Keep out of my personal life.'

He snorted. 'You take a command position with ConFleet, you don't have a personal life. Do you think he's telling the truth?'

'If he says he'll help us, he will try. But I don't know whether they can do what they promise. The Seouras weapons ...' We had both seen those weapons.

'What sort of a base do they want to make Jocasta?'

'He won't say. But it's not just our freedom at stake here.'

'You don't want to provide the possible catalyst for a movement that might start the downfall of the Confederacy.' He stated one of my fears matter-of-factly.

'No. Nor do I wish to provide an excuse for the Confederacy to crush that movement.'

That shook him. I was grateful he had not taken the easy way and merely pointed out that my duty was to gaol Henoit and get as much information as possible about the New Council.

'What do you think, Bill? Personally.' I was unsure if he'd reply at all, especially after his unexpected outburst yesterday about the Confederacy not helping us against the Seouras.

He scowled irresolutely at the dusty deck. On the Boulevard voices were raised in altercation, and there was a cracking sound as a construction AVG unloaded building materials. As I watched him Murdoch came to some decision.

'I'm glad to be alive now, y'know?' The expression he turned to me had none of his usual smirk. 'My people were treated as second-class citizens for hundreds of years. On their own land. It's taken us a long time to get over that.' A beat. His eyes stayed on my face but for once I didn't feel self-conscious. 'I don't want to be treated like that simply because I'm human.'

'I didn't know you were a separatist.'

'I'm not. I was talking to Griffis yesterday. He told me a bit about the EarthSouth movement in our place. Seems my people were more involved than I thought.'

'You didn't know that before?'

'Nah, I never saw us as revolutionary types. Too lazy, I always thought. But it looks like I was wrong.'

'Has it changed your mind? You think we should throw in our lot with the New Council?'

He grimaced. 'I don't like their methods.'

I thought of Henoit and the dead K'Cher trader on Rhuarl. 'Neither do I.'

'What do you think he'll do if you refuse?'

That was the other problem. 'I *know* what he'll do – try to take the station anyway.'

'Shit.' Murdoch stared rudely at the store-owner who'd appeared in the doorway next to us. The small Achelian

350

twitched her nose and slammed the door again.

'How will he do that? Bring in his fleet? Whichever way it goes, if they want Jocasta they'll have to get rid of the Seouras.'

'Exactly. We might as well make sure it happens on our terms, don't you think?'

'So you're going to agree?'

'Unless you can come up with a way to get rid of the Seouras first.'

He rubbed his chin thoughtfully. 'Why don't you ask him to prove he's sincere?'

'What do you mean?'

'He's a H'digh warrior, isn't he? Ask him to help us get rid of the Q'Chn.'

I considered the idea. If it worked, we would lose the Q'Chn menace, get rid of the Seouras, and become part of an alliance more immediate than the Confederacy. If it failed, the New Council would gain a base that had no operative systems and one resident monster.

'I don't know if he'd do it.'

'Depends how much he wants the station.'

I looked out on the Boulevard, a noisy, messy, volatile mixture of worlds. The lights flickered and the clamour increased as voices were raised in protest. I turned to Murdoch and broached the subject I'd been trying to avoid ever since I'd spent the hours since breakfast poring over holomaps of the engineering core.

'Bill, we're going to have to send another team up to the centre.'

'You're sure?' He looked as if he'd swallowed something bitter.

'Yes. We're running out of time. I've worked out the best route for us to take. With any luck, we won't be in any tunnels wide enough for the Q'Chn even if it's there.'

'Whoa. Who's "we"?'

'I know the core better than anyone else on the station.'

'No way.'

We glared at each other with ridiculous intensity. I broke it.

'I don't want to send anyone into a danger that I'm not prepared to risk myself.'

'Yeah, very noble. But we need the head of station here and alive.'

'I'm the best person for the job, dammit!'

'Then we'll send second-best.' He folded his arms with finality and I knew he had regulations and probably every other senior officer's opinion on his side. But he was wrong.

'Send them to me to be briefed then.' I turned away from him but he called after me.

'Wait a minute. Nearly forgot about this.' He reached into his belt pocket, glanced around to make sure nobody was watching, and held something out to me. A flat piece of round-ended metal about two fingers wide and short enough to be concealed in the human palm. Metal? It had a soft sheen, almost like clean fur.

'What is it?' I'd never seen anything like it, either tool or artefact.

'We found it on Jones's body but it was put in with his other effects. Forensic only checked it this morning. It had other human residue on it – Quartermaine's.'

I looked at him, shocked. 'This is what Brin was carrying?'

He nodded. 'We think Jones picked Quartermaine's pocket. Sasaki found a couple of people who said they saw Jones following someone the night before the Q'Chn attacked in Delta. And this morning I confirmed that Trillith offered to pay Jones to get it off Quartermaine.'

I took another step closer. 'Give it to me.'

Murdoch dropped the thing into my outstretched hand as if he wanted as little contact with it as possible.

'You're going to give it back to the Invidi.' It wasn't a question.

The thing nestled in my palm, faintly warm and furry. Was this the *nlitri* everyone was so excited about? Or simply the aid given to Quartermaine to find the information? As my fingers closed around it the decision was made.

'No. I'm not going to give it back.'

'No?' His voice rose a tone. 'What are you going to do with it then?'

'I'm going to find what Quartermaine was looking for.' I uncurled my fingers and looked at it. Strange little morsel of a forbidden alien feast. I might have smiled. When I looked up Murdoch was watching me, perplexed.

Maybe I shouldn't have told him. Officially any Invidi technology is strictly off-limits to us and it was clearly our duty to return it. Unexpectedly, he grinned.

'Good. It's about time we had some answers.'

Nothing, dammit.

'Nothing,' I said out loud to the empty room. 'There's nothing here.'

The space was too cramped even to echo back. After Security moved the contents of the *Calypso* salvage down from the Sigma storage bay where Keveth was killed, they'd erected a modular containment area here in one of the Gamma warehouses. The flimsy partitions kept any stray radiation away from other equipment but also meant that I had very little room to manoeuvre around or over the piles. I kept banging sore parts of myself on the corners of boxes and slipping on debris. My temper, already stretched, twanged and broke several times. But this was something that couldn't be done on a virtual screen.

The thing Murdoch had given me was an enigmatic flat oval, much heavier than it should be. I itched to find a join to pry apart and had run every test I could think of, but it remained as smooth and seamless as . . . as an egg. A mechanical egg. It was unlike any data storage device I'd ever seen, so I'd decided to try doing what Brin had presumably gone to the storage bay to do: use it to find An Barik's *nlitri*. I just hoped it was not set to respond only to Quartermaine's biosigns, or to a particular password.

I'd spent an infuriating hour or so moving it over every charred circuit, every pathetic piece of personal property – photographs of people long dead, an antique digital clock, unrecognisable blackened clothing that might have been knitted wool. Shards and lumps of console with threads of circuitry visible behind the pitted surfaces. These seemed the most likely candidates to contain An Barik's *nlitri*, and I passed the device over every millimetre. Without response.

What was I doing wrong? The device couldn't be that difficult to use or Quartermaine couldn't have managed – Brin had fought an ever-losing battle with all things mechanical. It probably gave off a signal when the object of the search was found. Sound? Light? Some sort of tactile response? I kept it in my hand, every sense spread in a net of anticipation.

Still nothing. Either I was using it the wrong way or there was nothing here for it to find. I squeezed down with a grunt until I was sitting on the deck beside the largest hunk of metal. From their main data processor. I went over this again, with the same lack of results. My next step would have to be to check the interior of *Calypso* in the same way. This meant suiting up and going over to the wreck. I couldn't get to the shuttle docks so it would have to be on a 'scooter', the tiny one-person engines we used to go quickly from the rings to one of Jocasta's surrounding platforms, or to make repairs to reflector grids – or just to joyride, in simpler times. Which meant telling the whole station I wanted something from the wreck. Although the station would probably be too busy to notice.

Why does An Barik need evidence of An Serat's interference in Earth's past? To get rid of it? But the facts will surface eventually. Griffis and the others are not going to be silent about what they know. And the *Calypso*'s presence is itself enough to prove the Invidi were actively involved in humanity's first interstellar foray.

It all depends on the nature of this 'evidence'. Perhaps it is in some way threatening to the Invidi in the present? That seems to rule out the cryostasis technology then.

I transferred the device – in my mind it was the 'egg' – from one hand to the other to scan a different area, fumbled, and dropped it. Looks like it doesn't break. I leaned back against the barrier, tired of getting nowhere. Tired of everything.

Have I really done all I could? When history looks back on these days and my actions, will someone say, but why didn't she . . . ?

It's not that I disagree with Henoit. Our isolation has made me question the assumptions I had always held about the Confederacy, Invidi technology, and the position of the Four Worlds as opposed to the Nine. Henoit is right about that – if we're not important enough for them to protect, then we owe them nothing. It's his means I can't stomach. I wish there were a middle ground. Veatch's neutrality option sounds attractive, but we can't do anything until we get rid of the Seouras. And as a neutral system with few defences, we would be at the mercy of whichever warlord or local pirate boss decided to move in. On the other hand, if I were to ask any one of the residents of Delta and perhaps Gamma too, they would surely say, 'Do it. If it means getting rid of the Seouras, what are you waiting for?'

I can accept the New Council's offer or not – only there's little 'not' about it, because I can't see Henoit getting back in a shuttle and politely vacating the station if we say we're not interested. Murdoch is right to be worried. The gamble was to accept the offer, and hope they can actually beat the Seouras. Hope, too, that they will not betray us. There might be time after for Veatch's neutrality option.

What would Marlena Alvarez have done? I'd laughed at myself for asking that when I talked to Henoit earlier, but it didn't seem such a strange question now. Alvarez had refused to join the armed opposition to the government, not because she supported the government, but because she did not agree with their methods of opposition. That sounded like our present situation, except that those women did not face the prospect of the very fabric of their homes unravelling beneath them. Our situation in space carries a new element of insecurity.

Alvarez also played one side against the other – often she used the media to advertise excesses on one side or the other. In the case of the government's attempt to physically remove Las Mujeres from the map, for example, she saved the village by making sure the opposition knew and would act against the government.

But I wasn't a politician. I had no idea how to play off two or more sides against each other and not get caught in the crossfire.

The damned implant itched and crawled. I sighed and rubbed my neck. It occurred to me that I did have the representatives of both parties here – the Confederacy and the New Council. I'd assumed Henoit would make no direct attack on An Barik because the Invidi would have protection of some sort. But I could confront An Barik with the prospect of our collaboration with the New Council and gauge his reaction. The trouble with that was that he might react by calling in ConFleet.

Isn't that what you want? I asked myself. *To have the Confederacy come and rescue the station from the Seouras. Haven't you been trying to ask them to do that for the past six months?* Yes, I have. And if that happens, presumably ConFleet would destroy the grey ships. Murdoch thinks they can, and he should know. Then the status quo would be restored. The station – if they allow Earth to keep it – will return to its orderly, stacked structure. The Four in the top ring, the Nine under them, and the refugees and illegals under the rings themselves, right down in Recycling, down in the shit.

Yes, the trouble with asking An Barik to rescue us from the Seouras was that he might agree.

'You'll carry a portable sensor,' I said to the Engineering team, 'that we modified from one of the outer arrays. It won't detect lifesigns – we can't break the jamming field enough – but it will tell you when that jamming field is operating. In other words, when the Q'Chn is approaching.'

They nodded solemnly and my heart sank as I looked at them. Three men and three women, all young, all experienced and nimble. They'd have a lot of crawling to do in this one.

'Tell me.' I sat down and Gamet, their team leader, took my place standing.

'We go up in one of the uplifts,' she said, her voice sounding light after my deep accents. Her slim, dark fingers traced the route on the holomap in the middle of the table.

'At the same time, Security starts their diversion by taking the uplift on the opposite side. They go up and we go across two sections on Level Six via bisecting corridors to the core and access it from a side door. We then drop three levels within the access shafts of the core to the opsys controls. As a contingency plan, if we detect the Q'Chn from the uplift we can access the maintenance tunnels from the hatch in the uplift and follow the wall tunnels into the core. It will take a lot longer than going down the corridors and means going around Level Six rather than across, but it will be safer because the tunnels are narrower.'

The weak point of this plan was when they got to the core. We knew the Slasher must have been there because it couldn't have caused some of the systems failures without doing so. But we had no idea which access network it had used. The ordinary maintenance shaft should be too narrow for it, but a freight shaft that rose from Level Twelve right at the bottom of the centre complex was a possibility.

'Your brief once you get there?'

'Is to be as quick as possible,' said Gamet. She caught my eye. 'This is important. We're not to try to repair everything, merely to reroute as many key environmental systems as possible to ring control and shut off core access to as many security systems as possible.'

'Thirty minutes,' I couldn't help adding from my chair. 'I don't want you in there any longer than that.' If they wore interface enhancements, the few we had left on the station, it shouldn't take them any longer. That was another reason all of them were young – the older humans get, the more our bodies reject enhancement, especially those of us who have used it extensively in our youth. Ten years maximum is all we get. I can't plug myself into an interface now without getting a migraine headache and an interface that needs initialisation surgery.

'If the Q'Chn does appear, we're to retreat immediately to the nearest maintenance tunnel and get back to the uplift as quickly as possible. Security will try to keep the uplift shaft clear.' We all knew what a hollow promise that was.

Gamet smiled at her team. 'Gravity will be off for the

duration of this exercise so the body armour shouldn't be too much of a burden.'

'Just don't put it on till we're in the uplift,' suggested a curly-headed boy, leaning back comfortably with his ankles crossed.

They all grinned, Gamet included. 'You put it on before we leave, Stuart. You ain't dressed right, you don't go.' She looked at me and I nodded. Nothing more to say.

'We start at 1400. Dismissed.'

'Good luck,' I said.

'Thanks.'

I sat at the table after she left, magnifying and reducing the holomap with one finger. What a lousy job I had. Telling young people to go and risk their long futures when there were those of us with less future to risk.

All this worry about alliances – New Council, neutrality, Confederacy – all that was bullshit. I was responsible for the lives on the station and my first priority must be to minimise casualties among them. First from the Q'Chn, then from the Seouras. An Barik and the Confederacy have demonstrated that they're not interested in helping. I should go to someone who will help, and if that is Henoit and the New Council, so be it. I had to forget the personal angle. After all, I'd forgotten it for seven years, I should have had enough practice.

Dan Florida found me as I emerged from the access hatch into the Hill.

'Commander!'

I whirled, adrenalin pumping.

'Sorry. Didn't mean to startle you. Guess we're all a bit jumpy with a Slasher on the loose.' His grin robbed the words of any sense of danger.

I waited a moment until my voice was steady. 'What is it? I'm on my way to a meeting.' I had come to find Henoit, to settle once and for all exactly what he wanted from the station and what he would do for us.

He looked hurt. 'You wanted me to do some research, didn't you?'

I'd forgotten. What had I asked him to do?

'In the historical database. On evidence of the Sleeper ship's journey?' he prompted.

'Of course.' I looked around. The Hill throughways were almost deserted. The stalls were battened down and doors on most of the dwellings shut. A couple of people talked to a Security guard at the end of this corridor. It was gloomy, most of the lights offline. Although the area had not been officially evacuated, most of the residents had moved by themselves.

'Can you tell me here?'

He looked around, then back at me with a pained expression. 'I suppose so.'

I folded my arms and waited. I didn't expect him to have found much more than I had.

He walked over to a bench by one of the abandoned food stalls and sat. I followed slowly as he pulled a handcom out of his jacket and activated it.

'I found some early records of Nguyen,' he began,

calling up an image. I peered at an unclear 2D represen-tation of a thin man with round, dark-rimmed visual aids.

'Sorry about the magnification. That's as far as it will go. It doesn't say much,' he said apologetically. 'Just that he quit NASA – that was one of the official aerospace organisations – and was starting his own company. That was 2001. The next bits are scattered here and there,' he glanced at my impatient face, 'but to summarise, the company, Sunline, completed a number of jobs, pro-gramming satellites for communications companies and foreign governments, developing small-scale space com-munication devices, and so on. This is over a period of ten or twelve years.'

'What about the flight itself?'

'Very little on it. There's an article in one of their specialist aerospace journals that Sunline was involved in a cooperative venture to repair one of the old skylab plat-forms and conduct manufacturing experiments there. It wasn't very clear on who the other collaborators were.'

'Rachel said they used one of the old skylabs to modify the ship.'

He shook his head. 'You'd think the government agen-cies would have detected them from the ground, or from one of their other satellites. Space technology must have really hit a low.'

'Either that or the Invidi provided some protection against surveillance.' It was one possible reason the *Calypso* had remained anonymous after it left Earth too. 'What about Confederacy records?'

He shook his head. 'Not so much as a whisper.

Although the Invidi kept a pretty tight hold on that sector until after Earth began space flight.'

'You didn't find a log entry by a freighter? Saying that they followed the engine trail of a Nukeni ship?'

'No, why?'

'I did. Do you mind?' I took his handcom and looked myself. Same database, same period, same search parameters – nothing.

'Where did you see it?' said Florida, when it became obvious that what I was looking for wasn't there.

'In the Confederacy historical database,' I said crossly, 'same as you.'

'On your office interface?' he persisted.

'On my handcom.'

'And when did you update your handcom?'

I felt my face flush with embarrassment. That handcom was one of my oldest. I'd left it inactive in the drawer in my quarters for ... months.

Florida grinned. 'I thought so. Now mine, on the other hand, was updated from the latest Confederacy records just days before the Seouras invaded. Along with the rest of the databases on the station. The databases that people bothered to activate,' he added.

I'd speculated that if I could find the log entries, anyone could. It looked as though this had happened. And that someone, who had the means to alter the official database, had decided to keep it to themselves or make sure no one else found it. Someone had wanted the Sleepers to stay hidden. Was it the Invidi? For the same reason they'd concealed *Calypso* all along? Whatever that reason might be – concealing evidence about An Serat's interference didn't seem motive enough. Or someone else might have altered the record, someone who also wanted to keep the knowledge of *Calypso*'s course a secret.

Florida looked shaken. I could understand why. How much of our other information, historical or otherwise, had been manipulated in this way? It's only the official database, I wanted to reassure him. It's always happened. Look at how differently they talk about Alvarez. We still have private and alien databases, and our memories.

'It's nothing to do with the Sleepers,' said Florida, recovering, 'but I found this incredible 2D vid fragment.' He tapped it onto the small screen. 'I thought with your family background you'd be interested.'

The screen showed an overhead angle on a large, square building with people gathered on a long flight of steps in front of it. The camera zoomed in to show a smaller group at the top of the steps. They were all human, mainly men but some women. The pale-suited man in the centre of the group was shaking the hands of the others in turn. With a start I recognised one of the women. It was Marlena Alvarez.

'Recognise it?' Florida's voice belonged to another world.

I nodded, unable to speak. I've known about this moment all my life, but never seen it. I'd never even thought to look in the database. The new president shook the hands of the person next to Alvarez. Then hers. She leaned forward and said something to him, at which he laughed. An incautious, genuine laugh, not politics.

'This was broadcast worldwide, you know,' went on

Florida, glad to have caught my interest. 'No wonder it had such an impact.'

All hands were shaken, all speeches made. The new president stepped forward and waved to the cameras. Marlena Alvarez stepped away from him to one side and looked up. She stood quite still for a second, then deliberately turned back, deliberately reached across the president so that the jerk of impact, the red blossoming of blood, was on her back and not his chest. The vid ended abruptly with people running and the security forces' belated attempts at control.

It happened just as Demora had said, except that it wasn't raining.

I found Henoit without any trouble. He was looking for me. We saw each other from opposite ends of the throughway and waved as if in some holovid drama.

'Come in here.' I dragged him into one of the communal halls on the boundary of Hill West. Although these places were never locked on principle, I clicked the magnetiser as we shut the door behind us. It was a low-ceilinged, dusty space with benches folded against both walls. There was a table at the far end with an ancient interface monitor and a vase full of flowers.

'Well?' He stood in his hunter's pose, hands loosely by his side, not quite facing me. 'Have you decided?'

'I told you, before I decide anything we have to get up to the centre and repair our main systems. Or there won't be any station to protect from the Seouras.' I walked up quite close to him and folded my arms. No more keeping discreet distances. 'To this end, I want you to help us.'

'Help you do what?'

'Help us get rid of the Q'Chn.'

He moved his head sideways, the equivalent of our laugh. 'How could there be a Q'Chn on this station!'

'I've seen it. So have a number of other people. As we speak it could be attacking more of my people.'

'It's nothing to do with me.'

I stared at him. 'It could attack you. Or your people if they ever get here. So are you going to help us or not?'

'I asked you first. Will you decide to join us or not?'

If I don't join them, went the unspoken corollary, he won't help us with the Q'Chn. I groaned inwardly. If I hadn't known what a difference a single H'digh warrior could make in a situation like this I'd have thrown the entire argument in his face.

'Ah, but I have an alternative. The Confederacy Council observer on Jocasta is an Invidi – but no doubt your sources have told you this. He will be very interested to learn that the New Council wishes to acquire a base within Confederacy territory. The general opinion seems to be that he could call for ConFleet any time, just hasn't felt like it yet. Perhaps this is what we need to motivate him.'

Henoit examined me carefully, from mussed hair to scuffed boots. Then he threw back his head and laughed aloud, a habit he had picked up around humans and used only when he was acutely uncomfortable.

'You have changed! You want me to risk my life to keep your own people out of danger and instead of guarantees you give threats.' He stopped laughing as quickly as he'd started. 'What is it you want me to do?'

I felt a small tremor of relief and unfolded my arms stiffly. 'Murdoch, the Security chief, is going to conduct a diversion at 1400 hours while the repair team go into the core. You'll have to hurry. We need you to go with the repair team.'

'I am no mechanic.'

No, you wouldn't know how to do an honest job with your hands, I thought, but kept it to myself.

'We don't have personnel to spare. By putting you on guard, we free at least ten security people to work elsewhere.'

He nodded, mollified. I'd put the ratio fairly high to flatter, but he probably thought one H'digh equalled closer to twenty ConFleet security guards.

'Where will you be? Coordinating?'

'No. I'm going to leave the station for a short while.'

'Leave?' He stepped closer. 'Where?'

'I'm certainly not going to take a stroll back to Sector Central, am I? I'm going to have a look in the wreck of the Sleeper ship.'

'Have a look for what?' He was close now, and intense – more so than when we'd discussed the Q'Chn or talked about the New Council.

'Nothing.'

'Halley, what do you know about that ship?'

I looked at him astonished. 'What do you know about it?'

'We know that it was last seen between Alpha Centauri and Earth. One of our sources in the innermost circles of the Confederacy Council informed us that it might arrive somewhere on the outskirts of Confederacy space.'

I didn't say they seemed to know considerably more than we did.

'Wait a minute. You're saying you came here because *Calypso* came, not because you want Jocasta as a base?'

'No, we do want you to join us. But we are also interested in why *Calypso* was sent from Earth so long ago. Or how.'

My head was spinning. I wasn't sure how much he knew about the Invidi side of it, about An Barik trying to rectify a mistake made by An Serat. 'Let me guess. Your source on the Confederacy Council is a supporter of An Serat?'

'I believe so.'

So the Invidi power struggle is definitely related to a ship that one of them sent from Earth a century ago.

'We think this An Serat may be sympathetic to our cause,' he continued. 'We hope to find something on the ship to confirm this.'

'But how did you know it would come here?'

'We did not. Other ambassadors were sent to other stations. But the likelihood of its being here was greatest. This is Earth's only far base.'

I needed to sit down but there were no chairs and the benches looked difficult to unfold.

'What do you think you'll find on the ship?' I felt the small, heavy shape of the Invidi device in my pocket. Surely this wasn't it.

'Think for yourself,' said Henoit. 'This ship disappears from the record before their flight is done, probably hiding behind Invidi shields until the rest of the galaxy is ready. Then it arrives here, thousands of light years away.'

Thousands of light years away. What technology could An Serat have given humans that would upset the other Invidi so much they'd abandon a valuable space station and risk other alliances? What was it that they want us kept away from most of all?

'A jump drive?' I said softly. It made sense. It would get the Sleepers here. If some of the Nine Worlds found it, they would have a foundation for changing the Confederacy. It would also solve the problem of which ship set off the jump mine. I wondered if An Serat had foreseen the mine or the Seouras. 'But why didn't An Barik just call in ConFleet and wait to seize *Calypso*?'

Henoit shrugged. 'We think it may be something to do with changing the elements of the ship's arrival. The timescape.'

So we've had to cope single-handedly with the Seouras for six months because An Barik was waiting to intercept a present from the past. I choked down the anger.

'Why hasn't he called ConFleet yet?' I said aloud. '*Calypso*'s been here three days.'

Henoit made a negative gesture with his head. 'I don't know, although it is fortunate for us. Perhaps he is waiting to confirm this is the ship.'

That was a good idea, come to think of it. If there was nothing on that ship after all, we were going to look like a bunch of idiots.

'I'll go and confirm whether it is or not. You protect our repair team. Deal?'

He hesitated. 'How do I know I can trust you?'

I put my hands on my hips. 'You don't.' It felt good to be getting somewhere with the mystery, to at last be close to understanding something. 'I can't fight Q'Chn. Can you recognise an alien jump drive?' He wouldn't know a jump drive until he saw the stars begin to sink beyond the window. He knew I could find it more efficiently.

Pleasure in resolving the mystery spilled over into the physical pleasure his presence still aroused in me. It was an incredible relief to be on the same side again.

'If we find it, will you join us?' He broke the spell.

'Let's deal with that later,' I said. I stepped away, giving myself a mental shake. I'd almost initiated something we both would probably have regretted.

If I found a jump drive on *Calypso*, we might be able to bargain on more equal terms. After all, this is my station. Salvage found here belongs here, and I wasn't about to hand it over without getting something worthwhile in return.

I found Rachel in the rehab centre, morosely flicking through some plans of the station on their library monitor.

'Are you free?'

She glared. 'Do I look like I'm much in demand?'

'Honestly, it's so depressing. I know I'll never catch up with a century of science and it hardly seems worth trying. Hannibal's quite content to go back to first grade and Ariel's too busy having fun with that journalist.' We walked along the quiet back ways of Gamma. The words poured out of Rachel as though my presence had tripped a release switch.

'With Florida?'

'I don't mean "fun" as in playing around. Florida's given him a job as researcher at the channel.'

It seemed that one of the Sleepers was managing to fit in. The one I'd have thought least likely to.

'I know the position is pretty bad here, and it makes me feel so powerless. I haven't felt like this since . . . since the Invidi came.'

'They made you feel powerless?'

'It's how I felt after the first few moments,' she said. 'Everyone remembers what they were doing when the Invidi came. It was how you identified that First Contact generation – whether you were old enough to remember it.

'I'd just joined Sunline and I was in Brussels getting

some equipment we'd ordered from the Europeans. I was in a café on the rue Hoffman – I even remember the name of the street. Black coffee and nectarines for breakfast. Everyone was talking at once and shushing each other around the telescreen. I looked outside and you could see the sun glinting on one of the Invidi ships, far, far up. I remember fear, joy, disbelief – emotions large enough to express what had happened. But it was also the beginning of a feeling of being trapped. That feeling has never gone away.'

'Why do you think they made you feel trapped?'

She shrugged. 'I don't know. Maybe it wasn't them exactly. Their coming made it impossible for us to go any other way but theirs.'

We'd reached the doorway to an emergency airlock. Rachel paused, one foot on the sill.

'Maybe that's why I joined the flight,' she said. 'To get away from that feeling.'

We stepped into the airlock and I gestured at the wrinkled pressure suits that hung there. The EarthFleet crew member in charge of them smiled as charmingly as an Achelian boutique-owner.

'Care for a walk outside?' I said.

'Are you sure it's safe?' Rachel's voice was scratchy in my ear pieces. Residual particles from the comet's tail were playing hell with the intersuit comm systems. Our suits were old, reliable, unwieldy things with portable airpacks.

'Perfectly,' I assured her. 'The Seouras have never shot

at anyone on a scooter. We use them all the time for repairs.'

She gripped me so tightly around the waist that I glanced down to check all my lines remained unsevered.

'Ready?'

'Yes.'

I pushed open the thrusters and the scooter left the airlock with an explosion felt, not heard. We skimmed along the surface of the ring, close enough to see darkened lines where the surface had been repaired, bobbing over protruding hatches and reflector lines. Rachel's grip slackened a little.

'This is fun.'

'Uh-huh.' I hoped it was not also a waste of precious fuel.

'How could they have put a drive on *Calypso* without our knowing?' She sounded properly resentful.

'The same way they kept the information from us – probably some sort of concealment field.'

We angled away from the ring and floated towards the maintenance platform. It loomed flat above us and the tethered form of *Calypso* seemed much more formidable than it had on a virtual screen. There's nothing like 'real' reality.

Our head-lights made the shadows dance in the debris. *Calypso*'s main cabin was familiar – I'd stared at the plan and our scans so much over the past few days that I could have drawn it all by heart.

Our salvage droids had removed most of the loose stuff

that could puncture a suit, so involuntary depressurisation was less of a problem than radiation – the warning patch on my sleeve had already begun slowly to stain from green to orange. When it began to glow red we would have to leave. We couldn't expect de-rad therapy back on Jocasta, for our few remaining radiation soak-ups were kept strictly for emergency use. They were another re-supply that never arrived from Central.

The main cabin was cold with ghosts of silent sleeping forms. I looked at Rachel with new respect. How must it feel to willingly give up all you know, everyone you cared about, for that cold and the uncertain interstellar dark?

Rachel's head turned inside her helmet.

'God, what a mess. I can't believe we lived here . . .'

'Where's the engine room?' The blackened surfaces, the debris, and the confusing light – from our helmets, the planet, the sun itself – all made it difficult to take bearings.

Rachel spun slowly, then pushed off from the 'floor' to a point close to a tangled mass of metal that must have been engine controls. Her gloved hand patted each piece of debris as she drifted past. 'My poor baby. I'd like to get my hands on the bastards who designed those mines.'

'They're long gone. From this space, at any rate.' I controlled my excitement with difficulty. Breathing too hard mucks up the air intake mix. Rather like my implant. 'One of the Confederacy's more impressive victories. I told you about the booby traps when we took over the station.'

I took the little Invidi device from my pocket and

moved it over the wreckage in hope of some response. Nothing.

'What's that?'

'I hope it's going to help me find the drive. Are you sure it was around here?'

She paused in front of a singed but unbroken panel in the back wall of the chamber. 'I know where the engine room was. But as for the other thing ...' Her voice crackled with tension and static in my helmet. 'Would you know an Invidi drive if you saw one?'

Touché. I placed the egg close to the panel but there was no response. I was beginning to think I'd have to take the ship apart module by module.

'I want *Calypso*,' she said. 'It's ours to claim, isn't it?'

'I suppose so. Wait a minute – you want to claim the drive too?' Theoretically it was possible.

'God, no. I just want the ship.'

'Why? It'll take a lot of work to repair.'

'What else have I got?' she snapped. 'At the very least, I can sell the parts for scrap. Or maybe we could put it on show and charge people to come and see. You know, see the fantastic hundred-year-old freaks and their ship. I could do a routine in a fake cryochamber and Ariel could sell the show through Florida's network.'

Her bitterness confused me. 'I'm sorry if you're unhappy here. When we get rid of the Seouras ...'

She laughed outright. 'You remind me of my grandfather. He had one phrase for the future: 'when the Jews leave'. When the Jews leave, we'll build our homes on the mountain. When the Jews leave, we'll beat our guns into something useful. When the Jews leave, we'll have enough money to send our daughters to college instead of sending our sons to training camps. Well, Grandpa, we had news for you – they didn't leave.'

She revolved a couple of times in silence. I couldn't see her face through the reflections on the helmet. When she spoke again her voice was less certain.

'I'm sorry. I just meant that I tend to want to do things now, not put them off. And if it makes any difference, I'm not unhappy here. I was more unhappy everywhere else.'

The egg jumped in my hand.

For a second I didn't understand. Then, barely breathing, I passed it again over the same area. A small, square section of the fused circuitry took on a different hue. I floated the egg carefully beside me, reached out, and prised the section away. It peeled off, like a strip of sealant three centimetres thick.

Underneath it was ... an area in flux. Perhaps circuitry, perhaps contained plasma. It seemed to have depth – could be the whole of the auxiliary chamber, which was the size of a small room. Shifting colours from all over the spectrum.

Rachel peered over my shoulder, her gasp an echo of my own.

I caught the device and brought it up to the same level as the flux. It quivered again and there was an answering shift in the colours. The egg pulled at my fingers and I let it lead me to the edge of the 'window'. I let go and it stuck there, magnet-like.

The pattern changed. It became ordered, mathematical, temporal in progression. Repeated itself. And again.

This is how they got here. Nothing complicated, nothing mysterious.

'Is that it?' Rachel's voice held awe.

'Must be. A Nukeni freighter wouldn't have anything like this.' My voice sounded faint, even in my own helmet. The pattern repeated itself, and this time I could see the subtle differences. I thought I could see it. Please, let me see it . . .

Not information about a drive but the thing itself. That's what the *nlitri* was. An Barik hadn't known exactly and Brin had given me a misguided translation.

I've got them. This is what An Barik wants – evidence of the Invidi helping humans, evidence that An Serat sent forbidden technology to the Nine Worlds. For whatever reason, he is helping us against the Four. No wonder the other Invidi are out to get him.

I threw my arms back, bounced off the floor and laughed aloud. I must have looked like an idiot.

'What's so funny?'

'What's funny is that now we have proof of Invidi interference. Now I have a bargaining chip to use against the New Council. Now we don't need to depend on the Four Worlds' ships for every bloody thing . . .'

It wasn't funny any more. This meant the potential to change everything. I remembered what Henoit had said. It was the breakthrough his group dreamed of. At the moment, the Four Worlds controlled the flow of resources and the diffusion of technology, but if everyone had the jump drive the New Council would be well on the way to achieving their objectives of fairer representation and greater autonomy for the Nine.

'That's nice,' said Rachel, in a tone that was anything but.

'"Nice"? This is the greatest breakthrough in human technological history since we began to use alien science.'

'A breakthrough. Funny, in my time a breakthrough was something you did yourself.'

I didn't say anything. She was right but I couldn't agree with her. Not in my present position.

'I don't know if you remember, but the vehicle An Serat shamelessly used to get this wonderful drive to you was also carrying passengers. We didn't think we were passengers, we thought we were explorers, but that's beside the point, isn't it?'

She paused for breath. Her air intake tube was probably recalibrating the mix.

I took advantage of the pause. 'What is your point? I don't see why you feel so betrayed. An Serat is obviously trying to help the Nine Worlds, for whatever reasons. Or at least, helping us aligns with his own plans, whatever they are. In any case, we reap the benefit.'

'There wasn't much benefit to the other people in our ship, was there?' she retorted. 'My friends and colleagues who didn't make it. Do you think An Serat didn't see the jump mine? Can you honestly say you think he would have cared either way?'

I shook my head in the helmet. I was almost certain it would have made no difference to the Invidi whatsoever.

'No, I don't think so either,' she said. 'So just don't expect me to go all googly over another piece of someone else's technology that we were sacrificed to get to you.'

'I'll take some scans,' I said, after an awkward pause.

We only had a few minutes before radiation levels reached critical. Enough to capture two of the flux sequences on an observation scanner. Not enough to work out anything important. The egg came off without resistance, and the window darkened immediately. When I looked back it was no more than another strip of burnt panel.

We returned to the station in silence.

We peeled off our suits with sighs of relief and I replaced my dirty uniform over sweaty inner clothes with a grimace of distaste.

Rachel was subdued, her face closed as she struggled with the unfamiliar suit fastenings. I was trying to consider all the ramifications of what we had found. When the airlock door opened, neither of us was prepared.

An Barik himself stood there, in full environmental suit. The suit's shimmering folds swayed as he stopped before us. The tiny lobby seemed full of alien.

'Governor Halley.' The volume of An Barik's voicer was louder than normal and his words made us both jump.

'Is something wrong?' My own voice sounded thin and unsteady. But I gave him no polite 'Master'.

'Yes.' The suit continued to shiver. I could imagine how the tentacles beneath writhed in distress.

'Halley?' Murdoch poked his head around the door. 'They said you were ...' He looked unhurt and good-humoured. 'Colonel Henoit here said you were going over to the wreck. Find anything interesting?'

Rachel snorted. Murdoch stepped into the room, followed by Henoit. Murdoch had spoken of Henoit in an easy tone, but there was a tension between them. The lobby was now so full we could barely move.

'You have that which belongs to the one,' An Barik boomed.

Presumably he meant the little device he'd been generous enough to lend Quartermaine, the 'egg' weighing down my inner trouser pocket.

'How did you know?'

'It tells the one. Where is it?'

He must mean it had given off a signal when I used it on *Calypso*. I hadn't thought of that possibility. 'I left it on the ship.'

'You lie to the one.'

Murdoch glanced from me to the Invidi in puzzlement. 'Halley, what . . .'

I hadn't expected An Barik to believe me. 'Yes, I lied.'

An Barik glided forward so that he was as close to me as he could get. Next to me, Rachel edged away. 'Give the *nlitri*.'

He said *nlitri*, not jump drive. 'You don't know what it is, do you? Anyway, I'm not giving it to you.'

The suit rippled. 'You must. You do not understand the consequences. But you must give before it is too late.'

It stopped me for a moment – the thought that he might 'see' a consequence of my actions that could worsen the situation, difficult as that was to imagine. The temptation to bow to second sight was strong. But then again, An Barik had said himself that 'individuals initiate paths according to their nature'.

'Give it.' His tentacle shot out with surprising speed but Henoit was quicker. He reached past Murdoch, grabbed my arm, and yanked me with painful strength to stumble between them. An Barik made no further move.

'It's not hers to give,' said Rachel. She folded her arms and raised her chin in defiance. 'It's ours. It was given to us and it's on our ship. You have no right to it.'

Theoretically she was right. But the time for theory had passed.

'You cannot resist.' An Barik's simulated voice held frustration but no fear. 'Confederacy forces come. The one calls.'

He'd been waiting all this time to get his tentacles on the jump drive. Or rather, prevent us getting hold of it. Now that he'd got the signal, he had called his ships.

'My forces are waiting too,' said Henoit. He turned to me, his hand still gripping my upper arm tightly. 'Give me the drive, Halley. I can get away before ConFleet gets here. We can still save it.'

'Oh sure. And you'll leave us to the Seouras and the Confederacy. This is what you've been after the whole time, isn't it?' I wrenched my arm from his grip and stepped back almost on Murdoch's toes. I've seldom felt such a fool. I'd thought we were working on the same side this time.

'No. We wished for an alliance if it was worth the price. But we will not risk a direct confrontation with the Confederacy. Not yet.' His voice grew colder. 'Give it to me now or I'll take it myself.'

'You can't *have* it,' I said, furious at his presumption.

'It's installed in *Calypso*. And don't try to take it. I left an explosive device set right in the drive window.' I didn't look at Rachel, and hoped she had the sense to keep a straight face.

'You lie again.' There was a shadow of anxiety on An Barik's voice. 'You do not risk harming the station. It is not your character.'

'Yes, well we're all acting a little out of character today, aren't we? I thought the Invidi were our friends.' I heard the vicious anger in my own voice and let it stay. 'The station will not be badly damaged in the blast. I do know how to set a charge, you know.'

Murdoch shifted beside me and I turned my head to him. Our eyes met for a long second, and I hoped he understood about the bluff.

I turned to An Barik. 'We need to sit down and talk about this. Whatever you do with the drive, part of the bargain is that this station is neutral. We'll declare separation from the Confederacy.'

'That is unacceptable.' It was probably the strongest statement I'd ever heard from him.

'What are you going to do about it?'

'If you didn't want humans to have this drive,' Rachel interrupted, 'why did an Invidi install and set it so that our ship ended up here?'

We all waited, but only the silver folds moved.

'Serat is misguided. He has little support.' An Barik finally answered.

'An Serat is still alive?' said Rachel.

The comm link on my wrist beeped.

'Halley here.' I half turned away from the aliens, trusting Murdoch to keep an eye on them.

It was Lieutenant Baudin's voice against unusually loud background chatter. 'The Seouras ship's moved closer and is maintaining that position. They want you to go over.'

Everyone was silent.

'Jeez, talk about timing.' Murdoch's mutter pulled me around slowly.

'Nobody leaves the station,' I told Murdoch, not that it mattered much, not where powerful aliens were concerned. 'Post guards around all the airlocks for platform linkups and keep the spokes evacuated. I don't want anyone to touch that wreck.'

'You can't go,' he said.

I blinked at the flat statement. If I didn't, they were capable of destroying us. 'Do I have a choice?'

'You said they read your thoughts.'

'No. I get images from them and speak out loud ... Oh hell.' I covered my mouth with shaking hands. 'The jump drive.'

'Are you sure they can't read your mind?' Murdoch sounded as desperate as I felt.

'I don't know.' How hard would they try?

'What's the matter?' Rachel frowned from one to the other.

'They mightn't need it if they already have some form of hyperspace drive ...' His voice trailed off. We both knew that wasn't the point. It was one thing to contemplate freeing the Four Worlds' secret within the Confederacy – although I was far from happy about this, either – but another thing entirely to let proven enemies take Invidi technology. Especially if they were advanced enough to understand and use it. Derive a defence against it.

We could ask An Barik for help, but by the time ConFleet got here the station could be destroyed. We'd lose the drive and they'd get hold of the New Council. We could make a deal with the New Council, use the drive as the price to get rid of the Seouras, but not in time.

Murdoch clenched and unclenched his fists. 'Destroy it. Use the charge. Boom, no more problem.'

He knows I wouldn't have thought of that. It makes me sick to think of losing the technology we've waited so long for.

'If we don't destroy it and I go over, the Seouras might force me to tell them or see the drive in my mind. But it's not certain.'

'Can you take that risk?'

'If we do destroy it they may still take the image from my mind and attack the station in retaliation.

'I'll put a tug field around the wreck, take it away.' Henoit was insistent.

'I'm to provide the diversion? No, thank you.'

A dull boom reverberated far off and the walls and floor shuddered. We looked at each other.

'What the . . .'

Another, worse shaking sent Murdoch staggering against me and Rachel into the Invidi, from whom she recoiled frantically.

'Halley to Command. What's going on?'

Baudin's voice coughed. This time in the background we heard emergency sirens.

'The Seouras ... hit the outer reflector and the old processing platform.'

'Did you confirm their message when we got it? Say I'm on my way?'

'Aye.'

'They're getting impatient,' grumbled Murdoch.

'Confirm it again ... Baudin?'

'Yes, ma'am.' The pickup went dead.

Why were they so impatient? Normally they'd wait while I readied the shuttle and left the station. They'd wait anything up to an hour before sending a second request. Today, there would have barely been enough time to get to the shuttledock. A reminder? I didn't need reminding that I'm at their beck and call and that the station is a hostage for a purpose unknown.

'Halley!' Henoit pulled me around with painful quickness. 'You must let me take it. Give me the Invidi device, it will help us decipher the drive.'

I pulled back in turn. 'Leave me ... What will your people do with it? Let everyone know about it? Not likely.'

'Better some of us have the knowledge than leaving it with them,' he indicated the Invidi with his chin. One of his hands snaked down into my trouser pocket. How did he know it was in there?

'Leave me ...' I tried to wriggle away, then his grip on my arms slackened.

'Take him to the brig,' said Murdoch to the two constables who had entered from the corridor. One of them stood next to Henoit, the other pointed a weapon at him from several metres away.

Henoit looked at them, then at me. 'You have one last chance to join us. Give me the drive.'

I stepped back. 'You wouldn't get it away, anyway.'

He looked at me for a long moment then turned on his heel and walked away. It looked like he was escorting the guards, not the other way. From Murdoch's frown, he was thinking the same thing.

I was already out the door when An Barik spoke. 'You must not give them the *nlitri*.'

'I have no intention of giving it to anyone,' I said angrily and tried to keep going, but he squeezed Murdoch aside and followed me.

'The moving ones have left their own turning,' he said. 'It must not be allowed to begin again.'

I groaned. 'Master, I have to go or they'll damage the station. I don't understand what you're saying.'

'They wait also. That which belongs to Invidi must not belong to them. The shadow comes again.'

I shook my head and walked faster. If I couldn't understand him, I couldn't help him.

Murdoch caught up with me. 'You can probably take one of the shuttles. We didn't run into the Q'Chn at all before. The repair team was in and out within half an hour. They said environmentals will hold for the moment.'

At least there's some good news. We reached the liftup and Murdoch opened the controls.

What am I going to do about the Seouras? I mustn't tell them about the drive.

The answer came as the lift moved and our feet rose from what was no longer the floor.

'You'll have to come with me.'

The glow lit Murdoch's face from above, flattened his deep eye-sockets and drained the colour from his dark skin. His mouth opened once, shut.

'Me?'

'Yes. We must prevent them gaining information about the drive. You'll have to stop me if that looks like happening.'

He let go the rail to wipe his hand over his head, and the movement started him bobbing against the wall.

'How the fuck do I do that?'

'That's your problem. Shoot me.'

'Bloody hell,' said Murdoch faintly.

'Will I be able to hear what you're saying?'

'Uh-huh. Sound carries. But you'll have to leave the helmet and use a mask if you want to hear.' I caught Murdoch's expression. 'The slime won't hurt you. It's just messy.'

This time the grey ship was too close to permit star-gazing. It was visible already, a small dot of menace against its indifferent backdrop. If I looked behind I would see the untidy world of the station

Murdoch pulled himself back from the aft locker with his half-mask. We both wore the soft, crinkly, 'veined' suits that could be activated in seconds in case of sudden depressurisation. Helmets at the ready, as per regulation.

'Tell me more.' He strapped himself in the co-pilot's seat.

I'd briefed him how we would dock, how the airlock took a while to open, how the slime was everywhere. How a couple of them would usually escort me to a different part of the ship, not far. I didn't ask how Murdoch planned to keep me quiet if I couldn't keep my mind off the jump drive and my mouth shut. He'd disappeared for ten minutes while I went through the shuttle's pre-flight routine, presumably to arrange something. It was better I didn't know.

'What do you want to know?' I was not thinking very clearly. I wasn't thinking at all because the tide of apprehension threatened to drown me even before we reached the ship. I kept running the same series of diagnostics on the shuttle's sensors. Engines, navigational interface, atmosphere ... How about an outside sweep? We need as much information about inner system conditions as we can get, considering the station's sensors are largely blocked by Seouras interference, not to mention residual blurring from comet dust ... I can't do this, it's too much. Eleanor's right, I'm too tired, my hands are shaking on the controls. It's supposed to feel good to reach a stage where there are no alternatives, no more decisions to be made, just action ... but please somebody else do the action.

'Why are they here? What do they *want*?' Murdoch stared at the grey ship as it grew in the forward screen. From being a speck it was now a flat wedge, no external features yet visible. The ships have unusually few external arrays, perhaps a function of their drive. Or aesthetics.

'I don't know.'

'Y'know, I had the feeling that An Barik was trying to tell us something.'

'Yes, but he's impossible to understand.' I snapped my mouth shut over the way my voice rose on those last words and tried to take deep breaths.

Murdoch drummed his fingers on the console and stared at the grey ship. 'You've been closer to the Seouras than anyone. When you're in this link, haven't you picked up any of their motives?'

'No, I haven't,' I muttered, and my hands shook so badly on the controls that I had to ball them in my lap.

His next question was one I keep asking myself.

'It's been quite a while. You've done this a lot. Is there

some way you could use the link to harm them, give us an advantage?'

What to say – I haven't tried? It's not that sort of link? Even thinking of it makes my heart thud in my throat. 'I don't know.' I didn't want to look at him. For a moment I hated him for touching a possibility that I wanted to ignore – had I left an avenue of escape unexploited? A path of resistance untrodden? I hated him because it might be the truth.

'We should have birds,' he said.

He'd certainly caught my attention. 'What?'

'Birds. On the station. In the ag section, maybe even in the residentials.'

I stared at him. I wasn't the one who had lost it.

'I was in the ag section the other day,' he continued, seemingly unaware of my response. 'The reflectors had just come on, and I thought, y'know, if this were planet-side, there'd be a dawn chorus. Couldn't we introduce a few species? It might help with fertilising the plants.'

I opened and shut my mouth a couple of times.

'They'd have to be seed-eaters.' I could see the appeal of birdsong. Logistically though ... 'Unless you want insects as well, and we've had enough problems with unwanted pests not to want to risk it again. And where can we get the breeding stock?'

'I'm sure the K'Cher have a catalogue.'

I smiled in spite of the tension. There's a sector myth that the K'Cher have catalogues for everything.

'When I was a kid,' he began, then shot me a quick, sideways look to check if I was laughing at him, 'we used to go up the country for holidays. It was always more "home" than Sydney. The first few mornings in the bush I'd have to get up with the dawn because the birds were so bloody noisy. After a couple of days I'd get used to them. Then we'd go back to town and I'd wake up at six or whatever and it'd be quiet. Too quiet, like nothing was alive at all.'

He looked at me. 'That's how it was the other day. Too quiet.'

Too quiet. I wished it was quiet inside my head. I'd told Murdoch that the Seouras had grown preoccupied, but the strange feeling of foreboding about them had grown to a hard ball of sick certainty. It was like a conversation in another room, or on the edges of sleep – I couldn't discern actual words, but the tone and direction was discernible. The tone was panic and the direction was an urgent imperative to do something. What, I didn't know.

'What were you doing before we left?' I'd assumed he was getting a report from Sasaki.

'Making good your bluff.' He sounded pleased with himself.

'What do you mean?'

'I asked Kwon to slip over in a scooter and put a bomb on Calypso for you.' He paused. 'It was a bluff, wasn't it?'

I couldn't believe he'd acted so quickly. 'Where ...'

'It's in the reactor chamber. Your security access code on frequency zeta will set it off. At that frequency it should sneak through the interference even from inside the Seouras ship.' He grinned. 'It was a great idea but I knew you'd never do it.'

Murdoch coughed and gagged. The smell must be penetrating the mask's filter. His suit was already coated with a dark, greeny-grey layer, the silver reduced to dull gleams as he turned around and back, disoriented. The mask was a round, clear plane clamped to the outline of his face. The raised box over nose and mouth, muzzle-like, gave his face a predatory quality.

I'd taken my suit, jacket and shirt off in the shuttle as usual. This time I kept a comm link in one pocket and the Invidi egg was in the other.

'This is it?' His voice echoed flatly through the mask's filter. There was an almost imperceptible time lag, or perhaps a trick of the murky light – his lips seemed to move out of sync with the words. 'Where are they?'

'They'll be here.'

He shook his head and shuffled closer. I shouted the words this time and he nodded.

Why had they called me now? Timing too unfortunate to be accidental. The apprehension that had been building in the back of my mind for days squeezed like the slimy walls. Squeezed out rational thoughts until I had to grind my teeth to hold in a scream.

Murdoch took a standard all-frequency scanner from his belt and held it close to his mask to peer at the readings. I could recite them by heart. In addition to this ship's shielding that prevented us contacting Jocasta and the dampening qualities of the atmosphere itself, there was another, unidentified biomagnetic field that had defied all our attempts at analysis since I took my first sensor readings back to the station. All we knew was that it had not been present on the original Seouras ships that were part of the Abelar Treaty.

Then two of them were there, filling the tunnel entrance – I've wondered if they scrape out the tunnels with their bodies as they move. Murdoch jumped and I heard his muffled oath. He stumbled backwards until his arm brushed my side. The glance he gave me was fearful, quizzical, amazed, and I saw them for a moment through his eyes.

I'd expected some reaction to Murdoch's presence but they did nothing, just moved around us a couple of times in their usual smooth inspection. Then the familiar tug at my mental sleeve.

Come.

They slid back towards one of the tunnels. I tapped Murdoch's arm and yelled, 'We follow.'

He nodded, but behind the mask his eyes were wide with shock. He'd read my reports back on the station of course, but that was nothing like confronting the real thing. He lurched and slipped behind me. The tunnel was claustrophobic, dripping, oozing, and seemed to go on for ever. Slime coated my bare skin in layers of itchy fluid.

I reached back for Murdoch's hand and eased off his glove. He grabbed it with his other hand before it could fall.

'What . . . ?'

I grasped his bare hand with a sigh of relief. I wanted

to hold warm flesh. To feel a connection other than the alien one that nestled in my brain.

Murdoch pulled in his turn so I spun around to face him. For a moment he stared, one hand gripping mine, the other cool on my shoulder in its insulated glove. What I could see of his expression through the mask was unexpected and, unexpectedly, set my pulse thudding with something other than fear. I smiled at him with the discovery and got a tense grin back.

Come.

I shook my head against the pain of the call, tugged Murdoch's hand and kept going.

We were in another chamber before it was clear the tunnel had ended. The edges of the space blurred back into layers of shimmering bodies, almost the composite shape of my nightmares. There were more of them here, more than I'd ever seen before. The mass seemed to move within itself without actually shifting position. Murdoch squeezed my hand.

'I didn't think . . . so many.' The slime sucked away his words.

I looked around. Seouras lined the whole chamber. The voices in my head had echoed, but surely not this many.

Come. The impact of the thought was so strong and the resulting pain so intense that I whimpered and staggered back into Murdoch.

'You okay?'

I shook my head, unable to concentrate on what he was saying. Pushed myself away from him.

The first two stood close. Awaiting an answer? It was close enough to see even through half-closed eyes that their body surfaces moved in a kind of pattern. For the first time it occurred to me that it might be their language.

'Where?' I choked out.

You will assist.

I was shocked at the clarity of the thought as much as its unexpectedness.

'Help you – how?'

'What?' Murdoch was trying to follow a one-sided conversation.

'They want me to . . . Ow.' I grabbed at him with one hand and my head with the other. He steadied me with a grunt. One of the two closer Seouras edged my way, then back again. Repeated the movement, an easy hint.

Come.

'No. Leave me alone.'

Come. The voice was stronger, and carried with it the sense of urgency I'd felt here earlier and before that on the station. Urgency, almost desperation. A sudden image, bright and precise, filled my vision with such completeness that I let go of Murdoch and fell back in the slime. The station. Around the white rings were the platforms and reflectors and all the attached paraphernalia that I knew and loved. I could feel their concentration as they showed it to me. Showed me a green, coruscating energy field reach out to devour it. Showed me its destruction, driving me to panic. Was that the image of what they were going to do if I didn't cooperate? Or, horrible thought, had it already happened?

'Why are you showing me this?' The spell broke and the image disappeared. I don't understand. The emotion

I feel from them is not satisfaction. *Hopeless, everything lost. All gone. Gone lost past still. We thought we could defeat them. We tried for so long. The last chance gone. All gone, still* ... I don't know if it's my thoughts or theirs.

Something touched me on the shoulder and my eyes snapped open. It was Murdoch. He gestured at the Seouras and pulled me to my feet.

'They want us to follow,' he mouthed.

Come.

It nudged us along. This had never happened before and I wondered if Murdoch's presence had changed something.

The light in this tunnel is strange, the wrong colour. *White light cold light no food no love light turn it off.* Get out of my head. The tunnel in the dream with a room beyond.

Go. You can go.

Go where?

Unlike in my dreams, it was a short tunnel and stopped abruptly. The line of slime reached up and around and back down to the floor, and on the other side white metal walls continued into a white metal room. A portal *go on go in you can go see help*.

The light was too bright after the gentle green and I stood blinking until my eyes readjusted. Even then the light was uncomfortably strong and I squinted into a large space, nearly the size of Alpha messhall. The near wall on one side and the far wall were lined with interfaces – control panels. On the other side benches jutted out into the room interspersed with large, solid objects.

A dozen steps into the room and I stopped, hands to mouth, as I realised that the objects were bodies. Seouras bodies. They 'stood' upright as when alive, but a live Seouras was such a continuously moving, shimmering, crawling thing that I hadn't made a connection between the two. Three, four, seven ... at least twenty bodies here.

I sucked in a deep breath to try to get rid of the sick feeling. Enemy or no, death is death. And why leave the bodies here? It seems an unlikely graveyard.

I'm breathing properly. Air whistles down nasal passages, fills up lungs. Lungs happy to filter and return unwanted bits, breathe out. The room has an oxygen atmosphere. It probably killed the Seouras.

'What the hell's this?' Murdoch's voice was comfortably loud.

I turned around to see him holding his mask. Our guide still waited in the doorway.

'You can't come in here, can you?' I asked. Murdoch looked at me quizzically then realised I wasn't talking to him.

Affirmative.

'What happened?'

The resulting jumble of images was too confused and far off, like someone shouting gibberish three rooms away.

'Wait.' I retraced my steps, keeping one eye on the still forms until I stood in the entry. If I stretched my arm I could touch the slime. I could close my eyes and feel the touch of their thoughts.

Stop fighting it I told myself as firmly as I could. You've been fighting for . . . forever, and where has it got you? Nowhere. You might as well try letting them in. Try going to them. Go on, try it.

I slipped into a long, gloomy tunnel but it's all right, it's talking voices lots of voices. The Moving Ones, that's what their own name means, 'Seouras' is a Danadan word, in itself a still thing. They don't like to leave the others here in the bright light and the cold, still. *Cold white hate hates us can't break free. We resist you resist help us.*

Too fast, too far. I'm being carried along out of control. You must let me take it at my own pace. A pause, then fewer, clearer images, not just chaotic loaded colours. There was a planet, torn with warfare. After that, grey ships lifeless and waiting to be used, to be taken, and the Seouras did. They crossed the void in the grey ships. But their own strife followed them and they began to divide into factions. And the ship learned that they were there. A lever was triggered in its programming and they were trapped.

Death powerless rage hopeless . . . The ships. It was the ships all along. I slid down the wall, shocked beyond sound.

'What is it?' Murdoch knelt beside me.

'They're trapped in these ships.'

'What?' He looked sceptical.

We have thought of the Seouras as 'the enemy' for so long, they have been our gaolers for so long, that it takes an immense effort to imagine that they could be prisoners too.

It was easier to talk to something, so I leaned on the wall and stared at the single Seouras in the passage as the representative of the voices. 'Why did you come here?'

We want to leave. A painful yearning. A picture of the Seouras outside the ships against an indeterminate background.

'Haven't you tried to leave before?' What followed was extraordinary – a whole history of resistance. Of despair and attack, counterattack, defeat repeated until it collapsed from exhaustion. They tried everything, and the ships grew stronger as the programming grew more knowing.

I shook my head, stunned. Our gaolers are actually prisoners and it's not enough to hate and try to destroy them – they must be rescued?

'You didn't need to kill my people.' Hate remained.

Surprisingly, the voices agreed.

Then I got a clear picture of a stick-like creature moving in exaggerated slow motion. That's me.

You must cause it to be still. We cannot.

'They want me to help them,' I said to Murdoch.

'You're kidding.'

'I know, but what if it means they go away? I should at least look at what they're talking about.'

He threw up his hands in confusion. I felt the same.

I forced my legs to walk back into the room, past the Seouras bodies like huge fossils to the system interfaces that lined the wall. This must be what they wanted me to look at. It seemed more menacing, more dangerous, the closer I got.

And more familiar.

Familiar? Why the hell should it have seemed familiar? I put out a hand cautiously, but there was no forcefield between my dirty fingers and the smooth, cool metal. No bolt of energy to strike me down.

The interface panel had to be that sunken portion with scattered triangular patterns. Then I knew why it was familiar – I had worked on a pattern like this before. In the first days on Jocasta, when it was merely Abelar Four Workstation.

The Seouras had said they found the ships. A likely story, part of me had scoffed. Now it was more credible, though, because these ships were built with Tor technology.

The Tor had destroyed the ecology of Abelar's inner planets rather than allow them to fall into Confederacy hands. It was unlikely that they would leave perfectly usable ships floating around for anyone to salvage. Unless it had been deliberate – they might have left the ships with their malevolent programming to catch someone. An elaborate booby trap.

'What are you going to do?' Murdoch stood behind me.

'Bill, this is Tor technology.'

'How . . . ? Do you think that's what An Barik meant?'

'I don't know.' I turned back to the interface. My mind was full of Seouras voices and I found it hard to concentrate on what Murdoch was saying.

I had to find a way for the Seouras to get away from

the ship. Quietly, so the ships don't notice. Just a quiet nudge to open the door. It all depends on how much I can remember of the Tor systems.

The interface is heat- and time-lag operated, like they were on the station. Be careful not to fall asleep with your hand on it, the joke ran. I would try the method we used to circumvent the jump mine programs, but it took time.

I could feel pressure from somewhere beyond the Seouras voices. It threatened to flood my mind. *Hurry up*.

I jerked back my shaking hands from mistakes, unsure of the pathways to follow. I couldn't think, couldn't find the right links. It had been a long time since I'd worked on Tor technology. The systems were like labyrinths, full of traps and dead ends.

I'd started to find a path when it happened. The chamber seemed to ripple as though a strong wind rattled the bulkheads. The pressure in my mind increased. I took my hands off the interface and held my head, trying to keep the pressure out.

'What is it?' Murdoch tried to peer into my face.

'Something . . .'

Then the voices were back in my head. But the coherence of the previous multiple thought was lost. Or rather, now that the single voice was scattered I could see what it had been. The new voice was strident, cold, inorganic.

Where is the new signal?

I'd never 'heard' such a specific question from them before. There was no mistaking its meaning though. An

Barik's signal from the device I used in *Calypso* must have had a long range.

'What do you mean?' I caught Murdoch's eye. It's time. He nodded.

Where is the new signal?

The force of it squeezed the breath from my lungs.

'I don't know.' There was an ominous silence that I hastened to fill. 'Really. Is that what you wanted me to ... ? Ahh.' I reached blindly for Murdoch's hand. Pressure – inside – worse – pain spurts all over. Greenish light spins behind my eyes crawling forms shapeless shaped. Murdoch's hand not here.

'In the ... I don't ... Bill.' Scream his name he's not here. One alien in front of me one behind I'm on my knees. Pressure unbearable a whole galaxy compacted within my skull not enough breath to sob help us help me don't

Where is the new signal?

'Find it yourself.' God, Murdoch, do something. Stand try and stand get out of the way it's so slippery. Murdoch a silvery blur.

Where is the signal?

The word rises like bile in my throat can't keep it back can't stop. '*Calypso*.'

Murdoch's there at last. He holds something in front of him. A weapon. My last thought as he shoots me is that I didn't mean it literally.

I'm choking.

Coughing, retching, hawking. Breathe.

A dream. It's a dream. Slime. A Seouras dream.

'Steady.' Murdoch's muffled voice.

That's right – Murdoch shot me. How long have I been out? Must have been some kind of tranquilliser and it's making me sick. Clever of him to remember he couldn't trust an energy weapon in here . . .

His warm grip levered me upright like a crane.

'It'll wear off in a minute. I gave you the antidote.' He let go my arms cautiously and watched as I swayed.

There was a strange sensation in my head. Empty.

'They're gone,' I said in astonishment. My lips felt numb and slurred the words.

'No, they're waiting . . .' He turned to wave his hand at the entry and his voice died away. There were no shimmering Seouras forms in the tunnel. He strode over to the entry and peered out, mask at the ready in case the containment failed.

'You're right. Can't see any of them.'

I tottered over to him. 'I can't feel them in my head.'

He drew the mask over his head. 'Come on. We gotta get back.'

I put a hand on his arm. 'I told them, didn't I? They know about the drive.'

He nodded. 'That's why we have to get back.'

He started to leave, then turned back when he realised I wasn't following. I couldn't move – the weight of failure seemed to drag me through the deck.

Murdoch removed his mask again. 'What's up?'

I stared at the slime-stained whiteness and couldn't move.

His free hand reached out and tentatively cupped my chin until I looked at him.

'It doesn't matter,' he said gruffly. 'They would have found it eventually. At least this way they didn't take the station to pieces looking for it.'

After a moment I nodded, but I didn't tell him of that earlier vision the Seouras showed me. I hoped they had not done just that.

Without our guide I wasn't sure if it was the right tunnel. The slick, uneven walls and invisible exits all looked the same. I kept slipping and lurching into the walls because I couldn't tell how close they were. No sooner would Murdoch set me upright than he would slip himself. Finally we emerged into the 'hall'.

'Airlock is . . . this way.' I had to clear my throat carefully to get the words out. Didn't seem to have enough breath to accommodate them. And something here smelled disgusting.

Murdoch pulled me along. My head was spinning and my chest ached horribly.

The air. Either the Seouras atmosphere itself was disappearing, or my implant was malfunctioning, which would explain . . . why I can't . . . I lost the thought and crashed into Murdoch's back, gasping. Not . . . a good way . . . to die . . . the world lurched as Murdoch lifted me . . .

Thunk. Swoosh of humid, stale air. Filters malfunctioning by the smell of it. I gulped in lungfuls of wonderful oxygen, coughing and spluttering. Murdoch leaned over me as the shuttle whined in pre-launch. 'Shit, you gave me a fright.' He straightened up and went to the controls.

I sat up slowly. My throat felt like a piece of frayed string. 'They cut off the implant. I couldn't breathe.'

'Yeah, I guessed that. Strap in.'

'Do you think the ship will let us go?' I peered at the readouts, ambiguous with the interference.

'Dunno,' said Murdoch. 'But I'm not going to sit around waiting for it to tell us.' The shuttle veered away from the grey ship in its programmed flight back to Jocasta. The aft sensors showed no fire from the ship. Two minutes. Five.

We looked at each other in disbelief. 'It's our lucky day,' said Murdoch. Then we realised how close to the station the grey ship had come. There were no Confederacy ships within view or as far as we could track on sensors, nor anything resembling a New Council fleet. They were all taking their time. And meanwhile the grey ship had come to take the prize from under all our noses.

'I reckon it's come to get the drive, it can't be bothered with us.' Murdoch echoed my thought. He kept one eye on the ship and one eye on the station, his hand ready to alter course if the ship opened fire. 'But if it wanted the drive, why not get it when we first picked up *Calypso*? Hell, why not pick up *Calypso* when it first arrived?'

I thought of the strident, inorganic voice that had

echoed in my head. 'I think it was waiting for the signal, the same one as An Barik. He had to have that confirmation before he could send for help.' I let myself float in the net. There was something I should be doing but I couldn't remember what.

Then I realised. 'It fits, if that really is a Tor ship. They always wanted Invidi technology, that's one of the reasons they fought. I can see how the Seouras could get trapped. I'd guess that they never really understood the programming. The Tor were cunning bastards. It's quite conceivable that they put together programs specific to these conditions.'

'You mean, to Jocasta?'

I nodded. 'If the Invidi can sort of see the future, why not their worst enemies? They might have been waiting for the drive too.'

'Speculation.'

'I know, but we'll never know the truth. Can you get a comm link to the station?'

He tried, then shook his head. 'Too much interference. No wonder, with that thing so close.'

Minutes later he brought the shuttle in to dock. We pushed ourselves out into the airlock, shocked at the gloom and stale air. The modifications to the environmental systems couldn't have lasted very long. Either that, or they'd cut off the centre systems altogether. This might make the Q'Chn uncomfortable, but I hoped it wouldn't decide to come down into the habitat rings in search of fresh air.

I kicked off around the corridor in the direction of the

nearest uplift. Murdoch drew his hand weapon and followed. He placed a finger over his lips and I nodded. Not that I didn't think the Q'Chn could find us by a variety of means other than sound.

The lights failed completely.

Murdoch cursed once in the sudden, directionless dark.

I hooked one foot over the handrail and peered at the peeling fluorescent paint of the direction indicator strip. Lift, this way.

The faint rustle of Murdoch's uniform followed me down the corridor. That faint sound and the pale line were our only reference points in a weightless, featureless universe. At least we wouldn't see the Q'Chn if it attacked now.

We reached the lift, tumbled in, and slammed the Emergency Close pad. The door closed with its usual maddening slowness.

Murdoch sagged back into the air, arms spread. 'I'm getting too old for this. I think I'm gonna retire.'

I retrieved my comm link from a slime-sodden pocket. 'Halley to Bubble. Status report.'

Baudin's voice. 'The closest grey ship is stationary off the platforms. From what we can tell, the others seem to be backing off. We picked up some small craft leaving the ship just before you did. Looked like life-pods.'

I glanced at Murdoch. The Seouras might have taken their chance to flee.

'Our systems?'

'At least fifty per cent of environmental is down. We think the Q'Chn is in the centre core.'

'See what you can reroute from other systems.'

'We're on it. Most of Security is on crowd control and patrol to stop panic.'

Murdoch twisted parallel to the door. 'Halley,' he said quietly, and his tone immediately brought me away from the link. 'The lift's not moving.'

The direction indicator on the control screen was still. The location indicator said Level Five. We wanted Level Six, where the uplift entries were. The door began to open. I tried to override the command but there was no time.

The Slasher hung there looking in on us.

Murdoch hooked one elbow over the rail and fumbled to bring his weapon to bear.

I stared at the Q'Chn with my mouth open. It really was beautiful. Colours from an alien spectrum ran through the chain mail–like surface of its thorax and the curve of its long forearms was clean and sharp.

The Slasher lowered a head the size of a human chest and focused upon me a multifaceted eye disturbingly like Keveth's. The eye was mesmerising, an immense orb with opaque, fiery depths. In one corner of every glittering surface, a tiny bipedal figure. The eyes were set in a foreshortened triangle, the small mouth hidden, like the K'Cher, on the lower side of the jaw.

'I've come to say goodbye, Halley.' Henoit's light voice broke the silence.

The Q'Chn swayed backwards a little to allow Henoit to brace himself in the lift doorway, graceful even in zero gravity.

'And to say that I'll be taking the *Calypso* with me, so

I'd like that Invidi toy you have with you. Please don't say you haven't got it because I don't like searching blood-soaked bodies.'

I took the egg out of my pocket and flicked it to him. He put out a hand to intercept it.

'You brought that thing onto my station.' I was so angry at him, I couldn't think of anything but the bare words to say. No expletive would have been adequate. If it had been me with the gun, I would have shot him.

'I did. My apologies for the mess it's left. We agreed to revive the Q'Chn but only if they agreed to modifications. It's supposed to follow orders more closely.'

'How could you?'

'Getting the drive is worth it.' His hand closed on the floating egg. 'You know that. You want it yourself. Don't deceive yourself, Halley. I know how much you want it.'

'Not enough to endanger the station,' I retorted.

'You betrayed me,' he said. His hand closed on the floating egg. 'You betrayed me many years ago and now I'm returning the favour.'

'Why did it kill all those people?' Murdoch asked.

I tried not to imagine what Henoit would order it to do now.

He made a short sound of impatience. 'It's not good at following orders. It came onto the station before it was supposed to, then killed the K'Cher that helped it.' Behind him, the Q'Chn moved its wings slightly. 'It doesn't like the K'Cher, as you may imagine. The K'Cher wanted its kind extinct.'

'What about Quartermaine?' Murdoch rasped beside me. 'That was after you got here.'

'My source said that Quartermaine had found the drive information and was taking it to the Invidi. I did not want the Invidi to call his forces until I had had a chance to confirm the existence of the drive myself.'

'Jones was your informant,' said Murdoch. 'Jones was in the storage bay and Jones asked Keveth to pick up the Q'Chn.'

'Yes,' said Henoit. 'But the human Jones was also betraying me to a member of the Four.'

Jones had dealt with Trillith. Jones had relayed all Trillith's information to Henoit but must have tried to play one off against the other. So the Q'Chn killed him too. What a terrible mess.

'I'm going now.' Henoit pushed back from the doorway. He looked at me. 'You will regret not joining us.'

'I agree with you, but I still won't do it.'

He looked at me again for a long moment, then the lift door shut.

'What the . . .' Murdoch peered over my shoulder at the controls. 'He sent us down. I thought we were mince-meat for sure.'

Funny how legs tremble with release of tension even when you're not standing on them.

'We've got no way of stopping him. Why should he bother killing us?'

'Maybe. But I'm glad I was with you and not alone.' His comm link beeped. 'Murdoch here.'

'Chief, the H'digh warrior has escaped from the brig.

He knocked out the duty constable and rerouted our surveillance monitor. Must have been twenty minutes ago.' Kwon's voice was breathless and apologetic.

Murdoch held his breath for ten. I could imagine Kwon doing the same on the other end of the link.

'That's all right, Sergeant. We're on it.'

When we got down to Alpha the uplift lobby and the corridors were dark and deserted, the air still and beginning to heat up. If the heat dispersal system was out, we were in big trouble. I could hear raised voices in other areas. The sounds seemed to carry further than usual – the background hum from recycling and maintenance that we never normally noticed was mute. Our footsteps echoed.

To see the station like this hit me harder than Henoit's betrayal, hurt more than the danger we still faced from the grey ships, made me feel worse than the thought of An Barik calling the Confederacy to come now that he had what he'd been waiting for.

They'd both been waiting for it. The Invidi and the Tor ships. An Barik had said that the Tor were dangerous, and he'd been trying to warn me in his obscure way before we went over to the grey ship. Veatch had said that the Tor had similar powers to the Invidi but in a different way. Perhaps it was not only the Nine Worlds to whom An Barik wished to deny the drive but the Tor as well. More likely, the Tor were the main reason he'd waited and the fate of the Nine was merely coincidental.

Henoit had been waiting for it too, curse him. The New Council calculated the station where *Calypso* would arrive and sent their best team. The team most likely to succeed, given who was head of the station. I wondered how much An Serat had been directly involved this time. Did Invidi 'retire'? At least An Barik's faction do their own dirty work. They don't use proxies like the New Council.

We found a working karrikar. It shuddered as it moved and I felt a distinct sideways drag. Inertia compensators are damaged. Hope the stabilisers are okay.

'Halley to Bubble.'

The comm link still worked. 'Baudin here.'

'A small ship will try to leave the station soon. It'll probably head for *Calypso*. Monitor it.'

Murdoch was speaking to Sasaki on his own link. He cut it and turned to me. 'We've got problems. People can see the grey ship coming and they're panicking. If we're not careful, some are going to try to evacuate. And that's likely to start a real panic.'

'Put out a message by all available means – use hand-speakers if you have to – that the grey ship is not going to attack the station. But if anyone attempts to leave, that's when they'll be attacked.'

He talked to Sasaki again.

We couldn't let the grey ship take the Invidi drive. I didn't want Henoit to have it either. But we had no means to stop it happening. An Barik claimed he'd called Confederacy forces – we'd have to sit here and wait until they came to the rescue. Was that all we could do? Wait until the big players fought it out and then line up politely for our piece of the spoils?

God dammit to hell.

They had proper lights in the Bubble, the emergency system. It was only two-thirds as bright as normal, and the blue or green glow of interface consoles lit faces from below. Every console was occupied, and I had to squeeze past two ConFleet ensigns to get to the upper level. Baudin turned to greet me, relief on his face. He even forgot to salute. Behind me, Murdoch strode to the Security console.

'Lieutenant. Status of environmental systems?' Keep it calm.

'Functions have stabilised at forty-nine per cent,' he began.

Murdoch cursed loudly. I nodded at Baudin to wait and peered over Lee's shoulder.

Henoit was leaving. At that moment all I could think was, I hope he's got the Q'Chn with him.

'Lock the docking mechanism. Don't let him go.'

Murdoch groaned. 'Can't. We've lost access to the entire docking system.'

'Deactivate the grid.' I could see as Lee tried it that we had no control. No control over what the grey ship did, or over what the Confederacy would do when it came. We'd almost had more control over our own fate when the Seouras were in charge.

'The ship is leaving,' said Lee. She connected the image to Baudin's big viewer in front of the central console and we watched the tiny speck break away from Jocasta's curved bulk.

'Tell him to pull back.'

Lee sent the message, then turned to me anxiously. 'No response.'

'How many lifesigns are there on that ship?'

Another agonising minute while she struggled with the sensors. 'We can't tell. It's a deflecting field.'

'The airlock records?' Murdoch looked over our shoulders.

'Non-operational. And we couldn't access them anyway at the moment.'

I glanced at Murdoch. No way to know if Henoit had taken the Q'Chn with him.

'Have we any contact with Confederacy ships yet?' If An Barik had really called them.

'No, ma'am. The Seouras ship is still blocking our sensors.

'Where's the grey ship now?' It was like watch-playing a game on holovid. Nothing to do but lie back and enjoy the fun.

'At the pace it's moving, in two minutes it'll reach the outer platforms.' Lee sounded as worried as I'd ever heard. They didn't know about the drive, and must think the ship was moving in to attack. Of course, it might attack after it got the drive.

'He's not going to be in time,' growled Murdoch, eyes narrowed at the screen. Henoit's little ship was nearly at the platform where *Calypso* waited.

'We'll be fine,' I said loudly. 'Keep an eye on environmental. Do we have repair teams organised?'

Baudin nodded. 'Chief McGuire is on it.'

I felt a momentary pang of envy for the chief engineer. I'd swap jobs with him any day, if I thought he could do mine as well as I know I could do his.

'Commander?' Lee's voice pulled me over. 'The small ship is activating a traction field. It's attaching it to *Calypso*.'

I squeezed in beside her to look at the figures, more precise than an image. Henoit was mad. How could he expect to steal the drive from under the Tor ship's nose? He didn't have time.

The grey ship fired before the smaller ship had properly attached the field. Henoit's defences lasted a few long seconds before the engines exploded and it came apart. A small flare, little bigger than the funeral pods. Momentum from the explosion snapped *Calypso*'s tether and sent her spinning outwards, away from the station and the grey ship towards the stars.

A confused exclamation from Lee, Murdoch's startled expletive, a sharp cry from someone else. I needed to sit down. There was a cold, empty spot in my stomach that threatened to rise and fill the space behind my eyes. Murdoch dragged a chair from the console beside Lee and pushed it behind my knees as they gave out. He muttered something about putting my head down.

Henoit was dead. It couldn't have been anyone else on that ship.

'The grey ship's closing on *Calypso*.' Lee tried to increase the amount of information the overtaxed sensors were sending us, but definition on the screen grew progressively worse. The gaze Murdoch turned to me was bleak. We'd failed to keep the Invidi drive out of enemy hands.

It was hard to see how things could get worse. But they did. The grey ship turned around and fired on the station.

The ship moved in, annihilating our options with each kilometre forward. The bolts it fired were familiar from that first attack six months ago. They had little destructive power but disrupted every electrical and plasma-based function on the station, causing total havoc.

The second bolt hit Alpha. The Bubble's lights dimmed and the room filled with greenish crooked lines of energy that danced over the interfaces and touched us briefly with sharp pain.

Amidst the groans and cries, the smell of smoke and crackle of severed connections, Lee's calm voice spoke.

'Ship has stopped moving.' Her interface was the best shielded and most heavily backed-up in the Bubble, but it was barely working. It gave her a trickle of data from our furthermost external sensor, the only one not affected by the grey ship's attack.

Everyone was looking at me. They'd done this when the Seouras first attacked too. As if they expected me to come up with a solution to the insoluble. As if I could pull a magic rabbit out of a hat, like an Invidi.

I leaned over Lee's console. 'Can we still send a short-range radio signal?'

'A radio signal?' Lee's training wavered for a second, then she quickly adjusted the screen. 'Yes.'

I made sure the frequency was zeta and tapped in my security code. I hoped Kwon had done his job properly, that somewhere inside the grey ship, the bomb in *Calypso* was activated. That the grey ship had not deactivated it already.

Nothing happened. Murdoch and Baudin staggered over to Lee's console, coughing in the sour smoke, and peered over our shoulders at the screen. I felt sick. So much for magic rabbits.

Then the grey ship began to list. It turned away from the station but wasn't making much speed.

'Their power output just dropped,' Lee's voice rose excitedly. Then her screen flared with glaring whiteness, which faded abruptly as radiation fried the sensor. A few seconds later we heard low booms as debris from the explosion began to impact on the station. Lee muttered, slipped over to another console, and tapped frantically.

I turned to Murdoch. 'Get down to Delta. They'll have the most damage.'

He nodded and left. I stood over Lee.

'I need a damage report, Ensign.'

'Yes, ma'am,' she replied, but it took minutes. I paced, stopping only to help one of the other ensigns make emergency repairs on his console.

'The grey ship's been heavily damaged,' said Lee finally. 'It's on a course that might take it into the planet's atmosphere.'

'What about us?'

'Environmentals critical. We've got' – she ran through them slowly – 'a Smoke ventilation failure.' That meant trouble for the residents and methane leaks into our atmosphere. 'In some of the outer areas damaged by the explosion we've got containment failure. The doors aren't coming down.'

'Shit,' someone said.

The possibility of a runaway containment failure was everyone's worst nightmare. Normally decompression in one part of the station could be contained, but not if the containment system itself was non-functional. Everything could blow open to space. There was no time to evacuate and no way to do so anyhow.

The containment system was up in the centre core. I could reinitialise it using the original program, the way we first began after modifying the Tor systems.

'Tell Lieutenant Gamet to meet me in the west spoke,' I said, and left Baudin in charge of the Bubble.

'We don't know if it's still there,' I said to Gamet, as the uplift jerked its way to the end of the spoke. 'We couldn't tell how many lifesigns were on Henoit's ship.'

Henoit would have had no reason to leave the Q'Chn, which was a valuable asset to the New Council. That's what I told myself. Then again, he hadn't seemed satisfied with the Q'Chn's 'modifications' and it was conceivable he'd left the alien here in a final act of vindictiveness. Besides, and I hadn't thought of this until now, would the Q'Chn have fitted into that little ship?

'You go through the tunnels, I'll try the corridors.' We'd decided to stick to the plan the repair team had followed before. 'Whoever gets there first starts the procedure.'

She nodded. We bobbed off the wall of the uplift as it bumped to a halt. Gamet removed the access hatch in the wall and gave me a thumbs-up before wriggling inside. I took a deep breath and opened the door, a sick feeling in my throat as I remembered the last time the uplift door had opened to reveal the Q'Chn and Henoit.

Nothing.

I let out the breath and pushed out into the corridor. It was still dark, but the pale direction strip on the wall was clear. I pulled myself along quickly, heart pounding out of all proportion to the severity of the exertion. The air was stale, but not that stale. The strip was cut off at regular intervals where doors opened into the corridor from each side. When the gravity field was on, this corridor was a stairwell. Most of the doors were shut, their round Confederacy logos glowing in the dark. Once I felt cooler air and an echoing space at one of the entries, and it took me a moment to gather enough courage to go past.

Main intersection, along into second corridor. The second corridor was the same, the light strip green. Only the dark and the handrail cold under my palms, roughened where paint had flaked, pitted where the original smooth metal had been replaced. The sense of dream, of otherworldliness was so strong I had to remind myself a couple of times what I was doing. Silently. It was tempting to fill the immense silence all around with words.

The end of the corridor came almost as a shock – I bumped my head on the wall and nearly missed the handrail on the rebound. I didn't want to flail around the middle of the corridor trying to get my bearings. There should be doors on right and left and an access hatch above my head. One hand on the rail, my other hand patted the smooth wall surface in vain.

They've moved the hatch!

Don't be ridiculous. Try upside down.

The hatch was there and I gripped the round pipe-handle with relief. The interface controls glowed faintly but, as I'd suspected, offered no response. It would have to be opened manually. My palms kept slipping with sweat and I had to wipe them twice on my trousers before the handle would move.

Into the narrow space. I swung the door shut and reached up with relief to activate the light strap on my head. The warm glow banished the surreal sensation of the corridor and resurrected the urgency of my mission. Get to the core, quickly.

Rungs in a tunnel. The air smelt differently here, metallic, more alive. My sense of smell had returned, now that the Seouras implant had stopped functioning. The rungs were for when the Invidi gravity field was operational and the core centre was 'down'. I didn't need them now and pulled myself along the rails with slippery hands. At my back was the cold, rough wall, on the other side of which lay the corridors and storage bays. There was a gentle hum in the air, but not as loud as it should have been.

Underneath the rungs of the ladder now, the delicate operational systems that ran the station for us covered the surface of the core in a filigree of metal. I looked around – it seemed inconceivable that the Q'Chn would fit in here, although perhaps it could fit further along where the relays were larger and the space for parts renewal and retrieval also larger. I had started on Level

Six, where all the spoke connections were, and needed to go across two levels, to Eight.

I followed the spiralling rungs of the ladder. Inside the narrow circle of light the opsys conduits and databoards flickered and shone. Outside the circle, the dark where the Q'Chn might be waiting. What did it think of all this? Was it simply glad of the excuse to begin its work of slaughter again? I imagined it must have found Henoit's orders very tame – a murder here, a murder there. Nothing like the glorious K'Cher wars of the past.

Level Eight. No sign of Gamet, but I'd sent her on the safer and longer route intentionally. I hooked my feet over the rungs, snapped my kit's lead onto my arm to prevent it drifting away, and began to work on the containment systems.

They showed no sign of outward damage – it hadn't been sabotage, then, but damage from the Tor bolts. You'd think that as the basic systems utilised elements of the original Tor technology, they would be less vulnerable to attack by the same technology. This didn't seem to be the case, although the opsys had always shown a certain hybrid vigour in day-to-day operations.

Something clattered further along the ladder and I started, watching a micro-tool float away. I'd been so immersed in the repairs that I hadn't kept one eye on the surroundings. Then a yellowish light illuminated the curve of the core and I slumped in relief.

'Gamet?'

'Is that you, ma'am?'

'Over here.'

She pulled her way over to me with neat, smooth strokes. 'This is it?'

I nodded and indicated where she could attach her enhancement connection. 'I've nearly finished modifying the baseboard for you. I didn't want you to use the connection otherwise. This system's very close to the original and I don't trust it.'

She smiled. 'No, I wouldn't want to let a Tor opsys into my head.'

That's what I'd been doing for the past six months through the Seouras, I thought, and touched the implant in my neck briefly. The sooner Eleanor gets rid of it, the better.

It wouldn't take her more than ten minutes to get around the containment system and reknit the program. Unfortunately it was five minutes later that I heard the Q'Chn.

It was the sound of a maintenance hatch opening. The slight squeal and creak was unmistakable – I'd made the same sound when I entered the core. It was impossible to judge distance in the echoing dark. Which level?

Gamet sat perfectly still with her eyes open, seeing nothing. The two connector leads ran from the lumps in the skin below her hairline to the baseboard where I'd made a safe initiator space. If I moved her now the connection would be broken and the system left in a worse state than when we started because it would be confused. If I forced her to go through the shutdown sequence, it would take five minutes, nearly as long as it would to finish the job.

Then I saw that Gamet had brought the portable sensor

that the repair team used in their previous mission. My ears pricked for more sounds, I ran a scan of the core. Everywhere but Level Six was clear. It showed an interference pattern that had become almost as familiar to us as that of the grey ships.

Level Six is too close. Don't panic, think, I told myself firmly. It will not fit through the same hatch you did. I don't care how fearsome it is, it can't bend the laws of mass conservation. Therefore it will try another way, probably the freight access in Level Twelve. We should be all right.

What if it just sits and waits until you come out? a nasty inner voice questioned. If you ask for backup, it'll mean more casualties. Are you going to sit here until ConFleet arrives? If they ever do.

I heard a new noise, one that sent cold waves of horror up my legs. It was the sound of ripping circuitry and snapping conduits. Crackles, hisses, and pops of small explosions. Ripples of light played over the opsys surface in front of me and Gamet blinked, frowned, and shivered once. There was a screech of metal being pulled beyond molecular limits and a resounding clang after that. I had a mental image of the hatch door being tossed into the corridor. It sounded like the Q'Chn was having a tantrum.

As I listened the cold fear turned to a flush of rage. Before my brain registered what I was doing, I had grabbed the sensor, hooked it onto my belt, and started pulling myself along the levels as fast as I could go. Nothing makes me angrier than wanton destruction of something that has been made with love and skill.

Murdoch seemed to think we could lure the Q'Chn with human bait. I hoped to hell he knew his job as well as I thought he did.

Nearly at Level Six. Ahead I could see the dark gashes across the surface of the opsys, like open wounds with light flickering on their lips. Loose energy discharges popped here and there, leaving a green afterimage on my eye. Slivers of metal and glass dust floated slowly towards me and I waved the debris away. The hatch was a dark oval, doorless as I'd suspected. I stopped several metres away, for I had no intention of getting within grabbing distance.

'*Hey!*' My voice sounded so loud after the long silence that I made myself jump. '*You with the wings!*' If I was going to indulge in bravado, I might as well do it properly.

There was no response, but the silence beyond the hatch was heavy with the Slasher's presence.

'It's about time you left my station alone. I'm not unreasonable though. I suppose Henoit left you because you were indiscreet enough to kill a K'Cher.' I emphasised the last word.

There was a movement behind the oval darkness, a soft touch of wing on wall.

'That doesn't bother me. There's a ship waiting in a dock on Level One. If you want to leave, go there.'

It probably knew there was no ship docked at Level One. But I hoped it would be curious enough to come and see what I was plotting. I also hoped it wouldn't kill Gamet first.

I turned and followed the opposite sweep of the rungs. Pulled myself along in a steady rhythm. Now that the thing was done, I felt sick. What have I let myself in for? I ran through Murdoch's scenario in my mind again and again – get to the airlock, lure the Slasher in, initiate depressurisation and, if you're trapped inside too, jump into the recycling tube. Don't forget to hold your breath.

I felt sicker. And getting to the airlock from the core hatch presented a problem too. I didn't want to pass through the corridors on Level One as I'd done earlier on Six. Not with the Q'Chn waiting for me. I'd have to crawl along the wall tunnels, which were too small for the Q'Chn. If Gamet could get to the core using those tunnels, no reason I can't do the same to get to the airlock.

I seemed to have been pulling myself along for hours. The surface under the rungs had changed, it was darker and rougher and had larger flat areas with no surface circuitry. The functions here had been routed to the rings' backup systems soon after the Seouras invaded and it had an abandoned look.

It occurred to me that I didn't have to worry about keeping comm silence now.

'Halley to Bubble.'

Murdoch answered. The link wasn't clear but I could make out his words. 'What's your position?'

'I'm in the core. At about Level Three.'

'I thought you'd be finished by now. Is something wrong?'

'Um ... The Slasher didn't go with Henoit, Bill.'

He didn't even waste time cursing. 'What can we do?'

'Some light would be useful. In the corridors.'

'I'm on it. Where do you want us to meet you?'

'I don't. You're to wait until I'm finished.' Not a good choice of phrase.

'What d'you mean?'

'I'm going to try your airlock idea. Got any after-thoughts that might help?'

There was silence at the other end and a muted roar in the background that might have been voices or machinery. Finally Murdoch spoke, slowly.

'No, I think we covered everything. Don't forget your decompression routine. But Halley . . .'

'Right.' I cut the link and tried to keep the sound of Murdoch's deep, reassuring voice in my mind.

Must be nearly at the farthest level. I was breathing heavily now, haven't kept up my zero-g drills. I found a maintenance access hatch. It was much smaller than the entry from the corridor proper and I felt reassured by the closeness. It was confusing, though, with passages stretching in four directions. I took the tunnel that must run along the bisecting corridor like the one I'd walked along in Level Six.

The thought of the corridor made me nervous. Could it track me through the wall? It might decide to cut through the wall to reach me. Would it be waiting for me when I came out?

The rungs here were much smaller and were set further into the wall – not much maintenance would be done unless the gravity field was turned off. It was a long time since I'd been in one of these. Being small helped. Someone as large as Murdoch would have been in danger of brushing the sides of the tunnel. The conduits on one side emitted a faint luminescence and an occasional *zzt* of energy crackled across the walls. I was more than halfway to the end of the tunnel and fear increased with every pull.

Without warning the world turned around.

What had been 'ahead' suddenly became 'up'. Something yanked viciously at my feet – I was falling. The gravity field had activated.

I tried to grab the rungs but the momentum was too strong and carried me straight down. I tried to turn, braced my knees and elbows and succeeded in partially reducing speed. A crackling noise, sparks, and the hiss of plasma escaping under pressure then pain shot through my legs and shoulders. An acrid smell of coolant. Rail, rung, grab anything. Can't stop . . .

Dizzy with shock and pain I hit the hatch at the bottom of the tunnel, back where I'd started.

Shit, shit, shit. I lay still and looked up at the faint glow of the hatch, now a good fifteen metres' climb away. Who the hell activated the gravity field? The alarm that normally precedes its activation hadn't sounded. Maybe the Q'Chn. Or maybe the system was glitching by itself.

Whatever. I lay still for another minute or two. It was dark. I'd lost the light band on my head. There were numb places all over me and I had the feeling that if I moved they'd hurt. On the other hand, eventually I'd have to make that climb.

If I did climb, it would probably be one of the last things I did.

I'd thought quite a lot about death in the past few years, and been close to it more than once. I had come to the conclusion that it wasn't something I should worry about too much. When the time came, I wouldn't try to sneak away from it. But it was definitely something to postpone as long as possible.

I could lie here until ConFleet came, but I was sick of waiting for ConFleet.

I sat up cautiously. I had trouble moving my right arm above shoulder level but nothing seemed to be broken. Everything hurt, though, and my nose was bleeding. I hate nosebleeds. I wiped it on my sleeve and started crying weakly. My body seemed so heavy after micro gravity, which made everything worse.

'Murdoch to Halley.' The scratchy voice came from somewhere above my head. After a moment I located the comm link, wedged between a rung and a conduit edge.

'Halley here.' My voice was scratchier than the link sound.

'We monitored your gravity field coming on. Are you okay?'

'Had a bit of a fall.' I leaned against the rungs. 'Did Gamet finish the repairs?'

'Yeah, we just heard from her. She's in the spoke and wants to know if she should wait for you.'

'Tell her to get out, now.' I didn't want the Q'Chn distracted. I looked up. Fifteen metres. 'Are the containment systems functioning?'

'Absolutely. We stood down the alarm.'

'Good.' I sighed. 'I'll be down soon.'

'For god's sake Halley, stay where you are. You don't need to do any more.'

He was right, and for a moment I hesitated. Then I thought of Henoit and how easily he'd taken me in, how for a short while I'd been so phenomenally stupid that I thought we might patch things up. Somehow the Q'Chn was part of Henoit's deception and getting rid of it meant getting rid of him too.

Not that I could say that to Murdoch, so I hedged. 'What would you do?'

He hesitated too long before replying. 'I'd get out of there.'

Of course he wouldn't. 'Sorry, Bill. Wrong answer.' I shut the link and put it in my pocket.

Climbing was surprisingly easy, once the first shock of pain wore off. I tried to keep an even pace. I counted about one metre per three rungs. Sixty. Don't think, just count. It was easy in the dark to keep track only of the next rung and not to worry about anything else.

Would the Q'Chn be waiting? There was no noise from above, only the mechanical background murmurs and the rasp of my own throat.

Once I swept my arm out in an incautious arc and hit a smooth surface. An instant jolt of electricity pulled the breath from my lungs and jerked me almost off the ladder. I dropped a couple of rungs then managed to cling tight.

I asked myself if I was really doing this to get back at Henoit and the answer was, not entirely for that reason but basically yes. I had the feeling it was one of those actions that, if we're lucky enough to survive, we look back on later and shudder.

Sixty. This time the opening was above me. Don't think, just do it. My fingers brushed the surface beside the hatch carefully. Remember the sequences – of course I remember the sequences, how many years do you think I've been using maintenance tunnels?

The hatch slid back with a slight creak and I ducked back inside the tunnel.

Nothing.

I hooked my good arm around a rung and peered out. The lights were on and their glare almost blinded me after the darkness. The corridor curved around until it disappeared over its little hill to continue around the other side of the centre. Before that, about ten metres away on the other side, was the airlock door. Round and solid, it looked able to withstand the assault of an army of Q'Chn. I hoped we wouldn't have to try. If all went according to plan, when the airlock opened, the rush of atmosphere sucked out into vacuum should take the Q'Chn with it and it would be unable to assault anything.

There was only one way to do this. I reached up for the rung above the hatch and used it as leverage to swing both legs over the hatch sill and slide out. Wishing my legs were steadier, I tiptoed to the airlock and examined the controls. Like all airlocks, its programming included a built-in safety mechanism that made it impossible to open the outer doors to a ship until the inner door had closed completely. There would be an easily accessible override control inside the lock too. I'd always found this comforting, but now it was a worry – if the Q'Chn knew about this it might be able to stop the outer door opening. I keyed in my code to deactivate the override. Hope it will accept the code.

There was a soft sound behind me. Dear god, if I ever survive this I'm going to have nightmares for years . . .

The Q'Chn's head and wingtips brushed the ceiling and its wings were like leaves.

The great head shifted and one of the forearms twitched in a flexing movement. Would it give me any warning?

The ceiling was too low for it to spread its wings either for flight or momentum. Two legs take off faster than four and a quick sprint might get me away from it and around the next corner. But I didn't want to run away, not this time.

It was so big, nearly three metres away and it could reach out and cut my legs from under me. You wanted to *talk* to this? The stupidity and arrogance of the idea rang faintly in the background of my fear. Murdoch's voice echoed there. 'They. Kill. You.'

I reached out two fingers very slowly and touched the controls. The airlock's inner door drew back with a ponderous clunk.

The Q'Chn was still. The next second it tensed inwards upon itself, almost shrinking. I shrank back too. Dammit, I got this far . . .

It did nothing more fearsome than stalk one, two paces closer to the airlock. It inspected the small space within and turned its triangular face 180 degrees to stare at mine. I stared up, grasped the airlock controls firmly in one hand, and gestured slowly with the other.

'After you.'

For a moment it stayed in the same position, with that same statue-like stillness. Then, with a movement more awkward than any I'd yet seen it make, lifted one leg over the airlock sill. It crouched to allow its whole body to follow, and the wings were curled tightly almost straight out behind. The other legs followed in turn.

I didn't believe it could be this easy. I held my breath as the last link of wing disappeared inside and hit the close pad. As the airlock began to hiss shut a feeler shot out and grabbed my leg.

I yelled in fright and grabbed the control box. It came away in my hand. Then I hit the floor and was sliding towards the half-open door. The feeler was like a band of steel around my thigh. I pushed frantically at it with one hand and flailed with the other but there was nothing to grab onto on that smooth deck.

I braced my heels on the airlock sill, hoping the door would shut in time and crush its feeler, but it was actually holding the door open with two vice-like limbs. My boots slid, I scrabbled for a foothold, got partly to my feet then crashed over the sill and into the airlock with the Slasher.

The hold on my leg released immediately and I slid to the other side of the room. It stretched a long killing-leg and snicked the blade at me. I crouched instinctively. The leg withdrew. I forced my trembling legs to stand again. It repeated the action and I crouched down, whimpering in terror. It's playing with me.

Think, damn you, think. Murdoch had said there was a recycling tube in the airlock. I couldn't see it. All the walls were bare, except for the override panel set next to the door, halfway between us. And the outer door activation panel, which was next to the round port, opposite the Q'Chn and close to my left.

The Q'Chn had tired of the game and drew both front legs up. I slid along the wall a little further away, but a part of me said, why prolong the inevitable? Open the airlock and finish it. Getting all the air sucked out of your lungs is a better alternative than having your throat cut . . .

The recycling hatch was on the floor between me and the Q'Chn. Of course it's on the floor, idiot. With the gravity field on, the wall becomes the floor, right?

With hope came fear. The hatch had a simple pullout opening for inserting material. It also had a magnetic seal that activated automatically when the outer doors opened. I'd have about twenty seconds after the door opened to yank it back and squirm inside.

Do it now.

As the Slasher snicked back its leg for the kill, I reached back to the outer door controls and tapped the short code to initiate emergency opening.

The bolts groaned. With a crack of release and a growing hiss of escaping air, the door opened.

I lunged for the recycling hatch at the same time the Q'Chn's feeler lashed for the override controls. I hoped I'd managed to deactivate them in the corridor.

The hatch cover came away so easily that I fell over backwards and had to grab the edge of the tube to stop being dragged out into vacuum. The hiss of air had become a roar out into cold nothing. My ears were popping and nose bleeding again.

I took two deep breaths, held the second, and pulled myself head first into the dank opening.

Hold the breath, wriggle, shoulders through, hips through . . . God, I'm not moving, it's got my foot.

The Q'Chn's grip was reinforced by the tug of outrushing air and slowly my leg was pulled back. Lungs burning and dark patches bursting behind my eyes, I braced the other foot against the lip of the hatch. Somewhere in the recesses of my mind I wondered why I was being so damned stubborn.

My boot slipped off.

The ancient synthetic suddenly gave out, its bonds unable to withstand such pressure.

I shot into stinking darkness and passed out.

After

Murdoch was in recycling to meet me with two constables when I slid out of the tube in a smelly heap.

They'd monitored airlock activity and worked out which vat top to hastily cushion. They laid me out on the deck and gave me something for respiratory distress and to pull my scattered senses together.

The first thing I knew about it was Murdoch's voice giving the Bubble a status report. I sat up with a groan and the constable draped a thermasheet over my battered shoulders. The room spun around gaily.

Murdoch didn't say much. I could vaguely feel his anger, and how he was trying to control it because I was hurt and exhausted and, after all, the Q'Chn was dead. No doubt he'd have plenty to say tomorrow.

'Is it . . .' My voice didn't emerge as directed and I had to try again. 'Is it gone?'

'As far as we can tell.' Murdoch seemed to deliberately leave distance between us. He motioned to the constable, who bent down to lift me, but I waved the man back indignantly.

'M'allright.' The room spun further as I lurched to my feet, but I didn't care. We'd finally got rid of the Q'Chn. The grey ships were gone. Containment must be secure, or we'd all be floating around outside, too. I felt light-hearted, as well as light-headed.

'Whoops.' I half-fell onto Murdoch and he grabbed me. Then, looking down, he caught sight of my bare foot and torn trouser-leg. It didn't look funny to me, but for some reason Murdoch started chuckling. I giggled, too.

We all stood there in the stink of recycling and roared with laughter.

An hour or so later, Murdoch sent a team to the centre to confirm the Q'Chn's death. It took them a while to find the corpse. Eventually they scanned it on the junction of one of the spokes, quite dead but clinging fast to the station's skin. We left it there for the time being – it was too much of an expenditure in time and personnel to go and get it. I think, too, we were all a little scared it might suddenly come back to life and start terrorising us again.

There had been no casualties from the grey ship's attack earlier, but many minor ones from the breakdowns all over the station.

I was in the hospital when An Barik's reinforcements finally arrived much later.

At first the Confederacy warship seemed to think our request for it to stand off was a joke. They ignored our warning and approached Jocasta. When we repeated the request an irate voice – visuals were still down – asked what the hell we meant and did we know who they were. I said that we knew who they were, but we wanted to talk about how many rights they now had here, and I repeated the formal declaration required by law. This stopped the Confederacy general – as he turned out to be – for a few minutes while he 'conferred' with his colleagues.

The general sounded more restrained the next time he

called. He suggested that while they contacted Con-Central for instructions, officials would board the station to appraise our situation.

'It means they want to make sure we're acting of our own free will, not taken over by aliens or terrorist groups,' whispered Murdoch. I snorted. If they'd come yesterday, I could have given them both.

We agreed to talk, and the general also wanted to speak to the Confederacy observer, so I told Lee to link him to An Barik's quarters. My eyes met Murdoch's and he nodded slightly then went back to his Security console. I didn't think he'd be able to access the Invidi's conversation, but there was no harm in trying. As it turned out, we couldn't break whatever code they were using. Later that day An Barik went over to the warship. In one of their shuttles, not in his own ship, which remained docked at the station. We assumed that he was not leaving us permanently.

The warship's captain wanted to dock for repairs and crew R&R, and she didn't understand why the request made us all laugh so much. We finally persuaded her that we had no equipment or materials to effect repairs and that if she wanted her crew to enjoy the station's hospitality, they'd have to, first, help us repair the facilities and, second, provide suitable supplies. The captain, who was a Bendarl, had no patience with the slow give-and-take of the neutrality negotiations, so by the time the official outline of the agreement had been drafted, she'd already sent three large teams of engineers who worked with great efficiency to restore normal functions to environmental systems. I suspect there was some conflict with the general over this, but Bendarl can take care of themselves and we never heard anything more on the matter.

The Fleet engineers had been less than complimentary about some of our many modifications. They laughed outright, for example, at the circuitry on the public recycle unit boards and the ringlift transport cars.

In return for this help, a trickle of visitors, mainly crew from the warship, appeared in the throughways of the station for the first time in more than half a year. They received such a delighted and riotous welcome that their reports when they returned to ConCentral were the start of Jocasta's undeserved reputation as a quaint stopover port.

I call our talks 'negotiations', but in fact what happened was a series of interminable, probing questions from the general, who was a military-turned-political officer. He was assisted by two officials from Central administration who wanted to examine our records in minute detail, an Earth government official who was nervous of everybody else, and the warship's first officer who had obviously been told to keep an eye on all of us, and did so. On the receiving end of the questions were myself, Lorna deVries, Veatch and his two senior department heads, and, to a lesser extent, Murdoch. It seemed strange to be under the familiar heavy hand of authority again, and I probably didn't answer all the questions as tactfully as I could have.

Murdoch and I gave them an overview of what had happened since the Seouras came. I didn't mention the New Council until the ConFleet first officer said they'd received information that several large ships known to be affiliated with the New Council were in the area. Had we seen them? I answered truthfully that no, we had not, as the Seouras hadn't let any large ships through. We gave them what information we had on the Q'Chn, but I did not mention Henoit and Murdoch, bless him, took his cue from me. They were happy to clean up the Q'Chn's corpse and bear it away. I could only imagine the stir it would cause and the problems that might arise.

By leaving it behind, Henoit had failed in his mission. Unless, and I believed this to be the case, he thought a New Council ship was close and left the Q'Chn to be picked up. This would explain why the Q'Chn was ready to believe my story of a ship waiting. But the New Council ship never came, and the facts of the Q'Chn revival, in the form of a corpse of a young Q'Chn, became known to the galaxy.

They wanted to move the Sleepers to the warship so they could be examined. I said no, they'd been examined already and they were Earth citizens. The Central officials said yes, the Sleepers were Earth citizens, therefore it was an Earth Outplanet Department matter, not ours. Lorna deVries said that under a certain article of the Cryogenics Revival Law, we could represent the Sleepers if necessary. The Earth official said we should ask the Sleepers themselves. I agreed, on the condition that Dan Florida was allowed to be present with recording and netcasting equipment. I didn't want Griffis, Rachel and Kloos to be persuaded into anything against their judgment. As Griffis had explained to me, the idea of being seen and heard live by large numbers of people has a restraining effect on officials. The general didn't like this, however, and the discussion was getting unpleasant when a message came from the warship, followed by their immediate withdrawal of the request. The Sleepers were free to come and go as they pleased. We all assumed the Invidi had something to do with this.

I found it difficult to have no debriefing. In all my previous experience, once an assignment had finished, I would present a report to my superiors, and they would accept it after going over every detail or perhaps order me to amend it. I missed that sympathetic acceptance, so unlike the scarcely concealed hostility of the officials' questions.

Late on ... I think it was the second day, I found time to stagger out of the main conference hall in the Bubble admin area, where the talks were held, and take the now-functioning karrikar over to the senior messhall. As I'd expected, the place was empty. Most of the ConFleet and EarthFleet officers were either doing double shifts, sleeping off their double shifts, or catching up on news from their counterparts on the orbiting warship.

There was a five-litre jar in front of the serving hatch labelled 'Real Coffee Compliments of the Boulevard Hoteliers' Association'. This must be the result of our initiating repairs on recycling first of all in Gamma. I could not imagine how the association had procured coffee so quickly or from whose contacts on the warship, but I poured myself a cupful gratefully and carried it over to the darkened corner of the room. Darkened in deference to the late hour, not because the lights were malfunctioning. Perhaps it was having lived for years with eccentric lighting, or the fact that I hadn't shut my eyes for far too long and the white light made them sore, but I felt drawn to the security of that dim corner.

I put the cup on the low table and sank into the worn chair. After sitting in the conference room chairs all day I was stiff, and all the bruises that Eleanor hadn't found were screaming for attention. I touched the side of my neck and had turned to check the wallscreen for the grey ships' position before I realised what I was doing. No need to check either now. Nor the Seouras – their escape pods from the grey ship had gathered and disappeared from our sensors somewhere in the asteroid belt. I don't know why the other grey ships dispersed, unless it was part of their programming, but we were glad that they had. Presumably ConFleet pursued them.

The disappearance of the grey ships seemed to have left an empty space, both out there and within me. I hadn't yet examined that space. It was adjacent to other, painful spaces that held images of death, monsters, and being trapped. I didn't have the energy to look at those images now and sat blankly, knowing that the ConCentral officials would return from the warship in an hour and that if I tried to sleep it would mean releasing a flood of reaction we could ill afford. It was an effort to lift the cup.

The coffee was wonderful. Its strength and mellow bitterness took me by surprise. It brought back memories of Earth and home with a directness that talking to the people on the warship had not. I gulped down the first mouthful and coughed as the heat brought tears to my eyes.

'That good, huh?' Murdoch put his own cup on the table and slouched backwards into a chair with such force that it creaked. He said nothing more, rubbed his chin tiredly and sipped the coffee. He then gave a satisfied grunt and stayed quite still, the cup held loosely in one hand balanced on his knee, staring at nothing with the same glazed stare as myself.

We must have sat there like two cryo-frozen mummies for ten minutes.

'Bill?'

'Mmm?' He focused on me slowly. He looked terrible – eyes bloodshot, skin tight and dry, the bones of his cheeks and temples too prominent. His jacket was unfastened completely and flapped over his belt.

'Have they finished the Hill recycling repairs yet?'

'This morning. McGuire said he told you.'

He drank down the rest of his coffee and looked at me, cup still in hand. 'Did you get that? Jeez, Halley, you look terrible. Haven't you had any sleep?'

I couldn't help grinning.

'What's so funny?' He was too tired to sound properly annoyed.

'I was thinking the same about you.'

He humphed and leaned back again. It took me a moment to restart the conversation.

'Did we ever charge Trillith?'

He thought for a moment. 'Yeah. But it can afford the fine. I heard it's negotiating the franchise for tourism in this sector.'

'Tourism?' We were like a couple of drunks, throwing an idea back and forth.

'Yeah, people coming here for fun.' He yawned hugely and rubbed the back of his neck, then looked at me.

'That reminds me, Veatch reapplied for his position here.'

'What?'

'I reckon they offered him a choice – go back to a reprimand and a demotion, or stay on Jocasta.'

'We still need a station manager.' At first the idea of working with Veatch was repugnant. Then I thought, what the hell, he's efficient and we know to keep an eye on him. Better the devil you know . . .

'Are you okay?'

'Yes.' I remembered the minutes preceding Henoit's death – the certainty we'd lost the jump drive, the crawling frustration of being trapped. And the relief of being able to act afterwards, over in the centre with the Q'Chn. I don't know what had come over me – as I'd suspected, it was one of those episodes where later you stand back and think, how could I have been so stupid?

I hadn't yet faced how I felt about Henoit's death. So far it was mainly shock at the suddenness. Regret at things left unsaid, there's always regret. And, if I'm honest with myself and at the moment I'm too tired not to be, relief as well. He'll never deceive me again.

Murdoch tapped the table to get my attention. 'Are you sure you're okay?'

'I'm still sore.' And my uniform still smelt faintly of recycling. I may have to get a new, navy one.

'What are you going to do now?' he asked over his shoulder as I refilled my cup at the hatch.

'Now?'

'After all the shouting's died down.'

I sat down again, uncertain. I hadn't thought about anything beyond the next step in the negotiations.

'Think I'd like my old job back.'

He stared, bemused. 'You want to go back to being an engineer?' He waved his arm around. 'Who's going to be head of this?'

It had been an unconsidered comment about my old job, but the more I thought about it, the more attractive it sounded. 'I'm no politician, Bill. If this independence idea succeeds, they're going to need an elected or otherwise chosen leader. Someone who can deal with both the Confederacy and the other factors.'

'And that's not you?'

'I don't think so. Dan Florida would be good. What will you do?'

He shrugged too.

'I'm not going to retire yet, if that's what you mean. I'll take whatever assignment comes.'

'You deserve an easy one after this.' I tried to lighten the mood but his face was serious.

He leaned forward and put his hands on my knees. They felt very large and heavy.

'Whatever you do, take care, huh?' And he kissed me.

I was so surprised that I let my lips kiss him back. Short, reasonably chaste. The kind of kiss old-time lovers give to confirm each other's existence.

He removed his hands, stood up. Unembarrassed, but he didn't seem quite steady on his feet.

'See you later.'

'Yes.' There were a lot of other things I could have said. But not yet.

The general and his officials said they were bringing us some visitors. The shuttle was a large one, and when Murdoch, Veatch, and I met them in the docking lobby, we found out why.

'An Barik you already know,' said the general. 'This is An Serat.'

'Call Griffis and Rachel,' I whispered to Sasaki, who was commanding the escort squad.

The general, after insisting that only his three guards be armed, which caused near-mutiny from Murdoch, made his speeches. The Confederacy acknowledged our declaration and promised to bring it before the next Confederacy Council. They also waived the courts-martial of the ConFleet officers involved. Which was hardly magnanimous, seeing that we'd saved their station for them.

Rachel and Griffis arrived. They looked at the Invidi, shocked, and Sasaki murmured a brief explanation for them. The two Invidi stood tall and silent in the cramped room. They looked different, although the suits' features were exactly the same. An Barik was ... neater somehow, taller, and more slender. The other was thicker and his suit had lost a lot of its bright shine. He must have used it for a century at least. There was a tension pushing between them, as though the opposing poles of two magnets were being forced together. If our suspicions about Invidi politics were correct, that was indeed the problem.

'I'd like to ask An Serat some questions, if he doesn't mind,' I said politely. I reminded myself that we were back in their world, the world where the Invidi wrote the programs that moved the rest of us around the board.

I was standing close to the two of them, Veatch beside us. Murdoch and Sasaki were a little to one side, and the general was talking to his officials, bored, behind the Invidi. One guard was with the general, one by the airlock door, and the third stood beside Rachel and Griffis, next to Murdoch. The guards looked bored too. They'd made their scorn for station Security clear.

An Serat glided forwards a half-metre. His movement was slow and he listed a little to one side.

As I stepped forward, one of his tentacles skated out without asking permission and touched my chest. I stopped myself from yelling in surprise. It tickled a little.

'You wish some answers, do you not?' His mechanical voice was lighter and warmer than An Barik's, with a completely different timbre.

I felt Rachel's eyes on me. 'You sent the drive with *Calypso*. You set it to arrive here.'

'That's right.'

'How could you be sure it would arrive here?'

'There is no surety. But the lines were relatively clear.' There was no hesitancy in his speech as in An Barik's, no confusion of tenses or subject.

'Do you remember us?' Griffis seemed shocked at meeting the Invidi again. His voice was small.

An Serat swayed. 'I do.'

'You used both us and this station to further some political end of your own.' Rachel was unforgiving.

'It may seem that way to you.'

'It does. Did you know about the mine?' How long she must have wanted to ask that.

He trailed another tentacle in the direction of her face. 'Not all things show themselves. It was far away.'

'Why here?' I had wanted to ask this for a long time too. 'What's so special about this place?'

'It is not the place.' His voice even carried an inflection of amusement.

'I don't understand. Is it this particular time?'

'Barik spoke to you of nodes?'

'Ye-es.' We all looked at An Barik, who made no movement.

'In his usual lucid way, I see.' An Serat rocked once. 'Pity him, if you can. He had to let the station be overrun and isolated because he dared not change anything that might interfere with the arrival of *Calypso*. Yet by doing nothing, he set you on a course that virtually guaranteed you would keep the drive and join the rebels, perhaps leading to the dissolution of the Confederacy.'

I could see what An Barik had faced, but pity was a long way off. I pitied Keveth and Quartermaine, and all the others who had died because An Barik wouldn't act.

'What are nodes?' asked Griffis.

'Nodes are a concentration of ... causes, which produce distinct effects,' said An Serat. 'They change the direction of the lines sufficiently to be visible to us.'

'Certain events have significant repercussions?' said Griffis.

'That is the result, as you see it. Actually, it is not so

linear. And events, in your understanding, are set in motion by the actions of living beings.'

'Like your decision to help Nguyen?' I suggested.

'And yours to change the balance of power here. Some nodes are living beings.' He touched my chest again. 'Like yourself.'

'Me?' I didn't like the idea of being a concentration of causes.

'I sent you the drive, although I did not know who you were.'

I stepped closer and spoke to An Barik. 'Why did you wait? I would have taken the drive if I could. You'd have lost your hyperspace monopoly.'

But it was An Serat who answered. 'Perhaps that would not be the terrible thing some of my compatriots believe.' The voice held humour also.

I groaned. 'I don't understand. Why not just give us the damn technology?'

'Because, as I have suggested, many of my compatriots do still believe it would be a terrible thing.'

An Barik shifted beneath his suit. So they did disagree. Henoit's information was correct. I was glad to think there might be an ally for the Nine Worlds among the Four, but as disturbed at his methods as I'd been at Henoit's.

'It doesn't matter. The drive was destroyed,' I said.

'You destroyed it.' An Serat made the comment without accusation. This time I didn't answer.

'And everyone goes back to what they were before?' Rachel's anger startled us all.

'We have disposed of the menace of the shadow. What

449

you called the grey ships, another legacy of the Tor. It would have been unfortunate if they had acquired our technology.'

'And where did the Seouras fit in this scheme?' I said, nearly as angry as Rachel now. If I'd felt manipulated by Henoit, it was nothing compared to this.

'They were an unanticipated factor.'

'They're probably dead. I bet they didn't anticipate that either.'

'You feel regret?'

'I feel . . . used.' I looked at Rachel, Murdoch, even Veatch. 'We all do.'

'We all do what we must,' he said. 'One of your elders once told me, "Our regrets are what define us."'

I phrased it as strongly as I could. 'I do regret losing the drive. I think you should give it to everyone.'

'There is no need of regret. You will find your *desada*.'

There's that word again. I remembered Quartermaine's words and knew that he'd got it wrong.

'*Desada* . . . there is no "special time", is there? It's now. It's always now. This moment.'

An Serat's whole body sighed, a leisurely shiver that anchored him more firmly to the floor. 'Your species has promise.' He moved his tentacle up slowly, preface to yet another quotation. I suspected he was just as irritating a conversationalist as An Barik, in a different way. '"If all time is eternally present All time is unredeemable".'

'I think all this far sight stuff is just a con.' Rachel pushed past me to stand close to An Serat, looking up. 'You want people to do things that you're too scared to do yourself. Non-interference my ass. You just can't bring yourself to be responsible for anything!'

She raised clenched fists almost as though to strike the alien. Griffis put out a hand to calm her down.

'Rachel.' She shook him off. I nodded to Murdoch over their heads and he whispered to Sasaki. Behind us the general and the others were watching. The guards stared into nothing, still bored.

Sasaki nodded kindly to Rachel and took her arm. They started to walk away, passing in front of the two aliens. Rachel shoved Sasaki hard in mid-stride, and she stumbled back onto the guard's toes. As he threw out an arm in surprise, Rachel grabbed the weapon he held in it. He looked at his empty hand with astonishment.

She pointed the gun at An Serat.

For a second we stared at her, uncomprehending. Then Murdoch's eyes flicked from side to side and the muscles of his face tightened. Neither the two guards nor the general standing behind us could get a clear shot at Rachel, for which I was glad. We all needed to remain calm. Griffis had stepped back in horror. Sasaki inched forward but Rachel jumped away.

'Uh-uh,' she admonished, and fixed her gaze on the Invidi again.

Murdoch might have reached her, but not before her hand closed on the firing pad. I cursed myself for letting the general remove Murdoch's weapon.

'What are you doing?' I let astonishment raise my voice.

She laughed, the freest sound I'd ever heard from her. 'What does it look like? Old biblical remedy, Halley. Eye for an eye.'

'I don't understand.' I hoped she didn't know how to use the thing.

'Don't try to buy time.' She chuckled and waved the flat end of the gun towards the Invidi. 'That's what these guys do. Use our time, use our lives. Now I'm going to take his.' The point stopped in front of An Serat.

'It won't work,' said Murdoch. 'They're wearing protective suits.'

My back was to the guards, but I could hear faint rustles of clothing and the squeak of boots as they manoeuvred for a better shot.

'This is ridicu— . . .' the general began.

I interrupted him. 'Rachel, put the gun down.'

Murdoch and Sasaki were silent. They knew the rules – don't crowd someone with a weapon, don't pressure them. One on one, gently.

'Are you sure their suits will protect them from this?' She twitched the gun.

Murdoch's poker face said he wasn't sure. I hadn't a clue. The weapon was small and discreet, one used by high-level bodyguards. I hoped they'd had the sense to keep it on the safe setting.

'The suits are sufficient,' rumbled An Barik's vocoder.

'Sufficient? What are you all looking so worried about then?' She was excited and bitter. 'Let's try it and see. A couple of people tried to assassinate an Invidi when they first came to Earth, you know. Remember what happened, Hannibal?'

Griffis shot me a look of dismay. He was as conscious of the guards as I was.

'Yes, Rachel. We protected them. They were guests on our world.'

She didn't like that. 'It was an invasion. Benign, but an invasion.'

'Rachel.' I took a deep breath and stepped forward. The guard behind us cursed under his breath. I'd deliberately ruined his shot on Rachel.

'No!' She raised the weapon in a firing stance. 'No further!'

I spread my hands wide. 'All right. Rachel, what's past is past. Leave it.'

'It's not past to me.' She looked at me properly then and the gun mouth focused on my chest. 'You're the worst,' she said. 'You know what they're doing but you go along with it. You betray all of us. You betray our history. Is it so hard to say to them,' she jerked her head at the Invidi, 'we don't need you, we don't want you?'

'It's a bit late now to blame us for your mistakes. We're trying to make the best of what you did to our world. If it was so easy, why didn't your generation say the words?' I snapped back at her in spite of myself. Her words stung more than I cared to admit.

Her hand wavered. 'Because we couldn't.'

Griffis spoke softly from behind her. 'Because we were in such a mess that we had no choice.'

'Rachel, if you kill me, are you going to feel better?' I let my tiredness show in my voice.

'No.'

'If you kill them, will it change anything?'

'No.'

'Then put it down.'

Her face crumpled and her hands holding the gun drooped. Murdoch leapt forward with an oath and grabbed her hands, pointing them down and away from anyone.

Then Rachel was crying, Murdoch snapped orders. The general countermanded them and issued different ones. Griffis comforted Rachel ineffectually and the red-faced guard stood stiffly to attention against the wall. The Invidi stayed motionless, like a pair of statues.

I walked away from them all, sick and shaky inside at Rachel's words more than her actions. I wondered if I'd have been able to do what Marlena Alvarez had done and step in front of the Invidi, to take the shot for them as she'd taken it for her president.

Rachel was wrong, though. This neutrality agreement is the beginning of something more. The Nine Worlds will not remain as they are within the Confederacy for much longer. It's only a matter of time.

Because I remember the Invidi drive. Not in detail, but the patterns move in my memory in the way the Seouras voices spoke in my mind; elusive, ambiguous, but nonetheless present. Given time, I will work it out. Everyone needs a hobby.